To Moe—Ezra wouldn't be the same pervy geek he is without you.

SWITCH IT UP

SARA BROOKES

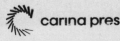

carina press™

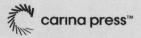

carina press™

PLEASE RECYCLE

THIS PRODUCT IS RECYCLABLE

Recycling programs
for this product may
not exist in your area.

ISBN-13: 978-1-335-01361-3

Switch It Up

Copyright © 2018 by Shree Finch

www.CarinaPress.com

Printed in U.S.A.

3 0646 00221 8893

SWITCH IT UP

Chapter One

This wasn't the first time Maddy had hacked into a kinky website. Porn sites weren't the easiest to weasel into, but certainly the most fun. Oddly, the task brought her a sense of accomplishment her day job didn't fulfill. It also provided hours of amusement on an otherwise boring Thursday night.

She adjusted the boom microphone on her headset as she waited for her business partner to accept the audio chat request. While she sat idle, she noticed a heavy layer of dust along one end of the long dining table she used as a desk for her dual computer setup. The fine particles' perfection was marred by a line of paw prints courtesy of her cat, Samoa.

"Hey, Maddy." Steve's baritone voice rescued her from her debate about the merits of attaching dusting pads to Samoa's paws. "I was just chatting about you to a potential client who insists his site is secure enough without our 'extremely expensive services.'"

"If it truly is, he wouldn't be talking to you," she replied. "Send me the details and I'll show him just how much he desperately needs us." Maddy tried not to sound eager about the idea of schooling some unsuspecting *n00b* who doubted her skills.

"That's my girl." A soft ding sounded over the line as Steve received an email. "And another satisfied customer who can't stop praising your work. You make this too easy sometimes, Maddy."

Fact of the matter was, most of the time this job *was* too easy. "Got a live one for you, if you've got the time."

"I always have the time for you. Finished up work for the night already?"

"You mean the exceptionally boring list of client websites I was given to intentionally break into? Pfft. Please don't insult me. Packets are already on the way, along with my billable hours."

She wouldn't have to mention how bored she'd been with the tasks. How the work lacked challenge. Steve would know their job of rooting around an assigned website for glitches and then putting together a solution package for the customer was work she could execute blindfolded. Even though the responsibility didn't give her the same exhilarating rush of infiltrating unsuspecting sites, it certainly paid the bills.

"Just grabbing a snack between meetings." He paused, a sign he was ingesting his go-to snack of Funyuns. No doubt there was a can of Dr. Pepper nearby. "Go ahead and educate me, wise master."

She verified they were the only ones on the private network he'd set up before she tapped a button on her keyboard to share her desktop screen. While she didn't doubt Steve's skill in the least, in their line of work it paid to double and sometimes triple check before execution.

"Holy shit." Surprise filtered through her earphones as Steve got an eyeful of her latest discovery. "Warn a guy next time."

Maddy winced. The XXX-rated splash page that displayed a nude woman bound with ropes of pink LED lights had probably shocked Steve's vanilla mind. She'd forgotten not everyone was as comfortable with deviant behavior as she was. Risks had been a part of her everyday world since the age of twelve, when she'd stolen her father's car and taken a joyride to Disneyland.

"Sorry." She drummed her fingers on her desk as she waited for him to get over his surprise. She didn't feel bad about scandalizing him. Steve O'Doyle wasn't just the co-owner of Devtag, working out of the East Coast bureau while she provided support out of her home office in California—he was also her ex-boyfriend. As far as a kick-ass gaming companion and business partner, Steve was the man. However, when it came to the matter of sex, the poor guy had "clueless" stamped across his forehead. Too married to his work to have normal, healthy relationships.

"Take a look at what I just ran across." She right-clicked to open a window for the source code, effectively covering the explicit image to preserve Steve's sensibilities. While he wouldn't care what the website was peddling, he would be interested in the strings of code used to construct the site.

"This is…whoa." Quiet whispers sounded as Steve read through the lines populating his screen. "I think you hit the motherlode."

She sat up straighter as Steve fell quiet. "Biggest steaming pile of shit you've ever seen, right? You'd think a sex website would have stricter security protocols."

Steve's loud snort came through her headphones. "My skills aren't top-notch, but even I know better.

Whoever coded this drivel should have their geek license revoked. No one codes like this."

"Except for maybe some pimple-faced junior high school dweeb working on a WYSIWYG interface," she responded as she wrinkled her nose at a string of characters she recognized from her basic computer classes freshman year of college, which had indeed had what-you-see-is-what-you-get software. She'd never seen programming code this disorganized and simplistic. It had been too easy to crack, and Maddy hated easy. Easy meant a loss of revenue. "They're just giving away their porn. Quality sex videos should never be free. Fucking amateurs."

"School 'em, Maddy-girl."

"You going to stick around to watch?" she asked as she pulled up a search on her second desktop computer. The one with the unmasked, fully legal IP address she used for her everyday browsing. As she read the extensive background on the About tab of the website, she recognized the name of the owner, Kochran Duke. "Hey, I know of this guy."

"Former beau?"

"Didn't you know I have lovers all over the country?" Maddy giggled at Steve's snort. "I didn't say I knew him, just that I know *of* him. The Duke family owned most of downtown San Francisco when I was in high school. Think my mom mentioned chatting with Kochran's parents a few times at the country club when she took tennis lessons Dad gifted her one Christmas. Also called them stuck-up prudes, if I recall correctly."

"Which is saying a lot coming from your mother."

Steve hadn't needed to point out the obvious. Her mom got along with everyone, and found the tiniest detail to like about the meanest, rudest person in the world. For her to express her aversion to the Duke family said a lot about how they conducted themselves.

The knowledge that Kochran owned the club wouldn't stop Maddy's intrusion of the website. He might have connections and nothing better to do with his parents' millions, but she had megaskills that trumped bored millionaires.

She cleared her throat, antsy to get started. "You never said if you're going to hang."

"I've got a meeting with a new client based in Japan at ten, but I can stick around for a few more minutes. Always a joy to watch Maddy Zane, badass hacker extraordinaire, work."

Maddy smirked. "All right. Let's see what this place is really all about."

A few keystrokes got her back to the front page of the website for a fetish organization near Sacramento called Noble House. According to the scrolling marquee across the top, it was a hybrid kink club with a physical location to serve members as well as the website.

"Unique concept, I'll give it that much," Steve said around a mouthful of snacks. "Odd name for a BDSM club, though. Not that I'm well-versed in that department."

Maddy had seen and heard plenty of BDSM club names, but nothing like this. As though Kochran equated his business to some modern-day fairy tale of sin where he probably saw himself as the ruler. Given her mother's description of his parents, it wouldn't surprise her to hear. "Think I'm going to snoop around a bit more. See just how lax things are."

She focused on her custom-built secure desktop with its high-level encryption that allowed her to surf without anyone tracking her geolocation and quickly added a bunch of random information to the membership database. When it came time to complete a sexual interest list, she blindly filled out a few pertinent details. Thankfully Steve couldn't see the screen of that computer, but no reason to tick off boxes for stuff she *actually* liked.

Once that was done, she had the system generate a random password. When a generic confirmation email arrived, she snorted loud enough to disturb the cat now sleeping on the corner of her desk. She glanced to the computer's clock. "Accessed and joined without spending a dime in forty-one seconds."

Mothertruckers.

"Looks like we've got another idiot playing with a toy he has no right to own." Steve's short burst of laughter signaled his amusement. While Maddy knew Steve wasn't into kinky sexual practices, she did know he got a thrill from illegally accessing websites. That shared interest was why they'd started a legitimate business together even after their relationship had fallen apart.

"Time to find out just how far down this rabbit hole we can go," Maddy stated as she assigned herself a screen name, choosing something she would have never dreamed of in real life. She pulled up a blank email and shared the username and password with Steve. "Just use this account for right now. No reason for both of us to be there if it's not necessary."

"Trixy Malone?" Steve asked a minute later.

The mocking tone of Steve's voice made her roll her

eyes. "Just poke around a bit to see if you can figure out the busiest sections so we can avoid them."

Though she could find out the information in a few minutes, it would keep Steve occupied while she hunted for the best spot to drop in a beauty of a program she'd written to allow her to return to the site undetected whenever she wanted. Most of the time the websites she hacked weren't worth a revisit, but who was she to pass up a free ticket to unrestricted porn?

"Based on the webstats, the video archive is the most visited area," Steve offered a few minutes later. "Members' message boards come in a close second. The archives would be the easiest place to drop in a virus, but also too predictable. Even with the rudimentary code, the website admin would quickly find the intruder. Then again, if it was the same coder responsible for this junk heap, maybe not. Taking the chance isn't worth it. Better to find someplace more secure."

Samoa jumped off the desk and wound between her legs, meowing loudly that it was well past dinnertime. "Yeah, yeah. Demanding fat cat, aren't you?"

"Hey!" Steve exclaimed, clearly offended. "I know I've let time get away from me, but no reason to insult a guy for a few extra pounds."

"My roommate is reminding me it's well past dinner time." Maddy scooped up Samoa and scratched between her ears. "Didn't you say you had a meeting? I've got this from here."

"Yeah," Steve said with a sigh. His reluctance to leave came through the line. Like her, he clearly wanted to explore further.

"I doubt we're the first ones to discover the hole, Steve. Not even sure it's large enough to notify Kochran. Probably just a fluke." Anomalies weren't uncommon on the internet, but she didn't believe that was the case. Something told her this couldn't be written off as a simple glitch.

"Could be a potential client," Steve noted. "All right with you if I stick around?"

That was the beauty of their partnership. Steve saw dollar signs and a possible new contract that would further expand their business. Maddy saw ways to pad her hacker resume. It was a win-win for them both. "Of course. Be back in about ten minutes."

She tossed her headphones to the desk as she rose. The brief break in the action would let her clear her head, concoct a game plan, and get some much-needed fuel. She made her way to the kitchen to grab a can of tuna for Samoa and a container of soup for herself. Not her preferred dinner, but certainly the easiest and quickest. And according to the note stuck to the cabinet, her only choice. She leaned a hip against the counter and noticed a second note affixed to her refrigerator. A third and a fourth on her coffee pot. All bright little slips of neon-colored paper reminding her she hadn't been grocery shopping in three weeks.

Restocking her cabinets took time, and now that she'd discovered a weakness, she didn't *have* time. With full access to the website, she wanted to exploit the flaw that called to her, as addicting as any drug. Groceries be damned.

If she'd found the way in, so could someone else. She wasn't about to let some jerk-off swoop in and claim this victory. Not when she'd rightfully done so. Steve wouldn't want that to happen either.

Some people found pleasure in whips and chains.

Madeline Zane got off on skirting the law. Laws were more like guidelines anyway. A line drawn in the sand just begging to be crossed. Maddy hadn't yet found a single line she hadn't been willing to leap over.

Samoa had already curled up in her worn office chair by the time she arrived at her desk again. Maddy gently nudged the cat away, settling down in front of her setup. Samoa strutted across her desk, leaving another line of tracks through the dust before settling in one corner. The cat's lemon-yellow eyes flashed, clearly annoyed plans for a nap in the comfort of the chair had been interrupted.

Pissing off her cat was the least of Maddy's concern. As she settled her headphones into place, she saw Steve was still logged in. She'd hope he hadn't been able to get out of the meeting he'd mentioned earlier, but it didn't appear so. "Find anything?"

"Despite the ease we got in with, everything looks well organized," he offered.

"At least something around here is done right."

She wasn't looking for anything in particular. Just a place where she could settle down for a bit and innocently interact with legal, paying members of the site. Sure, she'd broken countless federal privacy laws, but she had to entertain herself somehow. If she hadn't gotten out of San Francisco, her life would have been the typical upper-middle class life her parents had settled into. A brick rancher with a white-picket fence and a pool in the backyard. Days spent shuttling two-point-five kids to karate and ballet lessons. Nights entertaining the neighbors and gossiping about the same thing day after day. Rituals of civilized social interactions where she'd be expected to mask her truest desires. Nothing wrong with that sort of lifestyle, but Maddy had known at a young age she'd been destined for something else.

Shaking off the phantom threads of the life she didn't want, Maddy focused on the website. While everything looked interesting, she was especially intrigued by the four tiny blue letters in the top right of the window.

"Hey, Steve, you see the beta-testing section?"

"Logging in now."

She followed without hesitation. User-level testing meant that section wasn't fully functional yet, but the developer welcomed feedback from users. It also meant glitches that were prime for exploitation. Bugs that could be manipulated, as Steve would say.

Though the graphically intense section took a few minutes to load, the speed still surprised her. "Someone spent a lot of time constructing this. Reminds me a little of SimLife."

Steve laughed. "You know, it does."

SimLife was a quirky computer game she'd played as a teen where she'd spent hours meticulously developing a computer-generated character. The game hadn't kept her attention long, as the personality parameters she'd given the character had caused it to set fire to the house in a fit of paranoia and perish.

A towering building that resembled a fortress stood off to her left. Thanks to a quick round of Google-fu that displayed images of the actual building, she knew it was the BDSM club in virtual glory.

Thick, lush forest surrounded the building, the summer-green leaves blowing gently in a computer-generated breeze. It was a nice effect that added a layer of authenticity to the world.

"Guess we'll see just how close it truly is. Let me whip something up for us." The controls were easy enough to quickly figure out. She put together a character truly fitting of the handle Trixy Malone. Red flowing locks. Big boobs. Shapely legs that went on for miles. After a few adjustments—and the addition of a low-cut, tight fitting outfit she would have never selected in real life—she saved the character. Steve's wolf whistle confirmed she'd chosen wisely.

She dropped her newly minted avatar in the center of a pixelated cobblestone street. She used the arrow keys on her keyboard to steer toward a signpost at an intersection. Three arrows directed the flow of vehicular and pedestrian traffic. To her left was the club. To her right, a city center bustling with activity.

"Interesting," she said, tapping her fingers again the desk again. "Wasn't expecting there to be anything beyond the club in here."

"How about we split up?" Steve offered, "You can check out the town and I'll take a look at club."

Maddy glanced through the coding before asking, "Can we do that?"

"You're not the only one with skills, Zane." A second later a duplicate of her Trixy avatar appeared on the screen. "Simple enough to drop a loop into the code to trick the program into allowing us two av's of the same character. Go forth and explore. Let me know what you find."

She watched Steve guide the dupe of her sim toward the club building before she headed to the right. As she drew closer, she noticed mixed-use buildings that housed a variety of businesses. Strange for a fetish club website. She wandered around for a time, making small talk with the other simulated people through simple chat bubbles. She wasn't looking for anything in particular in this secondary world, just somewhere to settle into comfortably and put her observation skills to work. Steve hadn't said anything for a few minutes, so she assumed he was busy exploring the club. Or getting his mind blown.

She approached a pair of sims who were obviously not inhibited by the public setting. The female avatar sat on an ornate park bench, her legs spread. A man kneeled between her thighs, his face buried deep as he worshipped her. Just as Maddy passed, the woman grabbed the man's head and gave off a high, keening wail according to the little chat bubble that appeared over the sim's head. Of course simulated public sex would be allowed in an explicit virtual theme park.

When she noticed a yellow blinking light at the corner of her screen, she remembered her old computer game's need to be fed at regular intervals. "You getting the same notification, Steve?"

"Yeah, I see it. I was just going to ask you about it. Health depletion, maybe?"

"I think so. Give me a second." She steered her sim to a frozen yogurt cart to purchase a small tub. She clicked "eat" and her sim gobbled up the sweet confection in record time. The yellow dot changed to a red heart, her sim content with her life not hanging in the balance.

"Well, isn't that clever? Think we're good to go now." Easy to see how hours upon hours could be lost inside with members dropping a few cool bills in a short span of time. It was more than just a way to interact sexually with the club and other members. They could also have entire lives. Families. Jobs, for fuck's sake, as she thought about the sim that had sold her the treat. "Looks like there are two settings. A single payment system for an allotted amount of time and another game mode like this. Either way, someone is going to make a fortune when this program clears beta testing."

"No shit," Steve responded.

"How are you making out?"

"This place is unreal, Maddy. Never seen anything like it."

"Not offending your virgin sensibilities, is it?" She hadn't thought of it before, but perhaps it would have been better for her to explore the club aspect of the sim instead of Steve.

"Very funny. I'm a grown boy who can handle—holy fucksticks. These two guys are in a wrestling ring doing some seriously impressive MMA moves. This is better than watching Conner MacGregor in the cage… or maybe not."

"Okay?" Maddy asked, concerned Steve had gotten in over his head.

"Guy just came out of the crowd, grabbed the other guy's dick and started blowing him. They both took the first guy down. Time for me to move along."

Maddy giggled at the panic-tinged words from her friend. "Sure you don't want to switch?"

"No. Things can't get much worse than that. Let you know if I find anything else worth discussing."

She wanted to point out Steve was going to probably run into a lot he'd have questions about, but she left him alone for the time being. Instead, she angled

toward a theater and decided to go inside to see what
kind of moviegoers this place catered to. It wouldn't be
hard to guess, given the atmosphere, but she wondered
if the movies would be computer-generated as well.
As she slipped through a pair of swinging doors, she
found a darkened theater with most of the seats filled.

Up on the oversized screen, the images weren't simulated as she'd thought. Instead, it appeared to be a live
feed from inside the real club. It was an odd mix of life
and computer-generated simulator she found fascinating. Surprisingly, the video quality was remarkable.
The decor of the room on the screen was impeccable
and lush. The theater around her, though truly just an
artful arrangement of pixels, had the same attention
to detail.

A sign this place wasn't just some run-of-the-mill
porn site managed by a bunch of sweaty, kinky people looking to make some money. This was how these
people *lived*. They breathed bondage and domination.

Small conversations bubbles appeared over the
heads of several members. Though they appeared interested in the video playing on the screen, the hot
ticket for the night would be a session starring Kochran
Duke himself. If the accolades were to be believed,
Kochran wasn't just the owner of the club, but an active participant. The Hardcore King of Noble House
had quite a reputation, and a number of fans judging
by the chatter taking place among the theater patrons.
Evidently, he was the best at what he did. The only person she knew who was *that* good at what he did was a
comic book character, and she seriously doubted Kochran had an adamantium-coated skeleton or looked
like Hugh Jackman.

While she didn't consider herself a prude by any means, that was a lot of naked flesh parading around as entertainment for the audience while they waited for the featured scene to begin. They'd taken a page straight out of *Rocky Horror*—the avatars on the stage acted out whatever was occurring on the screen. Right down to the orgy. Thighs and shoulders and breasts and butts and cocks all came together in a pile of sinfully decadent human flesh. Loud moans and groans accompanied the sounds of flesh slapping together.

Outside of the sim, her body temperature rose. She was alone in her house, Steve couldn't see her, but that didn't stop her cheeks from heating as she watched the people writhing on both screens. She shivered. Goose bumps crawled up her arms, collected at the base of her neck, shot down her spine and punched her in the gut. She'd gone from world-class hacker to wanton sex goddess in two seconds flat.

Now she understood why Noble House was considered one of the premier fetish sites on the internet.

Chapter Two

By the time she turned her focus to the screen in the theater again, the featured event had started. It appeared she'd only missed the first minute or so, but already the woman was naked. She was crouched in the center of a room filled with people who were all dressed in various kinds of clothing, from jeans to elaborate formal wear.

In contrast, the woman only had pink ribbons tied around strategic points. Long trails of excess ribbon dangled from the pretty bows at her wrists and ankles. Matching cords of rope had been woven around her upper torso in an elaborate network of knots that perfectly framed and supported her breasts. In her hands, she balanced two silver serving trays that gleamed in the overhead lighting. One of the trays tilted wildly before leveling again.

The angle of the camera shifted, and the reason for the woman's struggle became clear. A low-profile box had been positioned between her legs and served as the anchor for a device that had been locked in place so it could be angled toward her labia.

A man stepped out of the crowd of people and placed a mug on one of the trays. Another man did the same.

placing his cup on the opposite tray. The woman expertly adjusted to the additional weight, though her legs continued to tremble from the stress. Despite the struggle, one glimpse at the woman's face showed the flush of her cheeks, the glazed appearance of her eyes indicating her arousal.

Another man stepped into the frame. Though he was only visible from the waist down, Maddy instantly recognized there was something different about him. While he stood with the observers, he wasn't one of them. Not different, just…in charge. As though—

Her thoughts ended when the man struck the woman's back with the short tails of a flogger.

"Steve, you still there?"

"Yeah." Despite his answer, there was a definite strain in his voice. "Think this is a little too much for me. Mind if I take off? You going to be all right on your own?"

"Of course. Do what you need to. I'll write up my notes when I'm done and send them to you." She already had plenty of information to build a report around, but she was invested in the activities going on around her. This may not have been Steve's idea of fun, but it certainly ranked high on her list.

She waited until Steve's name disappeared from the connection. Though she was no longer sharing her screen with him, she didn't want to take any chances.

Maddy adjusted her computer's sound so the video stream was the prevalent noise instead of the chatter of the observers in the theater. Judging by the noises of pleasure filling her office, she knew the woman enjoyed the pain.

Maddy's attention turned to the man as the camera

panned upward, finally showing his face. Kochran. He was dressed as though he intended to spend the day at the office, in gray slacks, a black button-down shirt and a gray tie. The only indication he was working hard was the fact that the sleeves of his shirt had been folded back a few times to expose his wrists and forearms.

Though he exerted little energy, his efforts were paying off in a big way as the woman's cries grew louder. Despite the fact Maddy was an interloper, she continued to watch as the man carefully landed hit after hit. He made a gesture to the crowd and several people stepped forward, each of them holding glassware of various shape and sizes.

Though her arms dropped a little from the weight, she kept the trays level as items were added. Her legs began to shake violently and her eyes lost focus. Kochran stopped hitting her with the tails and scooped his hand through the woman's long fall of raven hair. He stepped against her, tugging on her locks hard enough that she had to lean against him for support. Though Maddy wasn't there, she knew from the tremble of the woman's thighs the submissive had just orgasmed.

"Don't drop the trays, little subbie." Kochran held her shaking body through the quakes, giving her support. "You wouldn't want to displease me, would you?" The woman's face was a veil of ecstasy as one of the trays wobbled. "Don't disobey me, little one." The tray canted wildly to one side before being brought under control. Kochran clicked his tongue against the roof of his mouth. "Let me see if I can't bring you in line again."

When he spoke, it was as though the spaces between the words carried just as much weight as the actual commands. The deep quality of his voice roused something in Maddy, as though she wanted to be the woman on her knees pleasing her Dom.

Maddy blinked at the thought. The whole bondage, domination, submission thing wasn't a foreign concept thanks to her curiosity as a teen and parents who had no idea what she spent hours doing on the computer. But it was the first time she'd ever experienced that kind of reaction. The first display of dominance that made her want to hear the Dom say her name with that sinfully sensual growl.

The woman on the screen perfectly balanced the trays all the way through her release, even though her legs collapsed. Maddy marveled at the woman's control. Admired her strength. The woman held the trays in front of her as she struggled to keep them upright.

The camera zoomed in on the woman as her cries died. The close angle allowed Maddy to see that the woman wore a plain black collar decorated with a simple gold disk adorned with an emblem. Three lions surrounding a shield. The same graphic had appeared in the left-hand corner of the main pages of the website.

Before the woman had recovered or had the trays fully under her control again, Kochran spoke. "I didn't give you permission to stop sitting on the vibrator, little subbie."

Though the submissive whimpered, she angled herself on the vibrator again.

This time, instead of approaching her with the handheld whip, he flipped open a button and dropped the zipper on his slacks. Both the crowd around Kochran and the avatars around Maddy murmured with appreciation as he parted his shirt and stripped it away. The clothes had masked a bulk she hadn't expected. Every inch of him was covered in sculpted muscle, showcasing a strength forged from a man who took pride in his body. But his build wasn't the only draw for the audience. That penetrating stare of his possessed as much strength as his biceps.

It also exposed a large tattoo on his left pectoral. The black outline was the same three lions surrounding a shield crest she'd seen earlier. Obviously a brand the owner needed to have on him at all times. She wondered if all the members had the symbol etched on their skin, though she didn't see any openly displayed. That kind of solidarity wouldn't be too out of the ordinary for people connected on such an intense level.

Maddy wanted to go to her knees right there in her house. Her throat went dry as she realized the effect this show was having on her. She needed to stop watching and write the report. Playing voyeur had not been her intent on discovering this new world. The more time she spent on the interface, the chances of getting caught increased exponentially. But Jesus Christ, how could she not watch? He was un-fucking-believable. Everything she'd expected in a fetish club owner.

Energy thrummed through her fingers as they rested against the keyboard. Despite her vow to stop, she found herself enraptured by what she watched unfolding. The raw power that made her body ache for that kind of connection.

This wasn't about the sex. Wasn't about the people observing. This was pure, unadulterated trust.

He projected dominance with equal parts protection and confidence. He had an artistic perfection that came through the screen. It should have been impossible, but

Maddy sensed the connection between Kochran and his partner. Their chemistry was off-the-charts hot. Though she had no idea if they knew one another, they definitely shared an emotional link Maddy envied. Anticipation, along with a touch of wildness, thrummed through her as she watched the woman swallow Kochran's cock over and over. She'd never gotten this excited watching a fetish video before. Never experienced such a tremendous amount of intensity flowing from people she didn't even know.

That need to belong returned.

Maddy couldn't even begin to imagine what it was like to surrender and bring pleasure to a man at the same time. Maybe in her wildest dreams, sure, but this was actually happening right before her eyes. She was so caught up in the scene, she jumped when a man slipped into the vacant seat beside her avatar and began speaking.

"Hello, gorgeous, I'm Harry." His deep voice echoed through her living room. No way was anyone's voice tuned so perfectly that it sounded as though he was deeply aroused. Then again—he totally could be. That video playing was enough to excite even the biggest prude. It had certainly had a profound effect on her.

A quick glance at her sound showed that she'd forgotten to disable the direct voice chat feature when Steve had left. She reached over and adjusted the voice modulation in her profile. "Hi."

A feminine voice with a husky, breathy quality echoed through the room. Like she'd been interrupted in a heated moment of fucking. The stranger leaned closer, in a way that made her suddenly feel boxed in and claustrophobic even though he wasn't truly touching her. His eyes flashed dark, making her even more uncomfortable.

The reminder that she was in a safe place and not actually in the theater echoed in her head. Just an illusion. Still, as she watched the man's avatar reach over and stroke the side of her computer-generated face, Maddy shuddered. The slimy sensation along her jaw line wouldn't fade, her skin tingling despite the fact there had been no physical contact. A warning buzzed that she needed to remove herself from the situation before things took a turn she couldn't handle.

"I really need to go."

She directed her sim to stand, but the man wrapped his hand around her forearm and pinned it to the chair. Her heart rate sped as she tapped on keys in an effort to get away, but her avatar couldn't move.

"You'll stay right there and take what I have to give you, dirty girl."

Maddy slammed her fingers against the keyboard, willing her avatar to respond. She searched her screen for some kind of virtual safe word, but saw nothing that would allow her to forcefully stop the interaction. The guy had a strong grip and the only way she was going to escape was to—

"Go ahead, struggle. I really like that."

His face filled her monitor as his lecherous voice echoed through her room. Though she was a novice, she was savvy enough to know this guy bullied people into submitting to him. While she may not be in the lifestyle, she understood the difference between a predator and a Dominant. And this dude was a first-class *asssssss-hole*.

She killed the power strip, her entire computer setup

going dark as her heart galloped. Though nothing physical had happened, a sensation of violation swamped her. That the trust she'd extended, even marginally, had been ruined.

She pulled over a notepad and grabbed a nearby pen. *Safe word. ASAP.*

Her heart raced for another reason now, the back of her throat burning with annoyance. What if some unsuspecting, brand-new submissive had gone to the theater? Talked to Mr. Happy Hairy Hard-on? Gotten herself in a compromising situation where she didn't understand the power exchange dynamic?

Fuck.

She couldn't believe how irresponsible Kochran had been for allowing a beta test to commence without taking into account a safety net for the participants. Maybe it was simply an oversight, but she couldn't sit idly in her home office and allow the practice to continue. God only knew how many other people were at risk.

By the time her computers had powered up again, an angry heat had taken up residence in her chest. With a shaking hand, she navigated to the Noble House main page to look for contact information. While hacking a website rarely meant she came back for a repeat visit, this intrusion hadn't been normal. Kochran needed to be made aware of the predatory practices of one of his members before he allowed an expanded audience loose in the simulated world, and provide an escape if things took a turn for the worse. A word or a gesture. Just like in a real-life scene.

She continued to dig around the website as the phone rang in her ear. A second contact screen that gave the physical address of the club confirmed she'd missed its office business hours. Irritated, she hung up and jotted down the address. She debated the advantage of simply sending an email, but it could get lost en route or dismissed altogether. No way for Kochran to ignore her if she got right in his face.

Maddy noted the operational hours for the club and glanced at the clock. According to the schedule, they had open play for another three hours. If she got on the road for Sacramento right now, she could be there in an hour and half. An hour if she floored it. Just about the time Kochran would be all cleaned up from his scene.

Good. This shit needed to be cleaned up. Now.

Hunting through her computer's history, she located the audio-visual files and extracted the theater visit. Satisfied she had enough evidence, she dropped the record onto a zip drive to take with her. Perfect fuel to give Kochran and his irresponsible staff a piece of her mind.

Chapter Three

Kochran Duke hated being in charge.

At least tonight. All he'd wanted to do was lose himself in a bottle of his best bourbon and pretend the rest of the world wasn't trying to fuck him over. But duty called no matter his mood or health. The owner of Noble House didn't get to take a vacation.

He thought about ignoring his phone when it chimed, but with Tory in hospice care, he'd picked up the habit of keeping his cell phone close. As soon as he saw his business partner's name, warning bells sounded. Enver had drawn Dungeon Monitor duty for the night, which meant something important enough to warrant a call to Kochran had interrupted his rounds.

"Got a request for you in Court if you're not otherwise occupied," Enver said without waiting. "And if you are, why the fuck are you answering the phone?"

"Anything wrong?"

"Looks like she's ready to serve someone's head up on a platter."

He wasn't equipped to handle a bunch of shit falling apart tonight. Not with the emotional turmoil kicking around in his head. "I'll be right down."

The faster he got this taken care of, the faster he

could get back to finding the bottom of that curvy bottle seducing him.

Normally he would have changed into jeans and a casual shirt since he was off the clock for the night, but since his final destination was the heart of the club, appropriate attire was expected. Demanded, even. At times he hated the suit and tie as much as he hated being responsible for so many souls. As much as being the man in charge sucked sometimes, he had a business to run. When he was present on the floor of the main scene area, paying members—both virtual and physical—would expect Master Kochran in all his glory.

Whatever the fuck that means.

Noble House was known for its extensive and exclusive membership roster. Though the number of people who chose to visit the physical building was relatively small on most weeknights, the number had been growing thanks to the online component that made the BDSM club so unique.

Out of habit, he automatically scanned the room as he entered. Despite the late hour, Court was still a hive of activity. Most of the roped off scene areas were being used by a colorful assortment of characters, including Saint and Boyce, who'd exchanged their casual clothes for leathers. The newest addition to their relationship, Grae Burrows, had joined them. The silver knot-work of her collar glinted in the stage lighting as their bodies worked together in sinuous motions that would enrapture even the most vanilla person. Last Kochran had heard, they were planning an October wedding in Washington, near the college they'd attended.

Kochran spotted Enver standing near the center of the room, arms crossed and gaze intent as he watched members play. The formidable man was even more intimidating in his DM getup. Tight black leather pants. A matching leather vest unbuttoned to expose his impressive torso. If his Dungeon Monitor outfit wasn't enough to scare the members into compliance, his hawk-like glare would.

Enver met Kochran's gaze for a split second, inclining his head toward a nearby chair as he continued his watchful scan. Kochran ignored the signal. He'd known Enver Faust long enough to know something was obviously bothering him.

Kochran gestured toward Enver. "Your shoulders get any higher, you can use them for ear muffs."

"Been a long few nights." Enver's posture visibly altered as he responded, though his attention remained focused on the room and his duties.

The perceptible tension resting on Enver's shoulders had Kochran worried. Kochran had seen the latest footage when he'd been scanning through the dailies of a scene between Enver and the submissive he was training with his ropes. Their play at the club was becoming increasingly more aggressive. Not unusual, but Kochran had already made a note to check in with his friend to see if he could handle the historically uninhibited submissive.

"Take the rest of the night off. Get someone else to cover your shift."

"Already tried. Rhodes is overseas on a business trip. Tony didn't pick up his phone and Parker, the bastard, is MIA." It wasn't often the soft-spoken Enver cursed.

"I'll take over," Kochran offered, even though he didn't relish the idea. He would do what needed to be done because he had to. Businesses didn't run themselves. Members would lose their confidence in a disinterested owner.

Enver cut his gaze to Kochran for a split second. "You have something else to take care of. I've got a handle on things."

Kochran knew not to argue. But their longstanding friendship didn't mean he would allow the visible discomfort to go ignored. "You need a break, my friend. A long one. Preferably on an island somewhere with plenty of alcohol and a stack of good books. Maybe a long mindless fuck or three with a sweaty cabana slave."

Enver frowned. "Bracey's needs are shifting. She requires…more. I don't know what exactly, but I do know it's not a service I can provide. I could speculate all day long, but it's futile."

"So ask her."

"I have," Enver murmured. "She doesn't know either."

A conundrum Kochran understood well. He'd been down that path a few times with submissives he'd worked with. Taken the road himself, though he wasn't interested in revisiting that slice of a past he preferred to keep buried. "If there is anyone capable of figuring out a submissive's needs, it's you. The fact you recognize she requires something you can't give her means you care enough about her to see her happy."

Kochran didn't understand the why, but Enver had agreed to the partnership in Noble House, and to serve as a monitor and Dom, as long as it was clearly understood that he wasn't interested in participating in sexual intercourse inside the walls of the club. When

Enver was ready to confess his reasons why, he would. Perhaps.

Enver rolled his shoulders. "We've put it on the back burner for now to revisit sometime later…you know what, you don't need this right now. I don't either." He gestured to the corner again. "Go on. I've got this. No reason to keep her waiting for you any longer than we already have." He used his chin to point toward a woman sitting in a chair at the far end of Court. "She's feisty."

Kochran cut his gaze to his friend. "That good or bad?" His question was met simply with a lift of Enver's shoulders and a mischievous smile that deepened the lines around the older man's eyes. Kochran restrained further comment as he moved away. The grin could mean any number of things.

He slowed as he approached the woman so he could study her. She gripped the padded arms of the chair, alternately digging her nails into the fabric and stretching her fingers out. He almost leaned against a nearby post to observe her longer. Judging by her fidgeting, this was the first time she'd been to the club.

Her long fall of blond hair had been swept up into a ponytail. Fine hairs had escaped the restraint, falling around her face in wispy curls. As he watched, her big blue eyes never settled on anything for long, her freckled cheeks flushing an alluring pink whenever she decided she *had* looked too long, as though she would be scolded for getting caught watching people in the throes of passion. Hard to imagine this innocent-looking woman was the feisty being Enver had called him about.

"I'm Kochran Duke—you asked to speak with me?"

When that expressive gaze met his, Kochran's world slid sideways and then instantly came back into focus. He hesitated from saying more as her eyes darkened. The air around him snapped even as he was drawn to her energy and light. She stood, those small hands curling into fists at her side as she headed right for him. Startled, he couldn't move as she positioned herself toe to toe with him, and jabbed a finger in the center of his chest. For such a petite woman—her head barely came to his chin—she certainly packed a lot of power.

"So you're the irresponsible bastard who doesn't lock his shit down."

Ezra Snow liked to watch.

Men or women, in any manner of undress, and in any contorted position of pleasure. He wasn't the type of guy to discriminate. Tired of staring at the computer screen in his hole-in-the-wall office on the third floor of the club, Ezra had wandered down to Court. Though the scenes taking place around the perimeter of the room were fascinating, the real show was the sight of someone dressing down Kochran.

It was a rare occasion to see his boss at a loss for words, but he only seemed to be able to look at the woman gesturing wildly and speaking in elevated tones. Ezra had watched Kochran put more than a few submissives in their place with nothing more than a glare, so the visual unfolding before him was quite a treat.

Ezra couldn't hear everything she was saying, but considering the club was in full swing tonight, the fact he could make out even bits and pieces was impressive. The animated blonde either didn't realize she was yelling at the most powerful man at Noble House, or flat out didn't care.

Ezra hid a smile behind his hand when the woman started stabbing her finger into the center of Kochran's chest. From the lines bracketing Kochran's mouth, the woman was quickly approaching the limit on his patience. Still, it was a delight to watch. Not many people had the guts to go after a Duke, let alone this one in particular.

Kochran suddenly grabbed the woman by the arm and steered her to the nearest exit.

Ezra caught Enver's gaze, and the normally stoic man snorted and smirked. "She's complaining about your geek shit, Snow."

Ezra's interest immediately notched higher as he turned on his heel and followed the couple. At first he'd thought she was an irate member who'd had a scene go terribly wrong. But Enver's comment meant the club's extensive website, which Ezra was responsible for.

Ezra found Kochran and the woman standing in the hallway. "What the hell is going on?"

The woman ignored Ezra, directing her ire to Kochran. "Do you have any idea that you've got a skeezy predator prowling through your beta test, probably trying to pick off submissives one by one?"

Kochran rubbed between his eyebrows. "I have no idea what you're talking about. Noble House is the most secure adult entertainment site on the web." His gaze cut to Ezra. "Or so I'm told."

The woman tossed her hands into the air and groaned. "Mothertrucker. Seriously? You have no idea you're just giving your…*stuff* away for free? How stupid do you have to be to leave the back door open so wide someone with half a brain could just waltz right in? You've probably lost millions in revenue just because whatever half-rate code jockey you've got wrangling your data is a fucking imbecile and isn't worth his weight in overly caffeinated soda."

Ezra narrowed his eyes as he stepped closer. He'd be damned if he was going to sit idly by and listen to someone drag his work through the mud. "My code may not be the neatest or the prettiest, but it gets the job done."

"Out of all of that you're pissed off she insulted your code?" Kochran asked with a frown. "Bunch of fucking geeks."

Ezra crossed his arms, rocking up onto the balls of his feet. "Hey, it's your business she's insulting too. Or did you miss the part where she said we've got a prowler?"

Kochran frowned for a split second before his face was a mask once again. "Ms. Zane, would you calm down and explain with a little more detail what I'm giving away so freely and why you believe the safety of my members is in jeopardy?"

The woman ran her hands over her face.

"Ezra Snow." He stuck out his hand. "Fucking imbecile wrangler...wait, what was it you said? Half-rate code jockey, that was it, at your service."

The lines between her eyebrows deepened. "I can't believe you're owning up to that junk pile I cracked in forty seconds flat."

"Self-gratification isn't what it used to be, huh?"

"I'm going to let that slide. Once." She shook her finger at him, a gesture he found insanely sexy. "You've got holes the size of the Grand Canyon in your code. Any hacker worth their salt will be exploiting the breach. Surprised your ass isn't raw from the non-lubricated ass reaming you're getting."

"And with that overly pleasant thought, I'm going to excuse myself. Ezra, get this handled. Let Saint know if he needs to patch the security system and if I need to start revoking memberships." Kochran disappeared without waiting for confirmation, leaving Ezra to clean up this mess. Not surprising considering Kochran refused to change his passwords. The fact Kochran had turned the matter over to him meant he expected Ezra to make the complication disappear. One thing about Kochran Duke—he knew nothing about the technology that made half his club run. It was a wonder he'd managed as long as he had before Ezra and Saint had come along to provide the necessary platform for expanding the club.

A quick glance around the hallway showed they'd drawn a lot of stares from curious onlookers. The sort of attention Kochran wouldn't be happy about because it led to distracted members, and distracted members meant Dominants weren't as attentive to their subs, and submissives weren't as engaged in the scene. That kind of disturbance could lead to injuries or angry membership. Ezra sensed he'd already pissed off Kochran enough tonight; no need to add fuel to that particular fire.

"Why don't we step in there?" Ezra gestured to a nearby door. He had no idea what room he'd just directed the woman into, but anything was better than the public spectacle that had already played out to the curious crowd.

As he closed the door behind him, he realized being

out in full view was probably preferable. The room was
one of the spaces in the converted armory that hadn't
been remodeled after Kochran had purchased the building and surrounding land. At some point, the room
had been painted the standard military green. Flecks
of that same paint now littered the floor, exposing the
gray cinderblock beneath. A light bulb hung from the
ceiling, throwing harsh shadows everywhere. A sturdy
cage had been positioned in one corner, a five-gallon
bucket in the other, and several high wattage portable
spotlights by the door. Near the center of the room was
a single wooden chair rubbed bare in spots from years
and years of use.

Ezra had uploaded an interrogation scene that had
taken place in this very room to the website just last
week. He set his foot on a sturdy chest he knew contained ankle and wrist restraints, a spreader bar, a
TENS unit for electrical stimulation play, a first-aid
kit, protein bars, and several bottles of water. Appropriate items for taming the woman who was currently
giving him the evil eye if things got too out of hand.

He cleared his throat. "Sorry about the room, but
at least here you won't have to shout at me while telling me how much my skills suck and how lax security
for the club is. I'm sure my parents will be pleased to
know those four years of college were totally wasted."

She flipped her ponytail over her shoulder before
crossing her arms. "Sorry. I just get angry when people have such flagrant disregard for basic rules when
it comes to website structure and power exchanges."

The high color of her cheeks indicated her intrusion had been recent. "First of all, are you all right?"

When she nodded, he continued, "And when did this take place?"

"Around ten. This whole thing upset me more than I expected. I didn't mean to take it out on your partner." She extracted a zip drive from her back pocket and offered it to him. "There's footage on there I think you should take a look at."

Ezra's eyebrows winged up in surprise. "You drove two hours to shout at the owner of the website you illegally hacked into and hand deliver evidence that could convict you?"

"I wasn't thinking, all right? I just wanted... I wanted to be sure it was repaired as quickly as possible. That he—whoever he is—is stopped before someone really gets hurt." Her heavy sigh echoed through the sparsely decorated room. "I know I could have just sent an email but– -"

"You didn't want to take that chance." Ezra studied her closely, wondering why she'd gotten *this* agitated about a computer program. "As far as I'm aware, no one else has been fishing around our databases until now. Then again, something tells me I wouldn't have known you were in there either if you hadn't come barging into Court announcing your presence. We're pretty small fish, so what made you choose our little corner of the net?"

"Look, I... I do this for a living. My partner and I run a business breaking into websites."

"Websites that ask you to test their security and come up with a solution package. We haven't hired anyone to do that." While he was geeky enough to admire her skills when it came to unlawful entry, he was loyal to Kochran and the club that had given him sanctuary, which meant he needed to report the cybercrime. Perhaps locate Kochran and see if the club owner wanted to press charges.

Or he could work together with her to sort things out because he was interested in knowing how she'd wiggled through his firewalls, and seeing the footage on the drive she'd given him. If they went to the cops, he may never see what happened.

"Tell you what, since this is obviously something that is very close to you, for reasons you aren't telling me right now, why don't I contract your company to help with the patch? At a discounted rate, of course." When she gave him a skeptical look, he offered her a warm smile. "In exchange, I won't escort you to the nearest police station."

Her gaze shot to his. "You're not mad?"

"Don't mistake my offer for kindness." He wiggled the drive toward her. "I also want your help taking care of this guy that upset you."

She refused to look away from his unwavering gaze despite the fact her hands were trembling and her jaw was set. Whatever bravado she'd unleashed with Kochran had dissipated to give Ezra a glimpse of the woman beneath the mask. The one who had more guts than any woman he'd ever known. It had taken a great deal of courage to out such a criminal act to a group of strangers.

"How about I kill the whole system right now? Shut down the sim world and the website so no one can access it until we get this settled? Then you can use your obviously superior skills to help me untangle this and I'll convince myself to refrain from punishing you for calling me a half-rate code jockey."

His brain screamed at him for the foolishness in the words as they tripped off his tongue. This wasn't a submissive at the club. But she certainly was a woman who'd stirred things deep inside him.

"Deal?" he asked as he offered his hand.

She lifted the corner of her mouth in a wry smile, signaling those reins of command she needed weren't as far out of his grasp as he'd thought. "Can I still call you a code grinder?"

He'd been called that on more than one occasion all through school thanks to his penchant for wearing a tie and the clean code he used to generate. "Only on days that end in Y."

"Deal."

Chapter Four

A strange sense of comfort washed over Maddy as she stepped through the doors of Noble House on Monday afternoon. She couldn't explain why, but it felt like coming home.

Surprised didn't begin to explain her reaction. Those intangible layers of need and want coiled around things she had seen Thursday night, like sweat and tears and the indistinguishable cries of pleasure and pain. When she'd calmed down enough, the decadent smells of sex and leather had struck her, making her realize she belonged right in the middle of the energy that pulsed like it was its own power supply.

Though the decor was the same, the atmosphere wasn't as charged. And she didn't encounter the press of sex against her skin like last time. She fully intended the first order of business today would be figuring out who the hell the guy was from the theater.

True to Ezra's word, he'd shut down the entire network. Website and all. And kept it down the entire weekend while he and Steve had hammered out the finer details of the contract.

She made her way to the top floor of the enormous building that had once been an armory for the military, following the directions Ezra had emailed her. The club didn't look much different. Of course, now she was there totally on the up and up. Her temper had gotten the better of her, but Kochran had been so nonchalant about the breach, passing her off to someone else. For someone who obviously coveted the work he did, he sure had a blasé attitude. At least the other man had known and understood, even if he'd been the one responsible. Though Kochran was an extraordinary Dom, there was something about Ezra that struck a chord with her. A note that resonated through her all the way to somewhere deep in her center she couldn't identify.

For all the harmony she'd sensed with Ezra, she knew she had to squash whatever fantastical thoughts she had about him. She hadn't missed the two gold bands tucked securely in place on the fourth finger of his left hand. Married. Maddy was open to a lot of things sexually, could adapt easily enough to whatever the situation called for, but marriage gave her pause, even if he was in one of those open relationships.

Still, those rings didn't mean she had to stop admiring him or not find him an interesting case study. He didn't remind her of any code monkey she'd encountered before. No pop culture reference shirt or fraying jeans. He'd been clean cut, impeccably dressed and gorgeous.

She shook off the tingling sensations swirling through her lower extremities. Certainly she was experiencing the residual energy from being at the club when it had been in full swing the last time she'd been there. Curiosity had always gotten her into trouble. Interesting trouble, sure. But, as she reminded herself again, he was tied to someone for better or for worse. She wasn't interested in being responsible for the worse part.

When she reached the top floor, she noticed the decorations were much different than the floors below. Everything was so utilitarian. Stark and nondescript. Office space. Functional.

The directions stated Ezra's office was behind the door at the end of the hall, but the double doors in front of her drew her attention because of the cypher locking mechanism. A heavy-duty lock like that meant someone wanted to keep the contents of the room from prying eyes. A large slice of her wanted to know why. The part that wanted to pull threads until she'd unraveled the entire canvas. She suspected she could discover everything she wanted to know about the club and never have all the answers.

Ezra's office door opened. "Oh good, you're here."

She cast a longing glance to the double doors and made a mental note to explore later. He stood in the doorway, his gaze arrowed on her as though she was someone he'd always known.

She forced herself to swallow. "I am. I thought we had an appointment at one?"

"We do." He held up his mug, the bunching of his muscles obvious under the sleeve of his shirt. "Just going to refresh my coffee before we get started. Want some?"

She swallowed again, noting her throat wasn't as dry as before. "I never turn down a good jolt."

"Can't promise it's good, but it will certainly give you a decent buzz."

As she fell in step beside him, she was in awe of how dramatically her life had changed in just a few short days. Usually such life-altering decisions were thought about for days on end. She calculated. She weighed her options. She *planned*. But everything about Noble House so far had thrown her off her axis. Steve was the only one who knew where she was, and he was three thousand miles away. A dangerous prospect because she didn't know these people she'd agreed to help. These strangers who liked whips and chains and blindfolds and…who knew what else lurked in the shadows of a fetish club.

She'd willingly committed herself to fixing the problem at hand. They were paying her, but for one of the first times in her life, she was nervous. She'd broken federal privacy laws with the flick of her wrist and without a second thought. Yet the idea of sitting in a fetish club office with a man she hardly knew made her tremble.

Part of that anxiousness was due in part to the man walking beside her. He reminded her of an athlete, finely proportioned and just a bit on the stocky side. Even with his clothes on, he appeared strong and solid. Muscular. Those broad shoulders seemed to be capable of carrying the weight of the world, and then some. He had a quietness about him, a steady confidence that made her feel as though she'd known him all her life. He wasn't remarkably tall, but certainly towered over her petite frame.

As they entered the small kitchen, she leaned against the doorframe to wait. She was the newbie here and had no idea where everything was stored. Ezra, on the other hand, worked with a tidy efficiency she didn't believe she'd ever noticed in a man. Not a single movement was wasted as he prepared a fresh pot.

His hair shifted as he moved, a rich chocolate brown pelt that lay smooth against his scalp, worn a little long in the front. He flicked his head to the side each time strands of hair fell into his line of sight. And his eyes. The sort that observed every aspect in exacting detail. Thursday night they'd been green. Today, brown. She had no idea why, but she liked knowing his eyes changed color. She wondered if it was due to mood or nature. If a coming storm would darken his eyes to the same menacing shade as the thunderous clouds. The kind of tempest that was capable of stripping a woman down to full, wanton surrender.

Her gaze continued down to his faded denim shirt, the top button of which had been left open. Maddy suspected that button would be fastened if this had been a more formal meeting. Arms weren't something she was usually attracted to, but for some reason, Ezra's drew her attention as she looked him over. The way he'd carefully rolled back each sleeve of his shirt with equal folds that exposed his forearms and clung to his biceps and shoulders. Covered with a downy layer of hair, the muscles in his forearms stretched and bunched as he reached for each item he needed. His biceps followed each flowing, graceful movement bulking in all the right places.

His hands had a certain artistry. She wondered if they were as warm as she imagined, rough and thoroughly male. As he shifted to retrieve something from the narrow refrigerator tucked into one corner, his pants pulled tight across his ass. An exceptional specimen of the male form, to be certain, and one she wouldn't have minded observing without the covering of fabric.

She hadn't noticed all these things before, so why now? Why was it as though he was the only man in the world she wanted to pay attention to her all of a sudden? Despite her questions, she continued to unabashedly stare at the physique that made her mouth water and her brain dull like her skull had been stuffed full of tribbles. Yeah, he may be married, but she was going to ogle the hell out of him for as long as she could.

"Madeline?"

Oh holy wow. The way her given name tripped smooth and silky off his tongue with a voice tuned for sin. She hadn't noticed that earlier either. Easiest explanation was the fact she was standing on the top floor of a freaking fetish club.

"Sorry. Just thinking ahead to the job we have in store for us. You can call me Maddy. No need for such formality when I've been inside your code."

Ezra smirked. "Sounds dirty."

That devastating smile made things inside her come alive. "I have a feeling a lot of things said around here can be construed as dirty. Downright filthy on the right occasion."

"Hazards of the job, I'm afraid." He gestured to her with a mug full of coffee. "How do you take it?"

"No white stuff for me." She snorted at the implications as his lips twitched. Okay, she'd done that on purpose. No reason they needed to be all stuffy. "Seems pretty much everything you say can live in the gutter around this place."

"The gutter isn't such a bad spot if you have the right company. Ready to bang it out?"

She exhaled with a laugh. Quite a sense of humor on this one. A trait she found even more attractive than his physical stature. Brains had always been a turn on.

"Sure."

Chapter Five

The fascinating woman was a distraction of the first degree, an interference Ezra hadn't expected or wanted. Especially when someone had expressed her opinion quite loudly.

Half-rate code jockey. Madeline Zane certainly had a way with words. Now that she'd pointed out one of the amusing perils of working at Noble House, everything he thought was taken out of context. So far past left field out of context, it would be a struggle not to think dirty thoughts about everything they said.

As she followed him back to his office, her energy pressed against his back. That same energy had surged through him the instant he'd found her in the hallway. His body had come alive, and his dominant instincts had surged forward. Those same instincts had grabbed hold of the fear he'd seen in her eyes the other night. The sheer determination to triumph over evil. The need to bundle her close and promise nothing would ever hurt her.

"Sorry I don't have a better setup for you." As they entered his office, he pointed to the metal folding chair and card table he'd set up in the corner. "We'll find you something more comfortable by the end of the week."

"Just a short-term gig, right?" She shrugged as she passed. "Think I can survive. I'm going to get my stuff out of the car."

After she returned and set up her laptop on the small table, he realized his folly. The angle of the impromptu workstation allowed him the perfect vantage point to watch her work, though he doubted plunging headfirst into code would be hardship. Not when she'd admitted worming her way in through less than legal means.

He knew she'd seen the code she wrinkled her nose at before, but this time he'd given her the proper access authorizations. She'd waved those off as well, claiming she could slip back into the code faster than going through their firewalls. The point, he'd explained, was to patch those holes correctly. She'd reluctantly agreed and was now diligently working at her laptop.

Something told him Maddy didn't like taking directions. Didn't like to be told she couldn't do something when she had made her mind up that she could. Lots of possibilities with that kind of attitude around this place. Lots of ways to take advantage of it too, if she annoyed the wrong person.

Too bad he hadn't taken a submissive in years.

Though he kept his face angled toward the large monitor in the center of his desk, his gaze kept sliding to where she sat. Despite the fact he hadn't accepted this job at Noble House for the sex, he found he couldn't stop thinking about it since Maddy had stormed into his life. In fact, he'd accepted the job when he'd been approached because being around that much sex and kink would keep him focused on the job at hand and not how fucking lonely he was. Kink had been something he'd shut out of his life several years ago when his wife had died and his husband abandoned him.

He shook his head with a jerk, as though trying to clear the morose thoughts from his addled brain. The sooner they patched up the holes he'd been so careless with, the faster Maddy wouldn't be around anymore to plant such thoughts in his brain.

She turned abruptly, pulling her earbuds out. "You know there's a better way to structure your organization?" She gestured wildly at the laptop. "These files are a mess."

Of course he knew. Once upon a time, he'd exerted minimal effort in order to get Kochran the working website he'd requested because he'd made a promise. Helping a friend had been more important than dealing with his deep depression. His psychological health had been so poor, it had affected his physical health and landed him in the hospital. Story of his life. Ezra was paying for it now. He'd gotten a dressing down from Kochran about his attitude in regard to the security of the club's website the night before. Knew he had one still coming from Ford "Saint" Templar, co-owner of the club and the man responsible for the security of the network for Noble House, both online and physical. From what he'd heard, Kochran had already ripped Saint a new one because of the breach.

"Let's patch up these holes and then worry about the file trees." Better to tackle one thing at a time. "Unless you want to split up the work? Come at this thing from a few angles. You could clean up the organization while I patch the holes."

A soft clicking noise sounded as she tapped her fingers against the keyboard without using enough force to type. "No, probably wouldn't be as efficient or quick as if we work together to correct the breach. Just as long I get to be the one to kick that asshole out." She stuck her buds back into her ears as she turned to her laptop.

For a few minutes, concentrating on work was effortless. Then Maddy shifted in the seat, a change that pushed her shirt up to expose her lower back and his thoughts about piss-poor hypertext markup language and cascading style sheets tilted off their axis.

Her pants embraced her body rather than constricted. He'd never understood the fad of barely covering asses or exposing crotches. Leave a little to the imagination, for fuck's sake. Nothing remained a mystery anymore, a secret, sensual treasure trove to be discovered by covering areas that were uniquely female. Like the sloping curve of the two indentions in her lower back that called to him in a way he hadn't expected. Taunting him with the knowledge just a few short inches lower was the supple cleft of her ass. Those milky curves would give way to the heart of her heat and he would have an unobstructed view of the flushed folds that would beckon to him when she parted her thighs.

He would caress that wet heat just so, tease her with an infinitesimal touch as he feasted on the beauty of her sex using only his gaze. Her feminine gasp would fill the charged air between them. She'd clutch at the sheets he'd spread her out on, clenching her fingers into tight balls before flexing them as she fought against the sensations he forced her to endure.

She'd angle her head back against the mattress to expose the column of her throat in a tilt that illuminated the fine network of veins. He'd be relentless, continuing to torment her despite her pleas. In fact, those appeals

would only spur him on so he could experience each
and every one of her struggles. He'd work and work
to drive her higher. Enjoy the delicious torment that
would grip the base of his cock because he wanted to
position himself on his knees between her thighs and
drive into her tender heat.

He knew he wouldn't deserve such a treasure. He
was an average guy with an average job. In fact, Ezra
Snow was the epitome of the law of averages. He just
happened to wrangle code for the tech side of a kink
club at an abandoned military base. But in this second,
in his fantasy, Ezra was the man he used to be long
before illness, death and heartbreak had stolen everything he'd loved.

"Ezra?"

He jolted, upending a full cup of coffee he'd placed
next to his keyboard into his lap. "Shit."

He surged up, wincing against the burn soaking
through his shirt and pants. Maddy sprang into action, grabbing a roll of paper towels off the top of a
nearby cabinet before crossing the room to where he
stood dripping. He extended his hand to take the handful of sheets she'd torn off, but she evaded and tugged
his shirt free from his waistband. She wiped at the
liquid dotting his abdomen. The sudden shock of the
heated coffee had caused his erection to ease, but it
roared back with a vengeance as soon as her fingers
brushed against him.

A sudden rush of cool air grazed his skin, and he
was shocked to realize that she'd wrestled the button
of his pants free.

"I can do that." He covered his wet crotch with both

hands and canted his hips to the right so he wouldn't flash her any more than he already had.

"You need to get those in the wash before they're ruined."

Even with the exasperation in her voice as he evaded her again, Ezra would take ruined clothing over wrecked pride any day.

Kochran looked up from the folder he'd been studying to find Ezra shutting his office door. Stains mottled the button-down shirt that hung open. Kochran stripped away his reading glasses and used them to point to the front of Ezra's pants. "Unfortunate incident?"

"Nothing wounded but my ego."

Ezra's biting tone caught Kochran's interest. He hadn't been worried about Ezra pairing with Madeline in a working environment, even though the woman was quite a spitfire. He'd thought they'd complement each other nicely, both in matters of tech and sex. Though he hadn't heard their conversation after he'd left, he'd noticed an instant spark had flared between the two as they'd traded those initial barbs.

"Say something to piss her off further? If that's the case, you're lucky she only threw liquids at you."

Ezra frowned as he brushed at the stained fabric. "Just my carelessness."

It was Kochran's turn to scowl. Ezra wasn't usually so clumsy. He also wasn't like ordinary men. He'd been to hell, greeted the devil and fought with him on more than a few occasions. A fact Kochran respected.

He had hired Ezra when he'd expanded into the online footprint in order to give the man something to do with his time and his hands. Given the situation, the fact he'd made a few blunders wasn't out of the question. After the crack in their system had been exposed, he'd given Ezra a stern lecture about attention to detail and knew the situation would be handled. While he knew it was a fluke, he wouldn't tolerate another blunder.

Then there'd been the fact Kochran had had to work hard to shut his brain up when Madeline had been shrieking in a language he hadn't understood. Databases and mark ups and front ends and…something about server breaches. He'd wanted to snatch her over his knee and give her an unrestrained spanking, both for speaking to him so rudely and for her actions that had brought her to the club in the first place.

For the first time in as long as he could remember, he'd shut down his instincts and focused on the swirl of heat she stirred in his gut. It appeared as though Ezra wasn't the only one experiencing a connection.

"Think it will take long to patch?" Kochran tipped his reading glasses back to the end of his nose, took one look at the numbers that needed sorting for the accountant and promptly closed the file. As he stood, he tossed his glasses onto the pile of paper. The chaos of numbers wasn't going to sort itself out any faster if he spent another hour staring at them. "Or whatever it is you geeks do."

"A few days and nights of hard work should take care of everything."

Which meant the sweetly soft woman wouldn't be at the club for long. No more than the time it would take to educate the webmaster about his mistakes. A few nights, tops. Then she'd disappear like smoke. Too quick for Ezra to do anything about the obvious attraction he had toward her.

Sometimes Kochran wondered if the man was a fucking monk.

Chapter Six

Maddy groaned loudly as she stretched her aching back. Long hours hunched over weren't great for posture, but damn was it fun. So had been sniffing out the jerk who had tried to assert himself during her break-in of the simulated Noble House. Ezra hadn't argued when she'd insisted on taking the guy down, and she'd happily ejected him from the membership roster. Okay, she may have also sent a dozen vibrators to his house, but no reason not to use her power responsibly too.

Her glee in the task had started to wane when she realized the room had gotten warm and stuffy. She didn't remember ever being this confined. A quick glance down at the notebook she'd been scribbling showed she'd stopped midstream. Her brain was so addled she couldn't make heads or tails of the messy handwriting.

As she turned, she realized she was alone. Ezra's screen had gone dark and was cool to the touch. A sign he'd left some time ago. He hadn't left a note, and she didn't remember him telling her that he was throwing in the towel for the night. Didn't mean anything, though. She'd worked plenty of times oblivious to everything around her. She checked the clock hanging askew on the wall and saw it was close to five in the morning. Which meant she'd been at this for seventeen hours straight.

"No wonder I feel like I've eaten sawdust."

Hours upon hours of uninterrupted work wasn't unusual for her. But this wasn't her desk. Wasn't her preferred setup. It was functional at best, like the rest of Ezra's office. Plain and unassuming. Nothing like the man himself. She massaged her back as she stepped out into the hall. For shits and giggles, she tried those double doors again just like she had yesterday. This early in the morning was the perfect time to explore, right?

Still locked.

Were they ever open?

When she didn't feel like her head had been wrapped with bandages, she'd give that lock the attention it deserved. The only other open door on the third floor was a vast closet filled to the brim with every piece of clothing imaginable. She wasn't much of a clotheshorse, but a selection this exhaustive almost made her drool.

Since she didn't know her way around, she returned to the front entrance area. From the looks of everything, the club had closed up shop for the night. Wait... morning. Shit, she'd hit the stupid-tired phase. As she turned, she saw a set of doors she recognized. They led to the massive space that was the focal point of the club. Stupid-tired meant she had an excuse to walk toward, and through, those doors.

Surprisingly, none of the rooms she'd been in had reeked of sex. Expected for the office suite, perhaps, but the main room smelled...comforting. There was a pleasant aroma that permeated the spaces, even the workplace on the top floor. Like...her mother's kitchen when she baked. No, that wasn't it. A sex club that smelled like a bakery? She really was losing it.

The room was also cooler than she'd expected, and had a different atmosphere now as everyone had gone home. Well…almost everyone. A soft glow illuminated a corner on the far side and she headed for it, thinking it was Ezra. As she drew closer, she found Kochran balancing a laptop on his thigh.

She wasn't embarrassed for her outburst, but she wasn't proud of it either. Emotion had clouded her judgment, making her act as though she'd lost her flipping mind. As she stepped closer, his gaze flicked to her and he closed the computer with a snap.

"I didn't mean to disturb you," she offered with a sheepish smile.

"It's all right." He scribbled something on a slip of paper with a shiny pen before he set the laptop to the side and rose. *Unfolded himself* was more accurate. His full form had been compacted down into the small chair. With all the places to sit, the rust-colored piece of furniture seemed an odd choice.

"Finished for the night?" The paper and pen disappeared into his breast pocket.

"I guess so. I came looking for Ezra."

Kochran gestured toward the doors. "He left a few hours ago to get some rest when he realized he couldn't keep up with the workhorse he'd hired."

Maddy blinked. "I didn't even realize he'd gone."

"He said you were in a zone."

"You could have come to get me so you could leave." Great, now she was the flaky geek who'd gotten so caught up in her work, she'd made the big boss stick around. He probably had way better things to do than sit and wait for her.

"I don't have anywhere to be and I hate to interrupt hard work. I hear you cleaned a rat out of our membership roster. Thank you for that." He advanced toward her as he spoke. A sudden lance of panic stabbed at her gut as she stepped back. She wasn't afraid of him just...unsettled. The last time she'd seen him, she'd been riled up and snappish.

She bumped into a piece of furniture behind her.

"Watch out." He grabbed for her waist, setting his hand around her hip to keep her from falling.

"Sorry about that."

He released her once she had her balance. "No problem. It's dark in here."

Cold too. More so than she'd expected. "Where is *here* anyway?"

"This is Court, the main play area for the club. Most of the scenes take place here." He smirked. "Though I suspect you've already guessed that since you made such a memorable impression last night."

"The room is huge. Place is huge," she muttered. "Why the hell do people need such a big space to have sex?"

Kochran grinned. "We weren't at full capacity the first night you were here. Drop by on a Saturday night and you'll find out just how effectively the members use the space."

Maddy snorted. "I shouldn't have asked."

"Ezra didn't give you the ten-cent tour?"

"We got to work as soon as I got here." The weight of the day settled around her again as she remembered the number of hours hunched over the keyboard.

"Would you like one? Unless you need to go…" He trailed off, leaving the question to hang in the air between them.

She wanted to leave, but also wanted to spend more time with him. Kochran was the kind of man who made her blood zing in her veins. Had to be because she was tired and had been staring at the computer for too long. That was the only explanation she could think of for how she kept fantasizing about his mouth. The way his thick hair curled against the edge of his collar. Where it brushed against his brow. And the way he looked at her with a proprietary gleam that signaled he could feast on her for days.

"I think I should get home so I can shower and change." She wavered as she tried to turn, her balance still awry.

"You need some food."

A flush crept over her cheeks as his voice wove through her. Everything about Kochran was bold and unexpected. Enchanting in a way she wasn't usually attracted to. She certainly liked it in him, though. Silly, really, because Kochran wouldn't be too interested in her. Besides, he was in charge of a whole club. He had his pick of women or men to choose from. A man—a Dom—with those kinds of skills paired with his devastating good looks could have anyone he desired.

"Madeline?"

Oh man, that sounded exquisite coming from him. Velvety and smooth. Like her name was suddenly an obscene word. It made her feel vulnerable.

Her whole body gave a shiver she couldn't contain. When she looked up, heat flushing her cheeks, he simply waited for her response. The man was as dominant as they came, something that normally turned her off. She should have run from a guy who wanted that much control, but instead, she found herself completely and utterly intrigued.

Goose bumps erupted on her arms, and it wasn't entirely due to the way he made her feel. "Why is it so cold in here?"

"Bodies generate a lot of heat when they're having sex in a big room."

Her head spun as her mind flashed back to things she'd seen while working earlier. "I think I do need to eat."

What she needed to do was keep her head focused on the work she'd been asked to complete. More importantly, she wasn't a member. Feeling this way about a man she only vaguely knew—a man who owned a fetish club and was the son of one of the richest families on the West Coast—no matter how much he turned her on, was out of line.

Way, way out of line.

"Would you like some coffee? I made a fresh pot about a half hour ago."

Despite the little voice pinging a warning that staying was a Really Bad Idea, a shot of caffeine would help her on the drive. A quick buzz and she'd be on the road to her comfy, fluffy bed. Where she could fantasize about the two gorgeous men who'd made her feel sexy and…wanted.

"Actually, coffee would be great."

When he turned, she noticed the broad expanse of his back. Immediately, she wondered what it would be like to dig her nails into those muscles, have them ripple

and bunch under her finger as he plunged his cock…
whoa. Express ticket to horndog highway.

While it was obvious she and Kochran were the only
occupants, Maddy knew exactly what went on inside
these walls thanks to her cyber skills. Had seen with
her own eyes when she'd barged past the dude guard-
ing the door, her access granted because of her faked
membership. People had sex in full view of others. And
they enjoyed it. In fact, they even paid for the privilege.

In some small way, she admired the members. They
had a thirst for life she certainly didn't possess. She
wasn't hardwired for that level of kinkiness. Sure, she'd
had a few adventures with handcuffs and blindfolds—
what inquisitive human didn't? But her adventures
inside the bedroom were unquestionably vanilla com-
pared to some of things she'd seen during her forcible
takeover of the club's website.

She swallowed hard and followed him, expecting
they'd go back to the upper floor where she'd been
working, but instead he entered a small area that resembled a lounge. Tall café tables dotted the floor while
booths lined two walls. The wall behind the booths was
decorated with a large mural of the same logo she recognized from the club's website, three lions around a
shield. A door with a heavy-duty lock was nestled in
the far corner.

"How do you take it?" he asked as he stepped behind the waist-high bar.

She thought back to the conversation she'd had hours
ago with Ezra about this very same subject and gave
a quiet giggle. She smothered it with the back of her
hand and gave him a sheepish look.

"I didn't realize coffee preference was so amusing."

"My mind is wandering. Lack of sleep, I guess." She wrapped her hands around the mug to warm her suddenly cold and aching fingers. The first sip of the fragrant liquid made her cough. "This stuff will put some hair on your chest."

"I certainly hope not in your case."

She suddenly became aware of the fact she'd worn a low-cut V-neck tee. Sometime during her work, she'd stripped away her sweatshirt. When she'd accepted the coffee mug, the position had pushed her breasts together. Paired with his comment, and her exhaustion, her skin grew flush.

"How does one decide they want to own a club for kinky people anyhow?"

He grinned at her subject change. "Have to do something with my free time."

"I have to confess…there's a good chance our families rubbed elbows at the country club about fifteen or so years ago."

"Is that so?" Like Ezra, Kochran worked efficiently cleaning up the grounds he'd spilled during the coffee prep. Her revelation didn't give him pause. "I haven't been there in years. Much to my mother's displeasure."

"What do your parents think about this place?"

He leaned against the counter, ankles crossed, empty coffee mug with a faded bakery logo dangling from one finger, gaze thoroughly snagged on hers as he gave her a mischievous smile. "A man has to have some secrets."

Easy to imagine Kochran aiming that charming grin at a willing submissive who opened her legs for him in two seconds flat. He'd kneel between her spread thighs to bury his face in her pussy, his mouth and tongue working her until her cries carried to the rafters. He'd feast as though he needed to have her in order to survive. They'd be surrounded by the club's membership, performing and enjoying the audience. The submissive would open wider for him, allowing him to enjoy his fill as he pleased. He'd lift his hands to her breasts to tug and play with her nipples as he worshiped her.

A pull deep in her belly made it seem as though she was right there, experiencing the power and beauty of the moment. A dark thread of something Maddy didn't recognize hummed through her as her imagination kicked into overdrive. Took her to a place she hadn't expected. Now it wasn't a faceless submissive on her back, legs spread for the attentive Dom. It was Maddy. Naked and writhing under a man's attention while a group of strangers observed. And the man wasn't a stranger to her either.

She arched against Kochran's mouth, pleasure lancing through her as he wiggled his tongue against her opening. Forced her to experience a delicious pleasure that ramped up the temperature of her blood. She rolled her hips, desperately wanting to thread her fingers through his hair, but knowing she hadn't been given permission. That denial weighed her wrists down against the cushioned table she was spread out on as effectively as any pair of locked cuffs. The lack of physical restraint didn't hamper her enjoyment. In fact, it enhanced it.

Kochran lifted his head, his lips glistening with her honey as he shot her another one of those lethal grins again. "Do you like having my mouth on your cunt?"

Maddy blinked as the images that had formed in her mind dissolved when she realized Kochran had spoken to her. "What?"

He looked at her expectantly. "I asked do you like milk in your cup? You never answered how you take your coffee."

She had to count to fifteen before she was confident enough to answer without a wavering voice. Paused. Counted another ten, because the first exercise in patience hadn't been enough. She waved away the carton he offered. "I'm good."

She held out her mug with shaking hands to accept more coffee. The remaining tendrils of desire carried enough force she needed a few minutes. She was very aware of the slick, hot folds of her flesh causing friction as she shifted in the seat. Not enough to cause her to come, but enough to make her pleasantly conscious of the fact she was aroused.

She needed to shove this down. Way down. She needed to forget about it. Forget about him. And Ezra. Leave it to her to fantasize about a powerful Dom way out of her reach and his married employee. *Talk about fucked up, Zane.* Balancing her life was complicated enough without adding sex into the mix, let alone with two separate men. She reminded herself that her arrangement with the club was strictly professional. That it was built on the fact she'd weaseled her way into places she hadn't been invited.

"You sure you don't want something to eat? We're certainly not a top-notch restaurant, but we do well enough."

And with those simple statements, he'd ensnared her again with his caring attention. *Rein it in, girl.* "I'm sorry, I can't." The effort of speaking those four words had been immense.

He sipped his coffee, his gaze homed on her. "Can't,

or don't want to be alone with a man who likes to tie people up?"

The fact he mentioned his sexual interests meant a meal with him could easily lead to other things. "We work together. Office entanglements are a big no-no."

"Technically, you don't work for me. You're a contractor who works for my partner Saint. And you are repairing a flaw you found while you were busy breaking the law." Despite his accusatory glance, his voice was soft, his expression amused. Even with all his rough edges and the unapologetic attitude toward sex, Kochran wasn't judging her. She couldn't explain why, but she knew she could be honest with him.

Within the span of a few hours, two men—two complete strangers—had convinced her she was absolutely safe when she was in their presence. She'd come to the club to report a security issue she'd created, the dangerous lack of a safe exit and a jerkoff preying on innocent submissives—she hadn't been prepared for the unexpected pleasure from two vastly different men. Pursuing either of them would be double trouble. While Maddy loved skirting the law, she wasn't about to put her heart up as collateral. And why the hell was she thinking about both of them? Since when had she become the poster child for polyamory?

He touched the back of her hand with a gentle caress. "You're excited."

"What?" She jerked her hand away. "I'm just tired."

Kochran leaned closer, bracing his elbow on the bar as he angled his upper body toward her. "Your cheeks are flushed. Your breathing increased earlier and hasn't normalized yet. I'd bet it's safe to say your panties are wet, because whatever it is that you're thinking has gotten you all hot and bothered."

She swallowed. This boiled down to basics. What he'd said could be construed as forward and out of bounds, but she also felt safe around him. As though she knew he wouldn't overstep her limits and force her to do anything she hadn't consented to. "You're an attractive man, Kochran."

"And?"

"I don't do quick, hard bangs," she said matter-of-factly.

His eyes glimmered. "Neither do I."

Maddy wasn't someone who believed in instalove, but she did believe the zing of desire that she'd been keenly aware of since she'd walked through the club's main doors. The one that had made her appreciate finely built men such as Ezra and Kochran. And she also believed in the decadent heat winding its way between her legs. At the way it flourished and spun her higher with each cunning smile Kochran aimed her way.

"Madeline."

She jumped when she realized Kochran was standing right beside her. He was the sort of man who definitely knew what he wanted. That sort of focus from a man like him made her dizzy. Her body emitted a study thrum that was attuned to him. With him at close range, she was primed and ready. A single word was the key to a whole lot of answers.

"Yes," she answered, even though he hadn't asked a question. "You were going to ask if you could kiss me. I was just simplifying things."

"No." He paused, inches between their lips. This

close she saw his irises had golden flecks throughout. "The way you looked at me just now…you want something. Something you aren't sure you're allowed to have." He hummed softly. "I'm interested in finding out what that thing is."

She blushed. As desperately out of practice as she was at flirting, she was even more so when it came to sexual matters. "You don't beat around the bush." She snorted at her own joke as Kochran smiled. God, could she be any more of a dork? "You're very blunt," she amended.

"I know when I see something I want."

The power of his influence suggested this was more than a passing fancy. Wasn't as though she'd purposefully sought a man like Kochran, but the club certainly provided the perfect motivation. A hot and very sexy Dom stood just inches away from her, confiding that he was interested in knowing what she was thinking.

The color of his eyes intensified as his smile widened. She could devote hours to watching him—just like watching Ezra fix coffee. Looking at it from a different angle, maybe she just had a coffee fetish. Hot java was certainly a chosen drug, but so was being the focus of a handsome man.

"Since you won't tell me, I'd like to try a little experiment, Madeline."

"And that is?"

"I'm going to kiss you." His voice was a quiet rumble that pinned her to the chair.

The room constricted around her, causing her to feel too much, too fast. "Oh."

He swallowed the word by capturing her mouth. There was nothing easy or relaxing about kissing Kochran Duke. He demanded with each stroke of his tongue. Unapologetically took what he wanted with each brush of his lips against hers, yet still made her believe the entire thing had been her idea. Melted that instant flare of icy panic that had stabbed at her the second she'd realized what he'd intended.

Her head spun with how fast they were going. Their connection was undeniably hot. She could end up battered and bleeding by the time this was over, but she quickly found herself unable to care. She was only concerned about how damn good he made her feel.

He made her want to be fucked. To fuck him. To be observed while fucking. Nothing between them but the sweat and heat their bodies generated while moving. He also made her want the kind of surrender she knew he could give her because he owned a freaking S&M club.

Most of all, she simply wanted *him*.

With a groan, she opened wider to his exploration. Wrapped her hands around his strong wrists as he used his agile hands to angle her face. She adjusted, turning her body toward his, and her legs naturally widened for him. A rumble sounded, low in his throat as he wedged himself between her spread thighs. As he massaged his tongue against hers in a slow dance more sensual than any tango, she fell into the weight of his body against hers, the press of his erect cock hard against her inner thigh.

The persistent warning echoed in her head. But the pleasant clench of the inner walls of her cunt silenced that cautionary notice. She'd never been kissed with such ferocity and passion before. Such never-ending need as he sucked on her tongue. Nibbled and licked at the corners before diving back in for another consuming taste. He kissed her so ruthlessly, she was certain she was going to swoon. Fucking *swoon*.

He sucked in a breath and licked his lips as they parted. "You taste wonderful."

"And you sound surprised."

"Pleased." He kept his gaze on hers as he gave her a hasty peck. "Extremely pleased."

Hearing his approval on a desire-roughened voice made her core glow. Made her want to surrender to him like she never had to any man. She wanted a lot of things she'd only dreamed about before.

He smoothed his finger down the neck of her shirt, tracing her exposed skin right at the hem but never delving further. Oh, how she wanted him to touch her in any of the intimate places that were throbbing and on fire.

"You make me crazy," she whispered. "Make me want things I shouldn't want. Things I've only ever dreamed about. Fantasized about."

"Are you ashamed? Is that why you've never made them a reality?" He brushed her hair back from her face as he leaned closer and tilted her chin so she had nowhere else to look but directly into his eyes. "Tell me. What do you fantasize about? What were you thinking when you drifted off earlier? What got you so aroused?"

A blush rose to her cheeks. She'd underestimated his observational skills. She didn't know why she was so surprised by his attention to detail. Everything about this man was remarkable.

"Madeline, I want you to tell me what you were imagining."

His voice took on a hard quality that caused her to suck in a breath. She'd wanted him before, but *holy shit*.

"I was spread out naked on a cushion." She started speaking slowly, gaining confidence as she laid out her fantasy in detail. "You were between my legs, licking and sucking—"

"Eating your pussy."

She nodded, though she couldn't bring herself to repeat the harsher words. Someday she'd have the confidence to speak that way out loud. "There was a group of people standing around in a circle, observing. No one said anything, they just…watched. I felt something. Something I've never experienced before. I wanted to… I wanted to please you." Be like that perfectly poised submissive she'd seen him command on the video. "You wouldn't let me come. I wanted to, though. A lot. But you kept backing off just as I was about to blow."

"What turned you on more, knowing there were people watching us, or obeying my commands while I gave you a thorough tongue lashing?"

Everything.

The answer sat on the tip of her tongue. Envisioning the fantasy and describing it to the very man who starred in her mind porno wasn't easy. Silly, really. Kochran had undoubtedly heard it all. Had experienced more illicit things than her brain could even conjure. To him, her fantasy would be boring and unimaginative. And that was the root of the problem. Tempting as Kochran may have been, he should be with someone who wasn't frightened by her desires.

She gave him a half-smile. "I think I should go."

He stared at her for a long minute before he severed contact. She looked up, expecting to see his eyes dark with disappointment, but instead she saw understanding. "I'll walk you to your car."

He didn't play coy this time, or ask her if that's what she truly wanted. Gave her the space he obviously recognized she needed. Gooseflesh erupted down her arms. That knowledge turned her on perhaps more than anything else. He respected her limitations.

"You don't have to," she offered.

"I want to."

She accepted his hand with a nod. Though he may not be disappointed by her lack of sexual adventure, she was. This dude was totally into her and more than willing to help her realize her fantasies, and she was escaping.

The mid-June morning air greeted them as they stepped outside, adding a chili that said the last trace of spring wasn't ready to release its stranglehold just yet. That would change by noon, when the blistering hot sun melted everything it touched.

As she disengaged the locks, she noticed her car was the lone occupant in the parking lot. "Didn't you drive here?"

"I live close enough to walk to work." He stepped around, opening the door for her.

After she fired up the engine, she lowered the driver's side window. "Thank you." She didn't clarify what she was thanking him for. The coffee, allowing her to reveal part of her fantasy, or respecting her wish to leave.

"Are you all right to drive?"

"Yes," she responded truthfully. "The coffee is just enough buzz to fuel me."

He studied her for a few moments before being satisfied. "Well, good. Drive safe. Can I tell Ezra you'll be back later tonight to continue working?"

"Of course." Gah. Why did he have to be so...polite? So opposite of everything he'd been just minutes ago. He was a hard puzzle to solve, and something told Maddy she would never learn the key to figuring him out.

She pushed the brake and dropped the engine into gear, but paused when he gently touched her shoulder. He pressed a square of paper into the small pocket on her shirt. The paper's edge teased her nipple as he slipped it into place. She drew in a breath, unintentionally pushing her breast against his finger. Kochran met her gaze as he deliberately fanned his fingers to frame the roundness of her breast.

"So lovely." He gently squeezed until her breath was shallow and rapid. "So delicate and firm at the same time. Someday, I hope you find the courage to ask me for what you need, Madeline Zane."

He withdrew, pulling his fingers away with an exacting slowness that made her yearn for his touch immediately. She was headed straight for shark-infested waters without a life vest to help her tread, but she was too intrigued by the wild, out-of-control ride to retreat. God, in one day, two different men had made her feel as though she was the most important woman in the world. That heady buzz was going to be difficult to shake.

He pressed a gentle kiss to her ear. "I promise to make you come the first time I fuck you, Madeline."

Chapter Seven

Driving to the hospice first thing after a very long night wasn't Kochran's idea of a good time. He'd hated visiting when both his grandparents had been placed. He despised the task even more now that his sister was spending her last days cooped up in one.

A familiar kind of dread settled in the center of his chest as he parked, erasing any of the residual excitement running through him since leaving Madeline. He'd meant to come see Tory yesterday, but had gotten sidetracked by the certified letter from his accountant announcing his retirement, a crack in the tank in the water torture room and someone was stealing all the batteries from the toy supply closet. Add in the website breach and it was a wonder he had any sanity left. Now that he had the time, he realized he'd been intrigued by the spitfire who had brought it to their attention. She drew him in. Made him want to scorch his fingers because he'd gotten too close and wanted to play with fire.

His mind wandered down all sorts of interesting paths about her. Especially when she'd told him about that little fantasy she'd had about him. She hadn't pinged his radar all that hard when she'd been yelling at him, but she was certainly setting off all the bells and whistles now. So much so that getting a few hours of sleep after she'd left him at the club had been difficult.

His phone chimed again with another text from Adelita. A flood of panic erased the pleasant thoughts of bending the club's cyberhacker over his knee. With the preparations in the recent months, Kochran had been named as Tory's legal guardian, which meant he had to sign a shit ton of paperwork whenever she got a bug up her ass to change her will. Since his sister had the attention span of a gnat, alterations happened regularly.

He was exhausted today, so he didn't relish handling the task, or his irate sister when he talked her out of whatever she wanted to revise. The string of long nights thanks to the club responsibilities and several gigs with the band were taking their toll. But he'd do anything for Tory. Better than her trying to steamroll some unsuspecting paralegal.

When he looked up, Adelita was rushing through the sliding doors. He instantly knew something was wrong. The knot exploded to full blown terror as she came closer. The guilt he'd let eat him up inside gnawed through his gut as he cleared his throat.

He sent a silent prayer out to the universe. "Is she gone?"

"I should be so lucky." Adelita dabbed at her blood-shot eyes then tucked an errant strand of hair behind her ear. "She's being a cunt waffle. I was hoping you could talk some sense into her."

Kochran bit his lip as the tension tightening his body eased. "So it's a normal day?" Cunt waffle was a new one. He'd have to add that to his list of insults.

He wrapped an arm around his sister's girlfriend,

pulling her against him in a tight hug. Though Tory's
illness had been taking a toll on him, Adelita bore the
brunt. She'd lost weight, her skin was dry and her clothing wrinkled. Tension kept her small frame so rigid,
it was a surprise she hadn't snapped months ago. He
wondered when the last time anyone had taken care
of Adelita was.

She sniffed against his shoulder. "She demanded I
put her out of her misery again."

His panic returned. He grabbed Adelita's arm and
struggled to keep from forcing more information out
of her. "Christ, why didn't you tell me?" He released
her, pushing past to sprint to the sliding entrance doors.

Tory's demands weren't new, but that didn't mean
they were any less upsetting for everyone involved.
He understood his sister's desire to end her long battle
with a disease that was meticulously eating away her
heart cell by cell, both physically and in spirit. The
wait for the final visit with the Grim Reaper for Tory
Duke wasn't going to be swift, or kind. More like a
leisurely stroll down a path angled toward an end that
would never come. Facing that kind of reality had to be
daunting for anyone. Though she tried her best to keep
her frustration at bay, some days it was all too much.

Doors passed in a blur as he sped toward Tory's
room, ignoring the cheery calls from the nurses he
normally stopped and talked to. Tory's gaze met his as
soon as he stepped through the doorway. Her cracked
lips tilted at the edges as she tried to smile. "Hey, bro."

The room angled wildly as he tried to keep his emotions in check. Every day she looked a little closer to
the end. Long ago, her brunette hair had lost its luster.

The elasticity had been erased from her skin, making her appear much older than she should have.

Seeing his terminally ill sister lying so frail in the utilitarian bed clenched his heart every single time he visited. It never got easier. Not that he'd ever expected it to. But knowing she'd asked her longtime girlfriend to end things for her meant things were starting to take a turn for the worse.

Determined not to let her see his worry, he plastered on a smile. "I hear you're being a cunt waffle."

"Tired."

"I know." They all were. He made it a point to never show Tory just how much he wanted her to have the peace she desperately wanted. He ignored the overwhelming weight of judgment hanging in the stagnant air. "Mother was here earlier, wasn't she?"

Tory rolled her eyes. "She's still here. Pissy as ever."

No doubt Tory's request to Adelita had coincided with the visit. Enduring their mother's wrath took a toll on Kochran even during his best days. He understood Tory's craving for escape. To finally be free of the disease that had robbed her of a full life. Endless strings of doctor's appointments had driven Tory down the suicide path more than a few times as a teenager, and their mother had been too wrapped up in her own life to understand what her daughter was truly going through.

Kochran gave her a stern look. "You should have called me."

"She's refusing her meds." Adelita stepped beside Kochran, wrapping her hand around his arm for support he gladly gave. "Fought off the night nurse when he tried to force her to take them."

"Because she needs to take them, Adelita," said a harsh female voice. Noelle Duke swept into the room, her face as tight as the high bun she'd swept her hair into. Her diminutive stature did nothing to diminish her presence. "The nurse is simply following my directive."

"Did you buy him off too, Mother?" He tamped down on the urge to seek out the nurse and throat punch him. They'd had issues with that particular man not obeying Tory's DNR order. He'd complained to the center owner, but so far nothing had been done to reprimand the staff. Noelle's persistence that Tory's life be extended as far as possible, regardless of Tory's do not resuscitate order, was astounding. "I thought we'd gotten past this. Thought we'd agree to allow Tory to make the decisions about her care."

"No, Kochran, *you* agreed. I simply allowed you to live, once again, in your delusions." Noelle set her hand against Tory's forehead. "Mama knows best. Isn't that right, baby?"

"Mommy Dearest is more like it," Kochran muttered under his breath as he folded himself into a small chair beside the bed.

Noelle shot him a glare. "Don't be crass, Kochran. Not in front of your sister." She smoothed Tory's bed sheets, frowning. "These are the same linens that were on the bed yesterday. I swear, no one in this infernal place gives a damn about their responsibilities. Really, Victoria, I wish you'd go to the care facility in New York."

Despite Tory's glare, Kochran couldn't help himself. "You mean the facility that has your father's name etched in stone over the front entrance?"

"They had top-notch care. Tory would have everything she needed, including round-the-clock care, which is more than I can say for this place."

Tory set her hand on Noelle's arm. "Mom, I could use some water."

"Of course, baby." She swept up the pitcher and left the room.

He didn't unclench his jaw until the sound of her clacking heels faded away. "What do you need me to do, sweetheart?"

"Tell Mom to fuck off."

Despite his emotions pinging all over the place, he couldn't help but laugh. "Anything for you, dearest."

He kissed her forehead, noting the rough texture of her ashen skin. Her body was shutting down on her. Giving out one organ at a time while the one that was broken continued to beat. He knew she was hurting. Knew she wouldn't directly tell anyone that she was. He had never been able to find the strength he needed from her assurances that everything would be all right.

"I wish it was me," he confessed quietly.

"No you don't," Tory offered with a tight smile.

His heart clenched as fire burned in his veins. He hadn't meant to say it loud enough for her to hear. "I will always be here for you, sweetheart. Always."

Even as the words passed his lips, he knew he would never be able to fulfill the impossible promise. He'd have to sit vigil over her hospice bed to wait for the inevitable. Though it made him feel like a coward, until now he never allowed her to see how much pain he was in. How much her death was going to affect him. He treasured each moment she was still alive. Those instances were rapidly decreasing, however, and he knew he was going to have to face the truth soon.

Much, much too soon.

Chapter Eight

The past week had showed Ezra that Maddy wasn't a hobby coder. Though he didn't understand how it was possible, she had the ability to work on twenty lines of code at once. He braced himself on her desk with one hand, watching the numbers, letters and symbols appear on the screen at a staggering rate. As if she hadn't been fucking tempting enough—listening to her fingers fly over the keyboard made his cock so hard it was a wonder he was able to stand. If she'd known how much he longed to kiss that full bottom lip she tugged on while she concentrated, how he wanted to spend hours exploring her petite body, and how desperately he wanted to know how dirty her mind truly was, she would have bolted from the room screaming.

"You know you guys are the best in the game, right?" She paused, looking at him expectantly.

"Okay, I'll bite." He had no idea where this was going, but was interested to hear what she had to say. At least it would keep his mind off the way she looked when she worked. "Sure we are."

"I mean, come on." She gestured to the screen. "You have the market cornered because no one else out there is combining kink and geek. Who would have ever thought of an online BDSM club? It's brilliant. But it also means you're the alpha. You want to stay that way, so you protect your investment. You lock down your encryption tight with code the average hacker can't decrypt."

He'd never gotten so turned on by geek speak and been so ashamed of his reaction at the same time. She knocked him over the head harder than he expected. Made him feel all sorts of sensations he hadn't experienced in a damn long time. Not that he hadn't wanted to. He'd just elected to be extremely selective when it came to matters of sex and domination.

Ezra cleansed his thoughts lest his face give away the ideas turning over in his mind. "I'm getting ready to head out for the night. Want to grab a beer at Screwdriver in Ashes Fork? Take a break cleaning up my mess for a few hours?"

"I'd love to, but I can't. I'm taking the red-eye to New York this evening to work on some things with Steve this weekend." She logged out of the network and shut down her laptop. As she leaned over to shove her computer into a bag, her shirt hung open to give him the perfect view of her cleavage. "Unless you need me for something urgent?"

He hastily averted his gaze. "No, it's fine. I forgot you asked for the weekend off. Have a safe trip." It was better if they went their separate ways tonight. Safer. Too many raw emotions bubbling near the surface that he didn't want to dump on Maddy.

As he drove to his favorite bar, Screwdriver, he thought about how he'd refused to let anyone see when he was hurting for the longest time. The world favored strength and stoicism over compassion and tears. Let people know he was broken up inside because his wife died and his husband left, and they took pity on him. He hated pity with a passion. Then he'd seen it as the only defense against the constant barrage of questions thrown his way. Maddy, though…she was the first woman he'd wanted to show his scars to. At some point, it had become easier to let people believe he was something he wasn't.

Simpler.

The powerful reminder had driven him to exchange his desk at the club for a barstool.

Two hours passed and he'd only just finished the first round. Nursing a drink wasn't typical for him, but he hadn't come to the bar to drown his sorrows. Instead, he was avoiding his house. The stuffy confinement of the memories chasing him had gotten to be too much. He would have been better off finishing the bottle of tequila, but the numb of alcohol hadn't dulled the pain then, so it certainly wouldn't work now.

The last thing he wanted was to look at the world filled with fuzzy edges. He also hadn't been paying attention to his health as well as he should have—again—even though letting it get out of hand could have dire consequences. Besides, Duality was due to start their set in fifteen minutes and Ezra didn't want to be shit-faced. There were few things in life he found himself enjoying lately, and coming to see the band his boss banged the drums for was a good way to distract him from the shitstorm his life was starting to become.

Oz, the owner of the bar, eyed him. "You all right, man? Looking a little whiter than usual."

Ezra accepted the water Oz pushed his way. "Surprised you don't have a camera strapped around your neck to take pictures." Ezra gestured to the lead singer of the band breaking down their set. "You've been eyeing that one all night."

Oz snorted as he flipped Ezra off. The insults were a tradition between the men who had become friends shortly after Ezra had moved his office to the club. The bartender was also a popular Dom at Noble House, specializing in rough sex and total power exchanges. They'd had more than a few conversations about their shared interests whenever Ezra took up residence on a barstool. The banter kept him busy so he wouldn't have to think about how everything he touched inevitably turned to shit.

The thought of sitting at home made his skin crawl. So did being stuck drowning in bitter memories and soul-eating heartbreak. The memories of Nora and Kyle were always there, waiting in the rafters of his living room, the baseboards of his bedroom. Saturating the spaces around him so even thinking became a struggle.

Fifteen minutes later, the first few notes of Duality's opening song braced him over a dark rabbit hole. Some days were better than others. Today had been especially difficult since it was the anniversary of Nora's death. But the heavy beat drove away the temptation to wallow. As Charlie, the lead vocalist, began to sing, Ezra closed his eyes, losing himself in the melody and the husky quality of her voice. When she hit a chord, the fine hairs on his arm lifted as the resonance moved through him.

Demons he thought long banished rose from the shadows, wrapping around him in a suffocating embrace. He shook off the sensation, hoping the memories would go away. But as the band moved seamlessly into their next song, those cloying memories only sank their claws deeper.

Determined not to break, Ezra focused on the visceral way Kochran pounded on the drums, his biceps flexing and bunching as the tempo of the song increased. Ezra had always thought Kochran was most at home at Noble House, wielding his whip, but he'd been wrong. Banging out an infectious cadence on his drum set was Kochran's true home.

A sudden surge consumed Ezra, an intense desire to pound into Kochran with the same wild, untamed enthusiasm.

An unexpected gush of panic sped his heart rate. Sweat erupted across his brow, down the back of his neck. Inexplicable fatigue permeated his body. Muscles across his abdomen gripped with wrenching force, and the blinding need to urinate clawed at him. He gritted his teeth and clenched the bar.

What the hell was wrong? One drink wasn't enough to get him drunk. The noise of the bar sounded so far away, as though he was on the opposite side of a tunnel, train barreling toward him and he was tied to the tracks with unbreakable chains. He realized with a start that the music had stopped.

"Ezra."

Pressure against his shoulder did nothing to ease the swamp of memories he didn't want or need. In fact, his weakness only made them stronger.

"Ezra, it's Kochran. How much did you drink tonight?"

Ah God, not you. Don't be my rescuer.

Ezra attempted to assure everyone he was all right, but he fumbled the words, his tongue thick and cumbersome in his mouth. He was dimly aware of moving. Of his stomach roiling as he attempted to shuffle his feet. Coolness blanketed him, the drastic temperature change a wash of water over a raging fire.

Dazed, he struggled to fight back the inky blackness threatening to consume him.

A face appeared through the haze, handsome with a masculine curve of jaw covered with a sprinkling of dark hair. Deep green eyes matched the grass he was spread out on. His linen shirt hung open to reveal golden skin stretched tautly over washboard abs, and a dusting of hair in a dark trail that disappeared under the waistband of his jeans.

Kyle.

Feminine laughter sounded in Ezra's ears, and a cloud of white appeared as Nora jumped on top of Kyle. Her cotton dress billowed around them to expose the lovely, flawless curve of her breasts as she leaned over to press her lips against Kyle's. He cradled her, kissing her tenderly as she sank into his comforting embrace.

They are so fucking beautiful.

Ezra loved watching them like this. So carefree about their life. Their love. He called out, desperately wanting to be with them again. But they ignored him, rolling in the grass as though they were the only ones around for miles. Suddenly the two entwined lovers faded, then vanished.

Don't leave me.

He gritted his teeth as he surfaced, pulling in a harsh breath as he involuntarily sank again. The field was gone, the sun hidden behind heavy drapes that blocked the daylight. Nora lay on the bed, her skin sallow and parchment thin. Kyle sat at her side, clutching her hand.

Their earlier playfulness gone as they faced the inevitable.

"It's going to be all right, ladybug."

The reminder of Kyle's nickname for Nora stabbed Ezra hard in the gut, clawing and tearing at his insides. He tried to suck in air that wasn't there. Black spots danced before his eyes. A heavy weight settled on his chest, suffocating him with the force. The vision of his former lovers faded, leaving him feeling raw as though his skin had been scraped away.

"Please don't leave me," he whispered.

"Hadn't planned on it," a familiar voice said. "One breath at a time, all right?"

Ezra nodded, realizing Kochran was still on the ground beside him, one strong hand cupping the back of his neck, the other on his chest as a reminder to breathe.

But the knowledge his friend was there wasn't enough. An awful sound saturated with fear and pain scraped his throat as he tried to suck in deep gulps of air. Still drowning in the memories of a life that he no longer had, Ezra succumbed to the darkness.

Chapter Nine

Kochran rubbed at his eyes. Someday they wouldn't burn like he'd spent too much time staring at the midday sun. The reaction had nothing to do with his allergies and everything to do with the man sleeping in his bed.

The instant Kochran had seen Ezra stumble and fall, he'd abandoned his drum set and rushed to assist. By the time Kochran had reached Ezra, Oz was already on the phone with 911. The emergency training Kochran had had before he'd opened Noble House had kicked into gear the moment he'd seen the insulin pump taped to Ezra's abdomen. By the time the EMTs had arrived, they'd gotten some sugar in him and had averted a crisis.

Ezra insisted a trip to the hospital wasn't necessary, but Kochran refused to allow Ezra to go to his house alone. The unease clawing at Kochran hadn't decreased, so he'd sat in the chair next to the bed for the rest of the night. According to the wall clock, the sun had made its presence known hours before. This sort of vigil reminded him of sitting over Tory's bed. Only there was nothing he could do to stop Tory's health issues. Ezra, on the other hand, deserved a stern lecture on the value of a life where he had to monitor his blood sugar.

Ezra stirred, tangling the sheets around his thighs. He'd sweated so profusely during the attack, Kochran had stripped him before guiding him into bed. The displaced sheet uncovered the majority of Ezra's body, including his semi-erect dick. Kochran had seen plenty in his lifetime, but found himself staring at the sleeping man's more than he should have. Kochran liked to watch, but knew he was violating some level of trust by sitting here. Yet he couldn't stop. He tried to tell himself his voyeurism was strictly due to the fact he was tired. That he'd been so busy attending to everyone else, he hadn't taken care of himself. But in reality, he knew that excuse couldn't be further from the truth.

With a quiet curse, Kochran rose to pull the sheet back around Ezra's waist. Compelled by his protective instincts, he touched the back of his hand against Ezra's forehead, pleased when he found it cool and free of perspiration.

Ezra's eyes fluttered open. "What the hell?"

"You're fine now. Think you drank something that didn't agree with you. Or had too much." He decided not to mention the fact he knew exactly why Ezra had gone down. That was a conversation better left for when Ezra had his wits about him again. They could discuss that at the same time Ezra provided some clarification as to why he hadn't mentioned his condition on his required medical clearance for the club. Only a few members had balked at the need for the data, but if something happened during a scene, Kochran wanted to make sure information was on hand to effectively treat the patient. Emergency personnel were

only a phone call away, but Kochran required at least
basic level first-aid training for every Master and Dom
at the club.

Ezra scowled as he tossed back the sheet and sat up.
Kochran caught him when he swayed and muscled him
back into a horizontal position. "Take it easy."

Ezra screwed his eyes up again. "Everything is spinning."

Kochran kept his hand in place on Ezra's shoulder
just in case he decided to try again. "Relax. Don't rush
yourself."

Though Ezra frowned, he nodded and relaxed, tension bleeding from his muscles. Confident Ezra would
stay put for the time being, Kochran grabbed fresh
clothes for himself, dropped some on the corner of
the bed for Ezra and ducked into the shower area to
wash up.

Ten minutes later, Kochran went through the mindless task of fixing a fresh pot of coffee and flipping on
the burner. His stomach had protested the lack of food
during the middle of his shower. He couldn't remember the last time he'd eaten anything more than one of
the protein bars stashed in his desk at the club. A supply that was quickly diminishing because he'd been
spending more and more time at the club tending to the
paperwork that came along with business ownership.

He leaned against the counter with his second cup of
coffee as he listened to breakfast cook. The silence of
his home wasn't as pressing today. Most days when he
managed to drag himself out of bed, he flipped on the
sound system he'd had installed when he'd bought his
place. Today, the quiet burbling of the coffee maker and
the sizzle of the butter in the frying pan were enough

to soothe him. Then there was the fact he had an un-
invited guest. Given the open floor plan he'd worked
up when he'd bought the club—and the surrounding
land, so he could live on property—he knew any kind
of noise would be heard throughout the former missile
silo, so he'd erred on the side of caution out of respect.

He suspected there was more going on with Ezra
than diabetic shock. He'd been so damn relieved when
he'd realized Ezra was going to be all right. When he'd
realized he'd known how to help him. The whole thing
made Kochran want to punch a nearest wall. But he'd
stopped using concrete to solve his problems a long
time ago.

As he flipped the eggs, he heard movement behind
him. Ezra was shuffling over to the kitchen from the
bedroom. He only wore the ill-fitting shorts Kochran
had left for him, the insulin pump tucked into the waistband. The white patch of his injection site stood out
against his taut abdomen. His face was still drawn,
eyes bloodshot with dark circles smudging the skin un-
derneath. As foolish as it seemed, Kochran had hoped
all those things would miraculously vanish while he'd
been fixing breakfast. He wanted Ezra to be a normal,
healthy man who kept Noble House in touch with thousands of people across the world thanks to the internet.

Kochran cleared his throat, dumped the last of the
coffee into a second mug, dropped some cream in before handing it to Ezra and focused on the eggs. "Morning."

"Thanks." Ezra winced as he sipped the coffee, but
drank a second time. Then a third. "Now I know why
the stuff at the club tastes like shit." Ezra moved to the
table and folded himself into a chair. He hovered over

the coffee, closing his eyes as steam wafted around his face. In an instant, Ezra wasn't the helpless man who'd slept in his bed.

Kochran recognized the hard knot of desire that slapped at him and abruptly pushed it away. He cleared his throat again. "Coffee expert?"

"Did some barista work in college. Easy way to make some extra funds to get groceries for the week. Drink enough bad coffee and you'll drink anything. But now that I'm older and have a steady income, I don't have to settle." He sipped again. "This stuff is toxic. Could probably remove paint with it."

"Guess I've got a lead stomach." Kochran turned back to the stove.

"I know you like your sex rough, but damn, man, no reason to punish the eggs too."

Kochran looked down at the pan and noticed he'd burned the omelet. "Damn it."

He'd allowed himself to be distracted more than usual. Too many things keeping his mind occupied. His mother. Tory. Even banging on his drums hadn't given him the usual clarity. The only thing he seemed to be able to make right in his life was the club.

Ezra's hand appeared in Kochran's line of sight. "Give it to me. Can't save this one, but I can whip you up something that won't sit in your stomach for three days."

Kochran was so surprised, he handed over the spatula and stepped out of the way. He wasn't going to complain about Ezra's gesture because cooking had never been his strong suit. It was a miracle he hadn't poisoned himself yet. He moved to fix another pot of coffee, but Ezra stopped him.

"Sit down. Relax. Least I can do after you looking out for me."

Kochran started to protest, but after Ezra cracked an egg one-handed into the pan, he moved down the counter to quietly observe. Watching him from the side as he worked, Kochran found himself easily caught up in the fluid movements Ezra used to fix breakfast. It was also a covert way to look over the man's physique. Notice the way Ezra's shoulder muscles moved as he seamlessly shifted his efforts between the frying pan and the coffee maker. The sweeping planes of Ezra's chest and abdomen, broken only by the pump and patch. The defined arms and legs. Such elegant naturalness.

Kochran felt a stirring against his lounge pants. Having a half-dressed person a few feet away wasn't an unusual occurrence. He owned a sex club where people played out their fetishes nightly. Naked bodies were a part of the gig. But this moment was different. More personal. Intimate. Yeah, he tended to gravitate toward women when it came to sex, but he'd never sworn off the beauty of a man who snagged his attention. That particular desire hadn't risen in him for a long time.

In truth, Kochran only had one requirement when it came to his choice of sexual partner: they had to be able to handle what he liked to dole out. Most of the submissives at the club took it easily, and more than a few came back to beg for more. Finding that in a setting outside of the club, though? That was the crux of his nonexistent love life.

Ezra set a platter full of perfectly cooked eggs, golden-brown bacon and a few slices of toast in the center of the table. He retrieved two mugs of coffee and set one in front of Kochran before sliding into a chair on the opposite side of the table.

"Hope family style is okay." Ezra folded his legs up, propping his shins against the edge of the table.

"It's all going to the same place. Looks great. Thanks." Kochran sipped the coffee. "Can't believe this came from my machine."

Ezra wrapped his hands around his mug again and slowly inhaled the steam wafting up. That pang of something Kochran was growing all too familiar with clenched his gut again at the half-smile Ezra gave. Ezra finding pleasure in something so simple wrenched his heart.

"You're not going to let me eat all of this by myself, are you?"

Ezra waved him on. "In a few minutes. Just trying to shake off the last of the haze."

Kochran helped himself to some eggs, a slice of bacon and piece of toast. "Oz thought you were drunk or high at first. I saw the pump and figured out what was going on. Lucky quite a few of us there have emergency training thanks to my club policy for that." He gestured at Ezra's waist with his fork. "Best friend in junior high had one of those. He forgot to check on his pump before coming to class one day, and went down like a rock. Diabetic ketoacidosis?"

Ezra ran a hand over his face. "Yeah. Type one since I was a kid. Sorry. Let it get out of hand and I know better. And I'll apologize now for not putting it on my application. I…don't want it to be a burden on anyone. Have them treat me differently because of it."

The quiet way Ezra spoke signaled he didn't need a lecture. Kochran shelved that conversation. "I didn't think it was a good idea for you to be alone, so I brought you here."

"Where is here anyway? Some kind of warehouse?"

"Former missile silo." Kochran glanced around, understanding how the structure could be mistaken for an industrial building. His ceilings were nonexistent thanks to the soaring column. He'd left most of the storage tower untouched, remodeling only the bottom floor for the space he occupied. "Found it right after I bought the property and was trying to figure out where I wanted to build a house."

"Somehow I'm not surprised the control freak lives so close to the club."

Kochran hadn't wanted to live at home, or anywhere near his parents. "Government cutbacks closed the base down and I saw an opportunity."

"From military installation to castle of sin." Ezra shot Kochran a sly grin. "Lots of privacy and security, that's for certain. You've done some nice work." Ezra gestured to the space Kochran had allotted for a glassed-in shower, toilet and pedestal sink. "Spiffy-ass shower I'd like to take advantage of before I leave, if you don't mind."

"Be my guest." Kochran tried his best to forget the fact Ezra was once again going to be naked.

"Saw my kit on the nightstand. Thanks."

Kochran had used the keys they'd found in Ezra's pocket to grab the equipment for monitoring blood sugar stashed in the console of Ezra's car. "Figured you were going to need it at some point."

"Saw enough of the inside of a hospital before I was diagnosed." Ezra licked his lips before continuing. "I wasn't a person then, a kid who just wanted to play with his friends on the playground. I was numbers and tests and logs and logs of keeping track of every single piece of food I ate, everything I drank."

"If you need to get checked out—"

Ezra held up a hand. "I've had enough of being a specimen, thanks. Just be out of sorts for a day or so." They sat in silence for a few minutes before Ezra took an egg and a few slices of bacon. "Had a bad run of days."

"Need to talk about it?"

Ezra pushed away his untouched food. Kochran frowned, but bit his tongue. The last thing Ezra probably wanted was a lecture about his health. Given what he'd just said, he'd been hearing about it for as long as he'd been diagnosed with diabetes.

"Some days are better than others. Lately…been tough. Everything is going to cave in on me if I don't act quickly enough." Ezra blew out a breath as he shook his head. "I don't know why I'm sharing this with you."

Kochran decided not to speculate. "But you don't want to stop."

Ezra took a long sip of his coffee, staring at the platter in the center of the table for a few minutes before continuing. "I know we've talked about the fact my wife died a few years ago, but I've kept a lot of it to myself."

"You weren't ready to talk about her. I get it."

"Guess I'm ready now." Ezra ran his hands over his face. "She had cervical cancer. Spread like a virus. We only had a few months from her initial diagnosis. She refused treatment right from the start. No long, drawn-out complications, so that's something. Doctors didn't think it would work anyway. Cancer was too damn aggressive."

"Swift for her, but not enough time to prepare you for your new reality." Kochran pushed away his empty plate as the ghost of memories Ezra was being forced to relive filled the room. Kochran had known the basics, but hearing it firsthand was a reminder about the stark, cold reality of life.

Ezra lowered his head. They stayed quiet for a few minutes until Kochran rose, snagged Ezra's cup and topped off both of their mugs before he returned to the table. "You already know my sister was diagnosed with a heart defect as a kid. Been watching her die a little each day since then."

Ezra leaned back in his chair. Kochran understood a lot more about the man in the space of a few sentences and the weight pressing down on Ezra's shoulders.

"It just happened so fast. Like this out-of-control… event we knew was coming but couldn't stop." Ezra shook his head, pulled the plate back within reach and busied himself with the now-cold food. "Nora was upbeat the whole time. Like she accepted her fate from the start. Told us we needed to live the rest of our lives as though it was our last day. When *she* was dying, for Christ's sake."

"Us?"

Ezra blinked, shadows darkening his face. "What?"

"You said she told us to live the rest of your lives like it is your last day. Who's *us*?"

Kochran realized he was prying, but he couldn't stop. The blunder wasn't a slip of the tongue. In the brief conversations about Ezra's wife before, there hadn't been a mention of someone else. Kochran could usually size someone up in a few seconds, but Ezra was dancing around something.

The way his eyes glazed over when he talked about his painful past made Kochran want to cross the room to take him in his arms. He hadn't felt that way toward anyone outside of the club setting in a long time. In truth, he wasn't sure he'd ever encountered those emotions about anyone ever. The sensation was foreign and...wonderful.

Ezra met Kochran's gaze for a half second. He stood, grabbing the empty dishes to dump them in the sink. Kochran thought he was going to leave to avoid answering, but Ezra turned, leaning against the counter with his ankles crossed and his arms supporting him. His Adam's apple moved as he swallowed.

"We...had a husband too. A triad. A happy one. So goddamn joyful about life, like we didn't have a care in the world." He fell silent again, but this time Kochran let the quiet hang in the air. "We were trying—we'd decided the three of us were ready to have a family."

The puzzle pieces clicked into place. "That's how you found out about the cancer."

"Yeah," Ezra responded quietly. "She was having difficulty conceiving. We thought a few treatments with an infertility doctor would take care of things." And instead his world had crumbled around his feet. "Couple months later she was gone. Few weeks after that, so was he."

Kochran stood, fighting against the desire to blow the tenuous friendship of theirs out of the fucking water. "Sorry to hear that. I could tell you I understand, but you'd know I'm lying. If you want some time to get your head back on straight, take whatever you need. The website stuff will be there. Madeline seems to be competent enough to handle things."

"I like being busy. Keeps my head engaged." Ezra pointed toward the bedroom area. "Gonna take that shower now, if you don't mind."

Kochran forced himself to clean up the few remaining plates and wipe down the counters while Ezra showered. When the shower cut off, he stalled for another few minutes before moving back to the bedroom area. He was determined he wasn't going to let Ezra go so easily, not when he had the power to offer assistance. Kochran did his best not to think about all the reasons why he needed to offer Ezra a hand.

Thankfully Ezra came around the partition separating the shower from the bedroom wearing the clothes he'd been in last night. He avoided eye contact as he gathered his shoes and the kit.

"I could use a hand with a few things at the club," Kochran offered.

Ezra's gaze flicked over Kochran's body for a split second, but it had been enough for Kochran to see the instant flare of interest. That spark was enough to let Kochran know what kind of thoughts were playing out in Ezra's mind. Kochran's dick twitched in response. Definitely some curiosity there.

"What do you need?" Ezra tried to look everywhere but directly at Kochran. Under other circumstances, Kochran would have preened and taken advantage of the situation, but it was a bad idea on so many levels.

"Saint has been hounding me to expand the tech at the club by venturing into the realm of virtual reality. He has some kind of vision I don't understand, because I thought that's what you were doing."

"No." Ezra stood up straighter, obviously interested. "The sim now is just a user sitting at a computer directing an avatar. Virtual reality is immersive. It would certainly level up Noble House in the hybrid aspect."

"As long as you understand, that's all that matters. He gave me a few names, but I haven't had a chance to decide how to handle it with everything else going on. Think you could carve out some time and give me your thoughts?"

"Wouldn't Saint be a better choice?"

Kochran didn't miss Ezra's skepticism. "He's got enough to deal with right now because of the wedding, and this doesn't deal with security. He was offering suggestions, as you know he tends to do. You can interface with him if you're more comfortable and then have him present his findings to me."

"No, it's fine. I'll see what I can do."

Kochran located his pants, dug out his wallet and handed Ezra the slip of paper with Saint's neat list of names. Ezra didn't look as he tucked it into his front pocket. He barely glanced at Kochran as he tied his sneakers. The uncomfortable silence settled around them again.

Kochran left the area before he made an ass of himself. He tried not to think about the fact he needed the distance just as much as Ezra did.

He'd sensed Ezra had quickly been approaching an area he didn't want to discuss any longer. Nothing could change the fact he'd had the rug pulled out from under him when his wife died and his husband left. But Kochran sensed the many, many unresolved emotions Ezra was trying to deal with.

He needed space. Kochran wasn't against looking

at all the gorgeous window dressing, but Ezra needed something else. More than likely, the last thing he was looking for was a fucked-in-the-head alpha Dominant who had a secret past as a submissive. The safest thing to do was slam down on his arousal. The guy needed a few breaks in life, not more difficulties.

After his extraordinarily cold shower, he discovered Ezra had left. As he poured himself another mug full of the delicious coffee Ezra had prepared, Kochran didn't know whether to be relieved or disappointed.

Fuck me.

Chapter Ten

A week after her quick trip to New York, Maddy decided to take advantage of her day off with a stroll through her favorite stationery store, Take Note. This wasn't the sort of place where a consumer could purchase a plain paper ream for their everyday computer needs. It was the kind of store where paper was bought by the sheet. Where a patron could spend hours deciding between the delicate stacks of paper or the heavy weight of stylish enamel pens.

The small store in Fairfield also wasn't the type of place she expected to see the owner of Noble House shopping on a beautiful Sunday afternoon. But as she rounded a corner, she spotted Kochran studying a display of perfect-bound notebooks. Though he wasn't impeccably dressed like normal, his dark jeans and faded red shirt fit him as well as a tailored suit. The cut defined his broad shoulders, the short sleeves exposing his forearms. A watch wrapped around his right wrist. She'd never been so fascinated with a man's favored hand, but for some unknown reason, the fact Kochran was left-handed fascinated her. The sneakers on his feet were worn, but not dirty. He was a normal man on a normal day out shopping. His hair looked as though he'd just rolled out of bed. He also wore a battered brown leather belt, and she had a sudden, blinding image form in her mind of him stripping it off and using it on her. Not because she'd misbehaved, but simply because he'd known she would enjoy it.

Would she?

She'd never thought of pain mingled with the pleasure of sex until she'd agreed to work for Noble House. Until she'd had unrestricted access to the archives. As she approached, she wondered what his office at the club looked like. If he had one of those fancy stacked organizers filled with sheets of paper, sorted by color and style. Perhaps a box filled with a selection of fountain pens and pots filled with a colorful array of inks.

Or maybe that was just her stationery fetish. Most women could drop serious funds on purses, clothes and shoes, but office supply stores were Maddy's chosen place to binge shop. Pens, notecards and pads of exquisite paper in all shades of the rainbow begging to be used. Her deep, abiding love for the feel of expensive paper between her fingers was only matched with her fascination for ones and zeros. The two interests couldn't be more varied, but she loved them both equally. Coding notes written on expensive paper with a fountain pen? Her own personal nirvana.

When he reached out and touched the spine of a neon green notebook, his eyes narrowing as he picked it up and studied it intently, she stopped. He tucked it against his palm as though weighing the object's mass. The shock of color wasn't what she'd expected him to select, but he moved on to a display of pens with the notebook still in his hand.

The slip of paper with his personal cell phone number that he'd tucked into her pocket made sense now. He could have easily taken her phone to input his number. Most men she knew wouldn't be caught dead in this kind of package supply house, preferring to lurk around video game havens and comic book stores. Writing a note for him wasn't an act, it was an experience.

He used the same appraising look as he examined the neat column of writing instruments. He selected one, studying a cobalt blue jewel tone pen with an appraising eye, as though he was measuring up a prospective lover. Assessing if it was worthy of belonging to him. Her throat went dry at the idea of him choosing a submissive for the night in the same manner.

He returned it to the display case, shaking his head as he carefully examined the other selections. As he straightened, he faced her, his eyes going half-lidded as he smiled. The dark lashes framed his brown eyes intensifying the look of utter desire he aimed her way.

"I didn't mean to disturb you," Maddy stammered out as her cheeks heated.

"You are always welcome to bother me, Madeline."

His open appraisal coursed over her legs, her swaying hips, the movement of her body as she came to stand beside him. Just as she leaned one hip against the glass display case, his gaze reached her face. The heat kindling in his eyes made delicious things happen between her legs.

As Maddy took a steadying breath, she struggled to remember why she'd come to the store. Then she spotted something over Kochran's shoulder. Not what she'd come for, but instead a beautiful stack of notecards. The top edge was the palest blue and transitioned down at the bottom to a blue so deep it was almost black. Along the bottom quarter, nestled in that blue-black, was a row of sparkling stars and hearts. Matching envelopes sat in the display box next to the cards, the same stunning design in the left corner, shining against the deep blue, as though they'd been plucked from space and woven between the fibers of the paper.

Poppy Coverdale, the owner of the store, grinned as she presented the box to Maddy. "Just arrived Tuesday, special order from Japan. One of my regulars put in the order, but they weren't what she was expecting when they were delivered."

Maddy touched the stars and hearts, sighing at the texture. "Not really my style, but wow. Impressive."

"Hard to believe anything in this store isn't your style."

Maddy smiled at Kochran's good-natured jab. "They're too dark to be practical. You'd have to use a special ink just to write a note. I don't have anything like that in my supply stash."

"Hang on." Kochran disappeared around the corner, vanishing from sight.

"I got in a shipment of those adorable adhesive notes you like. Have them in the back for the next time you came in. Give me a second." Poppy scooted off, fumbling for her glasses, which were perched on top of her head.

Kochran returned, the cobalt blue pen he'd been examining earlier in one hand and a pot of metallic silver ink in the other. Maddy watched in fascination as he expertly disassembled the pen, filled the reservoir and fit the barrel back into place without spilling a drop.

"I would have been covered in silver. Given the Tin Man a run for his money."

"It's just a simple cartridge fountain pen. Nothing to it."

Maddy stared at him in wide-eyed wonder as he plucked a card from the top of the stack. He formed a few letters with precise and deliberate strokes. No extra flourishes or whorls that some people used to add decorative touches to their handwriting. Once he'd finished, he lifted the card, blowing gently across the surface to help speed the process. Maddy's skin pebbled with gooseflesh, as though he was breathing against her body. Somehow Kochran made the whole experience of writing sexual.

"There." He handed her the notecard.

The expensive paper had a high-grade linen feel. Unable to stop herself, she lifted the sheet to her nose, sniffing the faint musky cologne that clung to the corner where he'd rested his hand. The scent drew her in, a dizzying combination when mixed with the aroma of the ink and the new paper.

She touched the glittering silver letters Kochran had written. *Madeline.* A slow, tumbling roll like a child spinning down a hill on a long summer evening flipped her stomach. Did tingly things to her. If they'd been alone, she would have crawled up his body, spread her legs and shoved herself onto him. Stationery and pens had always been a euphoric experience for her, but Kochran had just vaulted it to the next level. And judging by his smug grin, he damn well knew it.

"I can't afford anything this lavish. And if you're going to say you'll buy it for me, I won't have any of that, thank-you-very-much."

"Don't be ridiculous." He swept up the entire pile and cradled it like a newborn baby. "I'm buying them so I can write you notes that make you look at me like you're eye-fucking me like you just were." He left her standing at the case alone as he walked toward the front register.

"Everything all right, dear?"

Poppy's question made Maddy jump. "Is it hot in here?" Maddy fanned herself as she scooped up the assortment of cellophane wrapped notepads Poppy had brought her without looking. Heat pricked at her skin as she waited in line behind Kochran. After he paid for his purchase, he waited at the end of the counter for her. The handle of her paper bag dampened as she approached him again.

Sweaty palms, Zane? You sure know how to take sexy to the next level.

"Care to join me for a cup of coffee and maybe a pastry? There's a good bakery in Ashes Fork," Kochran offered. Maddy bit her lip to keep from blurting out an immediate agreement. "You know there's no reason to be afraid of me."

She swallowed as she looked up to him. "What if I want to be?"

Dangerous thoughts surged inside Kochran. It must have clearly showed in his expression because she'd avoided eye contact as her cheeks flushed an alluring shade of pink. "Just coffee," he insisted as he tamped down on his desire.

"Fine," she said carefully. "But I'll meet you there."

Watching her walk away had taken a remarkable act of restraint. He hadn't intended to make a day of shopping, but once he'd seen her, he hadn't been able to resist spending more time with her.

He'd thought about her often. How her lips had pressed enticingly against his. How sweetly soft her body had been. How she had enough restraint to walk away from him even though the desire had been written all over her face.

The lighting inside Vanilla was golden and indirect, a homey touch that brought regulars around for miles. Kochran had directed her to a booth by a wide plate glass window painted with the bakery's logo. While he waited his turn in line, he watched how the afternoon sun streamed through the glass and highlighted the bits of gilded color in her blonde hair. He wanted to stare and drink in the fine features and grace of Madeline Zane. The way she took out the note he'd written for her on that ridiculously expensive notecard and gently traced the letters. The paper could have pure gold and he still would have bought it to write her notes. He'd never done that before, for friends, family or lovers. Never wanted to until he'd seen the way her face had lit up. How she looked at him as though she wanted him to take her right then and there.

"Well hello, stranger. Been a while since you've come in."

Kochran tore his gaze away from Madeline. The owner of the bakery, Charlene Husk, had spun up her strawberry blonde hair into a messy bun and painted her lips a vibrant shade of red that made her pale skin appear even more translucent. Though her makeup wasn't as heavy as on nights she worked the stage with the band, she still used kohl to rim her friendly blue eyes.

"You know I can't stay away from your scones."

"Long as you keep that girlish figure of yours to

bring in the women to the shows, you can have all the scones you want." Charlie pulled one out of the case, set it on an antique plate that she handed to him. "And for your lady friend?"

"One of those fruit tarts, and a vow you'll stop looking at me like that."

"Oh, come on." She affected a pout for a split second before her knowing grin returned. "You never bring anyone in here. Usually you're too busy taking up real estate on the couches reserved for paying customers, writing songs in those notebooks you love so much." She waved off the bill he offered as she keyed in his order and zeroed it out. She waved him off again when he held out his hand for the two mugs she'd filled with coffee.

A sudden terrifying thought stabbed at his stomach. "No. No, Charlene, no you don't."

"Oh hell yeah." Charlie ducked under the counter, expertly balancing the two very full mugs, and headed directly for Maddy. He swore under his breath as he scooped up the two plates with their pastries and beat a quick path to the booth. He made it just as Maddy was introducing herself.

"Kochran was just telling me you're the newest employee at the club I pretend doesn't exist."

Kochran rolled his eyes. "Charlie likes to pretend everyone in the world is having the same, boring, missionary style sex she *isn't* having."

Charlie stuck her tongue out. "Not everyone needs all the extras."

"Kink has its place. So does vanilla." Maddy bit off a corner of the fruit tart and groaned. "Have to

say, Charlie, your pastries are anything but plain and
unexciting."

"Thank you. Don't let this one convince you to do
wild perverted things just to satisfy his sense of adventure." Charlie waved over her shoulder as she moved to
another table to chat with one of her regulars.

Kochran blew out a steadying breath. "She likes
to butt in."

"She's sweet. Adores you, obviously." Maddy
brushed the crumbs from her fingers as something
shifted in her expression. "You treasure her as well.
Unless I'm mistaken about the familiar scent I caught
as soon as we walked in."

"What?" he responded, caught off guard by her af-
fectionate smile. "It smells like a bakery."

"It also smells like a certain club. Not the sex part,
of course. It's…warm and inviting. I suspect you use
some custom formulation at Noble House to help mask
the usual chemical aroma of cleaners so members don't
feel like they're in sterile surroundings."

"That's ridiculous," he said mildly. Even though she
was the only one who'd ever figured out the secret, he
wasn't interested in confirming. He'd spent a hefty sum
making sure it was perfect and he intended to keep it
that way.

She stared at him for a long moment before saying
casually, "How do you know each other?"

"Her family moved in across the street, much to my
parents' displeasure."

Maddy lifted her coffee halfway to her mouth,
paused and smiled back. "Riff raff dirtying up the
neighborhood?"

"Our sisters have been dating since right after graduation." As Kochran suspected, Maddy didn't bat an eye. Her open mind was one more trait he adored about her.

"Quite the scandal, I take it?"

"You have no idea." Kochran thought back to the day the family had discovered the relationship. The screaming demands to conform. Noelle loathed the idea of her daughter being a lesbian. If she knew the truth about her son, she would probably keel over.

"Are they still together?"

"For the time being."

Maddy frowned. "You make it sound as though they're having some troubles."

Kochran sighed. It never got easier taking about his sister's illness. "Tory, my kid sister, has a medical condition that will eventually kill her. Very soon, in fact." He grew somber as he thought about his last visit to the hospice.

"I'm sorry." A glimmer of sadness crossed her expression. "They must be very special women to stay together and endure something like that."

"They are." Kochran finished his scone, marveling once again at his friend's talent. "Charlie and I became friends when we discovered a mutual interest in music."

"Oh really?" Maddy's eyes danced with curiosity. "I can't imagine you with long hair and singing into a microphone in a garage."

"Hey, I looked damn awesome with long hair." He held up his index finger and pinky, throwing himself back into the days where hair bands and metal had ruled the music charts. "I play the drums, actually. And we set up in a shed in the Husk family's backyard.

Charlie's mom kept us all fed with homemade cookies and lemonade most of the summer."

Maddy held the last bite of her tart. "Must be where she's gotten her talent."

"The whole Husk family is talented." Unlike his parents, who were too busy hobnobbing with their elite, rich friends to bother with their children's activities. His father had given up on the idea Kochran would take over the family business. His mother…well, she lived happily with her delusions of grandeur. "Charlie is the lead singer. Paddy and Jolie round out the rest of Duality."

"Did you guys ever try to take it beyond the garage?"

Kochran shrugged. "We had a few agents talk to us early on, but I didn't feel right traipsing around the country when Tory couldn't get out and live her life." More like he wanted to be close to home and be the shield that protected Tory from their mother. On the road, he couldn't do that. "We're happy playing the local bars now. Lets us all stay close to home. What about you? Any legal activities your parents can be proud of?"

"Just the normal stuff."

"I assure you, Madeline…" He lowered his voice as he angled forward. "There is nothing normal about you."

"You know, from anyone else, I would take offense to that."

He couldn't help himself. He lifted her hand to his lips and kissed the back of her hand, flicking his tongue out to gently lick the delicate skin between two of her knuckles. "And you know, I'm not anyone else."

* * *

When the symbols on Ezra's screen had started to make his eyes bleed, he'd known it was break time. The weather was nice enough that he'd decided to take a stroll down Main to clear his head since he was working from home. It had worked too. Five minutes prior, the solution to a bit of code that had been giving him a fit, had presented itself.

He'd been in a rush to get home to work on the issue again, but came upon an inviting bench positioned outside of Three Mile Bookstore. It wasn't comfortable by any means, or visually appealing, with faded and chipping blue paint, but it was functional and that was all he needed. He retrieved his cell phone to pull up an app that would sync the information he typed in to his computer. The cloud-based application had saved more than one project when he had no access to his system.

The short blast of a horn broke his concentration. His neighbor, Mr. Astin, waved as Ezra looked up. Afternoon sunlight glinted off a nearby window, blinding Ezra. He shaded his eyes from the gleam as he remembered he'd left his sunglasses on the hook near his front door. On days he spent waist-deep in code, it was a miracle he even remembered his own name.

Ezra offered a friendly wave in return, ready to shield his eyes from the sun's glare again until he caught a glance into the store directly across the street. There, in the front window of Vanilla, between the painted cream and maroon letters of the bakery's logo, were Maddy and Kochran. They sat in the booth, their bodies angled toward each other as they leaned on their elbows. Their postures spoke of an intimacy beyond simple friendship as they talked over coffee and baked goods.

Ezra considered them for a moment, feeling something disturb a fierceness he'd buried when he'd faced the emotional upheaval years before. By mainstream standards, he should have been jealous Kochran was spending time with Maddy outside the club. Though he had no claim on her, Ezra knew the woman had definitely captured his interest beyond employee and supervisor. But there was no accusation in his thoughts toward the couple. No anger. Perhaps a little resignation, but only because he imagined himself sitting with them, sharing coffee and pastries. Listening to their stories and perhaps sharing a few of his own.

Ezra had no idea why he'd told Kochran so much the morning after the incident at Screwdriver. Why he'd felt the need to expose his vulnerabilities. Kochran had looked after him when he hadn't needed to. Taken up the task of ensuring Ezra was safe when he could have shuffled him off to the hospital for an overnight stay. Made him someone else's problem. Just like so many other people had done. And then there was Maddy... Ezra swallowed as he watched Kochran touch the tip of Maddy's nose with his finger. Felt something stir when Maddy's face lit with genuine pleasure.

Ezra's throat tightened. He would trade his soul to have her smile at him like that. She brought a vibrancy to the dreary landscape Ezra's life had become.

He sat there, heart in his throat, knowing he was going to fall for her. Hard. Do the wrong thing that would test their friendship, but fuck all if he cared. She was already inside his head. Somehow he knew she wouldn't allow him to get hurt again. In truth, it wasn't possible for him to hurt more than he had when Nora died and Kyle vanished. That kind of heartbreak changed a man. Maddy pushed him to want a life he hadn't claimed in a long time. Uncovered something powerful inside him that he didn't let out often. Kochran enhanced that desire too. Roused a beast who had been prowling around in a cage, desperate to make his mark on something he wanted. Even when he closed himself off and was being a prick, Kochran was a magnificent creature. Ezra wanted to drown in him.

A magical, rapturous need tore at him but he had to restrain it. He was also interested in finding out how skewed things could get for all three of them if they went down this path. Kochran had a legendary skill set that would force Ezra to up his game. Make him think outside of the box and work him like never before.

One thing was clear, Ezra wasn't going to sit by and watch Kochran sweep Maddy onto her knees. Not that he believed they wouldn't complement each other, or that Kochran wasn't an adequate partner. But Ezra knew he could give Maddy something Kochran couldn't because he understood her on a different level.

They both spoke fluent geek.

Kochran's inventiveness came through during his sessions with submissives, but Ezra and Maddy had connected on a nonsexual level Ezra could exploit. Use to his advantage. That was something he'd never done before. Nora and Kyle had never been interested enough in his work for him to consider integrating it into their play. Nora had been an English teacher; Kyle, an engineer. With Maddy in the picture, Ezra could use their mutual interest in computers to kick this into motion.

Fuck the repercussions.

Fuck them hard.

He rose, glancing at the window one last time as Kochran kissed the back of Maddy's hand and said something that made her grin. Hunger spiraled through him, collecting to constrict around the base of his now stiff dick. His plan would take some time to put into motion, but he could shove off the bulk of the work to Maddy, which would extend her time at the club.

Bonus level, for the win.

Chapter Eleven

Fourth of July weekend and Maddy was spending the holiday doing what she loved most. Even if her back hated it. She sat up to stretch out the kinks in her neck. The muscles were still unused to the unnatural angle of her less than ideal workstation. Not as though she expected posh desk chairs, foot rests and hot coffee on tap. Hell, even her desk at home wasn't that luxurious.

Ezra had left her alone some time ago to search out food and hunt down Kochran. He'd been complaining his back hurt as well. Though she needed to get out of the office, she wasn't interested in exploring again. She'd gotten into enough trouble last time.

The memory of Kochran's forwardness last month still lingered, but in a good way. Like she would compare all future men she was interested in by the way he'd kissed her. Made her feel safe and cosseted.

She'd always wondered what it would be like to participate in the lifestyle instead of watch from afar. Kochran had given her a glimpse and she was hooked enough that she'd dug deeper into expanding her knowledge about the lifestyle. She'd been pleased to learn a lot of what she discovered was right up her alley. Plenty of people around the club for her to ask for some hands-on assistance. She just needed to work up the courage.

A flashing icon at the bottom of her screen caught her attention. Someone had sent her a chat message on the club's intranet. The only person who knew her administrator account ID was Ezra. Possibly Kochran too, since he was in charge of the whole shebang, but she'd been around him enough to know he didn't have the passion for technology she had. There was a running joke about Kochran and his passwords.

She pushed the flashing icon and waited while a new browser window opened. Strange. For a moment, she thought she'd clicked on some kind of malware that could eat its way through the data, but instead a streaming video of someone walking into an empty room popped onto her screen. She didn't recognize the space, but she still hadn't gotten that tour. The lighting made it difficult for her to make out his features, but she could definitely see the towel he'd wrapped around his waist, and the outline of an appendage that clearly indicated this was a man.

He walked—oh, no, he *prowled* toward the chair that had been positioned in the center of a puddle of light. As he stepped fully into the light, his gaze lifted to the camera. Her heart stuttered as she leaned away from the computer.

Ezra.

The reason for the direct link became remarkably clear when he faced away from the camera, then stripped off the towel. The backside the fluffy fabric had kept hidden was—Jesus, she could have bounced quarters off his ass. He discarded the towel and settled in the chair.

The angle now gave her a view of Ezra and all his masculinity in profile. Shame unfurled through her, but that didn't stop her gaze as it mapped his defined jaw, the full bottom lip, the strong curve of his shoulders, the cut of his hip and, finally, to his stiffening erection. Though she knew she needed to close the link, she kept watching as he settled himself more comfortably and wrapped his hand around the base of his cock.

And oh, what a fucking magnificent piece of fully erect flesh it was.

A shiver traveled through her as he began masturbating. It wasn't as though she'd never seen a man naked before, or seen one manhandle himself on camera, but right this very minute, Ezra had sent her a link to watch him jacking off.

She'd assumed he was one of the members, but her cursory glance through the member list that first night hadn't turned up his name. To her, that meant he was an employee and didn't participate in any of the sinful activities at the club. But there he was, big and hard and stroking himself up and down, his hand and the hard flesh contrasting beautifully. As he dropped his head back, the flesh in his hand broadened and darkened, a sign he was clearly enjoying himself.

She closed her eyes and blew out a steady breath. *Turn it off, Mads. Walk away right now. Stand up, leave the room and walk the hell away.* The glint of the rings on his left hand reminded her he was married. Another reason she shouldn't be watching. But her fascination kept her rooted in place.

When she opened her eyes, she jumped. Ezra was looking directly into the camera. Directly at her. This couldn't be just for her, could it? Maybe he'd sent out the link to a select few. But that sounded…crazy. Suddenly, it didn't matter. The fact he intended her to see him like this was special and intensely intimate.

What is he thinking about? Is he imagining me in the room with him?

The idea of being right there, watching over his shoulder, stirred things low in her gut. Made flesh come alive that hadn't felt that delicious since…nineteen days ago, when Kochran had kissed her. Had promised to make her come when he fucked her.

The shame she'd expected with that revelation didn't come. She was thinking about a man kissing her while watching another jack off. Two men. Two beautifully attractive men she couldn't stop thinking about.

Not like you're having sex with either of them, Mads.

With thoughts of how Kochran made her feel just a short time ago filling her brain, she turned her attention back to the computer screen. Ezra's gaze was still focused at the camera. She saw a flash of emotion swirling through the depths of his eyes. Need. Desire. Perhaps loneliness.

The moment passed and he leaned his head back, closed his eyes and stroked himself with unhurried motions, as though he was luxuriating in the sensations. The answering silence of the room wasn't enough to distract her from the fact she'd gotten aroused watching a man jack off. No way could she close that window now. And no way was she going to pass up an opportunity to take care of herself.

The elastic waist of her sweatpants accommodated her hand easily enough. She released a quiet moan when she pressed her finger against her clit and an answering pulse shot through her. She hadn't expected to find herself this wet. This hot. She could have said watching a man take care of himself simply did it for her, but in truth, it was *Ezra* jacking off that pushed her buttons.

On the screen, he let out a deep groan as he cupped his free hand around his balls. He continued moving his hand up and down the shaft, palming the crown each time. He moved slow and precise, as though he had nowhere else in the world to be. More bang for the buck, so to speak.

Maddy snorted at her own joke.

As she focused on timing her hand movements to his, she imagined herself in the room with him. That her hand surrounded him as she sensually teased him. Given his size, she knew he would feel heavy and so hot against her fingers.

As she sank deeper into the fantasy, tension coiled through her muscles. Her heart beat in time to her throbbing clit as she continued strumming. Lifting herself higher. Muscles trembling with impending release, she leaned back in the chair. Her sweatpants were loose enough to accommodate the change when she shifted and dipped two fingers inside her opening. She used her other fingers to play with the petals of her sex, imagining someone's tongue dragging through her wet heat.

The fantasy shifted.

At first she'd thought the mouth on her pussy had been Ezra's, but she was surprised to imagine herself still working his cock. With a quiet groan, she realized it was Kochran's mouth on her. Kochran giving her pleasure while she sucked on Ezra.

A deep groan filled the office, and Maddy opened her eyes to find Ezra had quickened his pace. Tension coiled through her thighs as he planted his feet flat on the floor, tightness visibly straining his entire body as he worked harder.

Fantasy and reality merged before her eyes as she saw herself and Kochran in the room with Ezra. Her fingers quickened as she imagined herself still on her knees in front of Ezra, licking and sucking in earnest. Like the video she watched that first night, Kochran stood nearby, flogger in hand. The intoxicating lashes against her back, ass and thighs struck perfectly each time she swallowed Ezra whole. Then it all went supernova when Kochran tossed the device to the side, lifted her mouth and plunged his own over Ezra's cock.

She came in a rush, biting her lip to contain her scream, her body bucking against the chair as her legs jerked against the ancient wooden legs. Mothertruckin' holy Jesus. She'd never come so hard in her life. And she'd never imagined such a vivid fantasy before either. Not to mention, two guys being into one another like that? Definitely hadn't been on her radar before, but at the top of her very short list now. Not that it would ever happen in real life.

As the fuzz began to clear, she saw Ezra had also finished. She'd missed his release, but the telltale glistening drops dotting his chest and the rapid breaths and shaking hands meant he'd got off as well.

The screen went dark and she dropped her forehead to the desk as she attempted to set herself to rights. The answering buzz was enough to kick her over the edge again. She'd never been this wired, this tantalizingly achy for more. Like the orgasm hadn't been enough. Not even close to a bone-deep satisfaction she knew only one thing would sate.

She jumped when the office door opened. It took immense effort not to look guilty as Ezra slipped through the opening and gave her a curious look. She forced herself to focus on the screen and realized with a start she'd been sitting there for fifteen minutes. Her body still hadn't come down from the high.

"Found a small error in the PHP code," she said slowly. She set her fingers over the keyboard and desperately tried to quell the trembling. If she pretended the past forty-five minutes hadn't occurred, she'd be all right. Luckily, the scents she'd given off had faded enough that it wasn't obvious she'd masturbated right there in the chair. "Patched it up. Everything checks out fine now."

"Sound good. I'm going to give the message board a spin to check out the preprocessors there." He settled behind his terminal without further comment, his face a blank canvas.

He worked quietly, the glow of the computer screen highlighting the angles of his face as he diligently worked. She admired his ability to look as if he hadn't just jerked off on camera.

She needed to tell him. Honestly admit she'd watched something so personal. The fact he hadn't said a word so far meant she really hadn't been the intended target. As she turned, she was caught up by the way his hair curled against the collar of his shirt, the strands damp as though he'd taken a shower. There was something about a guy with strong shoulders hunched over a keyboard, clacking away.

"Hey, Mads?"

She jumped at the name. Too close to him. She needed some distance and space, from Ezra *and* the club. She never considered herself a prude, but this place had put sex at the forefront of her mind a lot. She'd just watched a video of the guy sitting a few feet away from her jacking off. Dear God. She'd taken a first-class trip to pervert city.

"Think I'm gonna call it a night." She ran a still-trembling hand through her hair. "Been working a little too much, I think."

His contemplative gaze focused on her. For the second time that night, she wondered what he was imagining. Wondered if he lay awake at night fantasizing about the same things she did.

Kochran brushed his fingers over his dry lips as he stared at his monitor. He shouldn't have watched the live feed that had appeared on his screen. Shouldn't have had to wrestle with the searing need burning through his veins.

The expanse of broad shoulders, muscles bunching and rippling across Ezra's chest, down to the tight flex of his thighs, the curling of his toes against the floor as he'd come, had made Kochran harder. Hotter. The agony of the burn was almost too intense to bear. Drove his lust for Ezra to levels that could make him insane. Good God damn, listening to the expulsion of breaths, the grunts as perspiration sheened smooth skin while Ezra jacked off had been spectacular.

He'd wanted to be in the same room with Ezra. Lay his hand on Ezra's chest to allow him to experience the texture of the flogger Kochran intended to utilize. Listen with a possessive satisfaction to Ezra's groan of response as Kochran stepped back and taunted him with the flogger. Order him to surrender to the pain.

But at the same time, a surge of desire to kiss each one of those welts he'd raise, and a bone-deep ache to have the roles reversed, shuddered through Kochran.

For as much as he wanted to take care of Ezra, Kochran wanted to receive the fiery strokes of the flogger against *his* chest, *his* back, and *his* thighs while he serviced Ezra with his mouth. He wanted Ezra's touch and didn't care if it was rough and brutal or playful and tender. More than anything he wanted his ass filled and stretched, pummeled with a ruthless force that made his knees collapse so he was presented in offering. The heat of Ezra's hand burning his skin as he slapped each of the taut globes. Ezra's voice, rough and thick, spilling over Kochran's back as he reached down to fist Kochran's cock.

It had been a damn long time since he'd wanted to get on his knees for someone, have another man force him to swallow his cock, worshiping the turgid length of it until he'd swallowed every jet of come the man had. Years since he'd been made to obey. If he closed his eyes, allowed himself to surrender, he could just imagine…

With the path he'd chosen, he didn't know how to change his role. Disclosing his true nature as a switch could cost him everything he'd worked hard to build. His reputation as a Dom was something the members counted on.

Despite his tormented thoughts, frissons of energy crackled up Kochran's spine as he continued to stare at the empty screen. Where was Ezra now? Curled up in one of the club's many recovery areas as he basked in the sensations flooding his body from the release? Back in the office he shared with Madeline? Possessive heat streaked through Kochran as he remembered the connection they shared with the remarkable woman.

Another illicit fantasy flashed behind his eyes again. He wasn't prone to bouts of imagery when he could have all he wanted just outside his office door. But the dominant needs that gave him life had been overcome by the wrenching desire to surrender.

This time, Kochran was on his back, his legs held open wide by restraints he could only feel and not see while Ezra filled him, stretched him with the firmness of his magnificent cock. They weren't alone in this fantasy. Madeline straddled Kochran's shoulders, wiggling and squirming and humping his face as he lapped up every bit of sweet juice from her pussy. Endorphins ran rampant as they blew his mind past all the bullshit worry. They knew how to fix him. How to give him a solid foundation to build the life he wanted upon. They became one, emotions inexplicably mixing so the experience became less about sexual release and more about the sensations threatening to overtake him.

Kochran wrenched himself back to the stark reality of his empty office. He could daydream all he wanted about switching for Ezra while pleasuring Madeline, but the bitch of it was, his worthless soul didn't deserve either of them.

Chapter Twelve

A high-level pass of the video stats indicated there had been two views. The numbers weren't concrete evidence Maddy and Kochran had watched from their admin accounts, though. Maddy, yes. Ezra wholeheartedly believed she'd seen it. But given Kochran's propensity for not resetting the generic system-assigned password, and leaving his computer unlocked and vulnerable while he was away, it could have been anyone.

However, the fact Ezra hadn't been ordered to report to Kochran's office gave him hope. If Kochran *had* watched, he would have to admit he had in order to scold Ezra. And that kind of information...

Ezra would have to find out more later, because it was obvious Maddy *had* done more. The guilty look on her face had confirmed her play time when he'd come back into the room. He could also smell the faint scent of her arousal while he'd pretended to work.

Had she imagined herself in the room with him? Watching? On her knees? Bound at his mercy? Ezra could give her each of those things. Could fulfill whatever fantasies she had. Give her the sweet edge of submission Kochran wasn't interested in because the man played so hard and fast.

Both men could give her the whole experience she perhaps craved.

Ezra was so far gone over this woman. Had been since the instant he'd seen her yelling at Kochran. He'd been determined to stay away until he'd seen them talking at Vanilla. The challenge had awakened something inside Ezra. An unshakable desire not to prove who was the more alpha Dom, but to see which of them could give Maddy what she craved.

Make her scream the loudest.

When he looked up he caught her staring. She blinked a few times but didn't look away. He'd gotten off imagining her working in his office without a stitch of clothing on. Fantasized about sinking between her thighs. Feasting on her while she fumbled through lines of code. But she wasn't the only one—he also thought about fucking Kochran. Holding the owner of the club in his arms, angling his body in such a way that allowed for deeper, harder thrusts. Power flooded Ezra, made him utter a guttural curse as he worked all three of them closer to the edge.

He hadn't thought about sex with two other people in a long time. Hadn't wanted command in equally as long. He couldn't resist anymore. By keying in that code, making sure they'd watched him pleasuring himself, he'd set a plan in motion that he couldn't walk away from.

Damn if he wanted to.

He shook off the trailing threads of his fantasy and focused on the reality sitting in front of him.

"I don't want things to get weird between us, Ezra, but I thought you should know I like you." She licked her lips, sighing. "I just—I'm not sure what else to say. You're married. Makes things complicated."

"Doesn't have to be complex." When she remained silent, he gave her a warm smile. "I'm a widower, Maddy. My wife passed a few years ago."

Her eyes lost focus for a second, then cleared. "I'm so sorry to hear that. You must have loved her very much."

"She was my life. My everything." This wasn't the time to purge a few more emotions, so he cleared his throat. "Does the fact we work together bother you?" She nodded, so he continued, "I'm glad we do. Since that first day, I haven't been able to stop thinking what it would be like to touch you. I leave the office every night with a hard-on because watching you work on my code makes me hot."

He watched her swallow hard as his blunt words sank in. She rose, walking toward him with those shapely legs taunting him with each stride. She paused at the corner of his desk, ran her tongue against the seam of her lips.

Fuck, that's an invitation if I ever saw one...

He raised his left hand slowly, toying with the loose ties of her sweatpants, wanting to see if she flinched. She didn't. She simply gazed at him with those round eyes. He tugged harder, his mouth watering at the sliver of skin he'd exposed. He pulled harder until her waistband wrapped her thighs. She sucked in a breath, her skin pebbling with goose bumps as the soft fabric trailed lower until it puddled around her ankles. Gaze still trained on hers, he traced his thumb over the seam where her thigh met her pelvis where her pulse beat. Her flush deepened, her breathing growing rapid.

"Do you like me touching you?"

Her lips parted, her tongue darting out to sweep over her bottom lip. He wanted to kiss the glistening trail she'd left.

"Yes."

Her answer was so soft he thought he'd imagined it. "Noble House isn't the place to be quiet."

Maddy couldn't believe this was really happening to her. She was seconds away from dropping to her knees for Ezra.

"Say it like you own it." His voice was level but hard, spearing through her like a jagged knife that cut straight to her soul. "Tell me without reservation, without hesitation, you enjoy me touching you, or we're going to both walk away."

She knew he would do exactly what he promised. Though she wasn't as well educated with power exchange play as most of the people at the club, the basic rules were simple enough. There could be no room for doubts. A few whispered words would shatter the need spiraling in the air between them.

"Yes. I like your hands on me. Watching you like this makes me all wet."

His Adam's apple bobbed as he gently stroked her sensitive skin with his knuckles.

"I need more. Need you to touch me more, hear that hard edge of your voice as you tell me what you want me to do."

She didn't care if the fuel for her hunger was his video, or the lingering sense of another man kissing her, learning he shared her crazy interest in stationery then spending the day with him at the coffee house.

Regardless if her time with either man was mundane or sexual, they blurred together to turn her into a hot ball of need.

"Good girl," he drawled out as he walked his fingertips around the swell of her hips, waiting to see if she flinched. But she didn't. She wouldn't. She needed him there.

A sly smile curled the edges of his mouth as he found she wasn't wearing panties. "Or maybe bad girl."

"I was in a rush this morning."

"No complaints from me." He angled his hands as he reached the opening of her thighs and wiggled one finger between her slippery folds. Her low moan filled the air as he made contact with the hard nub of her clit and moved his finger in a circle, slow and deliberate.

From this angle, she saw his cock had swelled against his jeans.

"Do you like me rubbing your clit as you grow damper while you look down at me?" Her moan changed to a quiet hiss as he delved deeper and found her opening. He toyed with it for a moment, with the same exacting gentleness he'd used on her clit. She scooted closer, but he adjusted to prevent his finger from dipping inside.

"Mmm. You really are a bad girl. Don't try to force me to go somewhere I'm not ready for just because you are." He stood suddenly, the adjustment pulling the denim tight against his crotch. She'd thought he'd been enticing sitting in the chair, legs slightly open to display the bulge, but standing… "I decide when I want to pump my finger in and out of this pretty pussy."

Desire stroking her courage, she slipped her hand

over the seam of his crotch. "Sure there isn't something else you'd like to put there instead?"

He didn't brush her away, but waited until she'd wiggled her way past the waistband and wrapped her fingers around his shaft. Before she could move, he slid closer so their hands were pinned and unable to move. Her free hand settled on his bicep and rested there. Not in an effort to push him away, but to seek balance as charged air snapped around them. They cradled each other, connected in the most intimate of ways without actually being inside one another.

His eyes took on a darker cast. "Say *red* if you want me to back away. It's the club's standard safe word." That gaze went harder when she gave him a confused look. "At any time, you say *red* and I walk. No questions asked."

Something clicked. A safe word. *Red.* Stop.

She released a quick breath, ruffling the hair she'd rescued from a messy bun. Encouraged, she squeezed his erection. This time he gave off a noise mixed between a groan and a muttered curse.

"Promise me, Maddy."

"Yes. I promise." With her gaze still on his, she settled her butt on the edge of his desk. She shifted her weight, angling so she could spread her legs. She dropped back farther, removing her grip on his cock and placing her hands flat on his desk. The new angle showed his tanned hand against the sweet pink flesh between her legs. "Ezra?"

"Yes, Maddy?" His seductive tone made her muscles clench.

"Can you promise you'll do things to me that I'll need a safe word for?"

He groaned, leaning toward her to lick her lips. The contact shouldn't have made her hotter except for the fact it took him an eon to trace his tongue from one side of her mouth to the other. By the time he was done, she was the one making unintelligible noises. God, sex with him would be soooo good. It would have to be. Any man who took that much time kissing a woman like that had to be good in the sack.

"Maddy." Her name whispered through his lips as he continued to tease her so tenderly.

No one had ever taken such care to kiss her in— well, forever. Kochran had, she reminded herself. But Kochran had taken her over, plowing through her defenses. Ezra filled the space between them with pretty words fueled by a lazy heat. Thoughts she had of a quick, hard bang against the wall wisped away as he nuzzled her cheek. Normally she wouldn't go for the slow, sensual tease, especially after watching so much aggressive sex lately, but for Ezra, it worked. And boy, did it work in spades.

"Follow me."

She blinked, stunned to realize she'd zoned out. He'd pulled her pants back around her hips and stood over her, extending a hand. A compelling strength fortified his request so that she simply had no choice but to listen. Her downtime at the club had allowed her to become familiar with the regular Dominants of Noble House, both on the feeds and in Court. He wasn't at all like those Doms. Or like Kochran. He possessed the same kind of powerful authority, but there was something extra special about Ezra Snow.

Ezra's gaze held a different kind of proprietary quality from Kochran's. A barely caged restraint that drew her in. Ezra exuded a quiet confidence that was the opposite of Kochran's aggressiveness, though she could sense Ezra had the ability to take charge of matters with little more than the well-angled look and a submissive would be putty in his hands. The overabundance of genuine charm helped matters.

He held her gaze as he guided her down the hall to a room she hadn't been to before. He smiled as he gently nudged her forward and shut the door. She barely had enough time to register the fact he'd brought her to the room housing the computer servers for the club before he'd turned her and pinned her against the wall.

"So…extra special, huh?"

"Shit." Her face heated. "Didn't realize I'd said that out loud."

"Well, now that you have, I know I have a lot to live up to. I mean, extra special and all."

The tension wrapping her hips grew stronger as he gently snapped the elastic waistband. The light slap of pain told her there was more, way more, beneath the surface of the mask Ezra chose to show the world.

Maybe he wasn't as different from Kochran as she'd thought. Both men possessed that innate ability to make her feel possessed and wanted at the same time. A brand that would mark her for all eternity whether she wanted it to or not. She'd never experienced that sensation from any lover before, and now that she'd had a taste, it wasn't something she wanted to go without again.

But wanting two men had to be wrong, right?

Chapter Thirteen

Ezra had his hands on her, shoving away those damned sweatpants again as his blood returned to a rolling boil. But this time he stripped them away from her completely. Her taste still danced against his tongue. That small sample had only ignited his need to have more.

Madeline Zane wasn't as innocent as she seemed. He would think about how much she terrified him later. No, not her—how she raised emotions and wants and desires he'd buried far down deep. Somehow he knew that even when he'd had his fill, he would never be cured of his desire for her.

She would submit, but she wouldn't be passive. Not Maddy. Something inside him soared. He'd never been the kind of Dom who wanted a sub who blindly accepted his care. He'd purposefully brought her into the server zone instead of one of the play areas because he hadn't cleared it with Kochran first to use one of the clubrooms. There were also no cameras in his office, no way for them to be seen. In the play areas, anyone could watch. But Ezra didn't want just anyone.

Only one person had access to the security cameras used in this room. A single admin account owned by the man who sat at a desk with a fancy, complicated computer setup he hated. He may not see them right away, but he would eventually when he made his nightly check through the system.

"Tell me why you really came to the club." He altered the tone of his voice slightly, layering in a thread of command. When her body went liquid against his, he knew he'd made the right choice.

"What do you mean?"

"You could have handled it over a phone call, Mads. An email. You could have let us untangle the knots and gone on with your hobby without a second thought. We would have never known you were in the system. What made you jeopardize access to all that free porn?" He boxed her in against the wall, curving his hands around the back of her thighs. "Why did you show up at the club?" he repeated.

"I tried to call, but no one answered." She tugged on her bottom lip a few times. "To be honest, I was going to ask Steve to keep quiet about it. I was planning to exploit the weakness I found and enjoy the free membership." Ezra's eyebrows rose, but she continued, "I looked around in the simulator world you have set up, saw some people talking about some king."

"Kochran." Desire flared hotter as their mutual interest was revealed.

"Yeah," she admitted quietly, probably more than a little embarrassed she'd gotten caught up in the hype of the man who reigned over Noble House. Problem was, it wasn't hype. Kochran Duke was a fascinatingly complex man with layers that hid so many things Ezra wanted to uncover. "I saw for myself they were right. So I kept exploring. Kept digging. Found the message

boards where the chatter was a bit broader, but still…
Kochran again."

He did a quick calculation in his head, counting back
to the last live show Kochran had given. "What did you
watch that starred Kochran?"

"How did you—" She stopped at his stern look.
"The video with the sub holding the platters, where
he used the flogger while she hovered over a vibrator.
Just the first section of it, before there was any sex."
Ezra smirked at the blush that rose to her cheeks. The
fact she knew there was sex indicated that she had
watched more than she'd admitted.

Ezra hadn't been there that night. He'd been home,
logged into the system and working on an update. Even
without reading the message boards, Ezra knew Kochran had given them quite the show. He always did.

"So Kochran is the reason you came to the club. You
wanted to see the man in all his glory."

"No. Yes. I don't know. He's…"

"Devastatingly handsome? Rakishly domineering?"

Her throat worked as she swallowed, her gaze landing everywhere but on Ezra. "Intimidating."

"He is, isn't he? He's also freakishly controlled, but
there's a wildness too. It makes you want to bow for
him. Be under his command at any cost." Though Ezra
hadn't kneeled for a Dom since his early days of training, he still understood the all-consuming sensation.

"You admire him." When he remained silent, she
pressed on. "Maybe it's more than admiration."

He ignored her statement, settling her thighs around
his waist. This wasn't about the knot of need sitting at
the base of his spine that had Kochran's name tattooed
on it. "Is this your first experience with BDSM?"

"I'm sorry, I shouldn't have—"

He silenced her with a finger against her lips. "Answer me, Mads." He knew that was absolutely, positively the last thing she wanted to do. She'd already been ashamed enough to begin with, but he made it worse. She didn't need his judgment, even though he had none. He was the last person who should judge someone for their sexual choices. He was going to keep staring at her, putting her on the spot until she answered.

"Yes." She averted her gaze once again.

"You like to watch."

She swallowed again. "Yeah."

"You like to be watched?" Though he'd asked, he already knew the answer. He needed to know she would get off on being watched as much as he did.

She took a steadying breath before answering, "Yeah, I do."

He tilted her chin and crushed his mouth against hers. Heat and wetness flared to life against his abdomen, but for the moment, he concentrated on properly kissing her. On tangling his tongue with hers.

He'd been right. She wasn't passive. She nipped at his lips and tongue, taking what she needed out of the kiss. More of that unique sweetness flooded his senses, though he suspected there were other parts of her that tasted even sweeter.

God, he needed to find out.

He wrapped his hand around her thigh, inching closer to the enticing heat pressed against him. He angled his fingers, dragging them through that heat, pleased when she gave an answering shudder. Those tremors expanded when he pushed two fingers fully into her cunt. He broke the kiss to suck in a gasp of air, then took her mouth again, desperate to keep contact.

He needed to fully take her over. To expose layers of himself he hadn't shown anyone in years. He tamped down on that urge as he slowly drew back. Those thoroughly kiss-plumped lips beckoned to him as her sweet face tilted up, her eyes closed in a blissed-out state.

"Some people like to watch, like you. Others like to perform. To be seen. Perhaps by an audience of one." She inhaled sharply as her eyes flew open, her gaze landing instantly on him. "I know you watched me jack off, Mads. I wanted you to see."

"What?"

He stroked his thumb over her jawline as his whole body became a tight ball of want. Maddy was going to be the death of him.

"Such innocence." He kissed her jaw, loving the way her muscles fluttered around his fingers. "I wanted to know if you like watching other kinky people, or you enjoy watching me. I could've asked, but where's the fun in that?"

"But you could have sent it to the wrong person. In fact, for a while, I thought you had."

He snorted with a soft laugh. "I know you think my coding leaves something to be desired, but give me a little more credit. Secure feeds over a closed network are child's play."

She ground against him, working her hips as he continued to plunge in and out of all that luscious sweetness surrounding his fingers. So damn tight and wet. His dick throbbed at the fucking beautiful display of submissive woman pressed up against him, turning herself over to him with such trust and admiration. Pleasure hammered against him, threatening to pound him apart with a madness that reminded him of the person he used to be. Emotions boiled to the surface, stark pleasure he wasn't equipped to deal with.

He slanted his mouth against hers again, the need to confess his intention before they went any further burning through his gut like a dying star. "Someone will see us on the security cameras, Maddy. See me finger fucking you."

He paused, waiting for that single word that would bring everything to a grinding halt. *Red.*

But it didn't come. Instead she continued to grind against him, her breath shuddering out at each plunge.

Knowing someone was watching should have bothered Maddy. But if there was anywhere in the world where her behavior was acceptable, it was Noble House.

He spread her legs wider, repositioning his hand so he had complete access to press the length of his body against hers. The position allowed her to feel the length of the cock she'd seen earlier, wrapped her hand around just minutes ago when they'd been in his office. Though his jaw and mouth were relaxed, approachable and non-intimidating, the impression vanished as she met his gaze again. Her pulse thudded against her throat as he swiped his tongue over his kissable lips.

"There's a few things you need to know about me, Mads, before this goes any further."

The statement broke the buzz spinning in her mind. "What do you mean?"

He considered her before answering. "I haven't actively participated in the lifestyle in a long time. It's still a part of me—that will never go away." His mouth lifted in a half-grin. "I also want you to know I'm bi-sexual."

He said it as matter-of-factly as telling her the sky was blue. Clearly the intent hadn't been to shock her. His sexuality was as ingrained in him as being a man. Surprisingly, this bit of information didn't unsettle her. Some part of her had known he was different in more than one way, her body answering to his in a thrumming note. A signal she was the kind of person he could confide in with absolute trust. She certainly couldn't explain the hows or the whys, but she just *knew*.

He feathered his lips against her cheek. "I also like threesomes." He said it so straightforward, she had to take a moment to process the statement. That information knocked her harder than expected even though she clenched around those fingers still buried inside her. "You're surprised by that and not by the truth about my sexuality."

Her surprise had been the result of the knowledge she'd been dead on during her spontaneous fantasy, not the revelation he liked multiple partners or had sex with men. She couldn't very well confess that news, though. She'd spilled enough truths about herself for the night. The insanity of it all was how much all these facets of Ezra worked for her.

There was an intrinsic rawness to him that made her want to uncover all her unexplored desires, as though she only recently discovered she'd been keeping herself locked in an impenetrable cage, and two men were breaking their way through.

"Why are you telling me all this, Ezra?"

"Because ninety-five percent of what goes on here at the club is right in my wheelhouse. The voyeurism, the floggers, restraints, and the toys. Being watched. But I haven't wanted to do any of those things in a very long time." He touched her collarbone as he confessed, tracing it with soft, even strokes. "Until I saw you giving Kochran a piece of your mind about the website that first day. I knew I had to have you."

His confession warmed her already hot core. He'd kept all the pieces of the puzzle locked down inside him, but had chosen this moment—chosen her—as the keymaster. "Why did you stop?"

His eyes hazed like the ominous clouds before a devastating hurricane blew on shore as he removed his fingers from her most intimate parts.

"When my wife died, our husband walked out on me. Said he couldn't stand the sight of me with her gone or some other bullshit." The confession spilled out in low, gravelly tones that signaled the weight of each word.

"Oh, Ezra." She cradled his jaw, pressing a gentle kiss to his warm lips. He returned her kiss, easing her against the metal rack housing buzzing equipment. Sweat pricked her skin and it had nothing to do with the unit near her shoulder pumping out heat through the cooling fan.

"It was better to be closed down," he murmured. "Better than dealing with someone leaving me again."

"Easier." She set her palm against his chest. "It was easier."

"I guess so." He took her mouth again, more insistent this time. More sure of her and the power arcing between them. "I feel safe with you, Maddy. One of the few people on the planet I think I can be totally myself with."

"I didn't think you liked me," she stated quietly as a rush of yearning pushed through the holes of her heart as it broke for him.

"I don't dislike you, Mads. You distract me. Throw off my game. Pull me into wanting things I haven't thought about in…" He blew out a long breath as he paused. "An exceptionally long time."

"And now?"

That alluring smile that made her want to drop to her knees, made her think about that mouth between her thighs, returned. It scared her half to death as much as it aroused her.

"I want to do it all." He tucked two fingers into her slick, hot pussy once again, that smile growing wider. "You're still drenched."

Pleasure pulsed as he added a third finger, then a fourth, and began to pump. Pressure built and built until she wasn't sure if she could take it anymore. But she could. For him. She bit down on her lip as the pain converted to pleasure, overwhelming her so that she was at his mercy. The world had gone hazy and light, edges blunted by the enigmatic, powerful presence Ezra had revealed.

She wanted to suffer for him. She bit back a moan even as she flooded his hand. Ezra swore, working his fingers into her with a ruthless pace that only made her hotter, wetter. The deluge of endorphins was new, but instantly addicting.

Addictive and disturbing.

Lovely.

"I want you to go to him, Mads." He continued fucking her with his fingers as he spoke quietly, his tone breathless but still firm. "Not right away, not with my smell all over you. Much, much too soon for that."

Ezra's body trembled against hers, as though he was already imagining that point in the future. "You won't restrain your desires for him at all, do you understand?"

Maddy's whole body gave a hard shiver at the weight of Ezra's darkly beautiful command.

"You fucking love being ordered like that, don't you? It forces you to be in the present instead of wrapped up in your head."

Maddy hung on the precipice of release, waiting and aching for the words she needed to hear.

"You will go to Kochran and you will do whatever he wants. Even if that means he fucks you in front of the entire membership. In front of me."

For a long, breathless moment Maddy was suspended in a pool of pure liquid fire. Ezra was her lifeline, his darkness drawing her in, exposing her own. Hot, aching desire buzzed through her as she realized she would do anything to please him because it would mean pleasure for her.

Anything for you.

"Yes."

Chapter Fourteen

Kochran's dick was in his fist as he continued to stare at the grainy security footage. He'd stopped trying to convince himself to turn off the feed when Ezra had told her they were being watched. That knowledge hadn't been a kill point for her. Hadn't made her run screaming from the club because of all the freaks.

Kochran wasn't the type to use porn as an outlet. Not that there was anything wrong with the choice, but he'd always had his pick of willing submissives craving his attention. Then again, the required contract—for employee or member—meant when they stepped through Noble House's front door, some degree of privacy had been stripped away. As owner, Kochran had the right to observe whatever he wanted, whenever he wanted.

Right now he wanted to watch Madeline and Ezra.

In his mind, he inserted himself in the server room so he could have them at his mercy. But the fantasized situation was…off. Maddy's display of submission lit a wildfire inside him that couldn't be contained. But Ezra…there was something glorious and irresistible about the man who challenged Kochran's way of thinking. Who made him want to surrender.

He commended Saint and Boyce for their flexibility

when it came to their choice of dominance or submission. How they flourished in both roles. Their ability to fluidly transition between the two states, even in the middle of the scene, was admirable. Grae certainly didn't seem to mind in the least that the men could easily command her one moment, then kneel beside her the next. There had to be a certain freedom in the choice.

The room closed in around him, his entire body surging with unbridled craving as the realization slammed into his core. The remnants of something he hadn't resolved threatened to choke him. The battle raging through his system caused him to go into complete and utter overload.

Anger. Desire. Loss.

The persona Kochran had so carefully crafted over the years cracked. A far-off sinking sensation he hadn't experienced in a long time swamped him so quickly, he wasn't certain he was equipped to deal with it. The shock to his system was too much to handle as everything began to make sense.

Jesus. Fuck. I want Ezra to be my Master.

Maddy inhaled sharply when Ezra dragged the tip of his tongue against the side of her neck.

"You got off earlier, didn't you? Watching me. Right there at your makeshift desk, you kicked back and touched your pretty little clit." He increased the pressure against her tender flesh as it gave a throbbing pulse. When he curled his fingers against her opening, her breath rasped against his ear as though she couldn't drag in enough air to breathe. She arched against him when he pressed deeper.

"You're not afraid of being around this lifestyle either, but you're shy and tentative. You like an intimate connection with the man you choose to bow before. Maybe not full-on friendship, but you have to trust and understand him before you'll offer him your submission. It's a gift to you. A precious treasure you don't offer up just to anyone."

She nodded.

"I want to tie you up, Mads. I want to expose your submissive nature fully. I want you to serve my needs and desires because while I think you're beautiful already, I think you'll be fucking gorgeous serving a Dom in a way that goes beyond orgasms and sex."

Warmth built between her thighs as he slipped deeper. She closed her eyes to bask in the pleasure he built for her. He shifted again and she groaned as he worked those fingers inside her fully. Explored the tight muscles quivering around his fingers.

"Who are you thinking about, Mads?"

Her eyes fluttered open and she met his questing gaze as his slow strokes continued to circle her clit. "You."

"Mmm, I don't think so. At least I'm not the only one you're thinking about. Not after all those ideas I planted about submitting to Kochran." He touched her chin, using just enough pressure to angle her face to the small overhead dome camera aimed their way. "You're thinking about him too. Imagining me spreading you out on a bed, restraining your hands and feet so you're available to us however I choose. Thinking you could really get off on a second body pressed up against yours, worshipping your breasts while I taste your clit. Perhaps you want to suck another Dom's dick while I put you on your knees and fuck you."

The world spun off its axis as her head spun. "Damn, you're good."

"I'm honest. I speak exactly what I see because I don't have time for games. And I see your honesty. You don't have time for games either. That is something you haven't had much of with your experience. Someone hurt you. Not a Dom, though, because you said you haven't been with another Dom."

"I just want to explore and play," she confessed. "I'm not looking for anything serious or permanent." Though she was looking for a connection of some kind, she couldn't handle anything more than casual. Her emotions were being pulled in two different directions at once, and she needed to delve deeper before she made a choice.

"I can give that to you." A strained whimper spilled past her lips as he twisted his wrist so he could press his thumb against her clit while he moved his fingers inside her. God, this man and his ability to make her lose her mind. "When I fuck you, I'm going to lay you out, make every part of you available to me. To lick. To taste. To do with as I please."

She knew he was capable of all those things. Better yet—she wanted him to do each one of those things.

"Kochran told me something similar. But he was… harsher. Dirtier."

"What did he tell you?"

"He promised to make me come the first time he fucked me."

Wet heat flooded his hand. "Good goddamn, Mads, I want to gorge on you." He held her gaze as he lifted his fingers to his mouth, and licked them clean. "Someday, I will taste your climax with my fingers buried deep inside your cunt."

She groaned. He muffled the sound by covering her mouth with his, overwhelmed her with his raw and hungry kiss. He replaced his fingers and immediately found the intoxicating rhythm that gave her life again.

"I didn't get to see because there was a camera between us earlier, but I want to see it now. Show me how beautiful you are when you come." Ezra pressed his mouth against hers. "Show *us*."

"Ezra," she ground out as the electric bliss of release crashed hard into her. Every nerve ending exploded in a wave of pleasure, lightning rushing through her veins at the sweet glide of his fingers against her delicate tissue as he pumped her through the release.

Even though she was convinced she couldn't possibly take anymore, Ezra increased his tempo, driving his fingers into her with frantic thrusts. Her muscles rippled around him, milking him as his low moan of approval sliced through the air.

"So fucking wet, Maddy." He sighed her name again as she went limp against him. She touched her forehead to his as he turned his back, sliding them to the floor and positioning her so she straddled his thighs. The world seemed to balance on the edge of a dime as he gathered her close.

He rubbed his hands up and down her back, her body continuing to quiver with aftershocks as he spoke. "Just as beautiful as I thought you'd be."

The blackness of the Keep swallowed Kochran as he stepped into the rectangular room. He turned on a single light so he could make out the shadow of furniture and made his way to the raised area on the far side of the quiet room.

Once, the Keep had been filled with a select few Kochran trusted the most, including the two men who founded Noble House with him. In the Keep, the demands of the business that tended to weigh him down didn't exist. Where he could enjoy the chosen aspects of the lifestyle he'd embraced after a few hard lessons in his early twenties. Free of any of the usual club equipment found down in Court or the private rooms, Kochran was liberated from the responsibilities of life.

He glanced at the chair he normally sat in. Chair, hell, it was a fucking throne. Annoyed with the power the oversized carved piece represented, he chose to sit in front of it and use the seat to support his back. The press of the cushion reminded him of the ache blooming across his shoulders thanks to his inability to move while he'd watched the security feed.

He'd sat there like some crazed, horny teenager with his dick in his hand, jacking off to the sight of people fucking two floors above him. Sex could be found anywhere in the club, but they were the ones who canted his world.

He attempted to organize his thoughts. Rest his mind. Stop the persistent, blinding arousal constricting painfully around the base of his cock. Ideally, he'd go home, stand naked under a cascade of freezing water, put a chokehold on his aching dick and jack away the discomfort. But with the persistent ache clawing at him, one orgasm wasn't going to be enough. Coming three or four times may not even erase the tenacious need. For that, he'd have to break into a bottle of bourbon and work his way through it. He preferred not using alcohol as a crutch to escape this kind of complication, but he had to do something to get the couple out of his system.

He was pleased Ezra had found a spark after years of shunning the lifestyle he'd once loved. Ezra clearly enjoyed the mind fuck aspect of the lifestyle. Kochran admired that approach—he'd done it enough himself. But Christ, it made Kochran's charade of having all his shit together harder to maintain. The blood hammering through his cock didn't give a flying fuck about good sense. It wanted somewhere warm and wet to burrow inside for a few hours or feel the hard press of someone else's cock pounding in him.

Fuck.

Nobody would ever believe Kochran liked to submit to another man. He'd built this club crafted on the fantasy that Kochran Duke bowed to no one. One slip of the truth and he risked losing everything he'd worked hard for. But the demand to embrace the submissive side of himself once again was becoming harder and harder to ignore.

He'd founded the club as a safe haven for anyone to explore their fantasies because he'd been convinced the life he craved wasn't attainable. His friends had surrounded themselves with love and affection while Kochran had submerged himself in the world of the extreme as a way to mask his pain. No fetish was too outrageous, no partner too extreme. Somewhere along the way, life had become about keeping the customer pleased, and less about maintaining his own happiness.

He'd missed his opportunity for happily ever after years and years ago because his life hadn't gone the way he'd expected. Instead, he'd transformed himself into something else entirely. Long ago, thanks to the one man he'd trusted, Kochran had decided he didn't deserve a happy ending. Those memories almost erased his apprehension about exploring that side of himself again.

Almost.

Chapter Fifteen

A week later, Kochran turned away from the trio of computer monitors Saint had installed in his office when they'd gone virtual. Kochran had insisted they weren't necessary, but he'd changed his mind when he found he turned to them more and more. If Maddy and Ezra had been together again since that night in the server room, they hadn't played where any cameras could sight them. He hadn't actively sought them out either, burying himself with the tasks of vetting new members, sorting out the club's accounting and spending precious moments with Tory.

When he looked up, Ezra stood in the doorway, holding two cups of steaming coffee. Their interaction was inevitable since Kochran had asked Ezra to handle the interviews for people developing new technology Kochran wanted to introduce at the club. Though there was already more than enough variety to keep the members interested, he knew the keystone to every business was the ability to grow and evolve. While he may not fully understand the tech that ran half of his club, he knew enough to hire people he trusted to keep it going.

"So what is the verdict on the virtual reality?" Kochran already knew the answer based on Ezra's frown.

"Not a single viable candidate in the bunch." Ezra shrugged. "Not sure what you're looking to do is possible."

"Anything is possible."

"You want to be up and running this time next year, you needed to find someone last week. There will be too much extensive beta testing that will need to be conducted to wait much longer."

Kochran tapped his pen against the desk. Despite Ezra's frustration, he was also clearly excited by the idea of the new project. Quite a pleasant change from the man who'd sat at his breakfast table two weeks ago.

Of course, Kochran wasn't the only one who had a say in the matter. "What does Saint think?"

"I have a meeting with him in a few hours. I would have met with him before this, but he couldn't get away sooner. There is one thing."

Always was when it came to the club. Kochran loved it dearly, but it sucked money from his bank account faster than a hooker looking for her next John. "How much is this setback going to cost me?"

Ezra snorted. That soft noise wrapped around the base of Kochran's cock and sank its claws into his need. Every time he thought he had a handle on it…he forced it down, determined to focus on the business at hand. The club wasn't going to run itself, and if he kept getting caught up in the needs of his traitorous cock, he'd never get any work done.

"I could use a hand upgrading the system to handle the load this new stuff will add to the servers. What we've got is fine, so you won't need too many purchases, but the expansion could use a second set of hands to code. Maybe even a third," Ezra added.

Kochran knew where this was heading. "You want me to hire Maddy permanently."

"Any programmer would work."

Ezra's noncommittal tone didn't fool Kochran. *Any* programmer wouldn't get Ezra excited. "That isn't your preference."

"She's already familiar with the system." Ezra shrugged. "Maybe even more so than I am, considering how she dug around in there before she even showed up. Having an expert at her level would speed the process."

Handy excuse. Kochran had no objection to Madeline being around longer to help with the system enhancements. He suspected Ezra's reasons weren't entirely geek related. He may not understand all the computer shit, but Kochran knew people.

He also understood the strange phenomenon that happened whenever Ezra was around. Kochran's dominant instincts rose to the surface, but for an entirely different reason than normal. He longed to give Ezra whatever he wanted, whatever he needed to heal, even if that included submitting. But as much as he wanted to fill the awful, glaring hole he knew existed deep inside him, Kochran couldn't afford that choice.

Madeline's presence would allow Kochran to fully dedicate himself to that promise he'd made to her in the stationery store. "All right," Kochran said carefully. "If she's agreeable, and available to extend her contract, she's more than welcome to join our happy little family."

The weight and meaning of that sentence hovered in the air as Ezra exited Kochran's office in a rush.

Maddy ran her fingers across the fluid scrawl of her name on the envelope she'd discovered tucked inside her laptop bag. The paper was a reminder that over a month had passed since she'd found Kochran in Take Note. When she'd asked him if he still intended to make good on his promise, he'd only smiled and told her good things take time.

Evidently, the time had arrived.

Her heart raced as she broke the seal and pulled out the matching card. Kochran's sweeping, perfect handwriting on that gorgeous notecard with the hearts and stars twisted something inside her as she read.

Take a sheet of your most expensive paper, and your favorite pen. Settle into a comfortable spot with a glass of wine. Write out your most explicit fantasy in filthy detail. Use your best handwriting for each and every dirty word. Deliver it to me the next time we see each other.

He wasn't much for poetic words, but his commanding tone came through the paper. The arch of each letter. The dot of the punctuation. Exactly what she wanted—and needed. Using his methodology that good things take time, she forced herself to wait at least two days before following his instructions, to think hard about the fantasy, getting aroused by it. Remembering how Ezra had ordered her to seek out Kochran, explore more of what he had to offer her. The instruction had been the key that had unlocked something deeply primal inside her, as though Ezra had known her secret desires as well as if she'd spoken them out loud.

It had taken her another two days to bring herself to deliver her fantasy to Kochran in person. She stood in front of his office door, certain the carefully folded sheet she'd written her fantasy on would burst into flames. As she started to knock, she had a momentary lapse of courage. Surely a man like Kochran would have heard every filthy, dirty detail imaginable. Had more than likely helped a few submissives live out those fantasies. Nothing she could conjure could possibly compare. But he'd asked. No, *commanded*.

Courage shored up with that knowledge, she lifted her hand again. She hadn't been able to stop thinking about him even though she and Ezra had continued to explore one another. Ezra had clearly indicated he didn't mind her playing with someone else at the club. In fact, he'd ordered it. Wasn't as though she wanted a relationship. It was just sex. Wild, kinky and outrageous sex.

After she'd followed Kochran's orders, she'd replayed the video of Kochran from the night she'd broken into the Noble House servers. This time, she watched from start to finish. She'd been riveted to her seat as the scene had played out between Kochran and the submissive. Though Ezra blew her mind, she also needed what she'd seen in the video. Kochran was the one to give it to her.

With a shaking hand, she knocked softly.

"Come."

The single word did wonderful, warm and perfect things that made her skin heat and her panties go damp.

She peeked around the door. "Have a few minutes?"

Kochran sighed as he looked up. "For you, sure."

He looked tired and stressed. Far more than the last time she'd seen him. "Is this a bad time? I can come back." If she had to, she'd lose her nerve. Burn the piece of paper in her hand in a fit of uncertainty and embarrassment.

"Of course not. Just stuff that will be there waiting for me."

"Two things." She stepped forward. "First, I wanted to know if I can revise my limitations list."

Kochran's eyebrows rose. "You actually filled one out?"

She shrugged. "I may be a cyber-troublemaker, but I wanted to make sure it was authentic-looking. I just randomly clicked boxes without paying attention."

"And now you want to officially have one on record that matches your true interests."

She licked her lips before replying, "My...situation has changed."

Kochran smiled slyly. "How so?" Even as he asked, he turned to his spread of computer monitors without a word. For someone who had the sort of attitude toward technology that he did, it was quite sophisticated. Clearly someone else was responsible for ensuring he kept a tight rein over his club. She remained quiet while he navigated to her profile. A few seconds later, the nearby printer came to life. He glanced at her over the top edge as he read the printout. "I know, you want to remove the selection about clowns."

"What?" She snatched the paper and scanned over it. Midway down the neat column: *Clowns*. "Shit. I thought you were joking."

"There is a fetish for everything." He took the paper from her, slipping the sheet into the feeder of a shredder.

"Um, I wanted to change that." She pointed toward the bin, where her list was now confetti.

He handed her a sheet of cream-colored paper and the fountain pen he'd purchased the day they'd run into one another at the stationery store. "Write out what you think your hard and soft limits are, straight from the gut without a tidy list prompting you. There are no mistakes either, so I don't want you crossing anything out." He held out his hand. "Let me see what you wrote while I wait."

His stern gaze arrowed straight to her heart, uncovering all her uncertainties. Compelled to follow the order, she allowed everything she'd kept locked away to pour forth. The unvarnished truth spread over the expensive sheet as though she'd opened a vein and bled on the page. He was still reading her note when she rose to get another sheet.

Without looking at her, he rolled his chair back, blocking her. "Sit down, Madeline."

His curt tone erased any of the biting words she wanted to fling toward him. She returned to the chair and settled. She waited until he'd finished, her temper quelled enough she could reasonably ask why he'd stopped her.

Those sharp eyes pierced her as he asked, "It's my job to see that you have everything you require, yes?"

"I didn't want to bother you."

"You're supposed to bother me, Madeline. To ask me for what you need."

So many meanings in that sentence. *What you need.* Like her fantasy, which he'd finished reading. And things in over half her already-transcribed list. "I'd like another sheet of paper so I can continue my list."

With an appreciative grunt, he handed her another sheet and went back to her note. She wanted to ask why he was reading it again, but there was obviously something in it he found interesting, be it her selection of paper, her horrible penmanship—no matter how carefully she wrote—or the fantasy itself.

She thought she'd already made herself vulnerable with the note he studied so intently, but writing her limit list was soul-bearing. The words staring up at her, the loops and lines of the letters that made up the words of the list permanent. An etching of her soul. She may as well have used her body as a canvas instead of the paper. After she set the pen on the desk, she folded her hands in her lap. He'd read her letter countless times by now, but she waited patiently until he looked to her again.

"You could have altered the list on your own, you know." His biting tone caused unexpected things to happen inside her. The elegant scent of his expensive cologne washed over her as his gaze pinned her to the seat. She fought not to squirm even though she was aroused. "The general membership can't, of course, but you have an admin account."

Sure, she could have. But she wanted to find out if Kochran meant it when he said he'd make her come the first time he fucked her. Revising her list this way was a convenient excuse to also deliver the letter he'd requested.

She handed him the sheets. "I have something else I wanted to discuss if you have some time."

Kochran gave it a once over before he tucked the

file into the drawer and rose. He came around the desk, leaned against the desk edge and crossed his ankles. From her seated position, she had an enticing view of his crotch. He may have been trying to appear aloof and calm, but the large bulge signaled he was anything but.

"And that is...?" He crossed his arms in front of him.

"What you said to me a few weeks back. I just wanted to know...if." She stopped, unsure how best to phrase it. How should she remind a man like Kochran he'd extended an open invitation she now wanted to cash in?

"Go on and ask, Madeline. I'm the last one to judge you."

"I don't know if I can."

"Of course you can. You're trying to understand what you want. You're surrounded by all these people day in and day out who know exactly what they expect from themselves. From their lovers. I can tell you're brave, baby girl, but your heart and your head are at war."

Once again, he'd pierced right through the heart of the matter. "You sound like you know exactly what I'm going through."

"The club has been my personal hell and my salvation." He shifted, sliding his hands into his pockets. The fabric tightened against his body, outlining his cock. The tissue between her legs swelled. She'd thought she was already aroused beyond measure, but he seemed capable of ratcheting up her desire with every passing second. "How about I confess something to you and maybe it will make you more comfortable?"

She swallowed. "Okay." Couldn't hurt to try. Strange how she'd opened herself fully on those sheets of paper, but couldn't seem to replicate the strength to speak out loud.

"I'm extremely attracted to you, Madeline. You do something to me, and it's not entirely sexual in nature. I don't know exactly what it is and that isn't a usual feeling for me. I'm compelled to explore."

She blew out a slow breath.

"That doesn't bode well for my confession."

"Oh! Sorry. I was thinking...how." She paused. "I thought you said what you did that first night because you said it to everyone. That I wasn't anything special."

"No, Madeline, I've never welcomed a new member or employee that way." He leaned closer, setting his hands on the arms of the chair to cage her in. "I would like to follow up that hot kiss with a spanking for thinking I'm so free with my greetings."

Those words silenced every fear and doubt she'd had about Kochran. "It was silly of me."

"It was cautious. Nothing wrong with that."

She moistened her lips. "I want to be honest with you."

"As I expect you to be."

"I... Ezra and I having been fooling around for a few weeks. No intercourse, but I...we've been...exploring."

"Exploring is good. You can learn a lot about yourself, and your partner, that way."

What she'd figured out was that her dependency on Ezra—and how he made her feel when he pushed her boundaries—was astounding. He was impossible to forget. Most of the time, she was surprised she could even get any work done.

"He had me masturbate for him," she admitted quietly. The admission gave her the strength to continue.

"Several times, in fact. With and without a vibrator. Last week, while he was uploading content to the website…he saw me watching over his shoulder." Damn him and that stupid spy mirror he kept positioned under his monitor.

His gaze evaluated her. "What did he do when he caught you?"

Not what she'd expected, that was for certain. "Ordered me to come sit on his lap. The video was one of your sessions in Court. You had a sub on her knees, her legs spread with her ankles and wrists restrained by wide metal shackles. She was bent back at such an extreme angle, she was almost lying down." She broke off, knowing she didn't need to explain the positioning in greater detail since he'd been the one to place the woman in the bondage. "I came twice. Once just sitting there. It surprised me. I've never had an orgasm without *some* kind of manipulation. But when you used a pair of vibrators to double penetrate her, I was a little overwhelmed."

"And the other time?"

"When you were flogging her a little later on, Ezra used his fingers to play with me. It was a little surreal, watching you and feeling his touch. But I… I liked it. When she climaxed, I did too." She held back the information that Ezra was partially the reason she was sitting in this chair. That piece wasn't essential to know going forward unless things took a turn.

Fulfilling his instructions to seek out pleasure brought her a sense of accomplishment. Just like writing her fantasy as Kochran had requested. Completing tasks given by two handsome and engaging men that she wanted to continue to please made her all warm and gooey on the inside. This whole thing should have been a giant, heaping serving of hell no with a side order of what the fuck. But she wanted it all anyway.

"I don't have rules that prevent employees from fraternizing during non-working hours."

She winced. Technically most of their play had been during working hours, but it walked an exceptionally fine line since they had no set schedule. "I just wanted it clear that—"

"You are with someone else," he finished.

"We're not together. Well, not together *together*."

"I appreciate your honesty, Madeline. As long as you are as honest with him."

Her head shot up. "I would never dream of lying to either of you about something like this."

"Good. I would hate to be the cause of ruining a good thing when you two obviously have chemistry." He touched the tip of her nose. "Don't look so surprised. I saw the footage from the server room. There is very little that happens in my club that I don't know about."

Embarrassment flooded her as she fought the urge to avert her gaze from his probing one. Ezra had told her Kochran was watching them in the server room, but she hadn't really believed him until this moment. A small slice of her had hoped it was the truth. Had even imagined Kochran sitting right in this very office, gripped by the sexual encounter unfolding before him on the monitors and taking himself in hand.

Things like this didn't happen to ordinary people.

Then again, these weren't ordinary men.

Kochran stilled his mind as he stood, wanting a bit of distance from Madeline. He needed to stop imagining the possibilities and focus on the reality seated in front of him. Reading the fantasy she'd chosen to share had been an exercise in patience. He'd wanted to give her those things she'd written about, easily imagining himself in the scene, guiding her through, taking the journey along with her. Even see her sitting, exhausted and spent, at his knee, a slight smile turning up the corners of her mouth as she floated on satisfaction.

The imagery formed by her words had been so vivid, he'd been pulled into the fantasy several times. He'd been so absorbed in the gift, he'd been afraid he'd missed something during the first pass. Then the second. And the third. In truth, she had an easy way with words that drew him in.

Her list of hard and soft limits hadn't contained anything beyond his experience level. Her penmanship had left something to be desired, but it had been legible enough for him to make out each and every item. Most of all, he'd been pleased to see the first few items on her list aligned with what he'd discovered so far.

"Sit up straight, please. Fold your hands in your lap again just like you did earlier." She settled into the pose within a few seconds. "Ankles uncrossed." She'd done it automatically, as most women did as soon as they sat. "Comfortable?"

She nodded her head slightly.

"Verbally, baby girl."

"Yes."

The single word came out breathy and soft. The three letters wrapped around the base of his dick and constricted it.

"Good. I like this position for you as well. Like you're waiting for a Dom to come along and sully you.

But not before he surveys you, sees the inflections in your breath as your body reacts to being watched. He notices the shape of your breasts under your shirt. Maybe sees the outline of the cups of your bra. How your breathing quickens the longer he watches you."

He hadn't needed the notes she'd written to know she had an exhibitionist streak a mile wide or to understand how she'd react to the position he put her in. He'd seen the way she'd come undone under Ezra's touch when he'd told her they were being watched. She hadn't pushed Ezra away. Hadn't pulled out the safe word he'd smartly given her. She'd allowed herself to be taken over.

Multiple partners. Surrender. Public sex. Bondage. She needed a Dominant who would handle her with a firm hand. But she also needed a Dominant who could see her other more sensual desires. Blindfolds. Soft floggers that only kissed the skin instead of marking it. He could help her explore a few of those things in one scene.

He offered her his hand and a companionable smile. She looked up to him, clearly confused but looking just as gorgeous as ever. "Do you want to continue in privacy, or go somewhere a little more…public?"

She licked her lips, her gaze darting around. Kochran knew she wanted everything at once. She wanted alone time with him, but needed the thrill of a public setting.

"Court, please." She responded so quietly he almost hadn't heard her. Clearly she was more comfortable with written words than her voice.

"So sweetly submissive. You like to be watched. Like knowing that people are imagining themselves in your shoes. Or mine. That they blend their personal stories with ours so we're all connected by tenuous threads of needs and wants. You know they are there, but you're also oblivious to them." He brushed his lips against the shell of her ear as he used his voice to ensnare her. "You want to experience the story as much as you want to tell it. You want to be the star *and* the chorus line. Either way, you should know when I scene with a submissive, she is my everything."

She gripped his hand tighter. He kissed the tips of her fingers as she accepted his unyielding support as she stood. It was easy to abandon the paperwork he'd been slogging through for the promise of what was to come with her.

He guided her out of his office, which connected to the lounge. The crowd in the social area wasn't as large as it could have been. A quick glance at the clock mounted over the archway entrance showed it was still early. Of course, once those there realized he was going to play with a submissive in Court, the crowd would increase exponentially. He didn't often come to the wide-open space anymore to play, but Madeline needed the accolades and the whispers and the rush that came with knowing other people were watching.

No reason in the world he couldn't give that to her.

Maybe he would find a little of what he needed as well.

Chapter Sixteen

Maddy's heart thumped hard as Kochran led her to a pair of decorative double doors. Her intent hadn't been to land herself a spot front and center in Court, but damn if she was going to back down now. The temptation to find out what he had planned was too appealing.

Though the activity level was low, the energy level was high. Almost visceral. As though every act that had taken place in the large room saturated the walls.

There were only two other scenes playing out as they entered the room. In one corner a Domme had positioned a male submissive on a short staircase. The naked man was draped over the treads like a piece of art, his well-toned body taut as he stroked his erection. Each time he didn't follow the Domme's instructions exactly, the Domme used a riding crop to strike the submissive on his thighs, arms or chest. As Maddy passed the scene, she caught the slight hesitations in the submissive's movements, as though he was purposefully disobeying so the Domme would be forced to use the impact instrument on him. Surprising given the dreamy quality of his eyes, a sign he was in the room physically, but psychologically he was soaring high in subspace.

In the other, a submissive was bent over a spank-

ing bench, her wrists and ankles secured to the heavy
wooden legs with thick leather cuffs adorned with intimidating metal spikes. A matching collar wrapped
her throat, its thickness being used to angle her head
and hold it in place. The bindings kept her open for the
machine behind her. A long extension pole was topped
with a thick pink phallus and was slowly working in
and out at a set pace. A man stood by her head, his cock
buried deep in her throat as he matched the movements
of the machine fucking the submissive.

Judging by the squeals, whimpers and groans, both
scenes would be coming to an end soon. Which meant
whatever Kochran had planned, he intended for them
to be the focus of attention. She was grateful the space
wasn't packed. Her nerve may have eroded if that were
the case. Yeah, she liked to be watched, but the thought
of that many people observing was intimidating.

The protective coating under her shoes muffled her
steps as Kochran led her to an area that had been roped
off in the center of the room. The concrete floor gave
way to a beautifully colored Persian rug that made her
want to kick off her shoes and dig her toes into the
velvety threads.

She glanced over to the stone columns used as support for the floor above. But that wasn't their only func-
tion. Large rings had been embedded in the columns,
inviting members to utilize them. She swallowed past
the dryness in her throat at the thought of such public displays. Sure, she'd thought about them hundreds
of times, used them as masturbation fodder on more
than a few occasions and, thanks to the club's website,
watched others get off on being viewed. But theory was
one thing. Reality, something else entirely.

"Not scared, are you?" Kochran's warm smile greeted her as she turned to face him. His hand was still wrapped around hers. She hadn't realized how much she needed that connection with him until now.

"No."

A loud bang startled her, and when she jumped, Kochran pulled her into his embrace. Maddy glanced over her shoulder to see a muscular man lifting a chair over the barrier. After he placed it on the rug, he turned to scoop up a pile of ropes and a cloth bag he'd dropped.

"Sorry. Arms were full." As he stepped closer, she must have made a movement because Kochran's arms tightened around her. "Enver Furst. Resident shibari expert for Noble House."

As soon as he said he was the rope master for the club, she recognized him as the Dom she'd seen in one of the videos who'd tied a submissive up to a nearby column and forced her to orgasm over and over.

"Don't worry, baby girl." Kochran touched her arm. "Enver is just going to give me a hand with some setup."

"I wasn't worried."

Enver smirked, an expression that made his older face even more handsome. "Yeah you were."

A shiver coursed through her. Her pulse jumped when she spotted the black square of silky fabric in Kochran's hand. "What is that?"

"I don't want you detached from this—from me." The flash of something hungry sparked in his eyes. "If you're uncomfortable, you need to let me know."

She eyed the neat coils of purple rope Enver had placed in the corner of the carpet. A glittering pile of panic snaps. The small bag near Kochran's foot. The chair. It was all so…surreal. This wasn't her life.

He cocked his head to the side. "Sure you're ready for this? We can take this to a private room, or have some coffee in the lounge to talk about your fantasy and lists a little more."

Ezra's command to move things forward with Kochran echoed in her head. More than anything, she wanted this moment. Needed it.

"No. This is all right."

Kochran's gaze turned frigid. "I have to hear you're more than all right, Madeline."

She squared her shoulders. "I'm just—afraid. This is cold and—set up. I need—I just need to feel the way I did that first night you kissed me." The way her body had come alive with his touch. His promise. That spark she'd experienced the instant Ezra had given her a safe word and commanded her with flawless expertise.

Kochran's expression changed. His eyes flashed again as he flexed his fingers around hers. "I can't guarantee that."

Her hope deflated. "Oh. Okay."

He eyed her, his jaw visibly flexing as he waited.

"Broody silence agrees with you." She swallowed hard as his gaze flashed. "I was living in my head again. Yes, I am—this is—more than all right."

She allowed him to lead her to the chair. It was plain and worn, obviously a tool used many, many times. She wasn't sure why she'd expected everything to be the same as that first night, when everything had been so new and shiny. Of course things would be different.

He released her hand, stuffed the fabric square into his pocket and turned her so she faced away from him.

He snugged tightly against her body, the swell of her buttocks pressing against the enticing ridge of his obvious arousal. "Since you're in your own little headspace right now, tell me what you see."

Unrestrained, her imagination took over. "Hundreds of people fill the room, silent and waiting for you to undress me." The loose edge of her tee crept up thanks to his deft fingers. Encouraged, she continued, "They marvel at the way you know my body so well, as though you've played with me a thousand times."

He kissed the shell of her ear. "I know what is mine."

She nodded even as a shiver dashed up her spine at the low tone of his words. "They start to whisper and talk, but you silence them with a glare. You don't want anything to take away from what you're doing. Don't want me to be distracted."

Kochran swept her shirt over her head, whisked away her pants. He banded his arm around her waist, as though he expected her to bolt now that she was only in a bra and panties.

"More people have come to watch," she added.

"Are there cameras?" he asked quietly.

She automatically layered that detail into her building fantasy. A spike of arousal stabbed through her at the knowledge now any member of Noble House could see them—virtually or physically.

Kochran huffed out a quiet chuckle. "I would say yes by the way your nipples just went hard."

With a shock, she realized he'd removed her bra and now cradled her bare breasts in his palms. She tried to remind herself this was just a performance, but her reaction was genuine. The sensations swirled through her rich and overwhelming.

He pressed his lips to her shoulder. "During a scene, my sub is my world. And I am hers." His captivating voice wrapped around her. His incredible charisma ensnared her, dragging her further into the fantasy. "I said I couldn't guarantee you'll feel the same."

"Yes." She licked her lips at the reminder when he swept his fingers up and down her torso, as though he were tracing an invisible line between her breasts and her pussy. Connected them in some way so she became an aching bundle of needy female.

"You won't feel the same." He tugged out the elastic that secured the braid she'd woven her damp hair into that morning. As she groaned, he combed through the thick locks with his fingers, untangling a few strands. "You'll feel better."

Oh God.

He increased the pressure, digging his thumbs into the base of her skull and massaging. "You spend too many hours hunched over the keyboard."

He pressed deeper, unknotting the muscles with brute force. This was a man who took what he wanted, and didn't apologize for his actions. She fell quickly under his spell, her body swamped with the sensations he gifted her with. Her nipples stood at full attention, her breasts begging for him to wrap his strong hands around them and give them the same powerful attention as her neck. She unconsciously tilted her body toward the stimulation.

He made a noise of approval. "You like this rough treatment."

Startled, she relaxed. He grumbled loud enough to cause her to straighten. "That's better, Madeline. You're a naturally sensual submissive, following your own desires while still yielding to a Master's command. Put your hands behind your back."

As she followed instructions, she realized she'd been hunched over. The new position allowed him access to her chest. A thrill unfurled inside her at the thought of his hands molding her breasts again. Teasing her nipples. But he didn't touch her where she wanted him to, at least not right away. He finished undressing her slowly, taking his time, as though she was a precious treasure.

She hadn't expected this type of careful treatment, given his commanding touch and the assertiveness he unleashed in his videos. Darkness closed in around her as Kochran slipped the silk over her head. Though her heart rate tripped a few times, it settled soon enough. She wasn't afraid of what was to come, but she was on edge. Still, she gave a shuddering breath as her world narrowed. Even with the spotlights aimed at the area, the only light that filtered in came from under the edge. The light dimmed when Kochran drew the ties together, closing her in darkness.

Her focus narrowed to the sounds in her immediate area. Muted voices as Kochran and Enver talked. Rope being shuffled against the carpet, the rasp of which raised the fine hairs on her arms. She should not have been aroused, but damn if she could stop. A few more moments of some kind of discussion and the air around her changed as someone approached.

"Doing all right?"

Until that second, she hadn't known it was Kochran standing beside her. The idea of so many unknowns thrilled her, adding a layer of excitement. "Yes."

"From now on, no speaking unless it's to use your

safe word," Enver instructed from her other side. She nodded, affecting the movement because of the covering. "Good. Just use *red* for now. Say that and you'll have more than enough rescuers coming to your aid around this place. If for some reason you can't speak, snap your fingers."

Enver's voice washed over her, allowing her to form an image of him in her mind while he worked. His hair had been dark, with a handsome peppering of gray at the temples. Though he was definitely older than her, he wore his age well. Like his hair, his eyes hadn't been a solid discernable color. Blue on the outer edges of the iris gave way to a deep green near the pupil. The steady heat of his touch gave her an anchor.

The scrape of rope against her wrist focused her attention there and not on questioning why she wouldn't be able to talk. Quiet blanketed her as Enver bound each of her wrists to the chair with knots that couldn't be slipped. He shifted, taking up her foot and lifting her left ankle to bind it to her wrist. Her heart pounded, her flesh heating with every knot and loop. She sank further into her own head. That same edgy neediness Ezra had given her before started to bloom. Being restrained was turning her on in the most fabulous ways.

Enver spread her thighs, positioning her ankle in the same manner against her right wrist. She sank again, becoming immersed in the sensation of the rope constricting her skin. Something brushed against her arm, more pulling and tugging of the rope. She lost track of the time as Enver worked. She wished she could see how she looked, what kind of shapes he'd used to decorate her body.

His movements weren't all methodical precision either as he took several opportunities to brush his nimble fingers against various pleasure points. As he banded a length of rope under her breasts, she wished again to see how spread and open and at his mercy she was. Over, around and under, he compressed her breasts until they were throbbing, aching globes of pleasure. A soft whisper of touch against one straining nipple made her whimper quietly. Extending her senses, she heard Kochran's measured breaths, sensed him standing near her right shoulder while Enver worked.

Her silent guardian. Her Dominant.

Enver paused when she inhaled quickly. "Does something hurt or pinch?"

Everything was exactly, perfectly right. "I'm fine. Please don't stop."

Enver continued to work, checking and adjusting the fit of the ropes binding her. She'd been taken aback by the realization Kochran was her Dom. Maybe not long-term, but for the duration of the scene. Even though Enver was the one working to secure her to the chair, Kochran was clearly the man in charge. He was watching out for her. Caring for her. Ensuring her safety even though another Dominant was present.

The idea of being the focus of attention to more than one person had only been a recent development in her life. Now that it had been planted, she hadn't been able to stop thinking about it. *Multiple-partner scenes* had been the first thing she'd written on the list Kochran had asked for, followed by *being under the guidance of a skilled Dominant.*

Enver split two lengths of rope around her labia, putting decadent pressure there, which she couldn't ignore. That feeling increased as he tested tightness and

stress to her joints as he made the functional task…
erotic. The overwhelming sensation washed over her
in a sensual avalanche.

Someone pressed a warm kiss against her shoulder. "You're magnificent, love. You'd make a fine rope
bunny," Enver whispered against her ear. "One I'd like
to truss up any day of the week. Something tells me
this one isn't going to let you wander too far from him,
though. Those ropes may be a comforting embrace, but
keep in mind your audience will want a show." He caressed her abdomen as he moved away.

Audience? She tried to focus on the word, but she
was too absorbed by the fact she couldn't sense Kochran or Enver nearby. She was smart enough to know
they hadn't abandoned her. A Dominant would never
leave a submissive in such a precarious position. Surely
one of them still had to be within arm's length in case
things took a turn.

As she listened for their breathing, a shift of clothing, anything that would give away their position, she
noticed something else. Everything inside her stilled.
As she tried not to think about the silence blanketing
her, she heard the murmur of voices. Not just Enver and
Kochran. There were more. Many more. So numerous
that she couldn't make out what was being said. Her
heart rate quickened as she thought about being presented. She fed on the energy the faceless strangers
gave her, using it to heighten her arousal.

The small amount of discomfort from being tied in
the odd position was…electrifying. Hands cupped her
breasts, and she jumped. Nimble fingers stroked over
her hardened nipples, and she relaxed, even though
so many factors of unknowns were spread out before

her. Her heart tripped when one of the hands lifted and slipped around her neck to stroke. He tilted her jaw up, angling it so she offered him free access to her throat.

"Hrm. Breath play was on your list of interests. Not surprising since you like dangerous games. Nothing too heavy, but how about a taste?" When she nodded, his grip tightened, restricting the airflow but not severing it completely. Arousal and excitement tightened her muscles. Though her legs were spread, she was so fucking stimulated. Open and vulnerable.

"Is this what you expected?"

No, it wasn't, but goddamn, was it exciting. She shook her head, remembering she wasn't allowed to speak unless it was her safe word. And the last thing she wanted to do was stop him.

Kochran released her throat and she gasped for air, her voice unintentionally sounding as he continued to fondle her breast. "Still with me, baby girl? You can speak now."

"Yes," she blurted, gritting her teeth against the pain as he pinched her nipple.

"Be as loud as you want now, Madeline. Your audience will appreciate it." As though on cue, a chorus of affirmatives filled the air. Far more people than when they'd entered the room, but still muffled through the rush of sensations cresting inside her like waves breaking against the shore.

His fingers disappeared and warm wetness enveloped her nipple. He licked and sucked the nub, hardening it even more though she was convinced that wasn't possible. When he bit down, gently at first and then with increasing pressure, she squirmed. His hand closed over her throat again and she automatically tilted her chin higher in offering. Her air supply slowly diminished the longer he sucked on her. Nips. Teases. She tried to gasp, but he'd stolen her voice along with her air. So she whimpered deep in her throat. His firm grasp released.

His touch against her nipple and throat vanished, leaving her a trembling mass of submission. "Do you like pain, Madeline?"

Butterflies erupted in her stomach. While she didn't know, oh, she wanted to experience it with Kochran. The item had been on her list. "I don't know."

A rush of wind sounded to her side and a slap followed a second later. She jumped before she realized he hadn't struck her. But he'd hit something hard and solid. The noise came again, and she heard a soft whistle. Was he testing something before turning it on her?

"Please hit me, Sir."

The slaps stopped. "I haven't given you permission to call me that yet."

Shit. "Forgive me." She'd gotten so lost in her head, in the scene being crafted, she'd forgotten.

She braced herself for a hit as punishment. Instead, he traced his fingertip over her shoulder. A sensual touch while the threat of more hung in the air.

"But I do like how it sounds."

Something tapped against her leg with enough force to make her jump. It wasn't painful by any means, but enough to get her attention. Her heart hammered away, the loud sound of it thumping in her ears. Cool air brushed over her heated skin as her head spun. There was something about this whole thing that was totally doing it for her. She suspected he would be correcting her quite a lot because she rarely remained quiet during sex.

She imagined those lovely eyes of his glowing as he brushed the curve of one breast. "You're trembling."

She hadn't realized it, but the shaking wasn't because she was cold. Far from it, in fact. A warmth spread through her, originating from her feet to wrap around her thighs, hips and waist. It coiled through her belly, lighting new infernos that blazed a path to her breasts, which he cupped tightly. Her breath caught when Kochran leaned forward and replaced one of his hands with his mouth again. Her voice stretched through the room as he massaged the tender bud with his tongue. Need spiraled through her as he sampled her. Suckled her with long, mesmerizing teases that pulled at her core. The heat of his mouth melted away into sensations she couldn't put a name to. The pleasure of it had her writhing against his hands. But he didn't command her to still. Her pleading noises changed to wanton moans.

He skimmed the gentle flare of her waist. Over the angle of her hip and between the thighs spread wide open by Enver's ropes. Kochran grunted softly when he probed between her pussy lips and found her folds slick with her desire.

"Since you like it rough, how about a pair of weighted clamps to adorn these tempting nipples? Maybe even a butterfly vibrator on this cute little bud that comes alive when I touch it?"

She gasped, fighting against the ropes to remain still. Enver had given her just enough slack to struggle, further adding to her arousal. Kochran continued to stroke her. She was naked and spread open for him, bound but still free to his bidding. But she was also on display for anyone in Court to stroll by and see. Available to the roving gazes of anyone who chose to observe the scene. Too caught up in her head, she couldn't discern if her arousal was due to being watched or everything Kochran promised her. She was alive, wild with the promise of what was to come.

Whatever the reasons, she knew he'd been right—he'd made her the center of attention.

When he lifted his mouth, she imagined how he would look with slightly swollen lips. She wanted to angle forward to kiss him, bite that tantalizing swell of his lip and tangle their tongues together. Instead, she remained in place, allowing her erratic breath to be the only sound between them.

He stepped back, severing his connection. She felt so exposed. So…bare as she rode the intoxicating wave of euphoria descending upon her. Her body pulsed with each beat of her heart, as though her entire being had been tuned to the unique frequency that Kochran controlled. The enormity of the sensations spiraling through her added a layer of intimacy.

"Please."

When he dragged his finger against her engorged clit, she sighed. He tapped and massaged, his intent clear. "Are you this excited because you're being watched or because of me?"

All of it, she wanted to respond as the urgency of his touch washed over her, but found her throat thick with the words. Instead an answering pulse surged through her core.

"Ah, you're dripping wet now. I think it's a little of both."

It should have seemed absurd—his words, being in front of people naked and bound. But the situation was so...normal.

Like she submitted to a powerful man like this in front of a captive audience every day.

Chapter Seventeen

Ezra's voyeuristic propensities had increased tenfold when Asha knocked on his office door to tell him Kochran and Maddy were mid-scene at Court. He'd done his best not to appear too anxious, but once the house submissive had left, he pulled up the live feed. Two seconds in and he'd made a beeline for Court, wanting a part of the moment even if it was only on the periphery.

He slipped in, noticing the crowd was larger than expected. Thursday nights weren't a large draw for the public spaces, but everyone present had been captured by the activity in the center of the room. It was easy to see why.

Kochran moved with a sensual grace that would make even the most devout think of sex. He carried out scenes as though they were religious rights, pure and sacred. That kind of presence didn't come along often. The preparation was as important as the actual scene.

The choice of clothing added another layer of decadence to the man, to the scene. The too-tight shirt outlined formidable shoulders, strained over the enticing curvature of pectorals and biceps. Ezra's gaze swept lower as Kochran turned his back and bent over, displaying the strong thighs and muscular arc of his firm ass. Kochran shifted again, this time so the creases of his pants drew the eye naturally to his crotch.

In his head, Ezra made no apology for the lingering glances he gave the groin area of those snug pants. A natural-born performer, Kochran intended to be ogled.

Not to be overshadowed was the submissive at his command. Ezra recognized Enver's handiwork that artfully bound Maddy to a chair. The position she was locked into displayed her to the crowd and gave Kochran access to any part of her body.

She was a beauty in her own right, a delicious display of feminine curves confined by the hard lines of inescapable bondage. If Kochran stirred things inside Ezra, Maddy brought them all into focus. Her blonde hair peeked from under the fabric Kochran used to block her view of the room and audience. It wasn't hard for Ezra to imagine her lush pink lips. The ones that made him think of sin and debauchery. To remember how obsessed he'd been since the moment he found out she'd muscled her way into his code.

Even with the distance between them, Ezra knew the heady scent of her arousal. He smelled it hanging in the air around him for hours whenever she left him. Every time, he'd been ready to take his aching dick in hand.

Kochran was an expert at balancing the physical as well as the psychological aspect of domination. He stood near Maddy, body still as his gaze roamed over her form, his feet evenly braced, his shirt pulling across the expanse of his chest and shoulders. His head was tilted, as though he was listening to something only he could hear. From this angle, Ezra looked at a man whose profile appeared to have been etched from granite. Though the distance and shadows made it impossible to see, Ezra knew those honed eyes watched Maddy closely.

His broad, well-muscled shoulders just begged to be used as handholds while he used someone as he pleased. Kochran knew this, but he didn't flaunt the power. He didn't have to. He just…was. People were naturally drawn to him. They were attracted to his open sincerity, which caused even the most withdrawn introvert in the world to open up like the petals of a blooming flower. Kochran was genuine. He was also sinfully sexy. The sort of man who captured the attention of everyone regardless of sexual orientation. For the members of the club, it was also because he was the leader they looked to in admiration.

The first strike came unexpectedly. Maddy jerked, but made no sound. Kochran struck again, focusing the impacts on her thighs. Ten lashes with the flogger before he stopped. Maddy breathed fast, the fabric around her head moving with each rapid inhale. Her wrists restrained, she opened and closed her hands as her body shuddered. Kochran reached down to play with her nipples, offsetting the pain with pleasure. She whined softly as he pinched one nipple, then the other.

Ezra found the development interesting. His time with Maddy in the server room had been purely sexual, playing on Maddy's desire to be watched while getting off. As had the blowjob she'd given him when she'd admitted to being turned on after watching a group scene they'd caught the tail end of after work one night. Even when he'd finally gotten his mouth on her pussy, tasting her release with his fingers deep inside her. Every other time they'd tormented one another, it had all been about sex. The scene unfolding before him was about control and surrender. Maddy could have been completely clothed and the session would have been as equally powerful. Ezra would have to commend Kochran later.

Kochran stepped back, delivered more strikes until her fingers clenched. Ezra knew Kochran wasn't a sadist, but he was skilled enough to tailor each scene to the submissive's need. He challenged himself with different techniques, expanded on his knowledge to compliment his preferences, like most well-educated Doms did. Though Ezra had known Kochran an exceptionally long time, he had no idea what those personal preferences were. As Kochran worked to peel back the layers of Madeline Zane, Ezra wondered what it would take to reveal Kochran's true desires.

Maddy's cries caught Ezra's attention. Kochran had pocketed the flogger and had placed a vibrator between her legs. Her body shuddered and jerked, her chest moving rapidly as a flattering flush crept between her breasts under the ropes. From her groans, Ezra knew Maddy was teetering on the cusp of release. Ezra had seen Kochran keep a submissive in that state for nearly an hour before he'd granted her climax, edging her past coherent thought to a place where she was only wanton desires.

A whimper pierced the charged air. Ezra swallowed. The strangled cry roused something deep inside him. Made him want to be a part of the scene unfolding on the stage. He wasn't content to be a faceless member of the crowd. But this was Kochran's show, his focus razor-sharp, completely homed on Maddy. Everything for him was how Maddy reacted to a hit, monitoring the ropes binding her wrists, the covering on her face.

Ensuring her safety. Guaranteeing she and the audience got as much pleasure from this as possible. A delicate dance fueled by intuition. Some things could be taught, but with Kochran, this was his very nature.

Maddy yanked hard against the bonds. Kochran continued his ruthless motions, not letting up this time, pushing Maddy further without words. Some in the audience would recognize it the second the agony purged her emotional pain, as though she was bleeding out everything she kept trying to restrain.

Suddenly, Kochran discarded the flogger and pulled on the fabric so Maddy's head was tilted back, her throat exposed. He covered her clit with two fingers and tapped there with enough force that she jerked in the chair, moving the legs several inches even though her feet weren't touching the floor.

He used exacting precision, alternating between his fingers and the oversized head of the handheld vibrator against her clit. He worked her higher and harder. Maddy gave off a sudden high-pitched wail, her climax unleashing an abrupt gush of fluid over the seat, her thighs and Kochran's hand.

Ezra suddenly wasn't content with observation. Neither was his dick. His rock-hard erection screamed for relief, pulsing with the need to have a slice of these two people.

When Maddy stopped quivering, Kochran continued manipulating her oversensitive nerves. She had ceased to make any sound except the rapid staccato of her breathing. Kochran held her, using his other hand to unlace the ties on the head cover to remove it. Maddy's face was flushed red, her hair an unruly mess of tangles. Kochran brushed the sweaty strands back, pressing a tender kiss to the center of her forehead.

"You've never been more beautiful, baby girl," Kochran said, loud enough for the audience to hear. He signaled for Enver's assistance, turning over the process of unraveling the bindings while he prepared for Maddy's aftercare.

Kochran looked over the crowd, as though he sought something in particular. The instant their gazes collided, Ezra knew. Unspoken need arched between the men. Ezra sensed Kochran had something to say, something vitally important to tell him. Yet, Ezra suspected they both knew exactly what type of animal they each were: two Doms teasing one another, with no intent to engage.

It wasn't so much what Kochran had done *for* Maddy, it was what he'd done *to* her. As though he could accomplish it through sheer force of will. The tools weren't simply an extension of Kochran, but they *were* Kochran. He hadn't been controlling the flogger and the vibrator, he *was* those things. That uniqueness was what drew so many people to admire him. Men and women, regardless if they were dominant or submissive, wanted that alluring spark Kochran possessed. Ezra understood Maddy's draw, why she simply had no choice but to surrender to Kochran.

He missed the intricacies of domination and submission. That need, that sense of belonging, had drawn him to seek out a job at Noble House. A way to still experience all the lifestyle had to offer without actively participating. Issuing the command to Maddy for her to seek out and explore, watching her follow it through with boundless enthusiasm, stabbed at something deep inside him. Had a more profound effect on him than expected.

Ezra exited Court. He tried to tell himself it was because aftercare was a private and deeply personal experience, but he damn well knew that was simply an excuse. He had to suppress the urge to join them, to cradle them.

The simplest explanation was that he was lonely again, a sensation fueled by the intense nature of the scene. By the knowledge he'd been the one to command Maddy to ask Kochran for the public scene. His resentment only stemmed from the fact he hadn't been a part of it. Looking back, he would have worded his order to Maddy differently.

Next time it would be all three of them.

Chapter Eighteen

After the scene in Court, Ezra returned to his office and buried himself in code. He'd wanted to pretend he hadn't been waiting for Maddy to come talk about her experience, but she'd never returned to his office that night. Probably too caught up in the afterglow. When he'd emerged from behind his computer screen at the wee hours of the morning, he'd discovered he was the lone occupant of the club. Not even Kochran was around. It wasn't an unusual occurrence, but it was the first time since he'd started working there that he hadn't wanted it to be. A strange phenomenon he was still coming to grips with Monday morning when he walked through the club's front doors.

After the death of his wife and subsequent abandonment by Kyle, Ezra had fallen into a pattern. He'd become a loner, happier with only himself than having to worry about putting on a facade in order to keep people from inquiring about his life. In the space of a few weeks, that all had changed. He looked forward to coming to the office, making small talk with the other members of the club and listening to their suggestions.

Most of all, Ezra looked forward to the time he got to spend with Maddy. She'd had to fly to New York for the weekend for more business meetings with her partner. He missed her in the days between the scene in Court and now. Missed seeing her face, smelling the unique notes of her perfume. Even more, he longed for the connection they'd shared every time they'd been together sexually. After seeing her play with Kochran, he wanted to expand things between them. If she was still interested, of course.

At the reminder of Kochran, Ezra detoured to the lounge and made his way to the door on the far side of the room. He passed a mural of the Noble House crest, looking at it with a new appreciation. Someone had touched up the paint recently, and the three lions were more lifelike.

The door had been propped open and he pushed it a bit without stepping inside. He wasn't looking to intrude if Kochran was dealing with club business. But the owner sat alone at his desk, staring off into space. The pen he held was poised in the air, as though he'd stopped in midsentence. It was uncharacteristic for Kochran to be in such a daze. Clearly something weighed on him.

Ezra had an instant flash of wanting to take care of the man, shield him from his trials and tribulations. Once again, he was compelled to offer comfort where none had been asked for.

Ezra tamped down on the compulsion and instead cleared his throat. The pen dropped to the desk with a heavy thud as Kochran blinked. "I can come back."

"No. It's fine." Kochran gestured to the chair. "Excuse me for a second."

He disappeared to the lounge, but Ezra knew it wasn't because Kochran needed a drink. The bar at

Noble House didn't serve liquor and never had. One of Kochran's strict rules for the club was no alcohol to dull the senses, or be the cause of questionable consent. The bar stocked a steady supply of fruit juices, smoothies and various caffeinated beverages if someone needed a buzz.

Ezra settled back into a smooth leather chair. Nothing in the room seemed out of place, a sign Kochran was in desperate need of a vacation. The position he held at the club had to be stressful. Handling the everyday workings, paying the bills, interviewing new members, in addition to taking part in scenes he'd been booked for. It was a wonder Kochran managed to find pleasure in this lifestyle anymore.

Kochran returned with two glasses of ice water, one of which he offered to Ezra.

"Long day?" Ezra asked before taking a sip.

"Long life," Kochran offered with a half-smile. "If I'm not here handling things, I'm at the hospice."

A reminder Kochran's sister wasn't healthy. Ezra had been down that road before, understood the ins and outs of watching someone you care so much for die a little each day. Knowing there was nothing you could do to control their descent to hell. "How are you doing?"

Kochran drew his eyebrows together as he blew out a breath with a snort. "No one's asked me that. Everyone asks about her, as though asking will make the situation better. Like they expect me to have a different answer or that science has suddenly found a miracle cure. Thank you. I'm as well as can be expected."

Ezra understood all too well. "People ask because it's the polite thing to do. They forget terminal illnesses take a toll on the loved ones just as much. Sometimes more. You'll get through it, being strong for her and then, when it's over, you'll fall apart."

Kochran's mouth twisted at the unvarnished truth. Maybe he wouldn't, but Ezra had watched Kyle, one of the strongest men he'd ever known, crack wide open when Nora passed.

"I came to talk to you about Maddy."

Kochran's expression softened. "Quite a surprising treasure."

"One you wasted no time exploring."

"Says the man who had the woman in question pinned to a wall in a server room while he finger fucked her."

Ezra smirked. "The King is always watching at Noble House." He took a drink and continued, "Nice job with her in Court on Thursday." No point in pretending he hadn't been there when Kochran had made eye contact. "We both obviously have an interest in her. Given the fact you know she was with me prior to then, you don't have an issue with sharing her."

Kochran circled around his desk, pulled a sheet out of a drawer and offered it to Ezra. "You may find that interesting."

Ezra took the paper and immediately recognized the handwriting as Maddy's. Though he was already interested in what Kochran had to share, that curiosity increased tenfold.

He strips away everything just as he strips me. I am naked. Free of any bondage because he pins me with nothing more than his gaze. His voice, stern yet tender at the same time, compels me to follow any command he issues. I know he has my best interests in mind, just as I know he understands what I need more than I do. I am on my knees for my Master, watching him open his pants with a hungry gaze that I know pleases him. The length of his already erect cock is so beautiful I want it inside me. It doesn't matter where—mouth, cunt or ass—as long as he is a part of me once again.

He denies me at first, taunting me with the tempting flesh. When he finally grants me the privilege of tasting him, experiencing the texture of him, I nearly explode. But I hold back, knowing I haven't been given permission to orgasm yet. Only my Master can grant that privilege.

His voice is low and sexy as I work the ridged head, the steel shaft, the velvety skin of his balls as he blankets me with his loving accolades. He cradles my head, holds it reverently as he fucks my mouth, my throat. He thrusts hard and I don't care about anything but bringing him pleasure. Not the lack of oxygen, the tears streaming from my eyes or the ache of my empty pussy.

My only concern is him.

With a quick rush of breaths mixed with visceral growls, he jets into my throat, forcing me to swallow a piece of him. I know I am blessed because I have been granted this exceptional gift he has allowed me. The power of that knowledge makes me long to have him everywhere possible, to be filled with him until I feel as though I am going to rip in two. And still, I want him to take

*me deep and hard, surrender to him in a way that
I've never surrendered to anyone.*

*I taste the flavor of his essence still lingering
on my tongue as he positions me at his knee, my
head cradled on his thigh in a position of total
subjugation.*

I am his.

He is all mine.

Ezra was tempted to read the words again, but he
set the paper on the corner of Kochran's desk. When
he adjusted in his seat, pulling the fabric that was constricting his dick, his gaze lifted to Kochran's.

Kochran smirked. "I had the same reaction."

Ezra wondered just how many times Kochran had
indulged in that little pleasure since Maddy had given
it to him.

"There's more," Kochran said as he offered Ezra a
few more sheets, printed on different paper. Ezra recognized the handwriting as Maddy's again. These words
were organized in a neat column, but far less care had
been taken to make sure the print was legible.

"What did you do, make her—well, shit, you did,"
Ezra said with a short laugh as he scanned through it.
Most of the items were common on most submissives'
lists. A few things stood out in relief against the beige
paper. "Seems like we're all on the same page without even trying." Given the way she'd reacted to hearing Ezra's suspicions about being watched, he'd easily
guessed her as an exhibitionist. Plus, she'd willingly
gone into a scene with Kochran after being with Ezra,
so her desire for multiple partners wasn't a shock either.

"Yes, it seems we are. But these certainly help understand her a little better, which is why I shared them with you. You two have a connection I'm not interested in tampering with. Not to say I won't use something I see between the two of you to influence her when she's with me, just as I'm sure you will." Kochran tapped his fist against the edge of the desk, holding Ezra's gaze for a long minute. "Which brings me to discuss a few things with you in regard to our resident blonde. Clearly she doesn't have a problem with experiencing a little fun. I was thinking this would be a good opportunity to work together."

"Play with Maddy at the same time?" Ezra stood, shoving his hands into his pockets. He rocked back and forth on the balls of his feet as he thought about Kochran's proposal. "Would tick a few of those boxes."

"Eventually. I was thinking more of what happened at Court. The scene we had."

"While I watched," Ezra finished. The thought sent a thread of hot desire unfurling through him. The idea of uncovering those slices he'd kept buried thrilled him. He hadn't realized how much he'd missed the sight and smell of a submissive. The taste of the commands as they slid off his tongue. It would give him the opportunity to delve deeper into his suspicions about the owner of the club and spend some quality time with Maddy, opening her up to the realm of possibility.

"I'm betting you want to know about sex given what she had written here." Ezra tapped an item midway down the list on the paper with his fingers. "And the fact she and I haven't had intercourse yet. As long as everyone is safe, I'm good for anything. If you're concerned about jealousy, I'm the last person you should worry about. The green-eyed monster hasn't visited

me since high school. Unless you're worried about how
you'll react?"

He held Kochran's unflinching gaze as a figurative
line in the sand etched the tense air between them. Ezra
had just thrown down the gauntlet, so to speak, where
the prize was unimaginable pleasure.

Kochran leaned forward, resting his elbows on the
desk. "I'm concerned you may not be ready for full
domination of a submissive. It's been a while, Ezra.
While I like a good challenge as well as the next Dom,
I have to put aside that mindset for a minute and con-
firm a friend isn't biting off more than he can chew."

The world stilled as Kochran aimed that penetrating
gaze Ezra's way. It wasn't an inquiry he'd expected Kochran to make. A rush of memories enveloped him, but
this time, he was prepared and handled them one breath
at a time. He still remembered how it had been waiting for the hospice nurse to pronounce time of death.
Nora hadn't been the type of woman who liked for
others to see her out of sorts, so part of her do not resuscitate order had been for her husbands to take care
of her. They'd given her a sponge bath, discarded the
housecoat she'd worn for nearly a week and put her in
her favorite dress and heels. Taken care to place the
bracelet the men had given her for their first anniversary around her wrist. Her wedding bands had gone
with her as well, though that hadn't hurt as much as
the silver necklace Nora had refused to remove even
when she'd been confined to the bed.

A lot of emotional and sentimental value in her collar.

After watching the hearse pull away, he and Kyle
had sat on the front porch. For the first time since she'd

been diagnosed, they'd purged every emotion kept hidden inside. The sadness that she hadn't been able to live longer in order to experience all life had to offer. The resentment that flared when the initial diagnosis had been made. The anger for what had been taken away too soon.

"Are you ready for this?" Kochran repeated in a low voice. For an inexplicable reason Ezra didn't want to waste much time evaluating, Kochran was offering him a lifeline. An escape clause.

Ezra sat again, unable to remain still. "I will never stop grieving the people I loved and thought I would spend the rest of my life with. Their memories are ingrained in me. Maybe not as prevalent, but—"

"Still there," Kochran finished.

"Always." Ezra swallowed. "I've asked myself that question more times than I care to count. To be perfectly honest, I never had an answer until now."

He sat up straighter as the phantom sound of Maddy coming undone rang in his ear. The sight of Kochran tipping her over the edge in front of an audience flashed behind his eyes at the same time. He needed both those things, and he wanted to explore the strange phenomena of the synchronicity they all shared.

He shifted again in the chair as a slender thread of anticipation wove through his stomach. If he was truly ready, he wasn't going to half-ass it or second-guess every decision he made. He would have to play a few hunches, hedging a lot on something Kyle had once told him about exceptionally strong Dominants—like Kochran.

That strength usually came from submission. Though Kochran may have preferred the dominant aspect of the lifestyle, Ezra suspected he had once found pleasure in submission. But given Kochran's attitude—and his reputation—he wasn't the type who would want others to know something he probably saw as a flaw.

As Ezra drew breath to ask a few questions of his own, he stopped. Kochran wouldn't answer even if asked directly. If he was really going to do this, he'd get more pleasure from allowing the path to unfold organically.

"Yeah. I'm good." He finished off the last of the water, noticing the look Kochran gave him when he licked a few drops from his lips. *Oh, this is gonna be fun.* "Real damn good."

As Ezra left his office, Kochran tried hard not to stare. Or worse, go after the man. He wasn't surprised Ezra had come to see him. In those last moments with Maddy at Court, Kochran had recognized that predatory glow to Ezra's eyes. He'd wondered for a time if Ezra was going to stake claim on the fascinating woman, and he'd hoped it wouldn't come to that because he was keen to watch Ezra scene with Madeline in a more official capacity.

He was genuinely concerned about Ezra's unique situation, but if this sort of arrangement was going to work, he was going to have to trust Ezra. Take him at his word that he was physically and mentally prepared.

Kochran spun around and tapped the keyboard to bring the monitors out of sleep mode. His routine at this point of the day was to scan through the feeds and gauge where the most activity would be for the evening. With this new facet, he had to guess where the most likely place was for Ezra to take Maddy for a session.

Court was usually the top choice, but for some reason, Kochran's gaze was drawn to the security feeds for a row of semi-private rooms. He checked the reservation logs. Only one name marked in a single room for Wednesday night.

Ezra.

Smirking, Kochran blocked off the entire row for the night. *Challenge accepted, my friend. Challenge. Accepted.*

For the third time that day, Maddy swore she'd imagined the last few conversations she'd had with Kochran and Ezra. All those not so subtle implications, those innuendo-filled invitations. The men had to be joking. She'd started it, allowing Kochran to claim a kiss her first night of work, and going a little further each time with Ezra. She wanted to crawl into a corner and die a few times of embarrassment. But then there'd been that scene with Kochran...

Neither man appeared put off by the fact they each had a place in her life. At least sexually. She reminded herself it was all just more harmless fun. It meant she wasn't uptight. That she was capable to letting her hair down and having a good time. Maybe she was seeing things through rose-colored glasses. She wanted the men to be attracted to her because she found them both incredibly sexy. She didn't want to have to decide because, *mothertrucker*, what they'd done to her still gave her the shivers days and days later.

The feel of Kochran's arms banded around her as he held her during aftercare still lingered. That soothing embrace had stayed with her, giving comfort where she hadn't realized it was needed. She'd been so focused on the scene, on how he'd made her feel, she'd completely forgotten about the period immediately following an intense connection. Having never experienced that level of care, she wasn't sure how to live without it now. It had immediately become as integral to her as the actual scene itself. She'd loved the sound of his breathing steady in her ear while she'd floated on the cloud of euphoria. Her words slurred, her thoughts broken, as though she'd been drunk on the finest wine. She'd never expected the simple pleasure to have such a profound effect.

But something else had penetrated this newfound intimacy. As much as she adored every gift that Kochran had given her, an ache of loss had been prevalent. Not enough to diminish her enjoyment, but enough to remind her a piece of something she needed was missing. For too long she'd channeled her desires into other things. Work. Video games. Cracking code. Kochran and Ezra had opened a new world to her and showed her how she could exist in both and still be who she was. By integrating everything together, she could truly explore the woman she'd become. She wasn't new, but enhanced. Madeline Zane 2.0.

She was still smiling at the thought when Ezra came into the office. "What has you so amused?"

"Just an upgrade I've been thinking about." The one that made her all tingly inside.

"To the servers?"

"Myself," she admitted.

When she looked up to his inquiring gaze, her heart gave a solid thump. Everything tightened at once, all in the right places. Her libido was pinging off the charts, but so was something else. Something she hadn't expected.

Her heart.

Love wasn't a part of her plan, but looking deeper, she realized she wasn't ready to rule it out entirely. It would, however, need to be pushed off to the side because she wasn't interested in exploring that particular aspect at the moment. The fact it was there at all meant she definitely had a connection with him.

As though he could see inside the deep recesses of her mind, Ezra scooted his hip onto her tiny desk. "Questioning everything that has been happening lately?"

"I wasn't expecting to find this kind of thing when I broke into the website."

"Well, no," Ezra said carefully. "This place has a tendency to pull forth a lot of things from people. But what you do mean...thing?"

Maddy tucked a few loose strands of hair behind her ear. At least her hands weren't shaking. That had to be something. "A new world that accepted me fully, faults and all?"

"Faults are open to interpretation. Just like what one person thinks is odd, another person covets. Weird is normal for some. Like you."

She blinked. "It's odd, hearing that I'm weird but that it's okay."

"I like weird. I like strange." Ezra cupped her jaw, cradling it. "Most of all, I like you."

His interest made a warm ball of fuzzy things glow inside her core. "I've had great relationships with the men I've dated. Hell, my business partner is my ex-boyfriend. But the whole spark thing has never been there. Sex was okay, but more like a way to relieve tension or something." Maddy cringed. "That didn't sound right."

"It wasn't fun?"

She blew out a frustrated breath. "I don't think I've ever had *fun* intercourse." She blushed at the admission.

"Ah, so that's your deep, dark secret. You haven't been hurt before, you just haven't opened yourself to possibility." Ezra held out his hand. "How about we change that?"

Maddy stared at his outstretched hand, unable to form words.

"You've already taken the first few baby steps. Waded a little deeper with Kochran. Discovered you liked what you'd been exposed to because you're still here. You didn't run from the building screaming about the freaks who get off on all kinds of kinky things. How about stepping up on the diving board with me and finding out just how much fun jumping off can be?"

"I don't know if I can." Though he'd described exactly what she'd hoped for when she'd written out her fantasy. "Some days, my mind is like a thousand tabs open on a web browser."

"An excellent Dom will focus your mind down to only one."

The analogy made her smile. She'd been drawn to him the moment she'd calmed down after yelling at Kochran, then even more so when she'd had her head about her that first day of work. Like his boss, there was something about him that wasn't intimidating, but totally was at the same time.

She couldn't shake the feeling they both could make her kneel with the right look. That something wasn't a thing she could define, but she knew she wanted it. She also knew both men could give it to her. Sure, it wouldn't be exactly the same, but that was part of the thrill. They could help define all those things on that list. Why had she written out the fantasy she had about sitting at a Dominant's knee and not one that was far tamer?

A woman could dream.

With Ezra and Kochran, she didn't have to.

Chapter Nineteen

Maddy held her breath as she stepped into the themed room dubbed the Cloud. This was the first time she'd been on this side of the glass in this particular area of the club reserved for semi-private play.

She'd hoped for this room and hadn't at the same time. It was light and airy and…romantic. Better than the gothic set up of the next room over, with its ominous shadows and walls comprising oversized, dark stone block with sconces hanging from elaborate hooks embedded in the stone. Or the sterile medical examination room at the end of the row. Or the one filled with all sorts of medieval torture implements on the other side of the hall. Or the makeshift garden that spanned the last two rooms.

Though she'd like the pain Kochran had introduced her to, she definitely wasn't ready for some of the more sophisticated, and darker, aspects of the lifestyle. The soft, dreamy air of the linen walls and sheer, draping curtains that hung from the ceiling and framed a gorgeous antique bed was more along the lines of what she needed tonight.

A fun perk had come along with her new status as full member of the club: access to the massive closet of clothing located on the top floor just down from Ezra's office, available to members. Maddy wore an outfit she'd found tucked between the gleaming stilettos and leather corsets. The white linen dress shifted over her skin like it weighed nothing. With spaghetti straps and tiny pink roses, it was the most feminine thing she'd ever worn. In ways she couldn't explain, it made her feel pretty. For a woman who lived in yoga pants and oversized tees, the dress was enlightening.

She made a slow circuit of the room, taking it all in. As she walked forward, she noticed something was affixed to the window, low near the floor. Though she'd passed the room many times, she'd never noticed it before. The window, sure. The pane of glass meant anyone could walk by and see what was happening in the room. Fine with her. She wanted people to see. Wanted everyone to know she had the privilege of playing with two of the finest damn Doms at the club.

As she stepped closer, she noted a circular item was stuck to the surface with suction cups and a loop of the same metal was connected to the center. It reminded her of the fancy towel holders she seen in the bathrooms here at the club. Unable to stop herself, she reached out and gave it a sharp tug. It didn't budge when she pulled harder. Huh. Strange.

The door opened and she snatched her hand away as though she'd been burned. Ezra stepped into the room, his hair damp. His stark white shirt hung open, revealing the lines of his abdomen and torso. Blue jeans. Bare feet. It was as though he'd stepped off the pages of a magazine and onto a beach to spend the day relaxing.

She suddenly felt overdressed and picked at the low

neckline of the gauzy dress. He smiled as he came closer and set his hand over hers. "Nervous?"

Lying to him would be silly. "A bit. Maybe I should have thought about my clothing choice a little more. You look so…relaxed."

He dragged his finger under one thin strap. "It's perfect." Everything inside her went warm as he pressed his mouth against hers. "Just like you are."

Need and relief made her weak all over.

"As much as I adore looking at you like this, the dress really does need to come off." Ezra whisked it away without preamble.

Her blood ran hot at the way his gaze coursed over her naked body. That gaze stayed focused on her as he lowered himself onto the overstuffed white couch against one wall. The soft light spilling over him showcased the definition of his shoulders, his pecs, the dark circles of his nipples, and the trail of dark hair her gaze followed to the bulge in his jeans.

Maddy licked her lips, imaging how Ezra would taste against her tongue.

"Come stand in front of me."

She did as ordered, feeling a little out of her body and grounded all at once. It was an interesting dichotomy. She burned for the promise of what was to come, need and fear and surrender a blissful mix in her system. He stared at her, the minutes stretching out for so long, she lost track of time. She sank into her head, that lovely, cottony blend of subspace that was as intoxicating as any fine wine.

"Bend over."

She did so without hesitation, loving the way the position placed her mouth directly over the denim en-

casing his straining erection. He wanted her as much
as she wanted him. But they had quite a few steps to
progress through before she would be allowed the pleasure of having him in her mouth.

She inhaled the heavy, musky scent of him, catching the traces of precome that indicated he'd been rock
hard for quite some time. The yearning to taste him increased with each passing second. When she pressed
her lips to the fabric, he cupped the back of her head
and tightened his hand in her hair. She gave a soft groan
when he tugged and pulled her away from his crotch.

"You're glowing, Maddy."

He shifted his hold, positioning her so she was
perched on her knees between his spread legs. With
his free hand, he tugged on his jeans, parting the fly so
she could see the fabric barely constraining him under-
neath. No help for it—her mouth started to water as he
tucked his thumb under the elastic waistband and pulled
down slowly. Inch by infinitesimal inch, he uncovered
his erection. She'd touched the length of it before, had
it in her mouth, so his size didn't come as a surprise.
But from her angle, she had an entirely different perspective of how long and thick it truly was once again.
He stood high and hard and proud and so beautiful.

"And now you look as though I'm the feast you want
to ravish."

She nodded as her gaze coursed over the shaft,
thickly veined and already beautifully flushed with
arousal. The desperate need to touch him, use her fingers to map him, rose to join the sea of sensations twist-
ing through her. She wanted to do everything at once.

"May I touch you?"

He tilted his head to the side as he released her hair.

"No." Immediately, a sense of dread knifed through her. He touched the skin between her eyebrows, smoothing away the tension. "Just your lovely mouth for the moment."

It was a diabolical strategy, granting her only part of what she craved. Still, the more he denied her things, the more turned on she became. Like a length of rope, they were twinned inexorably around one another in an erotic dance. So much of what Ezra did for her, to her, was like Kochran's commands, yet so different at the same time.

"Go on."

She sighed around that first contact between her tongue and the tip of his cock. Unable to help herself, she closed her lips around the broad head. Ezra grunted, but said nothing to admonish her. Parting her lips, she licked the slit, tasting the dampness there. Though he'd denied her the ability to touch him, he allowed her the freedom to explore with her mouth. She used the tip of her tongue to trace the underside of the crown, the ridge, and loved the contrast. Trailing down, the difference between the smooth velvety skin and the crest of the veins stood out in relief. She pressed her lips in an open-mouthed kiss against the base.

Ezra grunted again, this time gruffly, as though it was caught somewhere between a growl and a moan. The noise washed over her back, erupting a trail of gooseflesh wherever the sound caressed. Encouraged, she repositioned, and closed her mouth around the crown. His thighs quivered against her shoulders as she traveled over the heated steel with slow, dragging movements.

"Did you like when Kochran used the flogger on you?"

She pulled off, startled by the question at first, fighting the urge to look up at him to see his expression. "I was sore the next morning. But in a good way. Like I had this constant reminder, this trigger, that made me think about him, about what he did during the scene. Every time I did, it turned me on."

"Would it also turn you on to know I wanted to touch each and every one of those marks afterward? To press on them so you'd feel them even more?"

She looked up to him. His eyes had gone half-lidded, a dreamy expression painting his face, as though he'd gotten lost in his own imagery. "I'd like that."

Ezra's eyes snapped clear. "I needed to feel those marks, too. Feel them hot against my palms while I held you down and fucked you." The vivid pictures of that confession flashed in stunning color before her eyes. "Mmm, you like that idea. Your eyes just lost focus and your breathing is uneven. My little kinky coder."

The power emanating from Ezra was so intense, she lost her train of thought. She drew in a deep breath, enjoying the way that authority made her feel. Her hunger for him increased exponentially.

Ezra touched the hinge of her jaw, dragging his thumb down to the corner of her lips. She parted for him, tasting the flavor of his skin in her mouth, reminding her what it had been like to have his cock resting against her tongue.

"Take me into your mouth again, Maddy." He fed his cock between her eager lips.

She needed him with the same longing that she had to feel him nestled deep in her cunt. Her ass. Maddy thought she was going to die from the pleasure. The ache in her gut as the knot of desire drew tighter and tighter, a sign that when she was finally granted release, it was going to feel so *mothertruckin'* fantastic.

With Ezra in her mouth again, she looked up the taper of his abdomen, the mouthwatering terrain of his chest. Pleased, she focused on the part of him in her mouth, the length of which she was ready to lick like the finest, most delicious ice cream. Every inch of him pleased her and she allowed it to show by groaning softly as she opened more so he could slip into her throat. Ezra answered with a quiet murmur of pleasure. Instinct took hold of her as she savored him, sucking him slowly as though she had no need to breathe.

"Jesus Christ." Ezra's quiet words were like a prayer. He wrapped his hand against her nape, and Maddy reveled in the tremble of those strong fingers. She pulled back enough to inhale and then sank once again. The strong taste of his muskiness leaked from the tip, making her crave more. With Ezra deep in her throat, she entered an almost trancelike state, her enjoyment originating from the pleasure she was gifting him.

His cock pulsed and she drew back. This time, she used her tongue, mouth, and teeth to slowly slide up and down. She caressed Ezra, increasing the suction every so often to draw forth a hiss from him. The glistening moisture her mouth left on his length made it seem as though she was polishing him.

Her focus narrowed further so she was aware of only Ezra. It had been the same on the stage with Kochran, the knowledge that others were watching enough to give her exhibitionist streak a thrill. With her back to the glass, she had no way to know if others were present, but for the moment, she didn't care. Her only task was to gift her pleasure to him.

"You're so fucking good at this."

Maddy made an inarticulate sound as Ezra tightened his fingers and took total control of the moment. Her breath came out hard and raspy as he guided his cock against the back of her throat, pushing past her gag reflex again, growling as he nestled deep. He leisurely fucked her mouth, alternating between shallow and deep thrusts.

Just when she thought he was going to release down her throat, he pulled her completely off him, angled close and took her mouth with a fierce, urgent growl of possession. He tore his mouth away again, his eyes alight with an intense fire as he spoke. "As much as I love what you're doing, it's my turn to play."

Chapter Twenty

Ezra led her to the window, dragging a chair with him. He left her there, retrieving something from a cabinet near the door, and returned holding a long length of neon green nylon cord. "I'm not the artist Enver is when it comes to ropework, but I can manage well enough."

He came to stand next to her, positioning her by the glass, and gestured for her hands, bringing her wrists together in front of him. He started looping the soft rope around her wrists, winding up most of her forearms before he tucked the long trailing end of the rope up the coil and pulled it between her hands.

A smile played over his lips as he wound the free length around his fist and signaled for her to turn around. He reached between her legs, threaded the free end through the loop of metal attached to the window and then sat back up. When he did, he tugged and pulled her forward. He gave a satisfied grunt and then pulled more, until she was bent over in front of him.

"Oh, that's pretty." He touched the wet heat between her legs, dragging his finger through the dampness. She closed her eyes, reveling in the feel of his gentle touch against her aching flesh. "I'm tempted to keep you like this, but I have other plans." He tugged again and again, until her knuckles brushed against the wood floor.

He caged her hips, lifting them so he took a great deal of her weight. "Put your shins on my thighs." For a moment, panic swirled through her gut. Getting into the position he wanted meant she had to surrender total control. He didn't push her or coax her, simply waited for her to decide she was ready. She did, wondering what his intent was with the strange position. He eased her hips down, nestling them between his knees. "Lower your chest onto my legs so I can support you entirely."

He hooked the rope around the bottom of his foot, using that to lock her into place. The way he'd positioned them meant they were at an angle, everything on full display while allowing her to look out of the glass and see the hallway and rooms beyond.

As she relaxed fully, she gave a loud sigh. Being cradled against him this way was far more comfortable than she'd expected. He'd found a way to balance the harsh reality of being restrained by someone with how he'd positioned her against his body and tenderly took his time exploring.

"Mmm, that's a girl. You like this, don't you?" Ezra dragged his finger against her pussy lips. "I do too. Perfectly positions you for me to play however I want. I love your body." He spread his hands over the flare of her hips, and the gentle curves her thighs and butt made as she was draped over him. "It's more than that, though. I love hearing the way your breath moves faster when I touch you. The way it felt when I was deep inside your throat." He touched his thumb against her pulsing clit, circled it a few times. "I saw your desire in your eyes. Know you want me to fuck you without you saying a word. How you're willing to accept whatever I decide to give you."

He brushed his fingers against her slit, playing with her pussy lips while she was free to let her gaze roam to the hallway beyond the glass. This time she noted the space wasn't empty. Someone was standing in the shadows, the dim light in the hall highlighting the figure enough to make out the sharp line of an impeccably pressed collar. The golden glint of a wristwatch, and the sparkle of a clip holding a pen tucked inside the pocket of the shirt. A pen she'd helped pick out. Had used to write her incredibly long list of needs, wants and limits.

Kochran stepped out of the shadows and allowed her to see him fully. His eyes flickered in the low light, the intensity of his gaze washing over her even though they were separated by the pane of glass. If Ezra noticed they had company, Kochran's presence didn't stop him.

"Tell me what you like about Kochran and me sharing you."

She hadn't expected to have the conversation with Ezra like this. Then again, she was laid out on his lap, naked and spread wide for his pleasure while she stared at the other man she'd allowed to dominate her.

"If you don't, I'll stop." Ezra circled her opening, 'round and 'round, until she hissed. "C'mon, I know it has to be a good story if you're that hesitant." He paused again, waiting for her confession. She affected a pout so he could see it in the reflection of the glass. "You're cute when you do that."

"Enough to distract you?"

"Nope," he answered simply.

"Fine." Though she knew Ezra would never judge

her, she was still hesitant. Who wouldn't be, exposing such truths? "You're both forbidden. Intimidating. Sexy. Sometimes I feel as though I won't survive either of you. But then you do…things."

Though Ezra never stopped moving, his touch altered. Not rough, but certainly focused on what she had to say. "What kinds of things, Maddy?"

"Stuff," she muttered.

He tightened his fingers on her thighs.

Sensation curled around her. She needed him deep inside her but knew he wouldn't grant her that privilege until he was satisfied with her answer. "Things that are messy and out of bounds in normal life."

"Ah, but my crafty little code-wrangler, in Noble House this is normal."

Her thoughts splintered as she realized he was right. "This may be normal, but you two can out dirty me."

"Says the woman who keeps chasing her desire to explore. Just like in Court with Kochran. Right now with me, free for any member to walk by, stop and watch you." She gave a full-body shiver as the force of his touch increased. "Sex wasn't fun before, beautiful, because you didn't explore your kinkier desires. Didn't open yourself up to the wide, wide world of possibilities."

"I—Kochran had me write them all down." No reason to stop her confessions now. "Commanded me to write out one of my fantasies. I've never…yeah, I never thought this kind of thing would get me off." The admission had come more easily than she'd expected.

"But you can't imagine it any other way now, can you?" He traced his thumb slowly back and forth over her opening.

"No." Sex would always be fun as long Ezra and Kochran were involved.

He dragged his fingertips through her slick folds, playing and teasing her with those searching fingers. "This pretty little clit is just begging to be sucked." As he touched it lightly, she bucked against him. "Next time we're together, I'm going to hook your legs over my shoulders, map every single bit of your flesh with my tongue until I get lost. Then I'm going to slide inside you, feel you squirm on my dick. Kochran likes to keep you burning, make it so that you're taking the pain because you need it and not just because it's what he needs. I'm different."

He finally, finally slipped a finger inside her. She was frozen for a moment, basking in that incredible slick slide of his flesh against her aching tissue. "Not so different," she whispered, focusing on the pleasure pulsing through her as he slid his finger in and out. His soft strokes grew more demanding, "We haven't had intercourse yet."

Ezra slipped his finger deep, held it there so her internal muscles fluttered around him. "That could be taken a few different ways until I get a little clarification. Do you mean you want us to fuck you during the scenes, or do you want us to fuck you at the same time? Share you?"

The imagery of that hot fantasy she'd had where she'd been with both men flashed behind her eyes, heating already boiling blood.

"Mmm, think I know the answer without you saying a word. You want it all don't you?"

Noise pounded in her head so Ezra's voice sounded distant. She instinctually rocked against him, using her body to beg him for more, hungry and eager for whatever he decided to give her. She knew the answer too.

He uncrossed his ankles, the end of the rope he'd kept secured between his legs falling away. "Feet down."

Though she was disappointed he wasn't going to let her orgasm this way, she knew he had a plan. She was interested in learning what his devious mind had conjured.

He held her securely while she repositioned herself according to his directions. She had been in his lap, but now she straddled his thighs. He still had the end of the rope that was threaded through the metal loop at the window, and he used it to position her bound arms straight out in front of her. The position meant she had to rely solely on him for balance, trust him to keep her safe.

Her cunt was overly swollen as he entered her for the first time with his condom-covered cock, taking him all the way inside her. Sparks lit behind her eyes, blurring everything as pleasure radiated down through her body in a shower of light and energy. Ezra held her in the position he wanted, pinning her in place while he held himself fully within her, allowing her to adjust to his size. Then he was curling his fingertips into her hips, clutching them harder as he angled back, slowly withdrawing until just the crown remained. He filled her again, grunting as he sheathed himself to the hilt. Pleasure suffused her, colors pinwheeling behind her closed eyelids. Every sensation arched through her as though every sense was alive without shields.

Oh, hell, she was going to die.

Ezra pressed his chest against her back, pushing

her hair to the side to expose her ear. He kept himself buried inside her while he spoke. "Kochran's out there watching us. Do you want me to tell him to come join us?"

Maddy's inner walls clenched tightly around Ezra even as she shook her head.

"You like that idea." Ezra gave a dark laugh. "But you like the idea of him watching us even more, don't you? Like showing off for him while you ride me."

Her muscles fluttered then clenched again. Ezra hissed. "Christ, you're tight." He lifted her back up until just the tip of him remained inside her.

Kochran's eyes smoldered with a molten heat that reached her even through the glass. He slid his hands into his pockets, the tight stretch of fabric drawing her gaze to his obvious erection. As much as she wanted him to remain where he was, she also wanted him in the room. To stand in front of her, direct her mouth over and along the luscious length of his cock. Force her to swallow him over and over, just the same way she'd done earlier for Ezra.

"Are you thinking about him while I'm buried inside you? Imagining him here with us, ordering you to give him a blowjob while I fuck you? Fantasizing about taking us both inside you at the same time?"

She almost came at the questions, but she managed to keep a leash on her control. "Yes."

"Good." Ezra drove hard into her with such force, Maddy gave a keening wail. Before her eyes fluttered closed, she swore she saw Kochran's eyes flash, that tempting erection twitching under the fabric confining his interest. "I want you to think about him. Obsess about how much you want him, because he wants you too. Wants to be me. So we're going to give him a damn good show, baby girl."

The use of Kochran's pet name for her struck all the right chords.

Ezra plunged deeper, his full strokes hitting places she didn't know existed. She gave a long, trembling sigh as she absorbed each one of his thrusts. The world had slowed, not much more than a crawl of time passing by. She released a low, breathy moan as Ezra drove harder. She kept her gaze directly on Kochran as Ezra thrust deep, withdrew, and then thrust deep again. The full penetration caused a hot trail of need through her, spiraling around her clit as Ezra grunted his approval.

Maddy angled her hips higher in offering, loving the way Kochran's gaze fell to where she and Ezra were connected. She moaned and writhed, her palms sweating against the rope she clung to as she struggled with the desire to orgasm. She held back, determined to give Ezra pleasure before she sought her own. She tightened her inner muscles, pleased at Ezra's answering hiss, his fingers digging hard into her hips. She bore down again, as hard as she could so that each time he withdrew there was just as much resistance as when he shoved forward. A sharp crack resonated through the room suddenly, and Maddy gave a loud squeal as pain erupted high on her thigh. Ezra slammed fully into her, need bursting bright and hot deep inside her body.

"You will give me your orgasm, Maddy. *Now.*" He growled the last word, and it touched off something deep and primal. She wanted to hold on longer, prove that she could, but his guttural curses tipped her over the edge. She let go, her voice echoing back to her because of her close proximity to the window. Her cries melted into lusty pleas.

"I will give you as much as you want, beautiful. Whenever you want."

Even as she fell apart in Ezra's arms, she continued to move, riding wave after wave as they crashed into her. Pleasure throbbed as the dizzying power of the orgasm slammed into her with a rush, wild and heady. Ezra began to bang into her with hard, demanding thrusts as obscenities tripped off his tongue. She came again with a blinding explosion, the trigger Ezra needed to follow her into oblivion.

When she was finally able to open her eyes again, and her vision focused, her gaze collided with Kochran's. His face just inches from hers, separated only by the glass, his eyes wild and feral. Maddy leaned forward, resting her sweaty forehead against the pane. Ezra moved his hands over her, massaging away the strain that had developed in her shoulders from the odd angle, then held her until her legs had the strength to support her again.

"Stay there, love." As though she would even think of moving since the glass was the only thing holding her upright.

Kochran's gaze stayed with her as though he was playing protector while Ezra unwrapped her arms. Though he was clearly satisfied with the display he'd been witness to, tension lined his face. He touched the glass over her forehead just as Ezra returned with a warm washcloth and gently cleaned her. Her knees were trembling by the time he'd finished and he took her weight in his arms to lift her. She finally tore her gaze away from Kochran's as Ezra turned her.

Through the haze of satisfaction, he settled them on the cottony mattress. He cradled her, safe and secure, while she floated down through the haze of utter satisfaction. The soft glow of intimacy settled around them as she rested her head against his chest, heard his heart settling from its gallop.

"That was—"

"Fun?" Ezra finished with a soft chuckle.

It had been so much more than simple fun, but she wasn't sure how to articulate that. How to confess that she'd also had a link with Kochran despite the thickness of glass that had separated them. The trio had shared a connection she couldn't explain, couldn't label. What she did know was that she was quickly descending into a world where simple, friendly fucks weren't going to satisfy her. Her concept of normal was changing thanks to the men, and she didn't much mind.

She was worried that if she did say something, it would all shatter into shards and she wouldn't be able to fit the pieces back together no matter how strong a glue she used. Instead, she snuggled against him, allowing herself to be held, and slept.

Chapter Twenty-One

The rest of July passed in a blur for Maddy. As she'd dug deeper and deeper into the website's code, the more she learned about Ezra on a fundamental level. Pieces of his code were brilliant, laid out with a level of skill she admired. After she'd learned about how his marriages had broken up, she'd understood the reason for his lack of attention to detail in some places. Since she'd started working with him side by side, the quality of his work had increased exponentially.

It was as though Ezra had found himself again.

In between the hours she put in for work at the club, Ezra continued to put her front and center in the row of rooms with windows. He took his time exploring her likes, pushing her with gentle nudges toward things she wasn't sure about. She discovered her list of interests growing more varied after each of their sessions.

Kochran was there every time, watching with rapt interest from the other side of the glass. As though he not only got off on watching her with Ezra, but on the denial of his own pleasure.

Even two nights ago, when they had been in the room with the blacked-out window. She'd discovered it was a one-way mirror where the occupants of the room could see out, but no one could see in. That time, Ezra had used a microphone and speakers to pipe the sounds from the room to the hall. Kochran had gifted her with a lengthy note the following day, detailing his reaction to every single one of her screams. Her throat was still a little raw, but she found she liked the reminder of the intense scene every time she swallowed. Liked having that note hidden in her desk in Ezra's office, hers to look at whenever she chose. It had been the last thing she'd looked at before she'd gone home last night.

She'd come to Noble House a few hours before her shift Saturday afternoon to get a little extra work done, but had found a note taped to the office door. Her name had been written on the envelope in Kochran's gorgeous handwriting.

Come to Court.

Thoughts of working early vanished as she made her way down to the first floor. Nights of wishing and hoping Kochran would finally take their play to the next level had finally come to an end. She'd hoped that when he decided to take that step, he could continue with the open scenes anyone would be allowed to watch. Though she appreciated Ezra's subtlety, she also liked Kochran's brash openness.

She found him sitting in the same chair Enver had bound her to, but this time, a bench stood near his knee. Though the horizontal surface was padded, it was supported by a metal frame that had been painted a dull black. That small bag she knew he kept his toys in sat near his foot, and she eyed it, wondering what he had in store for her.

"What do you want, Madeline?"

A quick glance around the busy room and Ezra was nowhere to be found. Though she liked the way the two men segregated their play with her, her ultimate desire was still to have them both. That didn't appear to be happening tonight, so she pushed aside her disappointment and focused on the man who deserved her undivided attention. "Whatever you desire."

"I want to know what you're thinking about again."

"Having you inside me." His eyes darkened, taking on that familiar golden cast she'd come to recognize as arousal. "When you look at me like that it's all I can think about."

"Undress. Then get on your hands and knees."

One thing her time at Noble House had showed her—she didn't need pretty words or promises. She worked quickly, stripping each layer away until she stood before him gloriously nude. The power of the moment washed over her, giving her strength as she raised her head and their gazes collided. His expression was rich and powerful. Deep. As though he was freely offering her a glimpse into his soul.

He kept his gaze on hers as he rose from the chair, stepped over and sat on the bench. He was the one who took his time peeling away his clothes, exposing his firm and toned frame one inch at a time. By the time he was nude, she was a trembling mass of needy woman.

"Come to me. I want my mouth on those gorgeous tits." His harsh demand caused her breath to quicken.

She straddled his abdomen, sliding so his erection pressed against her butt. It was amazing how quickly she became consumed by his need, how being totally under his command made her body quiver with anticipation.

His gaze raked over her sitting above him, a hint of his impatience coloring his expression. "I'm waiting."

Quickly she leaned forward, sighing when he set his hands on her hips to hold her steady, offer support. The moment his lips met her nipple, she sighed again. He bathed the already tight nub with his tongue, his hot breath skating over her skin. When he flicked the hard tip, she jerked against him. He did it again and again. Her nipples grew tighter, loving the attention.

"I won't be slow tonight, Madeline, if you haven't already seen that. I've got too much pent-up energy I want to expend on you. Too much need for you that has to be sated."

"Oh, please."

After her plea, he drew back, his gaze aimed toward the breast he'd paid such reverent attention to. He circled his finger through the wetness he'd left on her skin. "Sit up. I want to see those pretty breasts on display."

As she did, he turned his hand over, fitting it between their bodies so he cupped her in his palm. She started to squirm against him, but stopped when he narrowed his eyes. She hung there in the cradle of him, his hand cupping her heat, cock nestled between her cheeks.

Kochran drew back his hips, lifting her slightly so he could reposition himself between her labia. She couldn't stop herself from rubbing against him, the slick wetness of her arousal coating his length as her excitement notched higher.

"That's it, Madeline. Ride me, but don't come."

"Not without permission."

"Mmm, that's right, baby girl." The nickname both men liked to use for her spilled out of his lips with a possessive growl.

Her internal muscles convulsed as she slid along the hardness pressing against her wet heat. She undulated her pelvis, pushing her pussy first against the heavy weight of his testicles, then against the tip, the friction pleasurably excruciating. She wanted to angle up, take him in her hand, to position him so that it would only take one perfect thrust to fill her all the way to his root. But she had to follow his orders.

As he gazed up at her, he wrapped his hands around her hips, taking control of her movements to work her over his cock. He wasn't going to make this easy, forcing her to continue as her response built hotter and faster.

She rocked against him. "Please. Please." She had no idea what she was begging for, only that she needed something, anything.

He switched the position of his hands and she was grateful for half a second until he started moving her in slow, sweeping circles. As her excitement level rose, moans and unintelligible pleas began to spill forth. Incoherent noises she couldn't contain as her body coiled tighter and tighter and…

"I'm close. So, so close."

He lifted her off him with an impressive display of strength and set her on her hands and knees on the bench. A crack split the air. A full second later, the sting of pain bloomed across her ass. The shock of being hit tamped down on her arousal.

"Who do your orgasms belong to, Madeline?"

She couldn't find the breath necessary to answer

right away and another hit struck her ass. This time, the pain merged with her fleeting excitement, giving it a sharp, dangerous edge.

"Tell me who."

She couldn't contain her gasp when he rubbed at the stinging pain. "You."

"Good girl."

She didn't want to be the good girl right now. She wanted the orgasm, wanted it so badly she nearly touched her clit. It would only take a few quick strokes to find the release hanging just out of reach. But she pressed her hand against the warm leather under her palm, forcing herself to remain still.

"Very good girl." Kochran curled over her back, the heat of his flesh pressing hard against the sting across her butt. "You want to climax, don't you? Want it with everything you are. If I just let you have that brief moment of respite, you'll be able to endure whatever else I have planned for you." He jerked his pelvis against the round curve of her ass, forcing her to feel the hard steel of his erection against the places he'd spanked. "But you'll only come when I command, isn't that right?"

She was starting to fully grasp just what kind of Dominant Kochran Duke was. Of course she'd seen it on the countless videos, been under his command before, but she now understood that he could take her past her limits in a short span of time. Show her how she was capable of stretching beyond what she thought so she could meet every demand. Those desires weren't merely physical. Mentally she wanted to please him as well, however and whenever he chose to make her fully and utterly his.

"Yes," she said quietly as her focus narrowed to a singular point of reference.

"There you go, nestling quite nicely along, aren't you?"

She nodded, unable to form the word again as warmth washed over her. The world blurred at the edges, blunted by the endorphins coursing through her at breakneck speed.

"Head down. Hips up." Though he maintained contact with her to provide support if she needed it, she easily made the transition to the position he wanted.

"This is your acceptance, Madeline. Forehead to the table, ass in the air. Someday I will order you to wait for me in this position so that when I enter Court, your pretty cunt will be the first thing I see."

She inhaled sharply. Such a position of subjugation would display her fully to him. Allow him to see the flushed pussy, the weight of her breasts. How ready she was for him to take her. The picture of the moment that formed in her head caused her to groan.

"Imagining it now, aren't you? The press of hardwood against your forehead and your knees as you wait for your Master to arrive."

At the sound of that word, she ceased thinking. *Master.* God, yes. A hot, needy sensation exploded through her core, rising to light an ache in her lower belly, her chest. Spirals of awareness unfurled through her as she vibrated with the desire to serve Kochran.

He cradled her neck in his palm, turning her face so she could meet his gaze. His penetrative look told her he recognized every single one of the emotions churning through her. "Does my claiming you make you wet, Madeline?"

"Yes, Sir."

"Good, I intend to keep you that way." He turned her face down again, pushed with gentle force to ensure she understood to keep her forehead pressed against the supple leather. When he set his palm against her lower back, she closed her eyes and let out a slow steady stream of air.

He parted her buttocks, exploring with that proprietary way that made her feel utterly his. "Have you ever been taken here?"

"No, Sir."

"But it was right there on that handwritten list of yours, wasn't it?" He traced the rim, dipping the tip of his finger inside her for a moment. "Fourth item from the top, if I remember correctly."

God, she hated that list almost as much as she loved it. Like it was a peek into her soul. In many ways it had been, on that ridiculously expensive paper. "Yes, it is."

His touch moved away, then returned, but this time it was cool and slick. "Just a little lubrication to help things along."

Everything was so new and foreign and exciting. She wanted to experience it all. Her focus pinged everywhere at once. Need clenched at her core, the aching desire to be filled by him.

"Shhh. Relax for me so I can do wicked things to you." The dangerous promise in his voice touched off new fires. In some crazy, thrilling way the idea of doing all sorts of insanely naughty things with him brought back a full rush of her excitement.

Something smooth touched her anus, and she released a shuddering breath. He stretched her with the pressure, opening her to him slowly with a practiced hand. The initial discomfort of the intrusion morphed into a hot need that had her angling her hips to accept more.

"That's it, baby girl. Take it all."

The item seemed to go on forever as it slipped deeper. Finally, her body accepted it, her asshole closing around the slender neck to hold it in place. He bent, brushing his lips against the small of her back. The tender gesture caused her muscles to clench around what he'd placed inside her, sending a hot lance of lust spearing through her core.

"You are a treasure."

She didn't know if a response was required, so she simply let the beauty of the accolade wash over her.

"Such beautiful, utter surrender." He kissed the small of her back again, then moved higher, brushing his lips against the knobs of her spine. A heavy object was set near her elbow before she heard the whisper of something being dragged across carpet. In her peripheral vision, she watched him sit in the chair he'd moved beside the table. He retrieved the object he'd set next to her, and now she could tell it was his cell phone.

Strange. She hadn't expected Kochran to have it so close at hand during a scene. Unless he needed it to be in contact with—a sudden vibration severed her train of thought. It had originated from whatever he'd placed in her ass. The strong pulse burst through her again, causing her to cry out.

"Music to my ears. I thought you would appreciate this little device as it appeals to your geek sensibilities. A plug equipped with the latest Bluetooth and Wi-Fi capabilities."

It gave an answering burst of power that made her

clench her teeth. The vibrator nestled deep inside her buzzed, travelling through her, relaxing her at the same time that it aroused her. The frequency of the vibration increased, building and building until she was certain she couldn't take anymore.

It stopped suddenly, leaving her panting. The ache of absence filled her. Amazing how she'd vacillated so quickly from never experiencing this sort of pleasure to craving it.

"Something tells me this will have your cunt gushing before long."

The fiercely intense build toward orgasm began again in earnest, making her shudder. The harsh, rasping sound of his voice charged the air around her. But she accepted his treatment, her legs shaking in response to the approaching climax.

She became more aroused, her clit pulsing even though there was nothing stimulating it. "Master... please."

"Keep doing that. Lift your ass a little higher." He made a noise when she complied, rotating her hips. "That's it. Goddamn, I could watch you go fucking mindless like this for hours."

"I'm going to come," she whimpered, fighting against the climax.

"You are when I say you can. Fight it, Madeline."

She wanted to comply with his command but her grasp on control was rapidly slipping. "I can't."

"Damn right you can't." He leaned closer, setting the phone directly in her field of vision. A quick glance at the screen showed he'd set it to the highest frequency without a pause programmed into the cycle.

"You're a fucking sadist, Master."

He laughed. "Damn right I am." His teeth gleamed as he grinned. "Seventh item on your list, I believe."

Come at the hands of a cruel Master.

Her body revved and eager, she screamed her pleasure as the orgasm tore through her. Her hips worked involuntarily to draw out her pleasure, and she rode the vibrant edge of the climax. When she came down, she realized she was making gasping noises that sounded like sobs. Kochran brushed her hair back from her face, heat turning his eyes all sorts of interesting colors.

"I'm going to fuck you now my sweet, sweet submissive, Madeline. And you're going to fly even further and scream even louder the next time you come, understand?"

The cell phone lit under his touch. At first she thought he was going to turn the vibrator off, but he tapped it a few times to queue up a preset pattern. "I'm going to leave this right here. Let you see the settings as they happen instead of wondering. Don't take your eyes off it."

He moved behind her, the sound of foil ripping as he opened a condom touching off new fires of exhilaration. She positioned herself automatically, the anticipation of him finally entering her almost too much to endure. As hard as it was to imagine him filling her while the plug was still in place, the desire to be doubly penetrated sent a strong pulse of yearning flowing through her.

A long string of unintelligible noises spilled from her mouth as he entered her. He was hard and thick, filling her with his sheathed cock in one stroke. Her vision grayed at the edges and she dug her fingernails into the bench in an effort not to come undone by the decadent sensations bracketing her on all sides. The combination of the plug and his cock stretched her to the brink, and still she wanted more.

When he withdrew, he repositioned her hips, shoving through the tight fist of her cunt to achieve full, deep penetration. The vibrations began in earnest, and they both gave twin groans as Kochran started moving with short, but still intensely effective strokes.

As the pulsing of the vibrator increased, her orgasm hung perilously close. Inside this space he'd built for her, she was consumed by him. Lost. Not in a bad way, but completely out of control and so unequivocally his.

"Yesss…" she hissed as the vibrations kicked high.

Kochran dug his fingers into her hips. "Fucking thing is malfunctioning. Should have stopped over a minute ago." The vibrator gave an answering pulse, the movements again growing impossibly stronger, this time causing her to gasp. The muscles in Kochran's thighs went rock hard against the backs of her legs as he tried to power through the cycle.

The vibrations ceased without warning and they both gasped at the same time. It pulsed again, softly this time, almost too softly. Her vision cleared enough for her to see the phone screen and saw the unit was supposed to be powered down. It buzzed with a strong pulse. The application in front of her hadn't changed. Though Kochran seemed to believe it had malfunctioned, her thoughts went in a decidedly different direction.

Maddy scanned Court again, searching for a familiar face. She found him close by, closer than she was expecting. Cleary he wanted to be found as he didn't appear to be masking his presence in any way.

Ezra stood ten feet away, leaning against a column, his cell phone in hand. Though his posture was relaxed, he was anything but nonchalant. He knew exactly what was going on. And judging by the ridge she could make out under the zipper of his pants, he was also astonishingly aroused.

Ezra's gaze lifted slowly, as though he was taking his time to enjoy the picture the two of them made together. When their gazes finally collided, a sharp stab of arousal bit her.

Kochran groaned. "You just went all hot and tight around me. Jesus, Madeline." He dug his fingers into her thighs. "Before we go any further, you all right with this?"

She glanced back over her shoulder, noting the light sparking in his eyes. He didn't appear bothered by the fact Ezra had muscled his way into the scene. That Ezra would have a say in the outcome of their pleasure. His gaze was on her, but she knew Kochran intended the question for both Ezra and her. This blended what had already happened between them, checking off more things on that list of hers. It also seemed like a natural progression to her, a merging of everything already between them.

Two Doms.

All hers.

Phew.

Her wildest fantasies had taken her to this place a few times, and now her real life was about to get a kick into overdrive. She met Kochran's gaze first, then Ezra's. "Yes. Please. Oh yes."

Ezra smirked and tapped the screen of his cell phone. The vibrator gave a powerful buzz that made Kochran tighten his grip and drive inside her. He pulled back and thrust forward, speeding toward release without instructing her to hold back her climax. He slammed hard into her, grinding his hips against hers as though he was an animal possessed. It triggered a powerful climax that had her screaming and crying at the same time, overwhelmed by the intensity. Kochran shouted his release, suddenly thrusting a few times. The movement sparked another wave of orgasm rippling through her, stealing the last of her energy so she went limp under Kochran's strong hold.

Through the haze of pleasure, she noted Ezra's fingers had gone white where he tightly gripped his cell phone. He made no move toward them, instead shoving the phone into his pocket and stepping back into the darkness.

Chapter Twenty-Two

It had been a while since Kochran had been this protective of someone. Longer still since he'd felt that sharp coil of need toward two people. Sure, he cared for every member on his roster like a protective father figure, but his feelings about this matter were different. He was downright giddy, still riding the pleasant buzz of anticipation and need twining together from his scene with Maddy a few days ago.

Kochran Duke hadn't been giddy over partners in a long, long time. Perhaps never. Having multiple play partners had never been something he'd dismissed, but it wasn't something he'd actively sought either. He'd left that to the resident ménage experts of the club, though Saint and Boyce had been taken off the market thanks to Grae. Because of a black mark on his past that still scarred him, Kochran had made a conscious decision to wait and see what fate brought his way.

Maddy and Ezra pinged his radar—hard. Penetrating so deep, the force had dislodged something Kochran hadn't expected would ever rise to the surface again. A slice of his past that he hadn't thought about in a long, long time. He wasn't ashamed of the kind of life he'd lived in his twenties, but he didn't talk much about it either. It suited his current path to keep quiet. The members of Noble House wouldn't expect the fearless leader had long-buried submissive tendencies.

A soft knock sounded on his office door and he smothered a growl. He wasn't in the mood for company. Not to mention he had a pile of paperwork so he could get to his gig at nine. It meant he had three hours. Enough time to maybe swing by the hospice to visit Tory.

The soft knock sounded again. Right. Business first. "Come on in."

He expected a house sub or one of the cleaning staff since they didn't officially open for another hour. Maybe even Ezra or Maddy, since they'd mentioned they were close to finishing. Instead, his sister's girlfriend peeked around the partially open door. "Busy?"

Kochran's heart leaped into his throat as fear churned his stomach. "Adelita. Is Tory all right?"

"Everything is fine. Don't give me that look." The petite brunette played with the strap of her purse as she arranged herself in one of his chairs.

"I know when someone is lying to me."

"Just like your sister."

The comparison warmed him. "How are you really? Not the bullshit answer you give everyone else either."

"As you'd expect." She brushed a shaky hand through her tangled hair. "Stressed. Horrible. Wonderful."

"And I thought I was messed up."

"Things are a jumble, to be honest," she admitted. "Some days I don't want to get out of bed."

"But you do." Because some days that was all you *could* do.

"I was all right until a few days ago."

Kochran knew that look. That one reeking of desperation and exhaustion. He'd worn it more often lately than he liked to keep the truth hidden from the people who meant the most to him. "My mother didn't start in on you again, did she?"

"I'm sorry." She rose, fumbling her purse as she did. "I shouldn't be here unloading this on you. You have more than enough to deal with."

Kochran snapped his fingers to pull her out of her string of apologies. He was quickly losing his patience with people deciding what he could and couldn't handle. "Adelita, sit. Tell me what happened."

"I was fired."

He wasn't certain he'd heard her correctly. "What?"

She brushed a hand through her unruly hair. "Too much personal leave, they said. And most of the time, if I did manage to make it into the office, I was thinking about everything else *but* work."

He examined the woman who had stolen his sister's heart. Her normally well-put-together appearance was frazzled and messy. Her shirt was wrinkled, half of it untucked from her skirt. A long snag in her hose ran up the side of her leg. "Do you need any money for food? Rent?"

"I…hated the job, to be honest." She offered him a weak smile as she waved off his questions.

"But it gave you something to do."

"It made me feel productive. Like a member of society. There are plenty of other firms I could go work for, but who is going to want to hire me knowing I'm going to take a lot of time off right out of the gate?"

He studied her. She was right. Adelita was the kind

of woman who would inform a prospective employer about her unique situation. She needed more flexibility.

He glanced toward his desk, at the piles and piles of paperwork he kept pushing to the side, and had an idea. "I could use someone like you. I send the club's books to an accountant I've been using for years, but it's well past time for us to have a full-time numbers nerd."

"I'm not your charity case, Kochran."

"You're not. One friend to another, I'm not a fan of all this crap I can't escape from. It's one of the drawbacks of owning your own business. So you'd be doing me a favor. Unless you think you can't work for a sex club."

She snorted. "I'm not a prude. I can't claim to understand everything that goes on here, or that I'm interested in finding out, but as long as you don't mind someone like me working here, I'm game."

Like her? He could only think of one thing. "A lesbian?"

"An old, boring accountant."

"Believe me, Adelita, you are anything but boring."

She pointed to him, the smile she aimed his way anything but humorous. "But we agree I'm old. I can start tomorrow."

He started shuffling papers into a pile that he could sort through later. Relief he would be free of that particular pain in the ass eased some of the ache pounding behind his eyes. "You can officially start when I say."

"I told you I'm not really into this whole dominance thing."

He came around the desk, crouching beside her. He gathered her hands in his, noting how cold and dry the woman's fingers were. She was too busy taking care of Tory to bother with basic necessities for herself.

"I'm saying this as Tory's brother. When you're completely available, you can start." He pulled her to stand, already thinking about what he could clear out on the third floor in order to create an office for her. Hopefully, he would have some time before she needed it. "What do you say we pick up some Thai and pay a visit to my stubborn sister?"

They arrived at Tory's room, arms laden with take-out, an hour later. Kochran frowned, setting the bags on a stand as he spotted his mother standing by the bed. He ignored her, brushing a kiss to Tory's cheek.

"Warmer than usual." He set a hand on her forehead, concerned. "Not running a fever, are you?"

"Hot 'cause my fucking gorgeous girlfriend just walked in," she said as she struggled with the sheets Noelle kept tucking around her frail body.

"Victoria, watch your language. And stop fidgeting, you need to conserve your energy."

"For what?" Tory rolled her eyes as she slapped Noelle's hand away. "The marathon I'm going to run later? The only activity I want right now is for Adelita to share her *nam tok mu* with me. Okay, that's a lie. I want her to share her grilled pork and then let her feast on my pussy. Dinner and dessert."

Kochran snorted at Noelle's horrified look. He dug through one of the bags, pulling out a container of pad thai, and a set of chopsticks. He handed them to Tory's other visitor, Grae. "Soy sauce and extra shrimp."

She accepted them with a grateful smile. "Thanks, I'm starving. Worked all day and came over for a visit before heading to the club."

"New movie?"

The redhead's eyes sparkled as she gestured to the screen where two people were locked in a passionate embrace. "Just finished up the dailies on my latest project and thought Tory would get a kick out of it since I signed her on as my official test audience." Grae had become a good friend to both Tory and Adelita since she'd come back into Saint and Boyce's life. The two had bonded over the blockbuster movies Grae performed computer graphic work on and cheesy one-liners that most people rolled their eyes over.

"Will you turn that obnoxious mess off? No one wants to see that man's butt." Noelle made a tsking noise as she wrinkled her nose. "Shameless Hollywood filth."

"That filth pays my bills, Mrs. Duke." Grae shoved a bundle of noodles into her mouth in what Kochran suspected was an effort to keep from telling his mother exactly where to go. Kochran also noted that while Grae didn't give in to his mother's request, she did cut the sound.

An annoyed expression flicked across Noelle's face. "They had to force Tory to take her medication again today. Since she won't listen to me, Kochran, you talk some sense into her. She needs to take better care of herself."

Tory's gaze cut sideways. "I'm trying, Mom. But you keep having your lackeys tie me down. I'm not the one who gets off on that kind of thing."

Kochran's vision sheeted red. Not at the comment about his sex life, but on the insinuation his mother had taken matters into her hands once again. "What the fuck is she talking about, Mother?"

"Watch your language, young man."

"Did you have the nurses restrain her?" The image of Tory pinned to the bed with wide leather straps, struggling with a man three times her size who forced pills down her throat, tore through his mind.

"She needs her medication," Noelle scoffed as she tidied the sheets again. "I know what's best for her. I'm her mother."

"You're an overbearing tyrant who is pissed someone doesn't want to fall in line. And despite what you believe, you don't have her best interests in mind." He didn't bother to modulate the menace in his tone. "Only yours."

Noelle's eyes flashed hot, her voice low. "You will not disrespect me, son. Especially not in public. If you can't respect my decision, you will leave."

He lifted a brow. "You can't respect Tory's decisions, so why should I respect yours?"

"This conversation is over, Kochran." Her voice had gone up an octave, becoming almost shrill.

The tone triggered a shudder through his gut, a violent urge to cut Noelle Duke to the quick. "Do you even hear how fucking selfish you are? Or are you just so blind that you don't see what you're doing to your daughter? What she's going through? Those choices are for her to decide, not you. As much as you hate to hear it, this isn't *your* life."

Noelle bristled at Kochran's outburst, the shock of his words reverberating between them. "I have entertained both of your whims long enough and it's high time it stopped. I know what is best for Tory and that's the end of it. Now, I'm going to start the process to move Tory out of this festering mount of dirt they called a hospice and transfer her to the facility in New York where they can properly care for her. When I come back, I expect you gone." Her jaw tightened as she gave a pointed look toward Adelita. "All of you."

"Tory needs me, so with respect, Mrs. Duke, I'll be here as long as I damn well feel like it," Adelita said quietly, never taking her eyes off Tory.

Grae turned the volume up on the television and reset the video to the beginning.

Noelle squared her shoulders. "Think long and hard about the consequences if you all continue to cross me."

Kochran swore he felt the room give a sigh of relief as his mother left. He shouldn't have taken it that far, but he was beyond rage that had goaded him into the argument. The New York facility named after his grandfather was Noelle's pride and joy. More so than her children. He reached for Tory's hand. "I won't let her move you anywhere."

"She's got a fight on her hands if she thinks I'm going anywhere. I know she means well, but Mom is… Mom." Tory's voice broke over the word. She cleared her throat, forcing a smile. "Now, my hot girlfriend is going to feed me some of that delicious smelling food and we're going to watch this couple covered in fake sweat get busy."

It wasn't often Tory had an appetite anymore, so he was pleased to watch her take a small bite of the sliver of meat Adelita offered. He watched them for a time, marveling at how Adelita expertly balanced the caretaker and girlfriend roles. Thinking about how she'd stood up against his tyrant of a mother for the woman she loved.

Grae touched his arm. "You need to eat too."

He wasn't hungry, but he accepted the plate piled high with food because of the stern look she shot his way. "Thank you for all you've done for Tory, Grae. You're a true friend to her."

"She likes my jokes. I like making sure she's happy."

"Unlike some," he muttered grimly, his gut a hard, aching ball. His mother was going to give him an ulcer.

"Your mom will come around."

"Want to bet?" They fell silent for a time, eating while the food was still hot. He thought of the care Grae took with Tory. The way she'd insisted he eat when he was too wrapped up in the fight with his mother. "Saint and Boyce are lucky to have you."

"They are, aren't they? Seems like you've had a run of luck in that department yourself." She ate for a few minutes, as though waiting for him to respond. But he didn't know how to. What could he say when each day was a struggle where he was convinced he couldn't be what everyone needed?

"I don't know what's going on, but I know when I see someone I care about in pain." Grae gave him a searching glance as she set her hand on his cheek. "Don't hide it from yourself. Or from whoever it is you're torn up about. Just…be yourself. I had to learn that the hard way. Because of my past, when something upset my stability, I bolted. Saint and Boyce called me out. Forced me to face it. Them. I thought I was trying to protect myself, but really I was just running from the truth."

Grae reset the video again and joined Adelita and Tory on the bed. They immediately fell into absurd critiques about the sex scene, each one trying to outdo the last with their comments.

Kochran wished he could open a valve and let all his insecurities and feeling gush forth in a rush. Confess to Grae how he constantly thought about Maddy, how those feelings consumed him. How he wanted to stitch up Ezra's wounded soul.

But as convinced as he was that they were exactly what he needed, he was also convinced he couldn't take the risk. The general membership of Noble House expected him to be every bit of the sexual Dominant he displayed during his shows. They didn't want to know their fearless leader was madly, desperately in love with two people who had the power to destroy him.

Chapter Twenty-Three

Kochran pinwheeled the drumstick for a few beats before banging it against the membrane of his drum. Duality had just started the last song of their first set, and from the sound Kochran was getting through the feed in his earpieces, they were rocking a house full of tourists celebrating Labor Day.

Screwdriver was one of Kochran's favorite places to gig because the owner was also a longtime member of Noble House. Oz had booked the band to play once a month for a year in advance, so Kochran gave him a break on the membership fees. It was a mutual agreement that suited them both, but also allowed a steady place for Kochran to delve deeper into one of his favorite activities. Because of the arrangement, and the close proximity of the town to the club, a hefty portion of the crowd at the bar were Noble House members. Which also meant the playlist could be tailored for the more open-minded clientele where they could experiment and test out new songs.

For the show tonight, they were debuting a song Kochran had been working on for the past three months. As the tune moved to the refrain, he lost himself in the throaty notes Charlie sang about the delicate balance between pleasure and pain. Charlene Husk may have been the most vanilla person Kochran knew, but she also trusted him not to steer her wrong when it came to songwriting. She also had a remarkable stage presence that said she was every bit the lead singer of a kick-ass band. She cocked her head to the side, her hair falling across one eye as she crooned about being the light of the sun and the moon. This song in particular had an ethereal alternative melody that was tempered with a gnashing, guttural distortion delivered toward the end. It wasn't often Kochran added more than a masculine layer under Charlie's voice as backup, but this song in particular belonged to him.

Losing himself to it, he closed his eyes and allowed the music to carry him away. Some nights, playing was a euphoric experience nearly as intoxicating as Dom-space. He drifted along with the melody, his arms and legs moving on muscle memory from hours and hours of rehearsal.

When the time came, Kochran joined Charlie, his voice layering with hers, further adding to the smoky quality as they sang about someone being alive when their weakest pleasure was pain. Her voice faded off on cue, giving Kochran the stage front and center. While he was no crooner, he had a decent voice with just the right amount of whiskey and smoke. As he sang about being aware he was a vicious tyrant who unapologetically took what he wanted from his partner, he scanned the crowd.

He made eye contact with a few patrons closest to the stage, the overhead lighting positioned in such a way that he couldn't see more than the first few tables near the riser. Didn't matter. He knew the place was packed, he just wondered if the two faces he wanted to see the most were out there somewhere. Then again, he would have had to invite them in the first place. Maddy wouldn't have known the band's schedule. And Ezra… the last time they'd played at the bar hadn't gone well for him.

As he broke off, turning the song back over to Charlie saying they were one in the same, he sank back into the raw, feral power of the last beats. By the time the set ended, Kochran was a wild, sweaty mess. His arms and legs burned as sweat dripped into his eyes. He grinned as the four of them stood to bow and Charlie invited everyone to stick around for their second set in twenty minutes.

"Really rocking it tonight, boss." Jolie, the band's bass player, doled out towels and bottles of water to the others. "Totally on fire."

"Thanks," he replied as he took a second towel from her and slung it around his neck. "Sounding good yourself." She was still struggling with the bridge of one of the newer songs that had just made it into regular rotation, but it wasn't the time to point it out to her. He made a mental note to discuss it during their next rehearsal as he stepped off the stage. Ever the perfectionist, Kochran was just as critical of his bandmates as he was himself. He believed in giving the audience a good show.

His still-burning eyes took a few minutes to adjust to the dimmer lighting of the main seating area as he made his way to the waist-high bar.

Oscar Nakamura had already set a glass with a few fingers of bourbon in front of Kochran's regular stool and waited until he'd downed half of it. "What has you so spun up?"

"Just working like always, Oz." Kochran dropped the towels and his soaked half-finger gloves onto the counter. Oz whisked the towels away, replacing them with a fresh one that Kochran used as padding so his sweaty arms wouldn't slide against the bar.

Oz shook his head with a smile as he spun a glass against a towel. "Working is what I'm doing, Duke. That up there? You were a fucking madman on some kind of mission. Seen you play a lot, man, but never like that."

Kochran shrugged and tried not to think about the possible reasons why. "New songs tend to be a little consuming."

"That wasn't a song, that was a fucking elegy." Oz eyed him as he moved off to fix an order one of the waitresses had shouted out to him.

From this angle, Kochran studied the man with a critical eye. No, not critical…curious. He wasn't tall, but his build was proportional. Kochran knew from experience Oz didn't believe in hours at the gym to keep himself in top physical condition, but he did subscribe to hard work. Oz also had the kind of charming personality women flocked to, which brought in a fair share of steady customers. With dark eyes, a full head of black hair, and golden skin, he had striking good looks. Unfortunately for the female population, he preferred more testosterone when it came to matters of love and sex. Kochran had only ever seen Oz dominate men at the club. And he was good at what he did. Remarkably good. Oz also played it rough, with most of his scenes ending with a very satisfied submissive who wore his marks for a few days afterward.

Kochran had just enough alcohol and adrenaline in his system to wonder if a quick fuck with Oz would clear his confusion about Ezra. Then he'd know his preferences when it came to sex had simply expanded a little again and he could move on with his life. But however impressive Oz's physique was, however charming his personality and attractive those preferences were with sex, Kochran wasn't drawn to Oz in the same way. There was nothing sexual, nothing visceral, between them. Broaching that topic with his longtime friend would only earn him a few minutes of embarrassment and a lifetime of heckling. Because that's what friends do when you ask for absurd favors.

More than a few times he'd thought about jetting off to parts unknown to take care of the persistent itch. Lose himself in a binge of booze, sex and bondage. He'd never hidden his wild living from anyone. He was the sex-hungry, hard-living and hard-drinking owner of a fetish club. Add in the fact he was the drummer for Duality, and the two sides of his life carried the added perk of an endless parade of partners to choose from. Yet, lately, he hadn't wanted anyone else but Maddy and that damn persistent ache whenever Ezra Snow was around. He kept pushing back the tenacious thrum of energy that pulsed through him when the other man came near. And damn the man if he wasn't being an obstinate pain-in-the-ass. Always on the periphery, as though he was aware of the reaction he caused. And that damn stunt he'd pulled hacking the plug. Kochran was still trying to convince himself the climax he'd experienced hadn't been one of the strongest he'd ever

had in his life. Maddy may have been the spark, but he
damn well knew Ezra had been the gasoline.

Kochran nursed the alcohol in his glass this time,
thinking about what Oz had pointed out. Something
had been different up there.

As he scanned the crowd from a different angle,
his gaze landed on a booth near the front windows.
His heart gave a solid thump against his ribcage as he
saw the way Maddy was leaning toward Ezra, listening intently to something he said. The two were fully
engrossed in a conversation despite the noise of the
crowd. As though they were in their own little world.
The second Ezra made eye contact with him, Kochran's
body came alive.

Yeah. You're so fucked, Duke.

Kochran grabbed his stuff as he pushed away from
the bar. He tucked the towel into his back pocket, noting he'd need it later once he got back under the stage
lights. For perhaps the first time in his life, he was nervous as he approached his friends. He was genuinely
interested in what they'd thought about the new song.
Though he valued most of his friends' opinions, it appeared to be especially true when it came to these two.
He played for thousands of people, put on show after
show for them as a Dom, but they'd all passed through
his life with little fanfare. He'd never wanted to impress any of those strangers as much as he wanted to
impress Maddy and Ezra.

As he slipped into the padded booth, he noted two
beers on the table, both within Ezra's reach. Immediately, his protective instincts roared to life. He studied
the man with a more critical eye, noting the smudges

were a little darker than normal, his eyes not as bright. Something was off again.

"Celebrating?" Kochran pointed to the bottles.

"We put the final touches on the sim tonight, so we're celebrating no longer being in beta testing. The new simulator is officially open for business and lining your pocket. Next step—virtual reality." Ezra picked the closest bottle and finished off the last of the contents. "Nice work up there."

Kochran's eyes narrowed. If he wasn't mistaken, a few of Ezra's words had been slurred. Not enough the average person would notice, but his diabetic buddy in high school had a bad habit of overstepping his bounds with alcohol trying to keep up with the rest of the teen-age partying. He started to issue a warning to Ezra, but stopped when Maddy leaned forward and captured Kochran's hand.

"I think I got a little wet watching you bang those drums during that last song." Her cheeks flushed pink as she drew her bottom lip between her teeth. The forward angle of her position had pushed her breasts together so her shirt gapped at the neckline and gave him a perfect view down the front.

"Oh yeah?"

She nodded as her gaze darted to Ezra, who remained silent, though he was clearly listening. "Low-slung jeans, black tank, biceps all bulging every time you hit the drums. The way your eyes got all unfocused when you were singing about being someone who got off on delivering pain." She paused, her own eyes going glassy. "It's pretty damn clear you love what you do."

Her giggle was music to his ears. "I'd warn you to be careful of giving a man a swelled head, but it's a little late for that." He shifted his pants, purposefully angling to draw her attention.

It worked. Her gaze darted to his lap, which she gave a long, lingering stare. Her smile fell, though. "Too bad I've already got plans for the rest of the night. A few of the girls invited me to come along for Grae's bachelorette party." She gathered up her cell phone and a light jacket. "Probably should have headed that way about twenty minutes ago, but I didn't want to miss the rest of the set." She pressed a lingering kiss to Ezra's cheek, then to Kochran's. "Walk me out?"

Something in her expression made Kochran slide out of the booth and follow her. He dodged the friendly greetings of customers with a smile, meeting up with Maddy again at the front door. "Everything all right?"

Her gaze flicked toward where Ezra sat. "Something's bothering him, but he won't fess up."

"I noticed." He remembered the conversation in his kitchen. Remembered the pale shade of Ezra's skin when he'd been laid out unconscious right here on the bar's floor over a month ago. "Did you know he's diabetic? Wears an insulin pump?"

"What?" She gripped his forearm, her nails biting into his skin. "No. I knew about his wife and husband. I thought that was the reason he was drinking like he needed to escape. Like he needed to forget."

He buried his reaction to the pain of her grasp. "He must have scheduled the times he changed his infusion site around whenever he was with you so you wouldn't find out." Careful calculation by a man who wouldn't let anyone truly in. Kochran knew that game well. He was a player himself. It was also damn dangerous since the pump should be worn at all times. Kochran hoped

Ezra took care to monitor his insulin levels when the pump wasn't in place.

"Judging how much alcohol he's had, I suspect this is the anniversary of one of those events. About the time you came to work for the club, he was here. Went into diabetic shock just as our first set started."

"That must have been the anniversary of when his wife died, and tonight…"

"When Kyle left." Kochran glanced back through the crowd, catching fleeting glimpses of Ezra staring off into space. He turned back to Maddy, his heart clenching at the concern darkening her eyes. "Go enjoy your party. I'll look after him."

"No. I can't go after what you just told me."

"You can and you will." He pried her grip off his arm, lifting her hand to his mouth. Her fingers shook against his lips as he kissed them. His voice had come off a little more demanding than he'd meant, so he softened it. "I can handle him."

"Are you sure?"

He shot her a lecherous glare. "I know how to put him in his place if he gets too obstinate. In fact, I think I may enjoy it if he does." He wiggled his eyebrows until the lines of worry between her eyes smoothed.

"Promise you'll call me if things get too bad?"

"Always." She didn't appear convinced. He stepped closer, touching her chin to angle her face toward his. "If I don't, you have my permission to sign me up for the dildo of the month club."

She chuckled. "He told you about that?"

"Sure did. Excellent work, baby girl."

"I know I overstepped there, but the asshole deserved something more than being kicked out of the club. He violated my trust. *Your* trust."

"You mean like having a few sheriff's deputies deliver a restraining order?" Maddy's eyes widened as Kochran spoke. "I don't take lightly to someone taking advantage of me. Or trying to get one over. He's lucky I didn't hunt him down."

Kochran watched her go, waiting until she drove away before turning back to make his way to the table. Ezra's expression didn't change as Kochran arrived, so that was something at least. "Going to stick around for the rest of the set?"

A waitress came by before Ezra answered, far too bubbly for the sour mood settled over the table. "Get you boys anything?"

"Another round for us both," Ezra offered before Kochran could dismiss her.

"You got it." She cleared away the empty bottles and the glass before flouncing off with a wiggle of her hips.

Tension filled the spaces between them as they waited. Kochran wanted to curse at Ezra, tell him how much a fucking fool he was being, but it wouldn't do any good. Ezra would just push back harder, determined he could take care of himself.

The waitress returned with a chilled bottle for Ezra. Her smile fell as she set a glass of water before Kochran. "Oz said you were cut off until the end of the second set."

"That's all right, thank you." Kochran took a few gulps of the water. "Tell Oz I appreciate him looking out for me."

When the waitress left, he gestured toward Ezra's beer. "Sure you should be doing that?" He put as much

consternation in his voice as he could without coming
off domineering.

Ezra scowled. "Stop being my babysitter, Kochran."

Kochran restrained his instinctual reaction to lash
back at Ezra again. Instead, he inhaled deeply, as he
took in the various smells permeating through the bar,
his drying sweat and Ezra's dismissive glare. There
were thousands of things he wanted to scold Ezra for,
but he knew every single one would fall on deaf ears.
He'd have been better off trying to coax the sun out
of the sky.

Chapter Twenty-Four

No matter how much Ezra tried to escape the past, it always found him, slamming into him with a force of a bullet train. Forced him to relive moments of his life he'd rather forget.

He'd thought the anniversary of Nora's death had been difficult to handle, but recalling the instant Kyle had walked out the door reopened scars that made him deal with the pangs of abandonment over and over.

Kochran set his empty water glass down with a sharp bang. "Set is about to start." He slid out of the booth, standing as he waved toward the stage. "See you when I'm done."

"Not worried I'm going to take off?"

Kochran held up a set of keys. "Nope, not worried at all." Ezra blinked as he slapped his hand over his pocket, found it empty.

Kochran swiped the beer in front of Ezra and exchanged it for the full glass of water a passing waitress had on her tray. He bent closer to her, flashing his most charming smile and kept his voice low. "Keep those coming for him, doll. Need him clear-headed and sober by the time I'm finished."

She gave him a knowing smile and nodded. No

doubt about what she was thinking. Ezra was sunk so deep in his bad mood, he wasn't going to bother correcting her.

He watched her walk away and then turned back to find Kochran still wearing that damn smile. The one that made things inside Ezra flash hot. "What the fuck are you up to, Duke?"

"Guess you'll find out at the end of the set."

As much as he hated the cunning smile Kochran shot his way, Ezra knew the man had done the right thing. He would have imbibed beer after beer in an attempt to forget. To erase the pain of the past. The heartbreak of the present. He enjoyed playing with Maddy. Found a great deal of non-sexual fulfillment working with her. But there were emotions bubbling under the surface he didn't want to deal with.

Then there was *him*. Ezra turned his focus to where Duality tore up the stage with their most popular hit among the locals. The song the band had debuted earlier struck a chord with Ezra as well. Made everything fuzzy come into clear focus. A focus he'd kept trying to dodge. He had feelings for Kochran that went beyond the typical boss/employee relationship. More than just a couple of buddies hanging out. The dance the two men had been playing with Maddy between them pinged all kinds of spots for Ezra. He'd been away from the lifestyle for so long he hadn't recognized his needs at first. But now that he had, everything was remarkably difficult. Problem was, Kochran bowed for no one. And Ezra desperately wanted to see Kochran on his knees.

After the set was over, Ezra agreed to allow Kochran to drive him home even though he could have easily walked the few miles. However, when they blew past the turn for his house, Ezra's annoyance returned tenfold. "You gonna tell me now what the fuck you're up to?"

Kochran's face remained impassive. The rest of the drive was conducted in silence and Ezra began to seriously rethink the situation. Annoyance continued to boil in his gut as Kochran parked the car and killed the engine. Since Kochran wasn't interested in chatting, Ezra got out of the car and walked to Kochran's front door. He waited there, listening to the soft hum of the locks disengaging as Kochran approached. By the time Kochran came to stand beside him, the panel had dropped and now slid back to reveal the stairs that would take them down into Kochran's hidden house.

Ezra stormed down the stairs and headed directly for the kitchen. To give himself something to do, he busied himself making coffee. He figured there was no way in hell that he was falling asleep there again. Unlike last time, he would be awake and aware. He'd sober up the rest of the way, and call for a ride.

He leaned back against the counter, scowling at Kochran. "You don't have to keep taking care of me."

"You're not taking care of yourself. Someone has to do it," Kochran said calmly as he sipped his coffee. "You keep going like this, won't be anyone to take care of."

Ezra scowled. "The last thing I need is a babysitter." He poured another cup before he faced Kochran again. "What I really don't need is an overprotective boss looking over my shoulder every chance."

Kochran lifted an eyebrow but said nothing. He drank again and again until he finished the contents. He rose, walked slowly across the kitchen space and came to stand by Ezra. Ceramic clicked together as Kochran set his empty cup in the sink.

"An overprotective boss may be the last thing you want, but a willing partner is what you need." Kochran angled his body closer, leaning his weight on one arm. "I can be that. Do whatever you need, because you and I both know I can take it. Use it. Use me. No one else knows what you're dealing with. That shit you have festering inside you is going to eat away at who you are. It'll tear you up, Ezra. Make you into a hollow shell of a human being. I've been there. I know. Don't let that happen."

Ezra knew what Kochran had said, had heard every single word with absolute clarity, but he couldn't believe the words. It was his wildest fantasies come true. Kochran Duke offering himself on a silver platter. He'd had suspicions, of course, but he'd kept writing them off as nothing more than his imagination. Chalked it up to Kochran's fascination with Maddy. Ezra had been collateral damage. Something Kochran had to endure in order to spend time with who he truly wanted.

"You don't know what you're saying."

"Don't dismiss me because you think I'm doing it out of pity." As Ezra watched, Kochran went down to the floor. He looked at the man lowered before him on one knee. Not absolute surrender, but enough to show Ezra that the offer wasn't empty or void of meaning, some hollow gesture born out of pity or contempt. "You inspire a lot of things inside my head, Ezra…pity isn't one of them."

"You ever gone this way before? Been with another man?"

Kochran remained silent, his gaze steady. The fact

he was attempting to be something he wasn't made Ezra's blood boil.

"That's what I thought. Don't tempt me with pretty words or offers unless you intend to follow through."

"There is something clawing away inside you, Ezra. Fighting to be free, but you keep denying it. Why?"

A cold sweat erupted over his body. He was worn out and frustrated, both mentally and physically. Most of all, he was tired of Kochran trying to placate him in an effort to play guardian.

"I have to." Ezra bit off each of the words through clenched teeth.

Kochran's gaze narrowed. "Says every other martyr in the world. Get the fuck over yourself and stop pretending you're the only man to ever lose someone he loves."

Ezra was a blur of motion, yanking Kochran to stand and pushing him against the refrigerator so hard Kochran grunted as he made contact with the steel. "You ever taken it up the ass before, Kochran? Know what it feels like to walk around the next day with some other guy's come inside you?"

"Yeah, I do."

Time stopped. Ezra's heart froze, pain blooming as the words sank in. His lungs ceased to work, that suffocating sensation choking him. When time restarted, slamming into him with the force of a concussive shockwave, his blood buzzed in his veins, as though he'd walked through a swarm of hornets.

He broke his strong hold, widening his eyes as everything inside him went still. "What?"

"Surprised to find out I'm not the Big Bad King Dom everything thinks?" Kochran averted his gaze for a split second, but long enough for Ezra to know the admission had come with a price. This wasn't the kind of information Kochran Duke gave up easily. "Back before I really got a handle on BDSM, in my early twenties, I banged everything with tits and a pussy until I forgot who I was. Somehow I could pretend I didn't come from an affluent family who wanted me to make something of myself when all I wanted to do was beat my drums.

"One night, I wandered into a less than reputable club in downtown San Francisco and it blew everything I knew about sex out of the water. These people lived at full throttle. Questionable consent. Lack of protection. Hard drugs. Edge and blood play like you've never imagined. And I wanted all of it. They welcomed me with open arms. Didn't judge me for my desires and fucked up needs. I sank so deep and fast, I didn't know who I was anymore."

"You found what you were looking for."

"Whatever the latest thrill was, I wanted it. And then I met him." Kochran shifted against the fridge, using it for support as he slid down to crouch. He considered Ezra for a moment, his chest moving rapidly, as though he was trying to catch his breath, find a balance between the here and now and the past that had carved him into the man he'd become. "He was… everything. This force I was drawn to. I fell and, ah, God, did I fall hard."

"Literally and figuratively, huh?"

Kochran smirked. "Miles was like nothing I'd ever seen. He was charming and charismatic. Chiseled face, sensual lips and lean, strong physique. God, he had a fucking beautiful body. That trademark tall, dark and handsome. Eyes that cut right through everything you were trying to hide from the world. He was everything I thought I could never be. Men and women flocked to him. Begged him for the honor of being in his presence. To exist in his space for just a moment in time so they could experience his greatness. They offered themselves freely with total disregard for anything else. Their only pleasure was to—"

"Serve him," Ezra finished as he wondered what it had been like to be there. To have seen people work so hard for attention. Then a sense of dread, sinister and consuming, washed over him. "What happened, Kochran?"

Kochran stared off into the dark for a long time before finally answering. "Something about me caught his attention. I don't know what it was and he never explained. To be honest, I never asked. I accepted it without reservation because I needed so much for it to be real. I became his."

"You were his sub."

"His slave," Kochran corrected as he met Ezra's gaze. "Complete and total power exchange. Unlike anything I'd ever seen or experienced, even now. It was the height of exhilaration that I'd been searching for. The drug I needed to mainline. I walked around with his collar around my throat and a huge attitude to match because I belonged to the baddest, meanest Master in the state. He owned me, through and through. If he didn't leave bruises when he fucked me, I subdropped hard. Stayed that way for weeks. I needed his marks to feel alive. To feel that someone loved me. Cared for me. Then one day, he was gone." Kochran snapped his fingers. "Vanished without a trace."

"You loved him." The weight of Kochran's silence stabbed at him.

When Kochran finally spoke again, his voice had dropped several octaves. "I convinced myself that I couldn't have the happily ever after because I would never find anyone who made me feel that way again." He paused, taking a deep breath. The sad, low sound of his voice knocked Ezra right between the eyes. "It took a long time before I was even marginally human again. Tory helped me a lot, taught me to deal with something that was out of my control. Once I dug myself out that hole, I swore I would never show anyone that vulnerability again. I learned how to give the audience what they wanted while keeping that piece of me locked away. Until now. It wasn't until we got to know one another better that I recognized you had what I didn't know I was still searching for."

The confession, even though spoken in low tones, hit Ezra right in the center of his chest. He hadn't been expecting it and sank to the ground, his leg muscles giving out. It was too many bits of information to process at once. It never occurred to him to think Kochran was broken. The man had seemed so limitless before. Ezra, and the majority of the Noble House membership, believed in everything the lifestyle had to offer and reveled in that fact. This bit of information made Kochran more like a man. A human being with wants and desires. The King of Noble House wasn't as hardcore as he'd led everyone to believe.

Of course, he could be lying too. Ezra had watched Kochran show his manipulative side more than once. He'd even admired the man for it. The mind fuck could play an integral part of a power exchange between consenting adults.

A gnawing started in Ezra's gut, chewing away at sensations he'd been struggling to bury ever since his marriage had ended. Strength regained in his legs, Ezra stood. He had to fight the urge to pound the steel above Kochran's head until it bore the impression of his fists. He wanted to destroy the past few moments, forget everything Kochran had confessed, and rip time to shreds so it matched the scraps of emotion inside him. He ached for what Kochran had said, for the pain the man had gone through that made him who he was today. Yet he wanted nothing more than to show Kochran he could be all those things he'd buried and more.

The pull between the two sides was too much to bear. Ezra spun on his heel, leaving the room to head for the entrance. Another few seconds, and they would become a tangled mess of arms and legs and dicks. He heard the whisper of sound as Kochran stood, the vibration of wood flooring as he followed.

Let him. He wasn't going to change Ezra's mind no matter how tempting the offer was. How damn tantalizing a sight Kochran had made on bended knee, the subservient side of the owner of the most prestigious club on the West Coast. Most people would have killed for the opportunity Ezra was throwing away.

"I'm broken, Kochran. On the inside and on the outside." Ezra let out a breath as he touched an assortment of items arranged in a neat line on a table near the staircase. A slender notebook, worn and folded at the edge from obvious use. A creased newspaper. Cell phone. Wallet. Watch. The method of arrangement made Ezra smile despite himself. Everything carefully lined up in a neat little row, just like the club Kochran watched over. The club he loved so dearly. It all made sense now. Kochran required control over everything in his life. Except Ezra stripped that need away and left the truth of a man who was struggling with his need to serve again.

Ezra knew that struggle all too well.

"You think you're the only one who has problems?" Kochran came to stand behind him. "Who feels as though the world is out to get them?"

Ezra knew it was a ridiculous notion, but he'd once lived his life to the fullest, and all he'd gotten was a lot of heartache. "I'm not a safe bet." He didn't want this hunger so deep his soul ached.

Kochran pushed Ezra against the wall. "Stop trying to make excuses and do it, damn you. Take me as your slave, even for just one night. I won't walk out on you or leave you to clean up the shitfest when something falls apart. Use me, damn it." Ezra's pulse jackhammered as he listened to Kochran confess, "This isn't easy for me, Ezra. I'm terrified of what I stand to lose with this choice. But I can't *not* want to throw myself at your feet."

"How long?" Ezra's voice cracked. He cleared his throat and tried again. "How long have you wanted to?"

"Since the first day I met you," Kochran admitted, his normal confident demeanor evaporating to leave a man weighed with emotion. "Saint told me he'd hired a guy to help with the new website. I didn't care who it was, just that it got done. I wasn't prepared for you when we met. Didn't know how to deal with the shit you churned up in my head. I chalked it up to the fact I was overworked, overtired. Pining for the past I refused to acknowledge out loud. I buried that shit down deep because I couldn't lose everything I'd worked so hard for. Knew you were hurting from something you didn't want to talk about either. We were both too damn broken to try to fix one another."

The truth was a forceful blow to Ezra's chest. "But now with Maddy…"

Kochran nodded. "She's this beautifully gorgeous creature who brings out what we're hiding from. You both challenge me with your fucking strength. Your glorious and irresistible strength that has the power to break me. To make me do…things."

Ezra whispered harshly, "What kind of things?"

"Anything. Everything." Kochran pinned Ezra with his gaze. "I don't fucking care."

Ezra recognized the enormous struggle tearing away at him. The temptation to free him from that conflict was too much to bear.

Ezra growled long and low before slanting his mouth against Kochran's. An explosion of heat and desire rioted through his already haywire system as their lips met. It had been too long since Ezra had filled a man. Too long since he'd had the rasp of stubble against his chin. Too long since another pair of wide, strong hands grappled with his to tear away clothing. They were both stripped bare in a matter of seconds, clothes in a pile at their feet.

When they finally broke apart to come up for air, Ezra looked down and peered at Kochran's undeniable erection. "That's, um…"

Kochran smirked. "What? Was I supposed to yawn and settle down with a beer and popcorn in front of a movie after a kiss like that? I meant what I said." His eyes narrowed to thin slits. "One favor before things get too out of control." He tapped the small device Ezra had secured to his waist with surgical tape. "This stays on. I... I don't want to have to worry about you."

"All right." Ezra leaned forward, brushing his mouth against Kochran's. "You're fearless, you know."

"Then explain why I feel like the fucking coward. Why I masturbated like a madman when you finger-fucked Maddy in the server room."

The memory of that night flashed behind Ezra's eyes. "I would have liked to have seen that."

"Came like I was Old Faithful," Kochran choked out. "The night you took her in the Cloud? I had to lock myself in the Keep. Again after the mock dungeon room. And just hearing you two in the cloak room? Jesus. Most damn action the Keep has seen in months. Since you two came into the picture, I think I've jerked off more times than when I was thirteen and figured out what this fucking thing was good for."

"Oh yeah?" Ezra reached out, touched the pad of his finger to the tip of Kochran's cock, glistening with a pearl of precome.

Kochran hissed. "Doing that isn't going to make it any less hard."

Kochran's unbridled masculinity could prove dangerous for Ezra. "You ever take care of this when it wasn't after a scene? Just a late night with nothing better to do?"

Kochran's eyes fluttered closed for a few seconds as Ezra explored. "Yeah." The single word came out as a throaty whisper that circled the base of Ezra's cock. "There's one that's been on repeat for a few weeks. A dirty cuckold fantasy where you chained me up so I was forced to watch you fuck Maddy." He shook his head. "Came so fucking hard and fast, I think my eyeballs were going to explode out of my head."

"So you wouldn't have a problem if I tied you up, put marks on you that no one in the lifestyle will mistake for anything but territory claiming, then leave your bed and go to Maddy?" Kochran's dick jerked in Ezra's palm. "That's exactly what you want, isn't it? You want me to take you every way I can and then fuck her."

"I want to watch you," Kochran confessed. "Share you. Dominate her. Care for you both." His throat worked as he swallowed. "I don't know how or why, but she's an integral part of this piece of me, just like you are. Miles taught me a lot of things that I dismissed as fluff, a Master mind-fucking his slave to get what he wanted, but he was right about one thing. Submitting to you like I want doesn't change the fact I still want to be her Dom, just like I want you to keep being her Dom too."

These facets Ezra had no idea existed in Kochran would be fascinating under normal circumstances, but under these extraordinary ones? He was absolute fucking perfection. So much so, Ezra knew he couldn't walk away, knew that what happened in the next few hours would either catapult their tenuous relationship into the stratosphere or drive them so far underground, they would have a dance contest with the devil. Kochran may have thought he was a jumbled mess of thoughts, but for the first time in a long time, Ezra saw clarity.

"One thing at a time, all right?" Ezra kissed Kochran low and slow, exploring the other man's mouth. Some part of him was screaming he needed to leave. The other part wanted to tear off the bindings he'd been restraining himself with and enjoy. Like Kochran, he'd kept pieces of himself buried because he couldn't bear to face the reality. It never occurred to him that he'd want to uncover it again. That he'd ever find someone who would want it too.

"Why?" Ezra licked his lips. "Why do you want to submit to me? I'm nothing special. Hundreds of other Masters at the club. Ones you could have sign confidentiality agreements if you're worried about privacy."

"I could fuck my way through the membership roster, but you and Maddy are the only ones I really want. Fact of the matter is, I'm aggressive. I'm a sadist. I know that. I get off on those things and won't apologize for them. One thing I have learned is that Dominant doesn't mean invulnerable. As a slave, I'm the other extreme, docile and a masochist to the core. Things I didn't realize I needed again until you came along. I'm a head doc's wet dream with how screwed up things are inside my brain. But you know just like I do that sometimes you've just got to let it all go."

"Yeah, I do." Ezra moved in again, slowly stroking along the length of Kochran's swollen shaft. Kochran's rumbling growl drove straight through Ezra and hardened his own cock. "I also know sometimes you've got to push someone past boundaries in order to allow them to be truly free."

Ezra held Kochran's gaze for a long time, giving him time to back down, escape, anything to turn tail and run as he stammered excuses why he'd made a mistake. Except Ezra knew Kochran didn't make mistakes.

He tightened his grip, increasing the force until Kochran finally winced. "I do something you don't like, I better hear *red*. Understood?"

He recalled what Kochran had said about getting off on the pain, so he released his hold and set his hands on the wall to frame Kochran's head. If he was as much of a masochist as he claimed, absence of pain was the worst hell.

"We'll talk about limits and work out some things later. A temporary verbal agreement is enough until I see how you react to being mine." Kochran shuddered again, a sign Ezra had made the right choice. "Right now, we're going to keep things simple. Nothing edgy. No heavy pain play either. And you're going to answer me, pet, or I will put your dick in a vise and twist."

The corners of Kochran's mouth lifted for a split second before his face was a mask once again. "Yes."

Ezra lifted one of his eyebrows, inquiring with a stern glare. Kochran had to be the one who took a step through the door Ezra had opened. "Yes, *Master.*"

"You're going to be saying that a lot tonight."

Chapter Twenty-Five

Kochran breathed slow and deep as he shifted his weight between his foot and the knee he was balanced on. He'd followed Ezra like an anxious puppy dog. Went down on one knee as he waited for further instruction. It thrilled him that there was no shame in the action. Slipping into the correct mindset was far easier than he'd imagined, though he didn't expect it would always be the case. He'd been a Dominant for so long, spent so many years pretending that Miles had never come into his life, he was hyperaware of failing. Yet, with Ezra, he'd wanted to tear off that mask and expose everything.

Pet.

The sound of that word had been the calm for the tempest that had been raging inside Kochran. He tried to use the sound of water falling as his focus, pulling on techniques his yoga instructor had spent hours hammering into his head. The fact the man he'd agreed to submit to stood just a few feet away in the shower complicated matters. Ezra's nude body was outlined in the fogged glass, providing a tempting view of something he wasn't allowed to have.

It may have been years since he'd been a slave to a

Master, but he knew and accepted the mindset. He recognized what it took. Understood sacrifice was necessary in order to surrender complete control. He yearned for Ezra like no one he'd ever wanted before. Even more than Miles, though Kochran didn't understand how that was possible.

The shower turned off and Kochran lifted his head. Streaks of water slithered down the glass walls, creating teasing glimpses of the man beyond, who didn't appear to be in a rush to exit. In fact, he stood facing Kochran, his arm the only movement.

The partition separating them opened. Ezra stood there, unashamed and unabashedly stroking himself, as though Kochran wasn't kneeling feet away. When their gazes collided, Kochran realized he was the reason Ezra was jacking off. He was using the image of Kochran kneeling to give himself pleasure. Kochran lowered his head, sliding his gaze to the tiles under Ezra's feet.

A soft sigh echoed through the space between them. "You know that position only enhances your erection even more."

A surge clenched his chest. "Not trying to hide it."

"I know. It's your way of surrendering some of your control, but not all of it. That's perfectly acceptable to me. It means I'm going to have to work for your true surrender." Ezra moved toward him. The slick sounds of his hand moving over his shaft sounded so close. So tempting. Kochran wanted to see what sort of inviting package Ezra had delivered, but he needed to wait for direction. "Look at me, pet."

A shudder filtered through Kochran as he lifted his gaze. Like Ezra, he took his time, enjoying the lines and angles of Ezra's physique. His gaze lingered on the hand still moving lazily, long enough to appreciate the way Ezra moved.

"Eyes up," Ezra ordered brusquely.

Kochran hadn't realized he'd been admiring Ezra's junk for that long. So long his mouth had started to water. Maybe full surrender would be harder than he thought.

"Open up." Ezra scooted forward, hand still wrapped around the base of his erection as he angled it toward Kochran's mouth. He was being tested. Accepting Ezra's dick in his mouth would be the ultimate gauge of his commitment.

Kochran kept his gaze on Ezra's as he offered his tongue and open mouth. Ezra closed his eyes for a split second when Kochran's tongue connected with the underside of his cockhead. He rested it there, in no obvious hurry to continue pushing into Kochran's mouth.

"Beautiful," Ezra whispered as he feathered Kochran's hair. "Thank you for this. For reminding me of everything I was keeping buried."

Kochran couldn't speak, knew he didn't need to. Ezra didn't need the words. Kochran simply needed to exist.

Ezra slid forward into Kochran's mouth with a groan. It was like a key had been inserted into a lock, and everything inside Kochran that he'd kept restrained fell away.

Warmth surrounded him like a comforting cocoon. Ezra had been inside another man's mouth before, but this was altogether different. Pieces he had kept walled off began to crumble. And as they stood in the ruins, he began to move, sliding in and out with the same slow, precise movements he'd used with his hand. He wasn't in the mood to rush this part. There would be time enough for that later. He intended to fully experience everything he knew Kochran had to offer.

He'd watched Kochran more than enough times to know exactly how much and how far he could push the man. He angled his grip to curl his fingers around the back of Kochran's head. The rumbling vibration surged through his oversensitive dick and up his spine. He pulled Kochran down, slow and steady, reveling in the feel of Kochran's lips sliding against his shaft. The man before him took everything Ezra had to offer and unapologetically waited for more.

"So fucking good. It's a wonder you don't give more blowjobs."

The answering snort shot a line of arousal up through the root of his cock and awakened dormant nerve-endings. He dropped his head back and basked in the feel of being surrounded by Kochran's mouth. Ezra quickened the pace for a few strokes, then pulled out with a quiet pop. He crouched, bringing himself to eye level with Kochran.

"I'm going to make you hurt, pet. Maybe even make you cry a little." Gazes locked together, Ezra touched his lips to Kochran's. They kissed slowly for a time, tongues tangling, gently massaging one another. In a flash, the moment shifted and the atmosphere became charged. Feral. Raw. Sexual.

Ezra had initially thought they could just bang it out of their systems, but there would be no recovery from this. They were going to come out of this irrevocably changed. They fulfilled a yearning that had no definition.

* * *

Kochran was grateful for the short reprieve Ezra had given him as he was led back into the main area and away from the humidity that had settled against their skin in the bathroom. But that gratitude faded quickly as Ezra made him kneel again. Like before, Kochran balanced on one knee, not in defiance, but stripping away every last vestige of his dominant personality in the span of an hour was impossible.

"You're getting stuck inside your head again, and not in a good way. You've got to let it go." Ezra ordered.

Kochran snorted softly. "If you're going to put on a blonde wig and start singing, we've got a problem."

Ezra narrowed his gaze. Shame heated Kochran's blood. Ezra was attempting to give him something to focus on and Kochran was trying to add levity to a moment where it wasn't warranted. His body began to tremble from anxiety and arousal. Surely something was wrong with him to want to experience the full wrath of Ezra's punishment. That stern, unforgiving glare aimed toward him and all Kochran could think was *yes, please.*

He fisted his hands, wondering if this was who he really was. Had he spent all those years dominating submissives, strutting around like he was a hot-shit Dom, when all along, at the core, he was truly a submissive? Try as he might, he couldn't uncover a reason why he desired a hard hand from Ezra. Why he needed such strict discipline from another person— *another man*—when he was usually the one dishing out the pain.

Was he that fucked up?

"You're disobeying me by analyzing shit again."

Ezra's normally calm voice came across as stern and implacable. He stood, circling to stand behind Kochran. A lash of bright pain streaked across Kochran's back. Holy Mother of God, what was Ezra using on him and where had he gotten it?

The jolt of heat stung him again, this time just to the right of the original impact. Another. Then another. A knife-edge that cut deeply and erased the doubts plaguing Kochran. The pain released a wealth of emotion as well. Feelings he hadn't realized he'd kept restrained. Kochran had no defense against the agony whizzing through him, so he simply accepted the ripple of response his body gave. A coil of something Kochran couldn't identify collected low in his belly as Ezra stroked him all over with gentle hands, the sensual feathering sensation a marked contrast to the brutality of the lashes.

A whistle pierced the air a split second before pain erupted against Kochran's back. He arched, not away from the hurt, but toward. This wasn't pain for pain's sake, but intended to deliver pleasure. Ezra knew how to balance on that fine line as he moved around, selecting different areas, never striking the same place twice, which only increased the intensity. Each blow chipped Kochran's dominant streak one hit at a time. Every nerve ending reached for Ezra, yet Kochran had a moment to wish the wall in front of him was mirrored so he could watch Ezra work. Another strike clouded his mind once again, stripping another layer away. Down and down he went, tumbling down the rabbit hole as though he'd imbibed the sweetest potion.

Kochran was so lost in his own head, he registered Ezra standing on his left side well after the man had approached. Ezra splayed his hand against Kochran's lower back so he noted the dichotomy between Ezra's flesh and the instrument he'd used to create the delicious burn spreading over his shoulders and back. When Ezra used his other hand to follow the curve of Kochran's ass, Kochran snarled with a possessive hunger. He'd heard plenty of submissives make that noise, and even been responsible for it, but somehow, it was altogether different coming at this moment.

"I'm going to fuck you now, sweet pet. And you're going to take every finger I shove into you."

Kochran growled, low and long, as Ezra slid three slickened fingers past the resistance. He held them there for a lengthy moment, allowing Kochran to adjust to the sensation of being as full as he'd ever been. When Ezra began to finally, finally move his fingers, the slow and steady movement made Kochran rock against his touch. Jesus, his cock was so fucking hard, Kochran was convinced he'd erupt like a volcano if Ezra commanded him to.

Then Ezra's touch vanished.

Son of a bitch. Kochran bit back the whimper of need clawing at his throat. Ezra touched his chin, gently nudging him upright, guiding Kochran into that single knee position. Kochran swayed slightly, but checked his balance.

"Eyes up. No looking unless I tell you otherwise. No coming unless I say otherwise either."

Kochran hadn't seen a goddamn thing yet, but he obeyed Ezra's command and focused on a point high overhead. His thoughts fractured when Ezra's mouth closed over his cock, and took him deep.

The marks on his back and shoulders burned hot as

desire raced through his system. Warm breath skated over his abdomen as Ezra swallowed more. When Ezra drew back, flicking his tongue against the tip of Kochran's cock, he couldn't contain his strangled gasp. He had nothing to hold on to, nothing to use as an anchor point as Ezra opened and swallowed him again.

"I can't..." Kochran trailed off as Ezra played with the underside of Kochran's shaft. Kochran growled deeply, fighting his body's reaction to spurt down Ezra's throat. Ezra simply took him deeper, ignoring him as he moved to create a slow friction up and down Kochran's entire length.

Ezra's mouth was both heaven and hell, a rapturous torment that held Kochran suspended between the two worlds. That torture was interrupted when something brushed against his rim. Ezra explored with his fingers again even as he continued to work his mouth over Kochran's shaft. Kochran grunted as Ezra slipped two fingers through his entrance, adding a knife of pleasure that flourished with each teasing stroke.

Unable to bear the tension any longer, Kochran rocked back and forth between Ezra's mouth and fingers. Ezra adjusted for the movements as they grew jerky, holding still to allow Kochran to move. Ezra's groan vibrated against Kochran's dick, and he couldn't hold back any longer. He made a strangled sound, unable to form the words needed to warn Ezra he was about to blow. Ezra took him deeper as he dug his hand into Kochran's hip. The bite of pain was the trigger Kochran needed.

Kochran cried out as he came and Ezra took the release, swallowing over and over as Kochran continued to jet down his throat. Kochran was still shuddering as Ezra pulled his mouth away.

It took a few moments for him to realize Ezra hadn't removed his fingers. They were still buried deep inside him, toying with the muscles constricting his fingers. Ezra thrust against the tightening, working to loosen those muscles again. The orgasm hadn't fully abated before the tingles indicative of another release started at the base of Kochran's dick. He thought he'd finished his climax, but the sensations Ezra raised signaled to Kochran he had a very long night ahead of him.

He blew out a breath, shuddering as Ezra worked another finger into his anus. Three fingers again, the burn and stretch making Kochran smile. Kochran had never been this open, this trusting of someone. He understood the submissive mentality now better than ever before. The full, absolute sense of belonging to another person. Knowing they had your best interests in mind. Knowing you were pleasing them.

"Quite satisfied with yourself, aren't you?"

"Mmm." Kochran couldn't form coherent thought necessary to arrange a response. All he could do was experience the sensations.

"You could take more, you know," Ezra said against his ear. "Little more lube, lots of patience, maybe another orgasm, and I bet I can slip my fist right into your greedy asshole."

The universe ceased to exist for Kochran as Ezra ruthlessly worked his fingers in and out. He pressed his lips to Kochran's throat, licking the perspiration that had collected in the hollow. He kissed Kochran's jaw. The point of his chin. "I could have you jetting come all over your nice expensive floors. Make you lick up every single drop like a good boy toy."

Kochran vibrated with unspent energy, overwhelmed by desire and need. He wanted to beg Ezra to use him as he saw fit, but he didn't know how because the moment they were sharing was too powerful.

"But not now. I want my cock to be the only thing that fills you tonight."

Ezra brought a washcloth and a bowl full of hot, soapy water when he returned. Kochran hadn't moved, though he had shifted position so he sat to one side, his legs bent and angled away from him. Ezra said nothing as he washed down Kochran's body, then his own. Refreshed, he offered Kochran a hand and tugged him up so they were standing facing one another.

Kochran's eyes were still glassy, a sight that caused a stirring deep in Ezra's belly. Watching Kochran's first release under his guidance had been nothing short of spectacular. He'd meant what he'd said about giving Kochran the kind of climax that would have him screaming and writhing and coming everywhere. He intended to do just that at some point. If he was going to expose Kochran to all the pieces of his soul, Ezra had many more doors to unlock. The pain had only been a small part of the process, but it told Ezra quite a lot. Kochran needed it in order to push through all the misgivings clouding his head. Past the weight of the years he'd spent convincing himself he didn't really want certain things. Others would be afraid they'd damage Kochran, or worse, they wouldn't be able to fulfill the man's need in the first place.

Ezra coaxed Kochran's lips open with his tongue,

seducing the other man with nothing more than a kiss. When Ezra increased the pressure, Kochran responded with a quiet moan and cupped his hand around the back of Ezra's head. Ezra added to the noise as Kochran slid his fingers through the strands, stroking the length of it.

He broke away, nudging Kochran toward the bed. He waited until Kochran had climbed in, then followed, positioning himself so they were groin to groin. Ezra had intended to take Kochran hard and fast, but something had shifted in the last few minutes.

A force clenched around Ezra's heart, thrumming with an emotion he wasn't equipped to deal with. The raw honesty Kochran gifted to Ezra meant there was much, much more than a Master/slave dynamic wrapping around them. The world narrowed until they were the only things that existed. The power of the moment was exactly what Ezra needed and exactly the thing he knew could someday destroy him.

Ezra elbowed Kochran to turn over. He did, moving with an easy fluidity as he maneuvered his ass in the perfect position to be taken. Offering without command. Ezra couldn't resist such a spectacular presentation.

He grabbed a condom from the nightstand, slipped it on and spread Kochran's ass cheeks. Kochran was still slick from Ezra's fingers, allowing Ezra to enter Kochran's ass in one solid stroke. Ezra began pumping immediately, denying Kochran the time he may have needed to adjust to being taken this way. Ezra pushed through the resistance, slamming the solid length of his dick into Kochran's body over and over.

"Come, pet."

Watching Kochran come was a beautiful display of

unbridled surrender. The growl he gave so deep, it vibrated the bed with its vicious power. Ezra came to the noise, pumping so damn hard he was sure they were going to end up on the floor.

Ezra's chest burned for oxygen as he fought to breathe. He held on to Kochran, using him as an anchor point while everything around them spun. Or maybe he needed to ensure that Kochran wasn't going to hop out of the bed and run.

They lay there for long minutes, their breathing and heart rates returning to normal.

Kochran cleared his throat, splitting the quiet. "This is going to get really complicated, isn't it?"

Ezra pressed a kiss to Kochran's shoulder. "It's whatever we make it."

Chapter Twenty-Six

Early mornings weren't Ezra's favorite part of the day. Waking before nine meant breakfast meetings. Traffic snarls. Subway rides. Things that had never fit him quite right. He'd never been one to box himself into a cubicle, logging in hours at an office job and answering to a stuffy boss wearing an even stuffier suit. Kochran wasn't that type either, so Ezra was surprised to find himself alone in bed.

It hadn't been a restful night. He'd surfaced several times, worried the entire experience had been a dream because he hadn't paid attention to his pump again. But, without fail, Kochran had been there each time Ezra stirred. During one of those moments, he'd found Kochran's head on his shoulder, his arm draped over Ezra's waist, as though he intended to pin him to the bed to prevent his escape.

Leaving had been the last thing on Ezra's mind. He thought he'd understood the full extent of what had taken place between them, but that simple, intimate gesture spoke volumes.

As expected, Kochran had been a demanding submissive, giving as much as he received. An active participant in the scene despite clear evidence who had all the power in the exchange. Ezra hadn't worked that hard to take a sub over since the last time he'd been with Nora and Kyle. He'd forgotten how addicting that sort of challenge could be.

He sat up, swinging his feet over the side. When he encountered soft carpet that tickled the soles of his feet, and spotted the white tee bundled near the nightstand, he grinned. He couldn't remember the last time he'd woken up being this…content. Whole. Muscles and joints achy because he'd spent a few hours attending to the needs of an eager submissive who had finally discovered what it was like to be their true selves. He'd forgotten how gratifying that sensation felt.

Kochran had been sinfully decadent before. With this new world Ezra had opened, Kochran was irresistible.

Ezra started to grab his kit, but tapped the face of his cell phone instead. A text message around midnight from Maddy asking if he'd gotten home all right. She was another interesting counterpoint to his need for domination, his craving to experience all that life had to offer again.

Struck with sudden inspiration, he responded, that stupid, shit-eating grin of his growing wider as he typed a message that could ruin the rest of the day or become the filler of a few lingering empty spaces in the people he'd come to care about.

Plan set in motion, he unzipped his kit and set to work. A few efficient steps told him his blood sugar was normal. A good sign after sleeping without his pump. Even though Kochran had requested it stay on, as things had gotten more heated, Ezra hadn't wanted it to get in the way. Hadn't wanted anything between them. He recapped the needle and set it in his kit to dispose of later.

Medical duties taken care of, the addicting aroma of coffee drew him to the kitchen. The space was empty, though there was still a cup's worth of hot coffee in the pot, a sign Kochran had been up for a while. Strange. Considering Kochran's late nights at Noble House, Ezra had never taken him for an early riser. Remembering Kochran's lack of skill when it came to brewing coffee, he dumped the remaining liquid into the sink.

He made a new pot, filling two mugs as his stomach growled softly. Breakfast would have to wait until he found out where Kochran had escaped to. One good thing about the open floor plan was the ability to see the entire space in just a few seconds. The disadvantage was that Ezra was noticeably alone.

As he neared the staircase that led outside, he saw the worn notebook was no longer there. Wallet, keys and watch were still lined up in their perfect row, which meant Kochran couldn't have gone far.

A burst of muffled thuds sounded overhead, providing a clue as to his location. Ezra carefully ascended the narrow staircase, balancing the two mugs, and stepped out into the mid-morning light. The rhythmic cadence continued to sound over his shoulder, and he turned. Kochran had set up his drum kit under a rectangular portico that kept the instrument protected from the elements. He wasn't sure how he'd missed it before because this wasn't something Kochran could have set up by himself in a short period of time.

Ezra approached quietly. Kochran had always been an interesting study to watch as he lost himself in the ebb and flow of the melody. Though hundreds of members at Noble House and music lovers at random bars watched Kochran perform on a weekly basis, Ezra knew he was one of the precious few who'd been granted the privilege of seeing Kochran in his unvarnished glory. He realized how truly prized this moment was and he refused to disturb the man no matter how much he wanted to. No telling how long before Kochran realized he was being watched, so Ezra stood there, quietly sipping his coffee.

He was just finishing when the resonance of the last beat made the fine hairs on Ezra's forearms lift. Kochran stuck the drumstick between his teeth and growled softly as he pulled a skinny, well-chewed pencil from its perch behind his ear and wrote something in that tattered notebook. The reason for the wear and tear on the book was obvious now—Kochran kept his music scribbles there. A way to trap the muse who took hold when the creative juices flowed.

God, Ezra felt like a teenager hoping to be acknowledged by his idol.

Kochran's gaze lifted, landing on him. A long moment passed before he asked, "Do you always walk around naked?"

Ezra stepped closer to the kit and leaned forward, noting Kochran only wore a pair of underwear. "You do all your gigs like that and I'm pretty sure your audience will increase exponentially."

"I've got a show tonight and I didn't want to disturb you." Kochran's eyes darkened as his gaze raked over Ezra's form and focused on his abdomen. "You're not wearing your pump."

"I'd commend your powers of observation, but I'm

too busy thinking about how much i want to fuck you again."

Kochran rose. Ezra searched his face for a glimpse of pain or regret in the smudge of dark circles under those captivating eyes. A specter of anger that would lead to Kochran demanding Ezra leave. But as much as he searched, he only found the need to be unraveled again—over and over. Ezra was perilously close to doing just that.

"I didn't tell you to move."

Kochran closed his eyes and blew out a breath as he sat again.

"Ass sore?" Kochran remained quiet, though he cut his gaze to Ezra. "Interesting problem, isn't it? Say yes and you'll show weakness. Say no and you run the risk that I'll spend the rest of the day making sure you weep every time you shift on the stool at your gig tonight." Kochran swore, which just made Ezra grin wider. "I may be a devious fucker, but I think we discovered how much you like my sadistic side a few hours ago. Or were you just begging me to fuck you harder so you could hear yourself?"

A dark thrill streaked through Ezra at the thought of fulfilling that threat, taking Kochran's ass so brutally he was uncomfortable the entire night. Doing so made Ezra feel profoundly good in a way that he couldn't put words to.

Kochran set his drumsticks across his knees and blew out a breath. "I wasn't sure I'd ever meet anyone who matched my level of mercilessness."

"Oh you have no idea just how ruthless I can be, pet."

Kochran opened his mouth to respond, but snapped

it shut with the sound of an approaching car. "What did you do?"

"Making sure your dreams come true." Ezra stepped around the drum kit to cradle Kochran's jaw. Eyes open, he pressed his mouth gently to Kochran's, enjoying the way his irises expanded. The staccato nature of his breath. Despite his surprise, he opened to Ezra, urgently accepting Ezra's tongue into his mouth. When he angled closer, Ezra muttered a few curses as hot coffee spilled over his hand. He dropped the now-empty mugs to the ground, their contact with the unforgiving surface muted against the roaring in his brain.

He cupped the back of Kochran's head, delving deep with his tongue, exploring and conquering with unspent passion. He was so fucking hungry for this man. Desperation was a heady drug that he wanted to mainline over and over.

Severing the kiss, he pressed his lips to Kochran's forehead, struggling to bank the fire roaring through his blood. Taking Kochran right there wouldn't be a problem, but he'd already set plans into motion he intended to carry out. "Unless you have a problem with the fact I invited the woman we're both fucking?"

Maddy almost drove off the side of the dirt road when Ezra leaned over and passionately kissed Kochran. Her hands were still shaking as she pulled next to Ezra's car and killed the engine, watching as the two men lost themselves as though they were the only people on the planet. Her cunt softened, heated and slicked at how unrestrained they were with one another. There was a sexy beautifulness about the way they moved together.

A depth of emotion and surety that they knew exactly what they were doing.

She'd dreamed of them, individually and together. Sexually and non-sexually. Lived up to that pervy stalker webgirl nickname she'd branded herself with over a month ago. But, oh, seeing them like this was so much better.

When she'd read Ezra's text, the weight of unspoken command had been evident. *Come to Kochran's house when you've had enough beauty sleep.* She certainly hadn't expected to see this when she'd arrived.

As Ezra stepped from around the drum kit, Maddy inhaled sharply. Ezra was completely nude, his cock rigid as it arced away from his body. No way to mistake the intent there. Arousal flooded the space between her thighs, dampening the crotch of the cut-off sweats she'd hastily thrown on, thanks to the fact she'd neglected to put on underwear. As Ezra drew closer, her nipples went tight against the soft cotton of her shirt. No bra either.

The need to offer herself to him, to find out what he intended, propelled her out of the driver's seat. As the door shut behind her, she fingered the hem of her shirt. She looked to him for some kind of clue, but he gave none. He only continued moving toward her.

Over Ezra's shoulder, she spotted Kochran standing behind his drum kit. He had a bit more modesty, surprisingly enough, and wore a pair of navy blue briefs. The fabric did nothing to cover his aroused state. In fact, the tight stretch enhanced it.

Given their naked states, it wasn't hard to ascertain the line of friendship had been crossed. But by how much? And had it simply been obliterated altogether?

She'd always figured they would eventually share her. A submissive with two Doms. But the King of Noble House had surrendered to Ezra.

The side of Ezra's mouth lifted in a wry smile a split second before he bent and scooped Maddy up into his arms. She squealed, but the sensation of being cradled was comforting. He captured her mouth as he turned and started walking back down the dirt path. She opened for him with a sigh, his musky scent an enticing blend of his and Kochran's tastes. It was too much and not enough at the same time. The questions she had evaporated as he took her over with that mesmerizing way of his. The one she'd grown so accustomed to. Adored.

He came to a stop and dropped her legs. As her feet touched the ground, he waved Kochran closer. After setting his drumsticks on his seat, Kochran maneuvered around the set up. He took Ezra's outstretched hand, winding their fingers together as he came to stand with them.

"You have paint in your hair." Kochran tugged on a few strands. "Just what the hell did you guys do for Grae's bachelorette party?"

The image of a gaggle of women, dressed in ridiculous old bridesmaid and wedding dresses they'd found at a local thrift store, dodging each other on a paintball course, made her smile. It had been just the sort of entertainment she'd needed for a few hours. The wild, feminine laughter as they'd bested one another game after game still rang in her ears.

"Played with balls." Both men blinked, waiting for further information, but she wasn't giving any up.

"Seems like maybe you guys have been playing with a few balls too?"

Ezra threw his head back and laughed. "Indeed we have," he retorted, leaning over to sweep a kiss against her cheek as he traced his fingers against the shell of her ear. "You'll get your turn."

"Sounds good to me." Anything concerning these men sounded ideal to her. She was anxious to hear about what had transpired between them while she'd been kicking ass in the eye-bleeding neon pink bridesmaid's dress she'd procured and then ruined. "So what first?"

"Breakfast." As if on cue, Kochran's stomach growled. "Definitely breakfast."

Ezra slipped an arm around her waist and guided her to the entry staircase. "Only if he doesn't cook."

She gasped in mock horror. "You mean there is something he's not good at?"

Ezra's eyes darkened. "He excels at a number of things. Sadly, feeding people is not one of them. A trip to the hospital is not on the agenda for today."

"What is?"

Kochran's stomach growled again, loud enough for them to hear even with the ten feet between them.

"Let's get some food in the growing boy first."

Chapter Twenty-Seven

The spread Ezra had whipped up made Maddy's mouth water. She folded her legs under her as she munched on a butterscotch chip pancake. "I can't believe I didn't know you cook."

He dismissed his talent with a shrug. "I've always been lucky enough to work from home, or have a flexible boss who let me set my own hours. Meant it was easier for me to have something ready when everyone else got home than to argue about what to eat."

It also meant Ezra had more control over what those around him ate. He could ensure they were eating healthy and within whatever dietary restrictions he had with his diabetes. It was a simple enough strategy she saw right through. She hadn't missed the absence of his pump when she'd seen him nude earlier. When they'd come downstairs, he had scooped up his clothes and ducked into the area partitioned off for the toilet. He'd reappeared wearing only his jeans. Still no pump in sight.

With Kochran in the shower, she decided it was as good a time as any. She reached for another pancake, gesturing toward his side. Though his infusion points weren't obvious, she knew the general area thanks to a flurry of research she'd done during a break in the action at the party last night. "Means you can control your food intake as well. Or rather, monitor your sugar." He glanced her way, but didn't say anything. "What? Think I didn't know? Truthfully, I didn't, until Kochran shared the info with me last night. Are you ashamed?"

"No. I just don't want to cause anyone to needlessly worry about something I have under control." He snagged a strip of extra crispy bacon and nibbled on the corner. "Enough other shit in the world without adding my own health issues into the mix."

She took the bacon from him. "How about from now on you let me decide what I can and can't deal with and I won't steal your bacon?"

"You wound me, woman." He slapped his hand over his heart and pretended to swoon. "Hit a man right where it hurts." He leaned over to press his forehead against hers and softened his voice. "Thank you for looking out for me. It means more than you'll ever know."

So many sensations and emotions washed over her as he looked into her eyes. She'd known she cared about the men, but hadn't realized just how much before this moment. And it wasn't about sex, or the connection the men shared now, but about roots. Permanence. No more drifting through life wondering if she was ever going to truly find her place in the world, if her quirks and habits aligned with someone else's. With Kochran and Ezra, she wasn't just an anonymous hacker with no life goals. They all shared an understanding, an affection that went beyond the club walls and had expanded into something magical and pure. Somehow, in ways she couldn't understand, they each added to what the other shared making them an intrinsic part of each other's lives.

Kochran entered the kitchen area still only wearing his underwear, and grabbed a mug to fill with coffee. He joined them at the table, but didn't eat any of the large selection of food.

She tapped the back of his hand where he was drumming his fingers against the tabletop. "I thought you were hungry."

"I am. But we've got to get some stuff clear first." The Kochran she knew and admired was back, in full control of himself. There were still shades of the man she'd seen earlier, but he was in full-on business mode now.

"Fine." Ezra grabbed a plate, piled it high with a little bit of everything and set it in front of Kochran. "But you can eat and talk at the same time."

Though Kochran scowled at Ezra, he picked up a sausage link and bit off one end. "Happy?"

"Are you?"

A wash of emotions passed through Kochran's eyes. "Yeah. I am."

Unable to stop herself, she twined her fingers with Kochran's. "Don't sound so disappointed in yourself."

"I didn't think I was the settling down type. I wanted to be, but…" Kochran paused, chewing another bite of sausage before continuing. "It's not easy."

"I get it." All the thoughts she'd had about being theirs hadn't been unsubstantiated. It wasn't just because she wanted to feel those things about the men, it was because she truly did. That sort of leap of faith could have shaken her to her core. "We're on this roller coaster ride. Everything is perfect and light and easy, and then the next…"

"Everything is out of control and on the edge," Ezra finished.

Kochran tapped the table with his now empty mug. "If I'm not mistaken, that happens when people fall in love. Certain they have it all figured out one second, convinced they know absolutely nothing the next."

She'd gotten to a place where she wanted to be with them every second of the day. Needed to be with them. It was as though pieces of her were missing when they weren't there. To her, that was the definition of love. Falling for the men had happened when she hadn't been looking. When she'd been busy having fun discovering a new world of possibilities.

"I've always known, I think. Somehow, some piece of me understood. It may be all new to me…" Her heart gave a kick that resonated deep. "But I get it."

"It's not new to me. I've been around it long enough, owned this club for so long, I know when it's more than play for the Dom and sub."

"And I've been in that kind of relationship before," Ezra said quietly.

"Oh, Ezra, I'm not…we're not…" She grabbed for his hand.

He gripped her fingers, reaching out with his other hand to take up Kochran's. "I never thought you were. Either of you. This…our connection is unlike anything I've ever experienced before. Not better or worse—"

"Just different," Kochran finished. "In more than a few ways. You want to take care of her just as much as I do. She needs us as much as we need her. Like it or not, we're all irrevocability intertwined. Even if we decided to walk away now, we wouldn't be the same people we were before Madeline weaseled her way into the club's website."

As she watched the two men share a lingering look, her curiosity finally won. "How did this happen? The two of you. I feel like I've missed a step. Not saying that I mind—I mean, come on, two hot guys going at one another is on my fantasy list—and I'm not leaving before I see that—but…yeah, missing something."

"You haven't missed a thing, sweetheart. I've had my suspicion about him for some time. Never told anyone 'cause how the hell do you explain *that*?" Ezra gestured wildly to Kochran, knocking over the maple syrup bottle.

She ran a few paper towels under the faucet before wiping up the sticky syrup. "No one would have believed you if you'd tried to tell them Kochran is submissive."

"Switch," Kochran said simply.

"What?" She stared at Kochran for a long moment, turning the word over in her mind. Familiar, of course, but certainly not a word she would have ever connected with him.

"Not submissive," Kochran offered. "Capable of moving fluidly between the two roles when the time comes. I'm not giving up what you and I have, baby girl. I still will want to lick you all over after he fucks you hard. Come all over whatever marks he or I leave. Want him to watch me tie you down and force you to come over and over. If that's all right with you."

Her arousal shot to melting point as Kochran listed things, though she wasn't entirely sure how that was possible. "Should I get you a pen and some paper? Hey, wait a second, that reminds me. I never asked why you needed the list anyway. Why did you have me write it out longhand like that? Everything I wanted was on your standard form, except the clowns."

"I didn't need it." Amusement shined in Kochran's eyes.

"Huh?"

He leaned closer, pressing his lips gently against hers. "You did."

The truth stung as though she'd been slapped. She *had* needed the list. The meditative preparation that had come along with the act of crafting each letter, as though her body had been the pen, the ink—her soul. The list had been the thing that had unlocked the door she'd stepped through that had brought her to the place where she was allowed to have the gift of being loved by two men. Submission was an art, and there was something oddly freeing about doing someone's bidding.

"And you?" She gestured to Ezra. "Are you a switch too?"

"Really? You're asking me that while leaving this whole area of clowns undiscussed?" Ezra laughed as he held up his hands. "Sorry to disappoint, but, spoiler alert, I'm dominant all the way."

Maddy turned the knowledge over and over, trying to resolve it on her own. "Hold up. You're telling me… this thing we have between the three of us, sometimes I'll have two Doms and sometimes Ezra will have two submissives?" She paused, looking between them as she waited for a different perspective. "Talk about a mothertruckin' jackpot!"

Kochran leaned closer. "I'll still want to have my

way with you alone, Madeline. I suspect he'll want some alone time with you and his toys as well. With me too. We'll only be limited by our imaginations."

It also sounded like a lot of fun. The type she desperately needed after a lifetime of not living her life to the fullest. Of hiding behind the code she generated on her computer screen. "Just promise me we'll all have each other, regardless."

Ezra clasped his hand around hers. "Always. So… about this matter of clowns. Do I need to go invest in obnoxiously oversized shoes and a red nose in order to fuck you silly?" She giggled as he kissed her knuckles first, then Kochran's. "I think it's time for Maddy to go sit on the recliner and show us that pretty pussy of hers."

Driven by the unfiltered pleasure pressing against her skin, Maddy made a beeline for the chair in the seating area and parted her legs as soon as she sat. The cool rush of air did nothing to dispel the heat collecting between her thighs. As she leaned back, sinking into the cushion of the recliner, she draped her legs over the arms.

She sat in that position as the men stopped about ten feet away. The way they looked at her with unvarnished desire made her want to run away and deny what they all shared. But she wouldn't exchange this kind of intensity for anything in the world. Those thoughts were further cemented when Ezra set his hand on Kochran's shoulder.

"Show Maddy how handsome you are on your knees, pet."

Kochran went, his expression filled with so much naked greed it stole her breath. She was tempted to sit there and watch Ezra and Kochran, but she'd been given a set of instructions she fully intended to follow. Being watched had always turned her on. But being watched like this? They made her feel like the adrenaline rush she'd experienced the one time she'd flung herself out of a perfectly good airplane. That same rush that came from racing toward the Earth at terminal velocity.

"And now you, baby girl, need to show my pet how seeing him like this makes you feel."

Kochran gazed at her as she slipped a hand between her spread thighs. She would have never expected to see such fearless vulnerability from a man like him, but now that she had, she wouldn't be able to imagine him without it. As her fingertip made contact with her clit, he gave a long, trembling moan of pleasure that resonated to her bones.

Ezra shuddered, moving his hand casually against Kochran's thigh as though this kind of scenario was an everyday occurrence for him. His voice dropped to a rasp. "Are you getting hard from watching her, or because I'm touching you?"

"Both."

"What if I told you I plan on giving you that little fantasy you mentioned last night?" He cupped his hand around Kochran's testicles, giving them a good, hard tug so Kochran hissed.

Maddy hadn't thought it possible, but the temperature against her hand grew hotter as she saw the glimmer of lust behind Kochran's unfocused gaze. She thought she'd been on edge before, but now…*mothertrucker*, they were perfection. Her perfection. Hers.

Despite the command she'd been given, she got caught up. Fascinated with the changes in Ezra, how easily he vacillated between Dom and Master. Enamored with Kochran's transformation to full slave, surrendering his position as Dom as easily and naturally as breathing. Knowing him, it hadn't been quite that simple or calm. They were both still the men who had taken her in front of the Noble House crowd, in the semi-private room.

Most of all, they were still hers.

"Maddy."

The stern inflection in Ezra's voice snapped her focus. "Sorry." *Not sorry. Not even a little bit.* She could watch them forever. A pulse of pleasure hit her as she began moving her finger again. The gentle strumming wasn't enough. "I need more, Sir. So much more."

"I know." He reached over to the nearby table to retrieve something. Kochran's gaze remained on hers while Ezra fit the length of leather around Kochran's cock and testicles. The effectiveness of the restriction was evident immediately as the shaft flushed an alluring shade of deep red. "Get her ready for me, pet. Fingers only. Give her as much as she can comfortably take in that hot little pussy of hers, and then add one more."

Maddy whimpered, petrified and aroused at the idea of being *that* full.

Kochran started to rise, but Ezra stopped him with a firm hand to his shoulder. "Crawl for her."

A brief flash of amusement moved Kochran's lips as he sank into position. Total power exchange was new for her, but watching Kochran come closer with all the grace and power of a predator stalking its next meal made her insides melt. She wasn't interested in experiencing that kind of surrender herself, but oh, observing was so, so damn decadent.

"Hi, pretty girl," Kochran whispered softly against her thigh before imprinting her skin with a warm, gentle kiss. He touched her with his index finger, circling her opening a few times before sliding inside. "You're so tight."

Ezra cleared his throat. "If you're going to speak to her, at least talk loud enough so I can hear how dirty my pet can be when he's talking to my sub."

A thrill exploded through Maddy at Ezra's words, jagged and bright as they sank in. Kochran's pupils had expanded, blowing wide open with the rush. He slid a second finger into her, her slick walls accepting the addition easily. She cried out, aching to move her hips for friction. Instead, she tried to shift her arms, seeking a way to take Kochran deeper.

"I don't think so." Ezra's voice came from above, and as she looked up, he wrapped his hands around her shoulders and pinned her to the recliner. Being held in place by Ezra while Kochran continued to slide in and out of her caused an explosion of primal need to arc through her.

Kochran withdrew his touch completely. She wanted to chase his fingers, force them back inside her heat, but Ezra's unyielding grip kept her firmly in place. She wiggled and writhed, but the movement only caused Ezra to clench tighter. The pain brought an added layer of excitement to an already charged moment.

"Master, I need a taste of her." Every consonant and vowel of Kochran's desperate plea was like a warm caress against her skin. Sensations rocketed through her, elevating her arousals levels so high, her thighs started to tremble.

"Mmm, I would like to watch her come all over your

face. Go on. But don't forget what I said about talking to her, pet." Ezra eased off his hold a bit as he touched his lips to Maddy's forehead. "I like hearing that filthy mouth of yours."

She expected Kochran to dive face-first into her, but instead, he slipped the two fingers inside her again. Those trembling muscles went taut as she fought against the overwhelming desire to orgasm. He rocked into her, continuing to work as she accepted his treatment.

"I need you," Maddy murmured.

"I know you do. I need you, too, baby girl. But so does he. Besides, you're going to have to loosen up a little. I've had Ezra in my mouth and I know—" Kochran bit her thigh, his hum of approval vibrating through her. "You just drenched my fingers. You're imagining me giving Ezra a blowjob now, aren't you?"

"Yeah." Her grasp of language was starting to break down.

Kochran touched his tongue to her throbbing clit, gentle at first, then with more insistent pressure.

"Tell us what that dirty little mind of yours has spinning around in it," Ezra ordered.

She knew she'd never be able to find the words. "I'd rather watch."

"Probably for the same reason I could watch him eat your pussy all night long."

Anticipation curled through her. "So could I." The idea of such unrelenting pleasure flowing between the three of them was almost too much to bear.

Kochran closed his mouth over her clit and fireworks exploded behind her eyes. He rocked his fingers deeper as he toyed with her, worrying the nub with his lips.

Blood roared in her ears, a freight train at full throttle barreling down the tracks. Everything tightened and coalesced. Ezra was beside her, whispering dirty, dirty things into her ear while Kochran bathed her with his tongue, working her lusciously deep. Kochran added a third finger. The pressure was almost too much to take, but she would—for them.

They both kissed her skin at the same time—Ezra, her shoulder. Kochran, the juncture between her pelvis and thigh. Two sets of warm, sexy lips gifting her with even more pleasure.

"Sweet, sweet girl. Taking our torment. Giving us back such love and devotion."

"Yes. Yes. Yes." She couldn't manage more than the one word, drunk on the sensations they were forcing her to experience. The force of her climax built and built, gathering like a hot ball of pleasure, collecting between her legs and radiating out.

"That's it. My slave is very gifted with his mouth, isn't he?"

She had no idea why, but the slave terminology was so doing it for her. Hearing Ezra claim Kochran in such a way tripped buttons she didn't know she had. That particular interest was definitely going to be added to that list of hers. The pain and pressure of the three fingers almost instantaneously converted to pleasure. She couldn't prevent her hips from churning, reaching for more as Kochran continued to torment her with unrestrained pleasure.

"Such a treasure, taking everything we have to give you."

"More," she murmured, her breath raspy.

Ezra's grip tightened on her shoulders. "Easy, pretty girl. Don't force it. Let us take you."

She succumbed to the dark thread of pleasure/pain roping through her, the release building hot and heavy between her legs. Ezra kissed her forehead, the gentle gesture in such wonderful, incredible contrast to the pressure and heat building inside her. He skimmed his lips against her jaw, over her chin as he angled closer.

"Let us swallow your orgasm." His mouth closed over hers at the same moment Kochran clamped his lips around her clit and sucked hard. The release slammed into her with concussive force, rendering her immobile as the men took what they wanted. As she gave them everything she was. Yet she wanted more. It made no sense. She should have been sated with the powerful release. Exhausted. Instead, she craved her next taste of what they had to offer.

"More," she repeated, the word slurred as though she was drunk. In a way, she was intoxicated on the delicious elixir. "Please, more. I need it so much."

"Sweet little subbie begging for more while she's still high on us," Kochran whispered against her skin.

She giggled, the noise burbling up and out of her throat before she could stop it. "Such good drugs." She cradled Ezra's jaw as she reached down for Kochran. Kochran kissed her palm before settling his cheek in her hand. "I never expected you. Either of you."

"But now you have us always," Ezra said before he scooped her up into his arms.

Her high squeal echoed through the space. Though she wiggled in his embrace, she didn't truly want to escape. He paused, glancing over his shoulder to where

Kochran still patiently kneeled and waited for further direction.

"Come on, pet. I want to fuck her in your bed." His gaze angled back to her. "Find out if she can soak your sheets."

Chapter Twenty-Eight

Kochran was already on the bed by the time Ezra arrived carrying Maddy. She had no idea how he'd made it there so quickly, but in truth, she didn't much care. He was there, waiting for them, and that was all that mattered.

Ezra stopped a few feet from the bed. She looked to him to see if something was wrong, but instead she saw an overwhelming sense of pride and love. Could she look at herself with that same kind of unbroken honesty? Unable to stop herself, she touched his face. "You look at him as though you've never seen him before."

"I haven't. Not like this. It's a gift I don't take lightly." He kissed her, tender and sweet. "You're a gift too." He deepened the kiss, sliding his tongue past her lips with a quiet groan. "Now get on the bed so I can fuck you."

He hadn't instructed her how she was to lie or sit, and as she climbed into the high bed, she realized that was the point. She was given instructions, but they were far less rigid and stringent than anything he'd commanded of Kochran. He guided her, but he claimed total mastery of Kochran. It shouldn't have made sense. Shouldn't have worked. A Dominant becoming a slave.

Another Dominant taking up the mantle after being away from this kind of arrangement for so long. But in so many ways, it did. There were no rules when it came to their desires.

The turgid length of Kochran's cock stood out against the vee of his thighs. Though she knew Ezra gave her some leniency, she wasn't sure how far to push. "May I suck him, Sir?"

"Though you've pleased me by asking, no, I have other plans. Sit between his legs, facing me."

When she settled into the position, Kochran's cock pressed against her lower back.

"Spread your legs," he ordered as he came to sit on the foot of the bed.

She did, noticing how the new position angled her in such a way she could lean back against Kochran's chest. It also allowed her to lift her face up and to the side so she could look directly at Kochran.

"This okay?"

"More than," Kochran said with a mischievous smile and a wink.

This close, she noted the glassiness of Kochran's gaze. Pleasure was clearly coursing through his body, keeping him nestled comfortably in a space where everything was cottony and hazy. She'd approached that same state a few times thanks to both men, but seeing Kochran blissed out made her arousal somehow sharper. More potent.

Ezra scooted closer, setting his hand on Kochran's ankle. "I have something I need to say to you both before we go any further." He paused to clear his throat. "You both scare me because I'm afraid I'm not good enough for either of you."

Kochran's body tensed under hers and she set a comforting hand on his thigh. Ezra needed to get out whatever had been pent up inside him.

"You both force me to be a better man. To be worthy of your friendship. To accept that I can't always be perfect, but I can be the man you both need me to be. The man I have to be for each of you. Thank you for giving that part of my life back."

Tears formed in the corners of her eyes and spilled down her cheeks. She wasn't sure what to say, but somehow, she knew just being there at the moment was enough. He didn't require anything from either of them except to give him the respect of listening.

"I love you both so much it hurts. I didn't think I was ever going to love like that again. You've changed me in ways you'll never imagine. I had a home once." His gaze lifted, meeting first hers, then Kochran's. "And now I have it again thanks to both of you." He bent and kissed the inside of Maddy's knee, licking mercilessly as he adjusted his position and settled between their legs. "You both scare me so much because I'm not convinced I can be each of the things you need from me, but I'm going to damn well try for the three of us."

Ezra rose up on all fours, kissing her neck first, then her nose and chin, before finally setting his lips against hers. She poured all the passion she could muster into the kiss, knowing everything was going to be all right between the three of them, even if they took a while to settle into the path laid out before them. It would take hard work and honesty, but she was willing to go the distance.

Her lungs started to burn for air just as Ezra severed the connection. Without pause, he took Kochran's mouth next. She loved the feel of being pinned between them, held in the cradle of their bodies while they connected on a deeper, more intimate level. With his mouth still on Kochran's, Ezra fit his body against her in perfect alignment.

They were seconds away from being connected on a new level and she didn't want anything between them. "No condoms," she whispered against Ezra's ear as he continued to kiss Kochran. "Nothing between the three of us, at least right now." Her birth control would prevent any unintended pregnancies. "I'm clean according to my last checkup. And given Kochran's stringent rules at the club, it's safe to assume you're both clean too."

"I think we've established we're anything but clean, dirty, dirty girl," Kochran said, his words slightly slurred.

She couldn't fight her smile.

Ezra's entry was rough, awakening nerves as her mind fuzzed. He pulled back, thrust home again, denying her from being filled with him completely. The shallow movements caused her to draw a shaky breath, release it with a near sob as everything inside her came alive. He withdrew a few inches, holding himself there over her, keeping his weight on his hands and knees. For a moment, the three of them were frozen, hanging in the moment where they'd all become beings of pleasure.

Ezra slammed so hard into her, she curled her toes against the sheet. He hissed, driving his hand under her ass to lift it, angle her so he could thrust deeper. "Fuck. Just like that."

Each thrust pushed her against Kochran's dick so

it was nestled between her ass cheeks. It moved with ease against her skin, his precome lubricating the path so Ezra's every thrust slid Kochran's slick cock against her.

"Come for me, baby. Come around my dick."

The tension collecting where they all connected finally hit breaking point and released. She dug her fingers into Ezra's back as she shattered. She bucked against them, rapture sweeping her away. Ezra groaned long and loud, his movements becoming jerky and erratic as he slammed into her over and over. His body suddenly stilled, and with a rough snarl that Kochran swallowed as Ezra kissed him, he came.

His release triggered another small but still powerful climax, and she cried out as it overtook her. Her senses opened, welcoming the all-out assault on her system as the pleasure of the joining boiled inside her.

She watched as the two men parted. "You have no idea how hot that is."

Kochran chuckled. "Oh, I think I do." To illustrate, he pushed his erection against her butt.

The movement awakened something inside her even though she was spent.

Ezra growled, his eyes narrowing as she clenched around him again. "You should see how hot it is when he swallows my dick." He pushed his pelvis against hers, grinding against her oversensitive clit. Small aftershocks assaulted her system, revving her for another round. She whined when Ezra withdrew, sitting back on his knees. The position framed his softening penis, the glistening sheen of her arousal coating him.

"God, you're both so fucking beautiful like that. Maddy thoroughly ravished. Kochran utterly frustrated." Ezra gave a sly grin. She'd thought seeing him hunched over the keyboard hard at work was hot, but this…damn.

"I think we could say the same about him," Kochran whispered in her ear.

She nodded as she touched the tip of her tongue against her top lip. She rose, overworked muscles groaning in protest as she went up on her knees and angled forward to kiss Ezra, tasting the flavors of Kochran on his tongue. She glanced over her shoulder, noting the angry red flush of Kochran's shaft. Despite that, he still wore a blissful smile. Amazing how he could still find pleasure out of all this when he was obviously in pain.

"You want him, don't you?" Ezra whispered in her ear. "Want his big, beautiful cock inside you."

"Please, Sir."

"I want nothing more than to watch you two fuck, but maybe in a little while. How about we both use our hands instead?"

The disappointment that had flared quickly vanished at the new proposal. They touched Kochran at the same time, Ezra's hand wrapping around the base, hers near the top fitting just under the flared head. The lube Ezra had slicked on made it easy to glide her hand, loving the heat pulsing against her palm. They worked in tandem, only taking a few strokes before Kochran's entire body tensed. The cords in his neck stood out as he fought, his fingers digging so hard into the pillows propping him up, Maddy heard the fabric give. She marveled at his control, admiring the sheer force of will necessary to withstand the orgasm that had to be clawing its way free.

"Give us your release, Kochran," Ezra said as he flipped the latch on the cock ring.

Kochran came with a roar, spurting all over his chest and abdomen, along with Maddy and Ezra's hands as they continued to fuck him with their fists. His voice echoed through the broad space, the only sound as Maddy and Ezra held their breath as they watched.

Ezra scooped her up, dumped her on her side next to Kochran and disappeared around the corner. He came back a minute later with two washcloths and proceeded to tenderly wipe everyone down. When he was finished, he discarded the rags on the nightstand and curled up behind Maddy, pressing her harder against Kochran. They filled the bed, leaving nothing between them but satisfaction and the promise of what they could all discover together. She tried not to think about what could happen when the afterglow faded.

Kochran's bed had never been this brimming with bodies before, and damn, did it feel glorious. He moaned as he sat up, saw the remains of the night scattered around the area like broken dreams. He knew there would be more of the same by the shower. In the main seating area. Evidence his two lovers had held nothing back.

A thrill surged through him as he remembered. They'd rested for a time before Ezra had finally given Maddy her wish. Kochran's dick twitched as the phantom touch of the hot warmth of her mouth sucking him off ghosted over his skin. Ezra had positioned her on her knees, driving inside her just as Kochran had been coming all over her tongue.

They'd showered after that, a task that had been made remarkably difficult as both men had traced her luscious curves with their soap-covered hands. They barely made it back to the bed before Kochran had finally, finally gotten inside her. Everything had melted into a colorful, chaotic kaleidoscope of sex where bodies tangled and roles had dissolved in a euphoric free for all.

He pressed a kiss to Maddy's shoulder as he rolled out of bed. Sliding back on into a mentality he hadn't embraced since his twenties had been remarkably simple. Then again, the pull toward Ezra made him comfortable enough that he could do anything. Be anything. Maddy strengthened that bond more than he'd ever imagined.

Kochran reached for his cell phone on the nightstand, found it under a pile of damp washcloths. When he scooped it up, he frowned at the screen.

Ten missed calls.

Shit.

Kochran rubbed his dry eyes, hoping the count on his phone was a mistake. A result of a late night with a near total lack of sleep thanks to Ezra and Maddy.

Ten. Not an error.

His heart gave a powerful thump against his ribcage. Bile coiled through his stomach, burning a path up his throat. He swallowed, but the acrid tasted wouldn't diminish. He glanced over his shoulder, noting Ezra and Maddy had adjusted for his absence already. He snagged a pair of sweats before moving off to the kitchen. He needed to find out what was going on instead of worrying, but calling meant the news he suspected was real. That the worst fear he'd lived with for the past few years had finally arrived.

He poured hot water into a mug, dumping a tea bag

in to steep. He picked up his phone again, noting the sweat coating his palm. The burn in his chest and throat flourished as the words on the screen blurred. Ten. Missed. Calls.

Ten chances someone had been trying to reach him while he'd been busy tangling with Ezra and Maddy. Finding his happily ever after. That kind of joy never came without a price. He closed his eyes, trying to push away the guilt settling into his gut. A cold sweat erupted over his body as he thumbed the phone screen and saw nine of the calls had been from his mother. The tenth call was the one that made his blood run cold. He tapped the button to return the call, his breath scraping against his throat as he waited. When the caller answered, all the oxygen had been stripped from the room.

"Dad?"

"Son. Thank god. You had us worried." The raw, broken tone of his father's voice told Kochran all he needed to know. "She's gone."

A long pause, filled with the raspy breaths that reminded Kochran of his father's age. Maybe he'd assumed wrong. Maybe the news was something else—

"About two this morning."

"I'll be there as soon as I can."

Kochran ended the call and let the phone drop onto the table with a clatter. Tory was gone. Dead. He hadn't been there like he'd promised. Hadn't been at her side to hold her hand. To crack jokes as she slipped away. To shield her, protect her like he'd sworn to do all those years ago when she'd been diagnosed.

Rage that he'd kept restrained inside him suddenly ripped forth and out his throat. He beat his fists against the cheap table, a satisfied crack of wood reverberating through the space. He screamed again and again, beating the wood over and over. The resulting cracks fueled his anger and his need. He shot to stand, kicking back the chair. He slammed his knuckles against the cracks, growling when the split deepened and lengthened. Caught up in the harsh grip of rage, he continued to pummel the table, pleased with each resulting shot of pain that fired across his knuckles and up his forearms. The wood gave with a loud snap as he pounded down, and the table fell to pieces.

He reeled around, an animal gripped tightly by a fury that knew no bounds. He spotted the counter Tory had helped him pick out. The appliances she'd insisted on paying for. Tory's mark saturated the room. He picked up the metal chair and started beating it against the counter, the fridge, in a desperate attempt to rid himself of the pain. The pings and cracks only fueled his ire.

A tight grip on his bicep prevented him from launching the chair at the stained-glass window mounted over the sink. He tried to wrench free, but the persistent fucker just held on. Kochran blinked, the red sheeting his vision bleeding away until he realized Ezra was the one holding him. Rocking him. Whispering soothing words to him. Something warm and soft molded against his back. Maddy. She added to Ezra's calming influence, breaking away the chaos screaming through his head.

The fight left Kochran, abandoning him to find a worthy adversary. The tears fell then. Hot and painful as each one tore itself free. His body collapsed, but still—Ezra and Maddy held him in their combined embrace. Offered their support without asking why he was falling apart. Anger gave way to utter desperation as he finally discovered what it felt like to have his heart break.

Kochran rapped his knuckles on the front door for a third time.

Maddy touched his arm. "Maybe she's at your parents'?"

"Doubt it." Kochran jiggled the handle again even though he'd already tried. "Adelita? It's Kochran. Let me in."

Silence.

"She's not here." Despite Ezra's statement, Kochran didn't move.

"Yeah she is." Kochran left Ezra and Maddy to make his way to the backyard. A quick glance through a hazy window confirmed Adelita was sitting on the couch in the living room, just steps away from where he'd been ready to pound the door down. The paint on the screen door was weathered and peeling, and the lock gave easily with a bit of force.

He didn't slow until he'd reached the sofa and scooped Adelita up into his arms. She clung to him like a monkey climbing a tree, terrified of the predator stalking it on the ground. He sat, taking her with him and listened to each and every one of her gut-wrenching sobs as she finally unleashed the same restraint he'd used for the entirety of Tory's illness. Unshed tears fell as he rocked her, soothing her as she trembled in his arms.

A shadow darkened the kitchen doorway and he glanced over to see Ezra and Maddy. A knock sounded on the front door and triggered a fresh torrent of tears in Adelita. She clung tighter. "She's gone, Kochran."

"I know, sweetie."

Maddy touched Kochran's shoulder as she passed. "I'll answer it." The quiet murmur of voices accompanied the front door opening, and then silence a few seconds later as she closed the door with a snap.

Kochran didn't know who it was, but the press of more people entered the room. He wrapped his arms tighter around Adelita as he turned to dismiss whoever it was. He stopped short when he realized it was Saint and Grae. Grae's pale face was red, tears streaking down her cheeks.

Thank you, he mouthed to her. She gave him a half smile before Saint ushered everyone out of the room. After a few minutes, Adelita sat up. He pulled a few tissues from a nearby box and offered them to her. She stared at them as though she didn't recognize what they were. He gestured her closer, and helped her blow her nose.

"Why are you here?"

Kochran gave her a level glare. "Because I knew the last place I'd find you was at my parents'."

"You should be with them."

"I'm right where I should be." His phone buzzed in his pocket. He knew without looking it was his father again. No doubt his mother questioning when he'd arrive and knowing he wouldn't take her calls. "I'll go see my parents later. Right now you need us more."

Grae appeared with two glasses of water. "Thought you guys could use something to drink."

Adelita turned as Grae came close and held out her arms. Kochran nudged Adelita out of his lap and the two women clung to one another as the quiet sounds of their hushed whispers filled the room. He signaled toward the kitchen and Grae waved him away.

As Kochran entered the kitchen, Saint gestured toward Kochran's hand. "You're bleeding."

"Doesn't matter." That earned him a trio of grimaces. He flexed his hands, biting the inside of his cheek at the flare of pain that caused black spots to dance across his vision. "Nothing is broken, I think."

Saint tossed him a gallon-sized bag filled with ice and some water. "What did you do? Try to beat down her door with your fists?"

"Kitchen table," Ezra offered as he handed Saint a mug of steaming coffee. "Dented the fridge, stove and dishwasher. Cast iron sink won the battle, though."

"Jesus," Saint said quietly.

Kochran barely remembered any of it. "Sorry."

Ezra waved his hand as he set another mug on the counter by Kochran's hip. Maddy appeared at the back door with an armload of groceries. Kochran knew the details from the past hour were hazy, but he hadn't been out of it long enough for her to go shopping. Boyce stepped into the kitchen seconds later, a few bags in his arms.

"What is all this?" Kochran asked.

"We have to eat." Maddy started opening cabinets and drawers as she familiarized herself with the layout. The shelves were shockingly bare. Of course they were, he realized. Adelita had been spending all her time at the hospice with Tory. She'd probably lived off cheese fries and greasy burgers, a fact he should have realized earlier.

"Thanks." He crossed to Maddy and wrapped an

arm around her shoulder. "I should have realized she needed all this stuff."

She paused, setting her hand on his jaw as she gave him a sweet smile. "You can't do it all, Kochran."

"What you did. Getting to her like that?" Ezra stepped against them, pulling them into his embrace. "That is exactly what you should have done." He kissed Maddy's cheek, then Kochran's lips before he snagged the boxes of macaroni noodles. "I'll get these started."

Kochran turned to find Enver darkening the back doorway. His longtime friend smirked. "About damn time, man." He pulled Kochran into a tight hug. "Really sorry to hear about Tory, though. I know it's been tough."

Saint pointed at the back door and Kochran and Enver followed him outside. "You need anything?"

Kochran glanced over his shoulder to see the silhouettes of Maddy and Ezra working together at the stove. "How do they know?"

"What?" Enver struck a match, the flame glowing orange against his face as he lit a cigarette.

"To do that? To know Adelita didn't have any food. To know—shit." Heat stung Kochran's eyes.

"Give yourself a break, man." Enver blew out the match he'd used. "You just lost your sister. You can't be expected to remember all the details. To be thinking clearly. Let them do what they need to so you can deal with your grief."

"You're their Dom, Kochran. They want to take care of you." Saint gestured toward Enver, wrinkling his nose. "You haven't given those up yet?"

"You have your vices, I've got mine." Enver took a long drag on the cigarette, clearly enjoying the act.

"I subbed to Ezra," Kochran blurted as he glanced between the men, looking for some indication he'd shocked them. "I'm not... I'm not the head Dominant in this relationship."

Enver blew out a steam of smoke. "Like I said, it's about damn time."

Kochran scowled. "Don't give me one of those bullshit speeches about how you've always known." He glanced to the house again to see Boyce had joined Maddy and Ezra with the meal prep.

"No, I meant it's about time you do something to make yourself happy." Enver picked the cherry from the cigarette with his fingertips, stomped on it a few times to make sure it had gone out, and palmed the spent filter. "Switch it up all you want, man. Go fucking crazy. Just...let yourself love them." Enver clapped him on the back as he clomped back up the porch stairs and disappeared into the house.

Love.

The word was foreign and...right. He hadn't sought it out, but he'd opened up to them like he'd never done for anyone. Yet there he was, a tangle of emotions because of Tory's passing, and these two people he needed most in this world were taking care of him. Not because he'd given into his desire to kneel as a slave to Ezra. Not because he still wanted to dominate Maddy. Because they were his as much as he was theirs.

"I'd appreciate if we kept this news under wraps for a little bit. Give me a chance to sort shit out." Kochran knew Saint wouldn't go blabbing the news, but he needed to get through the next week at least without worrying about the fate of his club.

"Members aren't going to care what the fuck you

do, Kochran, if that's what you're worried about. They just want to know they can count on you to give them a good show and that you are capable of competently running a BDSM club. The rest is—"

"Icing," Kochran finished. Still, confessing his submissive needs wasn't something he was ready for beyond his circle of friends. He hated that he needed them so much. Perhaps someday he would be able to cut off that self-preservation mode and just be. "Thanks. You guys didn't have to come."

"Soon as Grae told us, we knew this is where you'd be." Saint gestured to the house. "Adelita needs this. She needs you right now because we both know your parents are going to fuck with her world."

"My mother will, yeah. I can't shield her completely from that wrath. I can be a buffer for a little while, though." Kochran wished it could be forever.

"Adelita is a strong woman, Kochran. Just be here to get her through this, all the rest will happen like it needs to."

As Kochran and Saint came back into the house, they saw Adelita's sister closing the front door. Charlie dropped her bag and headed right for Adelita. Yeah, this was the best place for Adelita right now, surrounded by close family and friends who wouldn't judge and scorn her for her choices. But Kochran knew he faced some contempt as soon as he stepped across the threshold of his parents' house. Especially if Tory had followed through on her deathbed threat.

"Thank you for coming, Steve." Maddy lightly kissed her business partner's cheek. "Sorry it's under such bad circumstances."

He squeezed her hand, his gentle smile warming his boyishly innocent face. "How are you doing?"

"Worried." Watching someone she loved in so much pain made her ache as though something was broken inside her. Her heart twisted with the fear that Kochran would pull away or put her and Ezra at arm's length so he could deal with his grief in private. If that happened, Ezra could drift away as well. The tangle of emotions went deeper, but she kept her worries buried in order to give support where it was needed the most.

Steve pulled her into a tight hug. She relaxed against him, his chest vibrating against her ear as he spoke. "I can tell. Why do you think I'm here? Hate to see you hurting. Speaking of, how is your friend doing? I was worn out from a full day of work and travel, so I headed back to the hotel last night before I could ask if you guys needed anything."

Kochran's method of coping with his initial grief had been an explosion of emotion that hadn't returned, but the threadbare edges of his patience had begun to dissolve two days ago. Maddy and Ezra had been able to diffuse most of the tension by ensuring Kochran wasn't left alone with Noelle for long periods of time, but they'd known the funeral could be the breaking point for the family.

Maddy glanced over her shoulder to watch people offer their condolences to the Duke family. She attempted a lighthearted smile. "You saw how bad the tension was between Kochran and his mother at the wake." As expected, Noelle wouldn't allow the general public to know of the tension surrounding the Dukes, but cracks in her facade had started to show. Maddy and

Ezra had been the victim of more than a few of Noelle's disgusted looks when she thought no one would notice.

"This family makes mine look like angels." Steve shook his head. "Think they could all put it aside for a few hours."

Her heart clenched. "Is Will still mixed up with that bad batch of friends?"

A glimmer of sadness crossed his face. "Mom called the other day to tell me he was in jail again. Drugs or something. I don't know. Owes someone a lot of money. I tune it all out now." Though their relationship had been brief, Maddy had met most of Steve's family except for his older brother because of his time in and out of jail.

His expression cleared as Ezra joined them. "I didn't get a chance to introduce myself. Steve O'Doyle."

"So you're the other half of the business. Honored." The men shook hands. "Also honored you guys signed a contract to pair up with Noble House for the long term. Maddy has been a great asset to us."

Steve shook his head. "Always knew this one was meant for greater—" he dropped his voice to a whisper "—and kinkier things. Hear you guys rooted out a bad seed Maddy had the misfortune to encounter."

"Purged him from the system thanks to her dedication and loose morals when it comes to federal postal laws." Ezra smirked, tilting his head closer. "You're welcome to pay another, legal visit to the club anytime, Steve."

"Ah, no thanks." Steve held up his hands in mock horror. "I saw enough to last me for the rest of my life when she got in the system the first time. No kinky stuff for me." He cleared his throat. "If you'll both excuse me for a moment, I want to pay my respects."

As Steve joined the line to offer his condolences to the family, Ezra gathered her up in his arms. Though she was equally comfortable with both men, she sagged against Ezra. "I'm worried about Kochran." Maddy hugged Ezra tighter. "He hasn't said more than five words to anyone all day." Just that damn indifferent mask that hid the brewing internal war. Kochran had kept a lid on his displeasure with his mother's choices for Tory's arrangements, opting to keep the peace instead of calling her to the carpet.

"He'll be all right, Mads. We just need to get through the next twenty minutes."

Each of those minutes crawled by, but finally Kochran's father slipped through the front door to escort the last visitor out. Maddy started to rise, anxious to leave, but sat again when Noelle stepped into the room. The face she'd painted on for the general public had been replaced by a mask of hatred.

"Get out," she demanded as she folded her arms. "Don't think I didn't see you wrapped around that other man earlier, little girl. Absolutely repulsive the way you're using my son." Her gaze flicked to Ezra, her eyes narrowing as she looked him over. "And you, allowing yourself to be taken advantage of, all because she spreads her legs for you. Just like a man, thinking with his penis instead of his brain."

Maddy grit her teeth as she and Ezra stood at the same time. Kochran stepped in front of them, his body vibrating with restrained fury. "This isn't the time or place, Mother."

"This is my home, I will do anything I damn well

please." Her tone brooked no argument. "At least tell me that you will sell that dreadful, sinful place you run now."

Kochran's body stiffened. "What?"

Noelle waved her perfectly manicured hand, dismissing Kochran's palpable ire. "Your sister thought she was telling me something I didn't already know about when she wasted her last breath with her confession." She fluffed her hair, flicking away a strand that had landed on the shoulder of her expensive black pantsuit. "Honestly, I don't know what it is about the two of you. Tory dating that…*woman*, you owning that damned disgusting club, or the fact you choose to fraternize with people who are only around for their piece of the family money."

Ezra tightened his hold on Maddy's arm as her annoyance reached boiling point. "They need to hash this out," he whispered into her ear. "Long time coming."

Though she agreed with Ezra, watching this unfold made her uncomfortable. She wasn't easy to anger, but listening to Noelle break down one of her lovers had caused her to think nasty thoughts about the woman.

"Your father and I have kept quiet long enough about you whoring yourself out for these people." Her disapproving gaze flicked to Maddy and Ezra again. "It's time for you to grow up and act like a Duke for once in your life."

Kochran's back went rigid as he drew himself up to his full height. "Let's just cut through all the bullshit right now, Mother. Adelita loved Tory more than you will ever comprehend. More than you will ever hope to understand. Yes, I *whore* myself out. People pay me to have sex." Kochran's words came out fast and barbed, cutting straight through to cause the most pain. "Lots of sweaty, filthy sex, because I'm very good at what I do. I get off ordering people around, because I'm exceptionally good at that as well. And you know what I was recently reminded of that I'm extraordinarily good at?"

Kochran turned, grabbed the lapels of Ezra's suit and muscled him closer. For a second, Maddy thought he was going to kiss Ezra, but instead, he dropped his hands to his sides. Gaze on Maddy, he sank down on one knee and bowed his head. She heard the whispered "Master," but she wasn't certain Noelle did. It didn't matter—the meaning was clear.

As Ezra set his hand lightly on the top of Kochran's head, Maddy accepted the other hand Ezra offered her. He straightened before he said, "That club you speak of with such disgust is my home. It's your son's life. He built it from nothing, putting his heart and soul into the very foundation so others could have a safe place to go. You've spent Kochran's entire life trying to convince him he was insignificant. Unworthy of your love. And he was too damn proud to ask you to accept him—faults and all. You may find this hard to believe, but Maddy and I love Kochran, and we are prepared to spend the rest of our lives showering him with the devotion you denied him. Why is it so fucking hard for you to love him exactly how he is?"

Noelle's face colored. "I love my son."

"No you don't," Ezra said quietly.

"How dare you accuse me of such a thing!"

"I want Kochran to achieve whatever he sets his mind to do. Want him to embrace his desires, no matter how twisted and kinky they are. I want to protect him from people that have set out to tear him apart, like you. I love him for everything he is, Mrs. Duke. You hate him for it."

Ezra pulled Kochran to stand, and used his body to shield him. "With the utmost respect, Noelle, I speak for all three of us when I say fuck you."

Chapter Twenty-Nine

Maddy stood in the hallway on the third floor of Noble House. Those double doors that had taunted her from the first day called to her once again. Only, this time, as soon as she set her hand on the knob, she found that the locks hadn't been engaged. There would be no barrier to stop her from crossing over the threshold.

Kochran had been tenaciously vague when he'd delivered the invitation to her on high-quality card stock and printed in his neat, elegant handwriting. The love and care he'd taken with the gesture was sweet. Nervous energy pinged inside her like a pinball as she thought about the notes of affection he'd hid for her to find recently. Made her head feel fuzzy with how fun it was to show him just how much she appreciated each and every one of those pieces of paper.

The dreamy heat of arousal arced through her, her body in a perpetually heightened state thanks to Ezra and Kochran. The month since the funeral and his mother's outburst had been hard on Kochran, but he hadn't turned a cold shoulder to her or Ezra. In fact, he spent so much time with them, the general membership had to have certainly gotten a few ideas about just what was going on between the threesome. Since

Kochran insisted he wasn't prepared to share the news
of his status change, they'd confined their play to their
houses, steering clear of the club.

Even though she loved the exhibitionism angle of
the scenes they'd once shared, the choice gave the trio
the freedom to explore their desires at their leisure. To
peel away one vulnerable layer at a time until they were
naked, stripped and raw, with nothing left but their love.
But tonight would be different. She didn't know pre-
cisely how, but the fact Kochran had asked her to come
to the room meant something was about to change.

Her two favorite men were waiting for her.

As soon as she stepped through the doors, she forced
herself to wait one endless moment before she made
eye contact with Kochran. He was settled comfortably in an oversized chair positioned on a raised platform looking very much like the man in the video the
night she'd hacked the website. That cool arrogance
stared her down. For a single, heartbreaking second,
she thought she'd imagined the past few weeks. That
she'd dreamed up the connection the trio shared. The
sinful days and nights where they found solace in each
other's arms, and comfort in their bodies.

Ezra sat to his left, his posture relaxed, though it
gave her no indication of what was going on. Saint and
Boyce shared a nearby couch with Grae nestled comfortably on their laps. Judging by her faraway gaze,
they'd already been there for a while. They'd postponed
their wedding ceremony after Tory's death and were
set to exchange vows in just two days.

Nearby, Enver sat on a couch with a dark-haired man
Maddy recognized as the bartender of Screwdriver and
another man whose arms were covered from wrist to

shoulder with an elaborate network of tattoos. Several other members Maddy recognized but didn't know filled every seat in the room.

The atmosphere was markedly different from Court, the semi-private rooms, the lounge. In Kochran's private room of kink, the level of respect was tangible. These people didn't come to the club only to play or get off. They were friends. The kind of family not built on blood, but on the solid foundation of admiration and honor. They looked out for one another during the good and the bad.

She turned back to Kochran to find an intensity she hadn't noticed before. She'd been so busy focusing on other things, she'd missed the honed, sharp edge of his stare. The one that made her blush. Made interesting things happened to her body, her mind.

"They're here for you, Madeline. And they've been invited to the Keep because I trust each and every one of them implicitly. With my life, even." Kochran drew himself to his full height as he spoke, joining her in the center of the room. "Noble House has always been a safe place for anyone to explore their deepest, darkest needs and desires. The Keep is my private space inside that world."

"A personal playground of kink?"

The corner of his mouth lifted. "I shuttered the doors a while ago because I realized it wasn't a true representation of who I really am." Movement over Kochran's shoulder caught her eye as Ezra joined them. Kochran touched her chin. "But thanks to my gorgeous little hacker, I have everything I could ever need."

"Almost," Ezra said quietly.

Kochran nodded. For one terrifying moment, she

thought her world was spinning away from her. But
the pain wasn't reflected in their expressions. Instead
she saw the promise that they would burn the world
for her if they had to. Their complicated relationship
didn't make any damn sense, but she wouldn't have it
any other way. They would all keep going, one foot in
front of the other, for as long as they could.

She caught a glimmer and dropped her gaze. In Kochran's palm was a perfect circle of gleaming silver.
The solid metal was beautiful, elegant and eye-catching,
everything she'd once been convinced she wasn't. She
hadn't found those strengths in herself *because* of the
men, but *for* the men.

For a long time, all she could do was stare at the
item. An eternity collar. No end. No beginning. An
unbroken circle that was the ultimate representation of
the bond between Dom and sub. It meant permanence
and connection and…trust. Absolute, unwavering trust.

"My turn." Ezra picked up the collar, located the
hidden lock and opened the mechanism with a special
key. He slipped a pendant onto the circle and held it
up for her inspection. Looking closer, she noticed the
border was in the shape of two men and a woman, all
naked, hands and feet touching to form a heart. Despite the small size, the level of detail was astounding.
In the center, a sparkling blue gemstone mimicked the
heart shape, the letters E and K etched in silver on the
gemstone's surface.

The stark reality finally hit her right between the
eyes. They were really going to add a binding layer of
unbreakable commitment to their relationship. "I don't
know what to say."

"How about we ask the question first?" Ezra gave a

quiet laugh. "Maddy, will you do us the honor of wearing the collar we've selected for you? Openly display your devotion and commitment to us every moment that this is around your neck while you're at the club?"

It was the moment of truth. The instant where she had to open her heart or walk away from them forever. The collar would mean more than her agreement to surrender to them. More than simply a visual display of their union. It signaled she truly belonged to them heart and soul.

Maddy reached out with trembling fingers, and set her hand over the necklace. "I'm done spending my life holding back or being scared of how I really want to live. You've both instilled in me the courage I need to do that. You've given me so much I feel I don't deserve. Because of you both, I don't have to hide behind my awesometastic hacking skills or hide the unique love I have for you both."

Her eyes burned, words catching as her throat grew tight. "We're going to make a messy, complicated triad with Ezra as our Dom and Master, but I don't care. I want what the three of us have more than anything else I've ever wanted in my life. I would be honored to accept your collar."

She unconsciously leaned into their touch while they placed the collar around her throat. As they engaged the lock, she knew there would never be anyone else for her as long as she wore the piece. The heart settled in the hollow of her throat, tickling her skin every time she took a breath to serve as a constant reminder of their love and trust. Though she had nothing for them in return, she knew it wasn't necessary.

Instead, she looked at them and whispered, "I love it."

Kochran hooked his finger around the hoop, tugging her close until their lips met. "So do I."

As she fingered the metal roping her neck, she gasped. "Oh, Kochran, I'm sorry. So, so sorry. I didn't mean to out you like that." She bit her lip to prevent further confession. "That wasn't my secret to tell. I wasn't thinking. I just wanted—"

Kochran silenced her with a finger against her lips. "It's all right, Madeline. Tonight isn't just about your collaring ceremony. It took me a long time to get to this place, but I'm still not ready to give up everything. I'm not sure how the general membership will accept me as anything but a Master, but these people in this room… they are as much a part of my heart and soul as you are. They accept me for whatever I am. Even a slave."

Ezra pulled his hand from his pocket, and for the first time, she realized the two bands he'd always worn stacked on his ring finger weren't there. These men of hers certainly were full of surprises tonight. She grabbed his hand without thinking, rubbing her thumb over the slight indention the rings had left from long-term wear.

"It was time," Ezra said simply. "Just like it's time for this too."

He showed her a pair of rings. Both were silver, with three nude figures entwined together, as though they were locked in a passionate, carnal embrace, similar to the pendent Ezra had given her. She drew a sharp breath as she realized the rings were collars.

"I thought this would be something to bind the three of us together while we're at the club. For the past five years, there has always been this awful, glaring hole inside me. I tried a few different ways to fill it, thought

I'd come close a few times, but it was never quite right. And then you came along." Ezra slipped the ring onto Kochran's finger. "You ripped those holes wide open so I couldn't help but give you my heart. It scares me to feel this way about two people again, but I don't want to stop. Can't."

Emotion built in Maddy's chest as she noticed the slight quiver in Kochran's fingers.

Ezra continued, "I don't understand why you make me feel the things I do. Some days it's hard to process it all. But the one thing I haven't questioned is how I feel for you both. How we're all a part of each other whether we like it or not. I've never needed two people in my life more than I do right now."

Kochran reached for Maddy's hand, adding hers on top of Ezra's so they could slip the band into place. "We're certainly a complicated situation no one but the three of us will understand. Our dynamic makes us all a little insane, but there isn't anyone else in the world that I want to go crazy with. You helped me stop running from a past I thought I had to deny. With you both, I'm not the head of Noble House or the pet. I am neither Master nor slave. I'm simply Kochran. That is who I am and I can finally, finally accept that I'm comfortable in my own skin because I have two of the greatest loves I've ever known who have shown me the way." He glanced toward Maddy and nodded.

Her chest went tight, swelling with emotions so strong and deep they stole her breath. She understood what he meant about the complicated dance they were a part of. No one else may have fully understood how they would make it all work, but as long as the three of them did, that was all that mattered.

That same understanding made her look to Ezra, waiting for the small nod of permission before she proceeded. Emotion danced in his gaze as that approval came. The ring slipped easily into place, a sense of harmony filling her in ways she never expected as she looked at the simple band surrounding Kochran's finger.

Before either of the men could say anything else, she plucked the other ring from Ezra's palm. She snagged Kochran's hand, and together they slipped the ring into place on Ezra's finger. They'd surpassed the need for words as they settled the visual symbol of their union into place. As she glanced between the two men, she saw all the love she would ever need written in their eyes.

Though she'd never expected to find such adoration and understanding when she'd hacked into the club's website, this was home. They were joined together in the breathless moments of dominance and submission in a way only a select few could understand.

Chapter Thirty

Ten minutes later, Kochran lay spread out on the bondage table in the center of the Keep, the gorgeous lines of his body utter perfection before Ezra's gaze. Maddy waited patiently nearby. Part of Ezra was tempted to make her watch, but the sparkle of her collar reminded him how much he enjoyed being with them both. There would be time to exploit her voyeuristic tendencies later. Right now, Ezra needed them to cement their forever with their bodies against his.

Awareness of the room and all the people fell away as he pulled her closer, peeling off the flowy white shirt and dark blue leggings she'd worn. Her breathing quickened as he caressed the smooth skin on her stomach, moving his hands around to cup the delectable curve of her ass as he crouched. She leaned into him, allowing her body to speak her need when she realized his mouth was inches from her mound.

"Please," she whimpered.

He gave in, pressing a gentle kiss to her lower abdomen, right above the waistband of her underwear. Ezra stood again, loving the hazy spark in her eyes indicative of subspace. "Why don't you preoccupy Kochran while

I make sure he can't run away from us? But don't get him too excited. It's going to be a long night."

Her eyes gleamed with an intoxicating happiness. "Yes, Sir."

That kind of eagerness wasn't something Ezra ever wanted to vanish. Without hesitation, Maddy bent over Kochran's twitching cock and started to make sweet, sweet love to him with her mouth. That temptation to watch them rose again and Ezra knew he was forever theirs.

Ezra retrieved two coils of rope, working efficiently to bind Kochran's ankles and lower legs to the table. The intricate pattern Enver had shared with him worked beautifully in this instance, holding Kochran's legs wide so Ezra would have unimpeded access. Held open this way, his defenses were obliterated.

As he stepped beside Maddy, Ezra noticed the line that had formed between Kochran's eyebrows. More than just concentration as Kochran fought against need that was undoubtedly building inside him. Ezra had been inside Maddy's mouth more than once and knew how skillful she was.

Maddy pressed her mouth against the spot and whispered, "You all right?"

Kochran heaved out a breath, his torso trembling with the effort. "Yeah. Just been a while since I've been bound."

Ezra skimmed his hand along Kochran's side, reveling in the gooseflesh that erupted under his touch. "Forgot about that initial surge of panic, huh? The internal struggle your mind and your body have?"

"Fight or flight." Kochran smirked.

"That's all the restraint I'm planning for you tonight.

pet. I need your hands free." Ezra positioned himself beside Maddy and maneuvered her so she was aligned with the head of the table. He slipped behind her, kissing her shoulder as he looked down the line of Kochran's prone form. Shadows highlighted the definition of his muscles, his pecs and the dark disks of his nipples. "Isn't he gorgeous, baby girl? And he's all ours."

Ezra circled Maddy's waist, cupping a hand around one of her breasts and slipping his other finger under the ruffled hem of her panties. He flicked her clit with his fingernail at the same time he squeezed her breast. A soft hiss spilled from her lips, charging the air as Kochran's cock twitched.

"Lean forward, Maddy. Hands on the table, on either side of Kochran's head." Ezra tugged gently on her hips as she curled her fingers around the rolled edge of the table. "That's a good girl."

Ezra sank to a crouch, retrieving a string of cornflower-blue glass balls and a tube of lubrication he'd tucked into his pack earlier. He ran his fingers over each sphere and the connecting rope, even though he'd checked them over thoroughly when the package had arrived special delivery from Virginia. The glass craftsman he'd ordered them from was a genius who should have been paid triple his fee.

He tugged aside the fabric, teasing her opening with his wet fingers. "Spread wide for me, Maddy." The position placed her at the perfect angle. He worked the first ball past her tight muscles, loving the soft moan she gave when her body accepted the object. "That's it, baby girl. Gonna get this pretty little asshole of yours nice and stretched so both of us can fuck you at the same time." She took the last two globes with ease, the muscles of her legs quivering as the final one slipped into place.

When Ezra came to stand beside her again, her sleepy expression roused him further. Though she was already firmly in the grip of subspace, he needed her even deeper. She gasped, her eyes clearing, as he tugged one of her nipples and slipped a clover clamp into place. She was prepared for the second clamp and slipped back into a comforting embrace of his control once again.

"Hold Maddy's wrists," Ezra instructed Kochran.

"That was fucking gorgeous, watching you do that to her." One side of Kochran's mouth lifted briefly before smoothing.

He ran his knuckles along the inside of Maddy's forearms before caressing her wrists with his thumbs. She moaned softly, closing her eyes. Kochran wrapped his fingers around her wrists, anchoring the trio together with an unbreakable bond. Ezra cemented it further by hooking his finger through the chain connecting the clamps and brushing it against Kochran's lips. Kochran opened, the dangling chain slipping into his mouth. He gave an experimental tug that caused Maddy to hiss. The sound of it wrapped around the base of Ezra's cock, as effective as any cock ring he'd ever employed.

"Touch yourself, pet."

Kochran's face was a mask of emotions as he asked, "What?"

"I said there was a reason I wasn't going to bind your hands."

Kochran narrowed his eyes. "Thought you didn't want to watch tonight."

"Your Dom is showing, pet." Kochran blew out a heavy breath as he wrapped his hand around the shaft. "It looks like you're preparing for war."

"In some ways, I think I am."

Kochran dragged his fist up, stopping just under the flared crown. He held there, his internal struggle visible. Ezra understood. That initial surrender to his Master had come much easier because there hadn't been dozens of watchful gazes assessing and weighing every single movement or choice. Every misstep. Here, in front of his friends and trusted colleagues, Kochran Duke was becoming the pet.

"Fighting your instincts to take the scene over?"

Kochran shook his head as he worked his fist up and down a few times. A tremor worked through his abdominal muscles, up to his pecs and through his shoulders. "Fighting coming. Fighting begging for more. For less. Fighting for it all, Master."

Ezra touched Kochran's hand. "I know that well thanks to you, pet. I have every faith that you will perform beautifully and flawlessly."

Looking up the line of Kochran's body, Ezra knew he'd tamed a wolf. So perfect. All strain and hard breath, shadows and sweat-glistened skin drawn tight over hard muscles. Agonizing self-control. Kochran was pure, raw, animalistic sex lying on the table, skin flushed, one hand on his cock, the other locked around Maddy's wrist. Half restrained, half free and wholly his.

Once again, the need to observe rose so swiftly, Ezra had to tamp it down. He loved this struggle. Two of his chosen kinks warring with one another as though locked in some eternal strife. Collaring them should have sated him, but instead, it had awakened the need for more. It made him connected to Maddy and Kochran in ways that he couldn't begin to understand.

Ezra positioned himself between Kochran's legs, loving all the sensations brackcting his body. He touched the rim of Kochran's anus, pleased when his hips strained against the bondage. A low, helpless groan tripped past his lips, washing over Ezra. Kochran's aching need was tangible. Ezra used his fingers to slowly play with Kochran, timing his gentle prodding to Kochran's strokes.

Maddy groaned loudly, and Ezra looked up to see that Kochran had arched his neck, which tugged on the chain he still had clenched between his teeth. His knuckles were white where he continued to grip her wrist while he stroked. Maddy would wear those bruises for a few days. She'd love it.

Ezra focused his attention on Kochran again, working his finger against the tight pucker until Kochran accepted him with a loud hiss. Kochran's pace remained steady and he fucked his fist as Ezra worked another finger into him. Then another. His breathing had an edge of urgency as his hand moved faster and faster, his strokes rough. Maddy's name became a chant filling the air, and Kochran was so close to exploding, Ezra swore he could taste it.

"Stop," he ordered.

Kochran continued, his hips bucking wildly against the ties holding him down. For a moment, Ezra thought he was going to have to force his hand, but Kochran gave a deep growl that vibrated the air as he yanked his hand away. Maddy yelped as he grabbed her other wrist so hard the skin under his fingers turned white.

"Maddy." Ezra gestured for her to come over to him. Her worried expression nearly made him grin. Caught up in the power spinning around them, she wanted to obey the command, but she wanted to stay there and provide support for Kochran. "It's all right, baby girl."

Ezra stripped away her delectable panties, careful of the string attached to the anal beads still tucked securely inside her. "Up you go." She allowed him to lift her over the table, position her on her knees so her thighs bracketed Kochran's hips. "Stay just like that and watch."

He slicked a coat of lubricant over his condom-covered erection, inching forward until he set the crown against Kochran's opening. There was no resistance as he pushed forward, as he and Maddy watched Kochran accept all that Ezra had to give him.

He gave a few experimental thrusts, pressing deeper each time the walls of Kochran's channel rippled around his driving cock. Pleasure swamped him, so intense his ears started to ring. He had to pull back from the brink, remind himself he wasn't the only one who needed to get off. Still buried deep inside Kochran, he held Maddy poised over Kochran's straining erection. Though he would have liked to have watched her slide onto Kochran, Ezra was much more interested in her face. More importantly her eyes. As Kochran filled her, her expressive eyes flared, her pupils blowing wide open. That alluring red flush crept over her neck and chest.

"Like being that full, sweetheart?" She nodded, her hair brushing against his shoulder as she leaned on him for support. "Later we'll both be inside you filling you even more. Would you like that?"

"Yes, Sir." Maddy moaned as Ezra ground his hips against her and Kochran, her wet core slicking his abdomen as he pressed hard between her legs. Her whole body tensed as she dropped her head back, exposing her throat to him.

Ezra kissed her there, a tender brush of his lips against the beat of her pulse. The idea they were both open to him because of the position sent a tremendous thrill arcing through him.

"Oh, fuck. Yes."

Ezra snorted softly at the curse tripping past her lips, the pleading tone of a word he rarely heard from her. "I like how that sounds from you."

His balls were hard and tight and full, release screaming like a wailing banshee in mourning. All he could think about was the pressure across his groin. The release tingling at the base of his spine. How fucking fabulous this all felt. But he wasn't ready. Wasn't ready to stop burying himself in Kochran's ass, experiencing the delicious heat of Maddy's cunt against his skin every time he thrust home.

Kochran jerked as Ezra hit the sensitive bundle of nerves on his upstroke. "Master. Fuck. I need to come."

"No," Ezra ground out at his pet's pleading request, thrusting through the constriction around his shaft. Tight. So, so tight. He powered through the grip on his dick, slamming so hard into Kochran and Maddy that Ezra was sure they were all going to wear bruises for days. He gloried in that revelation. Maddy's thighs began to violently tremble, and he knew there would be no way to stop her.

"Maddy, come," Ezra whispered as he tugged hard on the chain connecting the nipple clamps.

And she did, beautifully. Her orgasm was stark and raw, slamming into her so violently, she bucked. Her fingers dug into Ezra's shoulders as she fought to maintain her balance, a desperate whimper sounding in his ear.

He banded his arm around her waist, taking her weight fully. "I've got you, Maddy. Go on. Come again for us."

Her body went lax as she gave herself over to the power of the moment. She came again, screaming as Ezra thrust into Kochran, which drove Kochran up hard and fast into her. Fueled by their sounds, Ezra urged himself to go quicker, deeper. He wanted to do his best not to hurt either of them, but *oh, fuck, yes, it feels too good.*

Kochran came without warning, his body freezing in mid-thrust into Maddy as he strained from the power of the release. Their combined climax tore through Ezra, making it difficult to concentrate on anything. They'd become beings of light and pleasure and he was incapable of doing anything.

So fucking close.

"Now you." Kochran and Maddy spoke together, their voices raw from the quick breaths and harsh cries, lost in the impossible area where command and surrender came together.

Pleasure and relief flooded Ezra in a hot rush of extraordinary joy as he pushed closer to orgasm. Nothing else mattered. He twisted and gasped, fighting the unavoidable wave because hanging in that space where everything was perfect was so damn good. He vibrated with need, his dick a jutting, achy pain that demanded attention.

He loved the struggle, the pain, the command and the surrender. Loved knowing he'd finally discovered the answer he'd sought. Loved knowing everything was once again as it should be. He couldn't wait any longer, hammering into Kochran once, twice, swept away by a climax that started at his toenails, gripped his balls, and finally jerked out of his cock.

The Keep, the scene, faded into the blur of sweat and heat and light. Ezra's world narrowed further, and he finally, finally knew there would be no one else for him. He'd found the people he wanted to spend the rest of his life with. Forever and always, because somehow their unlikely triad had come together to make a perfect circle.

* * * * *

Now Available from Carina Press
and Sara Brookes

At Noble House, fantasy has no limits.
Log on and enter a world of your most secret desires.

Read on for an excerpt from
GET OFF EASY,
from Sara Brookes's
NOBLE HOUSE KINK SERIES

Darkness surrounded Grae. In her life. In her mind. And even in her office as she leaned back in her over-stuffed, overpriced chair and yawned. The creature comforts weren't enough to keep her interested in the image flickering on her computer screen. Not that well-chiseled abs didn't do it for her. They totally did. But considering the fact she'd been the one to draw, define, and enhance each one of those tongue-licking indenta-tions, the final product had lost its appeal hours ago.

As long as the female audience members went wild, she would keep plodding along. Not to mention, if she didn't deliver, she wouldn't be paid her hard-earned check. As tempting as it was to continue, she desper-ately needed a break.

A quick glance at her trusty desktop clock showed she hadn't stopped for over thirty-six hours. Since she was on a deadline, her director's schedule won out over sleep and basic hygiene. Especially because she was under contract. If she wanted another shot at working with this director, she needed to have this guy's abs painted on and swoon-worthy in the next three hours.

One hell of a reward awaited her after she completed her work too.

As she made her way to the kitchen to refill her carafe, she tapped the reminder postcard that arrived two days ago against her chin. Fresh coffee would get her through. At least it had to. She'd worked under tighter deadlines, and on less sleep, than this project.

Thirty-six hours with no sleep was kid's stuff.

Her reward, however, was not child appropriate.

No way. No how.

Kochran Duke was throwing one of his famous parties tonight. The events, where participation was allowed by members both at the club and online, were not low-key and always the highlight of the month. It also meant there was a distinct possibility Saint and Boyce would attend. They never missed a party at the converted armory. No telling what they'd be doing, though.

It was always a surprise when it came to those two.

She shoved a fresh filter into the brew basket, dumped in beans and water, and realized she didn't care. They could sit and read nursery rhymes to one another, and she'd still get off. Wasn't as though she'd joined Kochran's exclusive website only to watch the pretty boys play with their toys.

Okay, well, it wasn't the *only* reason.

There was a touch of practicality to why she chose to spend her night watching porn.

And it had nothing to do with satisfying her voyeuristic tendencies.

Her former Master recommended the online dungeon when it became obvious she had all the desire and drive to submit, but none of the time. Noble House offered several levels of membership depending on participation or observation. The fees were steep, but it was a small price to pay for satisfying a guilty indulgence from the privacy of her home office.

Once she'd discovered two of her closest friends from college were Dominants at Noble House, her interest in the private club increased tenfold. Thanks to alumni updates from the university, she'd known they'd continued to date after they graduated. Even knew where they lived because of an article published six months ago in the yearly alumni newsletter about the building they'd saved from the wrecking ball and turned into an apartment complex. Knowing they were still together, and trying to change the world, warmed her heart.

And a few other strategic lady bits.

Someday she would visit Noble House. Though the idea of taking a vacation long enough to visit Northern California sounded absurd. With the constant trail of work following her wherever she went, taking a break was unheard of. Visiting friends she hadn't seen in more than a decade was even more ludicrous. As was confessing she'd seen every one of their broadcasted scenes since she'd become a member.

And hunted through the archives.

Several times over.

The coffeepot chimed. She dumped the contents into the carafe, then grabbed the French vanilla creamer. As she made her way back to her spacious office, her eyes slowly adjusted to the permanent darkness she'd created thanks to heavy light-blocking blinds. Day or night, the lighting in the room never changed. When she'd decided to leave the guaranteed contract with the big-budget movie studio behind and become a freelancer, she'd invested in all the bells and whistles. No sense working from home without the proper equipment.

Six monitors wasn't too much, right?

A quick check of the emails she'd been ignoring for the past few hours indicated the director was getting aggravated. Time to buckle down and turn out this masterpiece. Armed with a fresh cup of coffee, Grae leaned back to watch the fight sequence she'd been working on for the past week. She noted a few minor inconsistencies she could smooth over while she waited to see if she had approval. No need to waste her time if the director wanted to ditch the segment.

Task completed, she zipped the file, then dropped it onto her secure server. An email containing the link to the director was next and meant her part was complete. She flipped a switch to change over to her personal computer tower and waited for it to boot. When it finally beeped in greeting, she directed the browser window to Noble House's main site. A few keystrokes, and the splash page for tonight's event flashed onto the huge screen she'd mounted on the wall.

Two very familiar faces stared back at her.

Boyce Denali, the one on the left, wore heavy-duty leathers. Too bulky for working inside the club. These were the kind used for protection should he take a spill. Though she doubted he would ever be so careless. Boyce was the kind of man the pavement moved for. Dark blond, piercing blues, muscles to die for, and a chiseled bone structure even the most formidable Viking would find intimidating.

Ford Templar, on the other hand, was all dark and mysterious. Nicknamed Saint at the club, Ford was broody. Sulky. Dark hair. Olive skin. Lean muscles.

The dark to Boyce's light. Except his eyes. Those eyes. Eerily colored, they reminded her of glass Coke bottles. Rumor had it his gaze could pierce right through to someone's soul. While Boyce held a commanding air that demanded to be heard, Saint wore his power subtly but was still all dominant authority.

Seemingly connected at the hip, the two men scened together every week. Much to her delight. Grae didn't think she'd ever seen them work with a submissive alone. Not that the choice to only carry out ménage scenes affected their standing at the club. Not in the least. Every time they worked together, their scenes had been nothing short of spectacular.

"Let's see what you're up to tonight, boys."

The submissive Boyce had just finished securing to the bondage table struggled against her cuffs. Not surprising given the size of the dildo Saint had extracted from his toy bag. Boyce had been intimidated the first time Saint used it on him too. Damn thing had felt as though it had been about to split him in two. And he'd cursed Saint's full name the entire time he'd come.

Now *that* was a glorious memory.

Boyce tucked it away for later. Something to relive after this scene, when they were alone.

Saint's green eyes glittered in the stage lighting. Yeah. Saint was enjoying himself way too damn much to mention it. Not that Boyce would complain. He wasn't the one facing down the monstrous cock.

But he would definitely reap the rewards.

Boyce angled his face so the submissive and the cameras mounted around the room couldn't see him mouth *fucker* to Saint. That gloriously wicked gleam in his eyes darkened, transforming Saint from sadistic bastard to devilishly handsome sadistic bastard.

Definitely spending some time walking down memory lane later.

As Saint screwed the abundantly sized phallus to a long shaft attached to his custom fucking machine, Boyce crouched. Time to pay attention to a very worried-looking submissive. Face level with Asha, he stroked her cheek. Her whimpers grew softer, her breathing regulating as he caressed her. Her amber eyes unfocused, glazing over as he encouraged her attention to remain on him.

Boyce swept some of her blonde hair to the side, exposing the bright red flush that darkened her cheeks. That same flush had spread across her neck, the gentle swells of her breasts. She was smaller than Boyce usually favored, a tiny package of a woman who barely cleared his chest when she was upright.

But her petite size didn't make her any less desirable.

Boyce loved women—and men—of all shapes and sizes. Asha was a cute, little pixie who had more than enough enthusiasm to make up for her small size. She also had the wrath of Kochran Duke hanging over her head.

They'd planned a different scene entirely for the evening, but Kochran had intercepted them earlier in the day and called in a favor. One of the House submissives needed an attitude adjustment. She had a reputation for being mouthy with the Noble House Doms during a scene. Everything from topping from the bottom, coming whenever she damn well felt like it, and a few other infractions that went against club rules.

It appeared as though the owner of Noble House had

finally reached his limit on her bratty behavior. Boyce knew Kochran well enough to recognize this scene was just the first of many Kochran planned to subject the little bundle of energy to.

Boyce traced the flush of red across her torso, following it down until he reached the small triangle of carefully groomed pubic hair. "Eyes on me, sprite."

She giggled at the nickname he'd branded her with when she'd introduced herself earlier in the evening, before the cameras had been turned on. When they'd discussed limits. Punishment was punishment. However, it didn't include absolute no-nos.

And Asha didn't have many.

Boyce locked his gaze on hers as he scissored his fingers and spread her pussy lips. Out of the corner of his eye, he watched Saint performing a safety check to make sure all the mechanical parts were in working order.

"Open your legs wider for me."

She bit her lip as she complied. So accommodating. She knew she'd fucked up and was willing to accept whatever was thrown at her. If Boyce had to guess, he'd bet she'd done it on purpose just to gain attention. Wouldn't be the first time a submissive intentionally misbehaved.

Certainly was going to get her wish now.

Boyce pressed a gentle kiss to her knee. Legs still weren't wide enough to give the optimum view for the cameras once things really got going. He could order her again, but everyone was expecting a show. And he intended to give them one. Boyce hooked a second ring on a metal circle above her ankle, closing each of them with a snap, and made a few adjustments. Now her legs were spread wide, her ankles high in the air and secured by clips with panic snaps.

Safety first.

Boyce reached into his pocket. As he drew out a handful of clips, the sprite whimpered. "Courtesy of Kochran." He plucked two of the metal items from the pile before tossing the rest toward Saint. "Since she's on restriction, we should educate her accordingly."

"Works for me." Saint jiggled the clips, deep in thought.

Boyce returned to the head of the table to give Saint some time to formulate a plan on where he wanted to take the scene, as Saint was the lead this time around. Boyce would co-Dom for the night, picking up any slack where guidance was needed.

Which suited Boyce just fine. They'd been together long enough that most of the time, once they both dropped into the zone, Boyce could read even the smallest nuance and anticipate Saint's every move. They worked well together, which was probably the reason Kochran had enlisted their assistance.

"Please don't clamp me. Please, it will hurt." Asha's hair fanned out against the deep purple covering on the bondage table as she shook her head. Panic had drawn her slender eyebrows together and dilated her pupils.

Boyce loved seeing this kind of reaction. Loved watching a submissive struggle and beg. It meant he was doing his duty as a Dom. Fear—even controlled fear—was an excellent aphrodisiac.

"That's the general idea of punishment, sprite."

While she whimpered softly, Boyce turned his focus to her chest. She needed a distraction of some kind while Saint continued prepping. Leaning closer, Boyce

ringed one of her nipples, enjoying the way the pink
bud hardened under his tongue. A gentle squeeze had
her arching off the table.

Yeah. The little sprite enjoyed pain way more than
she let on. Not that Boyce doubted Kochran's word.
The owner always knew exactly what was going on at
any time in his club. Like he instinctively recognized
each of his members' wants and desires.

Freakishly so sometimes.

As Boyce continued circling, teasing and nipping, a
fine sheen of sweat coated Asha's tanned skin. When
he tightened the clamp around one of her erect nipples,
her eyes glazed over, her mind taking her to a place
where pain and pleasure were almost indistinguishable.

Too bad he'd given Saint the extra clips. Her dusky
nipples looked pretty clamped, the tips of the metal
fasteners trembling as he tied a thin string around an
open loop on one end and secured them to the clips at
her wrists. Though he admired the way her breathing
tugged and pulled on the string, he thought about an
artful circular pattern ringing her entire breast. Giving
her that pain she claimed not to care for.

Too late. Saint had beaten him to the punch in a
similar industrious fashion by taking the handful of
clips and lining them in a neat vertical row, pinching
her pussy lips together. Effectively locking her in chas-
tity. Saint pulled her ass to the edge of the table and
positioned her so he could use the entrance he hadn't
blocked.

"Inventive."

"Just being resourceful." Saint retrieved a tube from
his bag and slicked her with lubricant.

Boyce didn't distract her this time, but watched her

body and mannerisms with a keen eye as Saint brushed the dildo against her anus. Her breathing was steady, if a bit ragged. Her color had brightened as her arousal level grew. She kept licking her lips, as though she was preparing to say something, but each time, Saint would dip the toy into her opening.

The man was no fool. He was keyed in enough on her, on the scene, that he didn't even need to hear verbal protests to know when to push her. Saint's method of solving her problems was going to be barreling over her defenses to wiggle his way under her skin.

Boyce had seen it often, experienced it firsthand even more. And loved it each and every time, whether he was on the receiving end or not. His pride, and love, for Saint swelled, even though he didn't think it possible. The man continued to surprise him each day they were together.

As Saint slid the dildo in and out a few times, Asha unleashed a long, low wail followed by an inventive string of curses. There was the mouthy submissive they'd been tasked to discipline.

Boyce bit his lip to keep from grinning. She had a flair for the melodramatic, no doubt about that. Some Doms got off on that behavior. Some didn't. Asha needed to learn there was a time and a place.

Boyce caught the ball gag Saint tossed him. "Muffle her."

Don't miss
GET OFF EASY by Sara Brookes
Available now wherever
Carina Press ebooks are sold.

www.CarinaPress.com

About the Author

A native Virginian, Sara sold her first romance novel in 2009. Since that fateful day, she's published books in various subgenres of romance, been generously honored with several awards and saved the world from evil chocolate chip cookies.

She has won the PRISM Award from the RWA's Fantasy, Futuristic and Paranormal chapter for Best Futuristic Romance, and the HOLT Medallion award from RWA's Virginia Romance Writers chapter for Best Erotic Romance. She was also selected as a finalist for an RT Reviewer's Choice Award for Best Erotic Romance.

Though she may insist otherwise, Sara loves the places her mind conjures and has always been fascinated by the strange, the unusual, the twisted and the lost (tortured heroes are her personal favorite). She is an action movie junkie, addicted to coffee and has been known to stay up until the wee hours of the morning playing RPG video games. Despite all this geekiness, she is a romantic at heart and is always a sucker for an excellent love story.

You can find Sara on the web at www.sarabrookes. com, on Twitter at www.Twitter.com/Sara_Brookes, on Facebook at www.Facebook.com/brookesofbooks, her street team group at www.Facebook.com/groups/brookesbooktique and via her new release notification newsletter at eepurl.com/mbG31.